PRAISE FO... ...EN

"[Bowen] bolst...   ...ower, humor, and hea...   ...a huge fan and she's at the top of my auto-buy list. Everyone should be reading her books!"
                                        —Lorelei James, *New York Times* bestselling author

"Sarina Bowen is a master at drawing you in from page one and leaving you aching for more."
                                        —Elle Kennedy, *New York Times* bestselling author

"I not only bought this book and devoured it, I bought—and read—this entire NA series (The Ivy Years) in a WEEK. It is OMG-awesome-NA-at-its-finest."
                                        —Tammara Webber, *New York Times* bestselling author

"[A] terrific read."
                                        —Dear Author

"Bowen writes great dialogue and wonderfully realistic characters."
                                        —*Kirkus Reviews*

"This page-turner will have readers eagerly awaiting Bowen's next book."
                                        —*Publishers Weekly*

"So well done that I just want to read it over and over."
                                        —Smexybooks

ROOKIE MOVE

SARINA BOWEN

BERKLEY SENSATION
New York

BERKLEY SENSATION
Published by Berkley
An imprint of Penguin Random House LLC
375 Hudson Street, New York, New York 10014

ISBN: 9780399583438

First Edition: September 2016

Printed in the United States of America
1   3   5   7   9   10   8   6   4   2

Cover art by Claudio Marinesco
Cover design by Rita Frangie

For Elle,
who always reminds me that this job is fun.

ACKNOWLEDGMENTS

There are so many people who make this job doable! Thank you Mollie Glick, and Emily Brown and Jess Regel! This past year has been amazing.

Thank you Laura and Julie for bringing the Brooklyn Bruisers to life, and thanks to the rest of the Penguin team! (And where did you find that cover model? My readers want to know.)

Thank you Keyanna and Nina and Mike! You have all helped me so much this year and I don't think I could have done it without you.

Last but not least, thanks to my local writer pals: Jess, Sarah, Jenny, and KJ. Our dinners out always make my week.

ONE

TOP TEAM HEADLINE:

Will the Brooklyn Bruisers Name a Coach At Last?
Press Conference Called for 10 AM
—New York Post

Cobblestone streets did not pair well with high heels. So Georgia Worthington took her time walking to work through Brooklyn's Dumbo neighborhood.

Luckily, the office was just another block away. Her job didn't often call for heels and a suit, but today she needed to look authoritative. That wasn't easy when you were five-feet-three-inches tall, and every athlete and coach in the Brooklyn Bruisers organization towered over you. Today she'd need those extra inches. The press conference she'd planned would prove to the organization that they didn't need to hire another senior publicist to replace her boss, who had left two months ago.

Every day that went by with Georgia at the helm of the hockey team's PR effort was a victory. She only needed a little more time to prove she could handle the job alone.

Just like she needed a little more practice time in these shoes. Georgia was practically invincible in a pair of tennis shoes. She could serve a ball down the court at a hundred miles per hour. She could dive toward the net for a short shot, return the ball, and then pivot in any direction. But walking down Water Street in her only pair of three-inch Pradas? That was a challenge.

It was a sunny February morning, and a stiff breeze blew off the East River, though Brooklyn was especially beautiful at this hour, when the slanting sunshine gave the brick facades a rosy hue and sparkled off each antique windowpane. She turned (carefully) onto Gold Street, quickening her pace toward the office. The doormen of the buildings she passed were in the midst of their morning routine—sweeping the sidewalks, hosing off any filth that may have landed there in the night. That was more or less what she'd done herself for the past few years—leaning hard into the morning sunshine, banishing the darkness into the well-scrubbed corners of her mind.

In two hours she would host a press conference where the team's owner would announce that the newest NHL franchise had finally anointed a new head coach. She'd set the whole thing up by herself, and it needed to go off flawlessly.

They all had a lot riding on this announcement. As the youngest team in the conference, the team needed the visibility. It had been not quite two years since Georgia's boss had bought the Long Island franchise and rebranded it as a Brooklyn team. It was a risky maneuver, one that many sports pundits had already decided would fail.

As if the stakes weren't high enough for Georgia already, the new coach just happened to be her father. After twenty years coaching college teams and then a stint as assistant defensive coach for the Rangers, he'd just agreed to take the riskiest NHL job in the nation.

Having your dad show up and outrank you at the office wasn't exactly a dream come true. But Georgia had always been close to her father, and she knew this was a big step for him. She was just going to have to make the best of it.

And anyway, he was a tough coach, and she wanted her boys to win, right? No, she *needed* them to win. There was a chorus of voices ready to write the team off as a failure. They said the tristate area had too many hockey teams. They said the Internet billionaire who'd bought the team didn't know what he was doing. It was Georgia's job to help combat all those unwanted opinions with a polished public image.

Their critics were wrong, anyway. In the first place, there could never be too many hockey teams. And she'd seen signs that the young owner knew *exactly* what he was doing.

She climbed the steps to the team's headquarters and tugged on the brass handle. Georgia wasn't ashamed to admit that she loved the office building with the glee that other people reserved for obsessing over a new lover. She liked the weight of the big wooden door in her hand, and the golden sheen of the wooden floors inside. Like many of the buildings in this neighborhood, their headquarters had been a factory at the turn of the century. The team's owner—Internet billionaire Nate Kattenberger—had bought it as a wreck and had had every inch of it lovingly restored. Every time she stepped into this entryway, with its exposed brick walls and its old soda lamps overhead, she felt lucky.

Just inside the entry hall hung a wall-mounted screen showing clips of the boys winning in Toronto. Back when she'd just started as the publicity and marketing assistant, Georgia had edited that film herself. It gave her a private thrill to know that the first thing every visitor to headquarters saw was her handiwork.

Working for the Bruisers was her first job out of college. She'd landed it when Nate Kattenberger had just begun his tenure as owner. He'd fired nearly everyone from the old franchise and started fresh. That was a bad deal for the lifers, of course, but pretty lucky for a twenty-two-year-old new graduate. In the early days she'd done everything from fetching coffee to answering phones to arranging photo shoots.

Nate still referred to her as Employee Number Three. You had to know Nate to understand that the nickname was a high form of praise. At Internet companies, being an early employee was a status symbol.

Georgia didn't care if she was Employee Number Three or number 333. But she really wanted to hang on to the top post in publicity.

When the senior publicist quit eight weeks ago to move to California with his boyfriend, Georgia was given his job on an interim basis. But so far the general manager (Employee Number Two) had been too busy trading players before the deadline to shop around for a more seasoned PR replacement.

At twenty-four years old, she was (at least temporarily) the senior publicist of an NHL franchise.

Pinch me, she thought as her heels clicked importantly on the shellacked floors. From the lobby, a girl could follow the left-hand passageway toward the athletic facility and the brand-new practice rink that Kattenberger had built. But Georgia went the other way, toward the office wing on the right. The double doors in her path were made from wavy old bottle glass, and she loved the way they gave the hallway beyond an underwater sheen until she pushed open the door.

The first sound she heard on the other side of the door was her father's voice. And he was yelling.

Uh-oh.

Later, when she reran the events of the day in her mind, she'd remember this as the moment when the wheels came off. And it wasn't even nine o'clock yet.

"Why am I even here?" her father hollered. "You *said* I'd have veto power over your trades. But I'm in the building *ten fucking minutes* when I find out that you took a player I don't want?"

"Actually," another voice began. Georgia knew that voice, too. It belonged to Nate, the thirty-two-year-old owner of the team. The self-made billionaire had built a browser search engine in his dorm room eleven years ago which was now active on eight hundred million mobile devices.

Nate started a great many of his sentences with the word "actually."

"Actually," he said again, "we grabbed this player one day *before* you stepped into the building. Totally our prerogative. Read your contract."

"I shouldn't *have* to read my fucking contract!" her dad hollered. "I put my whole career on the line to lead a team that everyone thinks will fail. You said, *Trust me, Karl. I need you, Karl*. And then you pull this crap?"

"Legally . . ."

"'Legally' is for pussies. That's some underhanded shit you just pulled, and a real man admits that."

Oh Jesus no. She began skating in her heels toward Mr. Kattenberger's office, hoping to end this conversation. Calling the owner's manhood into question was not a good strategy. The boss was a little touchy about that.

Okay, a lot touchy.

When she rounded the corner into the outer office, her heart dove. She counted two or three bodies as she passed by them in a blur. If any of them were reporters, they'd just overheard every ugly word of the argument in Nate Kattenberger's office. If any of them *recorded* this dustup, her week had just gotten twice as long.

She ripped open the door to Nate's office and slid inside. "Gentlemen," she said quietly. As she feared, the two men were staring each other down, shoulders squared as if for battle. They were an interestingly mismatched pair—Nate with his steely eyes and his five thousand dollar suit on a lean frame, versus her square-jawed jock of a dad with his military haircut and I-eat-men-like-you-for-breakfast snarl.

"Princess!" her father barked. "I didn't know you worked for a weasel."

"Coach," she warned. She'd decided ahead of time that she would call him Coach at work. Because calling her own father by his first name was just weird. And calling someone "Dad" at the office was not good for a girl's image. "Listen to me," she begged. "We are expecting thirty or forty reporters in this building today. And there are people out there listening to you two chew each other up. That's *not* what we want in the sports section tomorrow. So you can have this argument using your inside voices."

"He just . . ." Nate began.

Georgia held up a hand. "Your publicist says to tone it down right now, or I'm sending both of you to the penalty box."

They stared each other down while she held her breath. Her father folded his meaty arms in front of his chest. "We're not finished with this conversation," he hissed. "If that kid's contract is unsigned, I'm tearing it up."

"Too late!" Nate said cheerily as her father's lip curled. "They sent us a scan of the signed file last night. Georgia, please add our newest player to your press release. We'll have *two* additions to the Bruisers to announce today." He reached across his desk and handed her a file folder.

"Yes, captain." The boss had a thing for Star Trek, too.

Her father gave her a look. But what else could she say? Georgia and the big boss had a great relationship, and that was because she'd figured out early on that Nate had no idea how to be a team player. When you make your first billion while other college kids are playing beer pong, it's the social skills that suffer.

And she'd *warned* her father that Nate was egotistical. You have to *handle* Nate. And shouting at him always failed. So she gave her father a look right back. *We talked about this*, she telegraphed.

He's such an asshole, his sneer replied.

And it was probably true. But when she looked at Nate she saw a kid who'd been shoved into lockers during high school. And now he wanted the last laugh, taking every opportunity to throw his (nerdy) weight around. He'd bought a hockey team, and he was going to make the jocks do his bidding, at least until the day he realized that vindication wasn't everything in life.

"Now," she said quietly. "Let's go over the announcement." She set her leather briefcase on the corner of Nate's egotistically sized desk and pulled a folder from the outside pocket. From inside, she pulled a page for each of them. "Nate will introduce you, Coach. I have him leading with your win record at the college level, because it's pretty spectacular." She winked at her father and saw him relax by a degree or two. "Then we'll hit your NHL years, for depth . . ." From her coat pocket, her phone began dancing a jig. There was too much going on this morning to ignore it. "Sorry, one sec."

She pulled out the phone and took a peek at its massive screen. Everyone who worked for Kattenberger was issued a big-screened, turbofast, ubersecure phone that Nate had designed himself. The call she'd received wasn't business, though. It was from her old friend DJ. It wasn't until after she rejected the call that she realized his timing was a little odd. DJ never called her at work. It made her worry that today's big announcement had already leaked to the media.

God, she hoped it hadn't.

"Georgia," her father grumbled, breaking her train of thought, "was this the shirt you meant for me to wear with this tie?" Her father tugged at his half Windsor knot. The tie was purple, of course—the team color. Georgia had messengered it to her childhood home out on Long Island yesterday. The fact that she still bought her father's clothes for him was not something she wanted to put in a press release. But Georgia's mother had passed away when she was six years old, and her father did not like to shop.

"You look dashing." She smiled at him, hoping he'd lighten up. "Now, can you two play nicely together until after the press conference? It's either that, or you need to double my salary, because I'll have to work twenty-four hours a day to undo the damage."

Coach Worthington sighed. "I won't shout anymore. But we can't keep this player."

"*Bullshit*," Nate hissed. "The kid is good. And I got him cheap."

"Quiet!" she whispered. "I'm begging you both. Now I need to head into my office for half an hour, before we're overrun with reporters. Stay out of trouble until the press conference, okay? I'll fetch you right before I speak to the players."

Her father set his jaw into a grim expression of acceptance. Georgia was fairly certain he wouldn't start yelling again when she left the room. He was passionate, but he was smart, too. "Okay, honey." He put a meaty palm on her shoulder.

Unfortunately, she picked up her heavy briefcase at just the same time, and the weight of his hand destabilized her. "Whoa," she said as she teetered on the stilts that passed for her shoes.

Her father reacted fast, catching her by the elbow before she could fall down. "Christ, Princess! Are you okay? Should you be wearing those things? I thought you swore off heels after that incident at your eighth grade gradua- tion . . ."

Nate snickered behind his desk, and Georgia felt her face flush.

She stood up straight again. "Coach, a favor? Don't call me Princess at work."

Her father tucked the strap of her briefcase over her shoulder, the way you would for someone who was about five years old. "Sorry, Miss Worthington." He grinned. Then he pecked her on the cheek.

Yeah, they were going to have to work on his style of office interaction. But at least he wasn't yelling anymore.

She made her way back to the outer office of the C-suite. Sure enough, a couple of the people sitting on Nate's exqui- site leather sofas tried hard to look bored as she passed through.

Not a good sign.

Georgia hiked her bag a little higher on her shoulder as she turned into the hallway. She gave a wave through the open doorway to the bullpen area, where most of the assistants and interns sat. "Morning," she called to Roger, the publicity assistant.

"Morning!" He waved. "I'm going for donuts in a few minutes. You want jam-filled or chocolate?"

Georgia dug into her pocket for some money, noticing that Roger had not asked if she wanted a donut. That was just assumed. Georgia's metabolism was well known around these parts. "Jam," she said, darting in to put a five on his desk. "Thanks. You're the best."

He gave her a salute as she stepped back into the hallway to open her office door. Her keys eluded her, though. She had to dig all the way into the bottom of her bag to find them. When she finally fit her office key into the lock and turned, it was heartening to hear the squeak of old wood giving way. At least for today, this office was still all hers. She stepped inside, but then dropped the keys to the floor, where they made a small metallic crashing sound. She bent over to pick them up, and had to smile because the ground was farther away than usual. *So this is what it's like to be tall.*

If she'd been just a little less clumsy, she might have missed the conversation at the other end of the hallway.

"Come right this way," she heard her coworker and roommate Becca say, the clomp of her Dr. Martens echoing through the grand old passageway. "The general manager is still sitting in traffic, but Nate is excited to meet you." Becca was Nate's assistant, and Georgia lingered half a second to wave her down and ask if she wanted a donut, too. But Becca didn't happen to look in Georgia's direction as she led a tall man down the corridor. Something about his gait snagged Georgia's subconscious. So she took a second look.

And that's when her heart took off like a manic bunny

rabbit. Because she knew that man. She knew the chiseled shape of his masculine jaw, and the length of his coal-black eyelashes.

Oh my God.

Omigod, omigod, omigod.

"How was your flight?" Becca asked him, oblivious to the fact that Georgia was spying.

"Not too bad. I got in late last night."

The sound of his voice fluttered right inside Georgia's chest. It was the same smoky sweet timbre that used to whisper into her ear while they made love. She hadn't let herself remember that sound in a long time.

Now it was giving her goose bumps. The good kind.

"Welcome to Brooklyn," Becca said while Georgia trembled. "Are you familiar with the area?"

"Grew up about thirty miles from here," he answered while chills broke out across her back.

Holding her breath, Georgia eased her office door further closed, until only a couple of inches remained. She could not be caught like this—freaked out and speechless, hiding behind a door.

The movement caught Becca's eye, though. Georgia saw her turn her head in her direction and then pick her out in the crack where the door was still open. Becca raised one eyebrow—the one with the barbell piercing in it.

All Georgia could do was close her eyes and pray that Becca wouldn't call out a greeting.

There was a pause before Georgia heard Becca say, "Right this way, please."

Quietly, Georgia stepped farther into her office and shut the door. After flipping on the light, she let her briefcase and pocketbook slide right to the floor. Only the folder that Nate had given her was still in her shaking hands. She flipped it open, her eyes searching for the new player's name on the page.

But she didn't even need the paperwork to confirm what her racing heart had already figured out. The newest player for the Brooklyn Bruisers was none other than Leonardo

"Leo" Trevi, a six-foot-two, left-handed forward. Also known as her high school boyfriend, the boy she'd loved with all her heart until the day that she'd dumped him. And now he was *here*?

"Thanks, universe," she whispered into the stillness of her office.

After tossing the folder on her desk, she gathered up her bags and shook off her coat. She sat down in her office chair, her back to the Brooklyn Navy Yard out the window behind her. Usually she stopped for a moment just to appreciate the view, but now her phone was buzzing again. It was DJ calling once more, and now she understood why—her old friend DJ just happened to be Leo Trevi's little brother.

The phone stopped ringing before she could answer it, but a text appeared next. *Call me? I need to tell you something, so you won't be shocked later.*

Georgia's answering text was only two words: *too late*.

The phone rang in her hand again, and she answered it this time. "Hi," she said. "How are you?"

"Pretty damn good," he said. "I'm on winter break in Aspen with Lianne."

"*Nice*. I sort of remember what vacations are like. Though the details are fuzzy."

He chuckled in her ear. DJ and his older brother sounded nothing alike, which was one reason she found it easy to stay close to him. Their friendship was totally separate from the past she had with his brother. "Gigi, are you okay?" he asked.

"Um, sure?" she said, convincing nobody.

"I mean . . ." He was quiet for a moment. "You never talk about him. Like, *never*. And whenever I mention him in passing, you always change the subject."

That was entirely true. "Why can't you be like other men, who don't notice things?"

"Sorry, girl." He snickered. "Have you seen him yet?"

"No," she said quickly. Because she was sure DJ was asking whether she'd spoken to Leo, and not whether she'd spied on him through a two-inch crack in the door. "All right, then. Since I never ask, give me the 411 on your brother."

"Well, the big news is that he's the newest rookie forward for the Brooklyn Bruisers."

"You're hysterical." Some warning would have been nice. But trades happened swiftly and secretly. That was the nature of the beast.

"He just got the call yesterday, Gi. I heard late last night when I finally turned on my phone and found a voice mail from my mom."

"Huh," she said. Her boss had been a busy man yesterday. Why had he bothered acquiring a new player the day before her father showed up? Even if he'd made it too loudly, her dad did have a point.

"Leo's been busting his ass on that AHL team for a season and a half. He'd been hoping to get called up to Detroit, but a trade gets the job done just the same."

"What else?" Georgia asked, wincing at the vagueness of her own question. The things she really wanted to know were the things she did not have a right to ask. Did Leo ever talk about her? Did he have a girlfriend? Or worse— was he engaged to be married?

God. That idea made her shudder. If there was a fiancée in his life, she needed to know now so she could work on her game face.

"I dunno what he's been up to this season. I haven't seen him since Christmas. But I guess I'll be coming to a Bruisers game pretty soon. If they're really going to play him in the big house."

"Come anytime," she said. "Can't wait to see you."

"Let me guess—that's not what you would have said to Leo."

Busted. "Well . . ." She cleared her throat. "It's hard."

He went quiet again. "Maybe it doesn't have to be. It's been more than five years, you know? He'll probably be really happy to see you."

She doubted that very much. The last time they'd

spoken was the day she dumped him. "We'll get through somehow," she said, praying it was true.

"Hang in there," DJ said. "Call me, okay? Lianne and I aren't skiing today. We're too sore from yesterday."

"How will you fill the time, then? Just the two of you in a hotel room . . ." She giggled into the phone.

"No comment," he said, laughing. "Bye."

"Bye!" She hung up the phone with a smile, but it faded quickly. Talking to DJ was easy. Talking to his brother would not be.

And she had a press conference to throw. Pushing Leo's file folder away from her on the desk, she tried to get to work.

TWO

For Leo Trevi, the last twenty-four hours had been a wild ride in the best possible way. He could hardly believe he was standing just outside Nate Kattenberger's inner sanctum.

On the taxi ride over from the hotel, he'd wondered what to expect from the great Kattenberger hockey headquarters. Leo had pictured the Internet billionaire as the sort of guy to command the entire penthouse floor of a Manhattan skyscraper, with his desk in the center of a grand, rink-sized room. And maybe that's the setup he had at his corporate headquarters in Manhattan. But this space felt more like a sound stage on an old movie set. Leo kept expecting guys to step out of the shadows in bowler hats and sporting handlebar mustaches. Instead, there was the friendly female office manager with purple hair and Dr. Martens.

It was all very unexpected.

Twenty-four hours ago, he was still working the line on an AHL team in Michigan, earning a salary of $42,000 and busting his ass for a shot in Detroit. Then, just after the morning skate, he got the big call from his agent. A few hours later he was on a flight to JFK airport. His paycheck?

More than ten times higher than it was before the phone rang.

This morning he'd woken in a fancy hotel room a half an hour from where he was born and raised. It had been the most exciting day of his life so far, and it wasn't even ten o'clock.

Standing there in his best suit, Leo didn't have anything better to do than to admire the cool old factory building, with its exposed bricks and its industrial-looking ironwork. A couple of other guys sat perched on chairs by the windows, typing rapid-fire into their laptops. Whatever they were doing, it looked urgent.

Mr. Kattenberger's assistant went to sit behind her desk, and for a few minutes nothing happened.

To amuse himself, Leo Googled "Dumbo" on his phone. He didn't know why this Brooklyn neighborhood was named for a Disney elephant. As it turned out, Dumbo was an acronym for Down Under the Manhattan Bridge Overpass. The O for "Overpass" was stuck on there for aesthetic purposes, he guessed. Without it, the neighborhood would be called "Dumb."

Keyed up as he was, this idea hit him as hysterical. He actually snorted to himself as he put the phone away. Hell, he'd live in a neighborhood called "Dumb" if it meant he could play for this team. In fact—they could put "Dumb" on the back of his jersey if they felt like it. He wanted this opportunity badly, and he could barely believe that it was finally happening.

It was about a minute later when everything went south.

His first clue was an angry growl from the owner's office. The assistant—purple-haired Becca—peered nervously at her watch. She was perched on a chair behind a modern, kidney-shaped desk and stealing glances at her boss's office door. "I'm sure he'll be right with you," she said. "We're going to have a crazy day today—there's going to be a press conference announcing the brand-new coach."

"Oh?" This was news to Leo. His agent hadn't said

anything about that. Everyone knew the Brooklyn Bruisers had been interviewing coaches for a year now. It was something of a joke in the press. Pundits had written that maybe Kattenberger wanted the job for himself. "Who is it?" he asked.

She winked her right eye at him—and the diamond stud in her nose twinkled under the antique lighting. "I could tell you, but then I'd have to kill you."

"That would shorten my career," he joked. "I guess I'll live with the mystery."

Though it turned out he didn't have to. Because somebody began yelling behind Mr. Kattenberger's closed office door. "I don't want this fucking player! Find a way to undo it!" And, *damn*. That voice sounded familiar.

Someone argued back in a low voice that Leo couldn't quite make out.

"Oh yeah?" The first voice again. "We'll just see what the lawyers say. Send him right back to Michigan or where-the-fuck-ever."

The realization that he was talking about *Leo* hit him like a crosscheck into the plexi.

And just to extinguish any lingering doubt, Becca leapt out of her chair and scrambled to tap on the office door. Then she opened it a crack and stuck her head inside to say, pointedly, "Mr. Trevi has *arrived*, sir."

If only. His big entrance suddenly seemed a hell of a lot smaller.

There was a murmured reply, after which the door was yanked all the way open. That's when Leo saw him—the coach who had once been his mentor, until the man had decided he wasn't anymore. Coach Karl Worthington leaned forward, searing Leo with his beady gaze, grimacing as if Leo were a cockroach who'd just scuttled in.

For one fraction of a second, he felt like one, too. But then his blood pressure spiked. This was a big day for him—or it had been until a minute ago. It had always been a mystery to him why this man had turned against him. And now he'd been hired as head coach of the Brooklyn team?

Hello, roadblock. But fuck that. He wasn't going to let Worthington ruin this opportunity for him, not without a fight.

"Hi, Coach," he said. And maybe Leo's smile was more of a grimace. But it was the best he could manage right now.

The moment dragged on while Leo stood there wondering—what *was* the shortest NHL career in history? Two games? One? If Coach Karl had his way, his might be a single hour. Leo fingered his phone in his pocket, wondering whether he could call his agent this early in the morning. The man was on West Coast time, but this probably qualified as an emergency.

Coach Karl returned Leo's greeting with nothing but a nod. Leo bet the two of them looked like a pair of angry dogs who were trying to decide who'd be the first to attack.

Becca cleared her throat. "Nate, would you like Mr. Trevi to wait in the lounge?"

The team's owner stepped in front of Coach Karl and offered Leo his hand. He looked just like his photos—a lanky man with untamed hair and shrewd eyes. "Pleasure to meet you, Mr. Trevi. I've been following you for years. I'm a Harkness College man myself."

Leo offered his hand for what turned out to be a surprisingly fierce handshake. "Hey, I remember reading that. Which house were you in?"

He gave Leo a grin. "Turner. Inner tube water polo champions of 2006."

"Congratulations."

Coach Karl didn't like that bit of alumni bonding at all. While Nate Kattenberger smiled, he actually let out a little growl.

But fuck 'em. The owner was trying to give Leo a chance, and he was grateful enough to do a little harmless ass-kissing. Even if Coach already had steam coming out of his ears. "I still have a couple of Frozen Four T-shirts from last year. I'll bring you one."

"Awesome," the billionaire said, clapping him on the shoulder. "Now if you'll excuse us, we have a press conference to prepare for. You'll be briefly introduced at the end, before Coach Worthington's Q and A."

"Thank you. That sounds great." Since Becca had drifted toward the door, Leo knew he was supposed to follow her. But instead, he stuck out his hand toward Coach Karl. "Good to see you, sir."

There was a very awkward beat while Leo waited to see what he'd do. The coach's eyes narrowed, as if sensing a trap. Then, having little choice, he grasped Leo's hand, giving it a bruising shake that threatened to break his arm in half. He muttered something that was supposed to be a greeting, and Leo refrained from giving him an inappropriate smirk.

Having survived the handshake, Leo turned his back on him and followed Becca into the hallway again, feeling victorious.

"I'm taking you to HR first," she said. "There's paperwork. And then someone will walk you into the lounge, where the rest of the team will gather for the press conference."

"Thanks," he said, tugging at his necktie. He was experiencing a very quick comedown from the high of forcing Coach Karl to be civil, because playing for a man who hated his guts would probably end in disaster. He'd been so ready to celebrate this milestone, but now that seemed premature. Instead, he'd be putting in a call to his agent to discuss disaster scenarios. If Coach Karl wanted to be a dick, he could send Leo back to the minors. At least his signed contract probably meant that they'd still have to pay his NHL salary. Unless there was some loophole Karl could activate—a way to send him back to the minors empty-handed.

He sure hoped not.

In the HR office, Leo filled out approximately seven thousand forms. There were contact forms and health forms. Tax documents. A public relations survey—favorite charities and past experience. The stack of paperwork was endless.

Yet if Coach Karl had his way, he'd be on the next plane to Michigan.

When Leo took a break to raise his agent on the phone, the man confirmed that Coach Karl could send him back to the minors at his whim. "They have to honor the financial parts of your contract," he said, "so you'll make the big bucks for two years, no matter what. But they don't have to keep you in Brooklyn. They can stash you in the minors."

"That's the worst that can happen?" he asked.

"*Pretty* much," the agent hedged. "I mean, if the new coach really hates your guts, he could prevent you from being traded to another team that wants you. But that would be both expensive and extreme."

Jesus. "Good to know," he grumbled.

After that uplifting conversation, and his hour in the HR office, Becca brought him a shiny box. "Here," she said. "Everyone on the team gets a party favor." He lifted the lid to find a large, sleek, nearly weightless titanium phone. At least he assumed it was a phone. "I'm going to port your number onto the Katt Phone . . ." She covered her mouth. "Whoops. That's our nickname for them. The real name is the T-5000. Anyway—you'll carry this for as long as you're a member of the team."

"Okay." If only he knew how long that would be.

"The big app on the front page will always know everything about your schedule—where to be, and when. When you're traveling, we push local weather and traffic information to you, as well as cab company numbers and restaurants. The floorplan of every hotel where you'll stay. Your room number. Everything."

"Got it," Leo said, fingering the device's cool edge. Talking on this thing would be like holding a large slice of bread up to the side of his face. But that was a small price to pay to join the team.

"There's a narrow light strip all around the phone that changes color when it wants your attention," Becca continued. "You'll see. If the edges of the phone glow yellow, there's an update you need to see. If it glows red, there's an emergency, or an important change of plans."

"Groovy."

"And one more tip?" Becca offered. "When you ask the phone a question, if you say Nate's name first, you'll get a priority hyper-connection. So don't just say, 'What time is the jet leaving?' Say, 'Nate, what time is the jet leaving?'"

"Got it."

"That feature will even swap you onto another cell phone network if you don't have enough bars. It's awesome. If a bit egotistical." She whispered this last bit, and Leo grinned. "Well." She clapped her hands once. "Let's get you to the players' lounge."

She led him past a big open room which was set up for a press conference—with a table at one end and rows of folding chairs lined up all the way to the back of the room. Beyond that, she opened another door to reveal a large lounge area, with sofas and a pool table. It was a gorgeous, comfortable room, and it was full of hockey players wearing suits and purple ties—the team color for the Brooklyn Bruisers.

Several heads turned in his direction, and Leo was confronted with the reality that this should have been a really exciting moment for him—meeting his new NHL teammates. But Coach Karl had robbed him of that joy. In order to become a true member of this team, it would be an uphill battle against all of Karl's objections.

He didn't know if it was possible, but he'd die trying.

And hey, he comforted himself, scanning the guys in this room, *at least if Karl succeeds at tossing your ass by the end of the day, you'll never have to wear a purple tie.*

"Gentlemen," Becca said, clapping her hands. A couple of conversations stopped, heads turning in their direction. "This is Leo Trevi, a forward, and Mr. Kattenberger's newest trade."

There was a murmured chorus of "yo" and "welcome."

"Hey, man." A player waved from the sofa, and Leo recognized him as the team's current captain, Patrick

O'Doul. At thirty-two years old, he'd been scoring for this team long before Nate bought it and brought it to Brooklyn. They'd had a difficult couple of seasons, but it wasn't O'Doul's fault.

"Hey," Leo said. "Glad to be here." He wanted to be a member of this team so fucking bad. But walking into this room wasn't a moment of victory—it was more like the preparation for battle. Knowing that didn't make Leo feel like the friendliest guy in the world.

"He doesn't have a locker yet," Becca said. "Will you do any rearranging? Or shall we give him the, um, open spot?"

O'Doul transferred a toothpick from one side of his mouth to the other, gazing up at Leo with his hands at the back of his head. Maybe he affected an easy disposition, but Leo could still see him sizing up the new guy, looking for weakness. "Put 'im in the open spot," he said finally.

Until that moment, Leo hadn't properly appreciated the fact that getting a crack at the NHL was like being the recipient of a donor organ—someone else had to suffer to give him his big break. Hopefully he wouldn't be offering up a lung to some other soul before the day was out.

"The publicist will arrive shortly to brief everyone on the press conference," Becca said. "Until then, make yourself at home."

"Thanks. I appreciate it."

"So where you from?" O'Doul asked lazily.

"Here. Grew up in Huntington on the North Shore. Been watching this team forever. When I was five is the first time my dad got season tickets to the . . ."

O'Doul held up a hand to silence him. "Don't say it. Kattenberger doesn't allow anyone to speak the old franchise name."

"Sorry?"

"Inside this building, you can only call us the Bruisers." O'Doul winked. "See? I can say it easily now. Took me a year to break the habit. I mean—Kattenberger is a bit of a whack job on this particular point. It's like a Voldemort thing. The Team That Shall Not Be Named. But since the boss man paid his left nut for the franchise and changed the name, he can do it his way. If you want to avoid his wrath, you never say that old name."

"Um, thanks?"

The captain had an evil grin. "I know it's weird. I still have all the old pennants in a box somewhere. If Kattenberger knew, he'd probably send one of his ninja minions to my apartment to have 'em incinerated. Where else you play hockey?"

"Drafted by Detroit. Sent down to Muskegon's AHL team for two seasons. Harkness College before that."

O'Doul's expression chilled. "Aw, an Ivy League boy. That's cute."

Somebody has a chip on his shoulder. Looking for a change of topic, Leo nodded at O'Doul's purple rep stripes. "Did the owner choose the new color, too?"

O'Doul tugged on his tie. "You betcha. Him and a bunch of million dollar marketing gurus. We call it indigo, 'cause that sounds better than purple."

Leo laughed. "Thanks for the tip."

"Stick with me, kid. Might want to grab yourself a bottle of water. If you're the new guy, they might make you say a few words at the press conference. Publicist will let you know. Though maybe they won't get around to it, because the whole coach thing is a pretty big story."

Ugh. "No kidding."

"The last guy got fired—what—a year and a half ago, now? Kattenberger had to do it. The guy was a good coach, but you don't trash-talk the new owner like that. Then an interim coach got cancer. So now it's on to Worthington. He's another Long Island guy. Could be worse, right?"

No, actually. It could *not* be worse, even if the coach was his dead aunt Maria Theresa. "Where did you say that water was?"

He pointed to the corner. "Espresso machine is over there, too, if that's your thing."

"Thanks." Leo made his way over to the corner, stopping every few feet as the guys reached out to shake his hand.

"Thanks," he said a half dozen times. "Great to be here." But he probably wasn't all that convincing. Wait until they watched a snarling Coach Karl ship his ass back to Michigan. That would be a fun moment. They'd all be wondering what the hell he did to piss off Coach.

Leo would be wondering, too.

Once upon a time, he and Coach Worthington were tight. Karl had been a college coach then, but he'd done some development work with Leo's high school team. The man had taught him a lot, and had always had time for Leo.

At the same time, Leo was dating his daughter, Georgia. There are some dads who hate their little girl's boyfriend on principle. But Coach Karl hadn't seemed like that sort of dad. And anyway, Leo had treated Georgia like a queen until the day she'd broken his heart. When Leo looked back on high school, loving Georgia was actually the one thing in his life he knew he'd done right. Maybe he wasn't as good a big brother to his siblings as he should have been. And maybe he was a pain in the ass to his teachers. But Leo had been really good to Georgia Worthington, from the moment he asked her to the homecoming dance their sophomore year until the day of high school graduation, when she cut him loose.

It wasn't quite as simple as puppy love running its course, though. A few months before graduation, something terrible had happened to Georgia, and Leo wasn't around to stop it. The last part of their senior year, they'd both suffered. And sometime during those dark days, Coach Worthington stopped approving of Leo. At the time, Leo had been too worried about Georgia to wonder much about her father's change of heart. His disapproval meant nothing to Leo—there'd been only Georgia and her pain. He'd stuck by her side, loyal to the very end.

Goddamn it, he was good to her. Then she'd pushed him away.

And now Leo was standing in front of a glass refrigerator full to the top with water and Gatorade, his fists clenched, upset all over again by the anguish he'd tried to put aside for the last six years.

"Just open 'er up and take one," a voice said beside him. "Anytime you need."

"Thanks," he said gruffly. He realized he'd been staring at the row of bottles as if they'd provide the secrets of the universe. He yanked open the door and snagged a bottle of water.

"I'm Silas Kelly," the guy beside him said, thrusting out a meaty hand. "Backup goalie."

Leo shook. "Good to meet you. How long you been a Bruiser?" God, that sounded ridiculous.

Silas grinned. "This is my rookie year. Spent some time in Ontario on an ECHL team. Got traded in September."

"Cool."

"I've played four games. Hoping the new coach is a fan so I can get off the bench a little more often."

The backup goalie job wasn't an easy one. "I hear you," Leo said. "Gotta say, if Coach Karl likes you, that'll make one of us."

He laughed, and it was big and loud. "Really? You two have history?"

"We have a little." *Even if I'm not quite sure what it is.*

"How'd you get called up, then?"

Leo shook his head. "No clue."

The door to the room banged open. "Gentlemen," said a female voice.

He turned toward the doorway, his fingers freezing midtwist on the cap of the water bottle as he stared at the girl in the doorway. No—scratch that. At the *woman* in the doorway. His chest seized, because *Jesus Christ.* Georgia was even more beautiful than she had been six years ago.

She addressed the team. He thought so, anyway. But he didn't hear a word she said, because he was too busy cataloging everything that was familiar about her. Adulthood had thinned her face a little, revealing cheekbones so shapely that they might have starred on the cover of a magazine. His ex had always been a pretty girl, but now she was stunning. Her blond hair had darkened somewhat, but it was still shot through with golden streaks. He knew exactly how silky it would feel under his hand if he brushed it away from her face.

There were unfamiliar parts to this picture, too—her stern expression, for one. He'd always hoped that Georgia had gone on to find her smile again, even if he wasn't the lucky recipient. But he didn't see any evidence of smiling now. And she was all dressed up in a suit and filmy blouse. And *heels*. His Georgia never wore stilts like that. They made her legs look a mile long. They were killer. But they weren't her.

". . . We'll begin in fifteen minutes. Coach Worthington will thank Mr. Kattenberger for the opportunity to lead the team, and he'll say a few words about how excited he is to work with all of you. All most of you have to do is sit up straight and clap. Any questions?"

His brain was still playing catch-up. If Georgia was talking about the press conference, she must work for the team. An assistant? A publicist?

O'Doul raised his hand, a goofy smile on his face.

"What is it, captain?" Georgia asked with an edge of impatience in her voice.

"Is it a coincidence that our new coach has the same last name as you?"

"Yes and no," she said, eyes on her clipboard. "It is a coincidence that we both work for the same team. But we have the same name because Coach Worthington is my father."

O'Doul grinned. "Thanks for clearing that up, babe. Is he pretty, too?"

Her expression darkened. "You can decide for yourself, Mr. O'Doul," she said coolly. "And you'll have a good view, because I need you sitting on the dais up front. After Coach Worthington gives his remarks, you'll say a few words of welcome. I've drafted something for you here."

She flipped to another page on her clipboard and extracted a sheet of paper, handing it to him. She actually had to lean down a bit, because her shoes made her so much taller than usual.

Leo was openly staring now, but he couldn't help it. She looked both the same and different. Her legs, always shapely from playing tennis all her life, looked ten miles long in those heels. But there was something about her that was . . . harder. She seemed more brittle than he remembered.

She hadn't looked at him yet, either. Did she even know he was here?

"Do I have to say this exactly as it's written?" O'Doul asked, skimming the page.

"No, as long as you sound warm and articulate."

"Just like I am every day." He chuckled. "Fine. What else?"

"One more thing." She cleared her throat and shifted her weight. "I need you to welcome a new player after you welcome your coach. Georgia dropped her eyes to the page in front of her again. As if she needed notes to get Leo's name right. "Mr. Leonardo Trevi, rookie forward, formerly of the Muskegon Muskrats. Traded from Detroit to Brooklyn for a second round draft pick this spring."

"Got it," O'Doul said.

Leo saw Georgia gather herself together. She took a deep breath and looked straight at him, as if she'd known exactly where he was the whole time. They locked eyes for a nanosecond before she blinked and broke off their staring contest. "Why aren't you wearing a purple tie?" she demanded.

After six years, that's what she wanted to say first? Her terseness took Leo by surprise, delaying his answer by a beat. "Sorry. Didn't own one. Muskrats don't wear purple ties." He smiled at her, hoping to put her at ease. *I know this is weird, Gigi. But we can survive it.*

But, damn it, her face shut down even more. "Someone trade with him," she snapped, looking down at the watch on her smooth wrist. And, *hell*, he knew that watch. He'd bought it for her with nearly all his savings. It had been a graduation present. He'd stood in Saks Fifth Avenue for a long time trying to figure out which was the most beautiful. He'd been so desperate to make her smile that spring. He would have done anything. Given her anything.

It hadn't worked.

"Two minutes," Georgia said, her voice gruff. "I want you to file into the press conference in *exactly* two minutes. Your seats are reserved in the two front rows. Do not take any questions on your way in. We'll start the conference the moment you're seated." Then she turned around and strode out of the room in those unlikely shoes.

"Dibs on giving the rookie my purple tie!" Silas yelled. "I called it."

Leo watched Georgia disappear. And then he took off his perfectly good green silk tie and took Silas's ugly one.

THREE

As Georgia left the lounge, the words she'd said to Leo echoed through her head. *Why aren't you wearing a purple tie?* God, was it cocktail hour yet? She'd actually *snapped* at him.

But she'd been caught off guard. As in her guard was on the G train to Queens as soon as she'd gotten a proper look at that chiseled jaw and those big dark eyes, with lashes so thick that there was practically a breeze whenever he blinked.

Now she'd have to take Taylor Swift's advice and shake it off, though. There was a press conference to throw, and it didn't matter if her knees were quaking. She walked straight into the press room to find fifty reporters shifting in their seats, hoping that Georgia would get the show on the road so they could file before lunchtime.

Checking her watch one more time, she took up a stealthy position on the side wall, out of sight yet near enough to the dais so that she could put out any fires or provide any necessary information. Everything was in place except for the only thing that mattered—all that was needed now were the team, the coach, and the owner.

Luckily, Nate Kattenberger appeared in the doorway. On his way to the front, he stopped for a moment in front of her. "Good crowd, Number Three. Well done."

The unexpected praise from a self-made billionaire made her stomach flutter. "Thank you!"

He moved on, stepping onto the raised platform and rounding the table to the center, taking the power seat and smirking at the reporters. Seriously, she needed to work on this man's RSF. Resting Smug Face. It wouldn't win him any points with either the media or his players.

Coach Karl was the next man to enter the room, and when he did, all the journalists leaned forward in their chairs. Then they all reached for their phones and began tweeting or texting or whatever it was journalists did first when they were in possession of today's latest bit of sports gossip. *Karl Worthington is the new coach of the Brooklyn Bruisers.* Their forefingers began hammering out the scoop as quickly as possible. In two minutes this would be old news, so they had to get it out fast.

As she watched her strong, capable father mount the dais and take a seat, for one golden second she forgot to worry about anything. She'd always loved growing up in a sports-centered household. It was a good life, and she was proud of her dad.

But then, right on schedule, the players began entering the room, passing her on the way to their reserved seats in the first and second rows. One by one they filed by in their suits.

Georgia wasn't blind—the men whose public image she guarded were hotter than the scotch bonnet peppers at the Borough Hall Greenmarket. But at work, she made it her habit to be a bit frosty. Okay, a *lot* frosty. Getting them to like her wasn't the goal. Getting them to *listen* to her was everything. It was her job to keep the players in line and out of trouble with the media, and she couldn't do that if they saw her as their buddy. It didn't help her credibility that she was younger than many of them, either. So she always brought her most professional self into the room when addressing the players.

She braced herself for the arrival of the final two players, but no amount of preparation would have been enough.

A broader, superhero version of Leo Trevi walked past, not two feet away. And he looked *ridiculously* hot in a dark charcoal suit. *God.* Seeing him was a sucker punch to the gut. Once upon a time he'd loved her. And then when he'd stopped, it wasn't really his fault.

A girl could get seriously lost in her memories staring at him.

Without wanting to, Georgia began cataloguing all the ways he looked different. His hair was shorter than it had been, and the trim made him look older. The scruff on his chin was new. She wanted to stroke her thumb across his jaw to see if it was rough or soft.

One of his big hands clutched a bottle of water. *No wedding ring,* her mind offered up. She remembered how those hands felt on her body . . .

Someone coughed on the dais. That's when Georgia realized she was staring.

Jesus, girl. Get a grip. She just needed to get through this press conference, and then she could go back to her office and be alone for a while to deal with her shock. She would need to form a game plan for coexisting with Leo Trevi. It would take some time to get used to him walking around this place. And it wasn't only that he looked like a sexy, A-list movie star. Seeing him dredged up thoughts of the scariest time in her life.

Maybe it wasn't rational, but she didn't like the idea of Leo invading her little world. Yesterday, Brooklyn had belonged to *her.* The Long Island 'burbs where she'd grown up had felt far away from the brick streets and renovated factory spaces of Brooklyn. In this job, she'd felt truly independent, putting down her own fragile roots in a new place.

Fast forward twenty-four hours, and her daddy had joined the workplace and her ex-boyfriend had shown up to remind her of all that she'd lost. Really, a girl could be forgiven for feeling slightly hysterical.

Not that there was any time to panic. Right now she needed to focus on the press conference and look like a professional—at least a half-nauseated professional in uncomfortable shoes.

The crowd made their last-minute adjustments, flipping open their reporters' pads, focusing their cameras. A low murmur of expectation hummed throughout the room.

O'Doul had been the last to enter the room, following closely behind Leo. His eyes met Georgia's as his hand landed on Leo's shoulder. Two paces later he rasped something into Leo's ear. "You gotta stay on the good side of the publicist." They were moving away, their backs to her. O'Doul tried to keep his conversation private, but she still heard his final whispered comment. "She's a total bitch on wheels."

The comment didn't startle Georgia at all. Nor did it even offend her. Forthright men in the workplace are revered for their strength. Women? You can either be a doormat or a bitch. Take your pick.

But what happened next was a surprise. And not the good kind.

The whole thing seemed to happen in slow motion. First, Leo and O'Doul rounded the corner of the table where she had carefully positioned their chairs and microphones. Leo's expression darkened, and she saw his eyes narrow at O'Doul, his beautiful jaw hardening. At the same time, he sat down in his chair . . .

Georgia gasped as he opened his mouth. It was like those dreams where you couldn't move fast enough to save yourself—she lunged forward, raising her hands in the universal sign for "stop," hoping the motion would alert him to the disaster that was coming.

But he didn't see her. Instead, Leo leaned toward O'Doul, as if in confidence. But that put his mouth *way* too close to the microphone. "If you want to keep breathing, don't *ever* call the love of my life a bitch."

There was a squeal of feedback, or maybe that was just inside Georgia's head. But either way, heads turned. Because that mic was *live*. The whole room heard what he'd said.

Georgia watched in horror as Leo realized his mistake, sitting back in surprise. As if moving farther away could undo what he'd just done.

O'Doul turned his big chin slowly in Leo's direction, a lopsided smirk on his face. For a split second she was terrified that he'd fire back at the insolent rookie who had just threatened his airway.

But at least now the gods were merciful. O'Doul held his tongue, because he'd been on the press conference circuit for years, and he knew to shut up and move on, at least while the cameras were rolling.

Which they were.

Like an army of giant, buglike eyes, every oversized lens in the room swung over to focus on Leo Trevi. The telltale sound of shutters firing issued through the room. And from the other end of the table, Georgia's father turned to give Leo a glare which outshone every flashbulb.

And just like that, she lost control of the meeting, and therefore the message.

Leo lifted his chin, his posture defiant. But she saw a red flush creep up his neck. Unfortunately his gaze swung in her direction next. He set his jaw defiantly. As if he weren't to blame for this problem.

As *if*.

But the press didn't care who was at fault. After gaping their fill at Leo, those cameras swung farther, following Leo's gaze, and landed on *her*.

That's when Georgia decided it might actually be possible to die of embarrassment. Or at least to wish for it. Reeling, she had to thrust out a hand to steady herself on the doorframe. Nate Kattenberger tapped the microphone, his mouth in a grim line. When they're trying to make a statement, billionaires don't appreciate seeing their hard-won media audience pulled in the wrong direction.

"Holy shit," a voice whispered beside her. It belonged to Becca. "You are in so much trouble."

She was right. The whispers and camera shutter sounds

only grew louder. All those eyes, all in the wrong place. There was only one solution.

Georgia turned and fled the room.

Nine hours later the reporters were long gone. But the horror of the world's worst press conference was still achingly fresh.

Georgia let herself into the apartment she shared with Becca, a bag of takeout food dangling from each hand. "Honey, I'm home," she called out. It was the first joke she'd made in hours. Today was almost too awful even for gallows humor.

She kicked off her evil high heels and staggered into the living room.

"Finally!" Becca squawked. "I'm dying!"

"Of hunger? It's only seven thirty." They often ate much later during hockey season.

"No, moron. *Curiosity.*" Becca snatched the food bags out of her hands. "This does smell good, though. How many kinds did you get?"

"Five. Three from the Garden and two from the Foo." Say what you will about Brooklyn—it's too crowded, it's too trendy, it's way too expensive—but when a girl needed some excellent Chinese dumplings, Brooklyn was the place to be.

Becca squealed. "Yay! I mean—I'm sorry that you had a five-kinds-of-dumplings day. Put on some yoga pants and I'll pour drinks. Go! Quick like a bunny! Because you have some explaining to do."

Georgia was too tired to argue. She went to her room and did as her roommate ordered.

"Our fridge smells weird," Becca called from the tiny kitchen.

"Yeah," she grumbled. "That mango we never ate? It's gone bad. I need to clean it out. Not right now, though."

"Ah." Becca didn't even have to shout, because their

apartment was small enough that they could hear each other from anywhere. "Hey—when I was answering your phones this afternoon, you got a call from some skydiving place in New Jersey. They had a cancellation for next week and offered you the spot. But I told them you'd be away on business."

"Thanks," she said, rooting in a drawer for flannel pants. Georgia had a lot of outdoor hobbies—skydiving and hang gliding and rock climbing. She was a bit of an adrenaline junkie, but most of those activities had to wait until after summertime. She could barely get to her dojang for tae kwon do once a week during hockey season. "How many nights is that trip next week, anyway? I'm afraid to look."

"Six. It's a doozie. And you have to pack a day in advance because the benefit is the night before."

"Of course it is."

"Now get out here and tell me everything about Leo Trevi."

Georgia took her time changing. She didn't really want to talk about it. Yet she was starving, so returning to the living room was inevitable.

At least when she got there, she found a candle lit on the coffee table and two places set. They didn't have a lot of furniture in their living room—just an enormous but terrifically ugly sofa—brown velvet with pink roses. They hoped to replace it someday soon. Until then they played up its odd color scheme with pink floor pillows for extra seating. Becca had pulled one of these up to the coffee table for Georgia, who liked sitting there.

This is where they ate when they had time for a leisurely meal. Lately, dinner had been either consumed at their desks or eaten on bar stools at their kitchen counter. Their apartment lacked a proper dining table. There just wasn't room.

"The first thing I need to know," Becca said, helping herself to the steamed chicken and cabbage dumplings, "is why have I never heard the name Leo Trevi before?"

Taking her first sip of wine, Georgia realized the question wasn't an easy one. She'd known Leo her whole life.

And then in high school, they'd been inseparable. The Golden Couple. Somewhere in her father's Long Island home there was even a clichéd picture of the two of them being crowned homecoming king and queen.

This morning, which now felt like a hundred years ago, she'd scoffed when DJ had said she never mentioned Leo. But she'd lived with Becca a year now, and never brought him up? Point DJ. The fact that she never mentioned Leo hadn't seemed at all strange to her until today.

"Well," she began, reaching for the jade dumplings, "Leo was my high school boyfriend." It sounded so inconsequential when put that way, though. Leo loomed a lot larger in her life than a teenage crush. He was her first date. Her first kiss. Her first love.

Her first *everything*.

"He's *so* hot." Becca sighed. "Were you together long?"

"Three years. I dumped him on graduation day."

Her friend gave a low whistle. "Jeez. Why?"

"Well . . ." Again, it wasn't going to be easy to explain. "You know I had a really difficult time my senior year." She'd long since told Becca that story. A few months before high school graduation, she'd been raped on a college campus where she'd spent spring break at tennis camp.

"Yeah. That must have been a terrible year, sweetie."

"No kidding. There are parts of it that I don't remember very well." The first ugly weeks after the attack, she'd been a terrified wreck. It had been a blur of police reports, a hospital exam. Her father's rage. Georgia didn't like remembering it. It had taken her a long time to feel normal again, and dwelling on the past felt like inviting the shadows back into her life.

"Was Leo around after it happened? That would be a lot for an eighteen-year-old boy to take." Becca rose up on her knees to refill her wine glass.

Georgia tried to decide what to say about that time that was fair to both of them. "Leo was amazing," she admitted, reaching for more dumplings. "I didn't go to school for a while. He'd come over afterwards and bring me the homework assignments. He brought me cupcakes and movies to watch. He just sat there on the sofa and held my hand for about six weeks straight. And then when I went back to school, he drove every day and walked me into the building and then out again afterwards. So I'd feel safe."

Becca sighed into her wine glass. "That's pretty inspiring. It's almost enough to restore my faith in men. *Almost.*" She hadn't been lucky in her dating life, which was one of the reasons she and Georgia spent so many of their Friday nights eating takeout on the coffee table. "So why did you dump him? Or shouldn't I ask? Please don't tell me he cheated while you were laid up. I really hope this story doesn't end like that."

It didn't, though. "No, he was perfect. Except that we'd been so happy before, and now we were both sad all the time." There was a cloud over the two of them that hadn't always been there. Before, Leo had always looked at her with laughter in his eyes. Whether they were playing tennis on the courts in the park, or singing along to the radio in his car, it was all fun and games.

That was all gone after her attack. Even as he held her hand on the sofa, regret seemed to permeate the air. All their jokes were gone—stolen for good on one brutal night in Florida. His laughing eyes were gone, too, replaced with concern and regret.

And as the weeks ground onward, Georgia knew it would never be the same again. Hour by stifling hour, she had literally watched their wild, passionate love affair dissipate. Leo became the best friend she'd ever had. But the passion was gone.

"I always thought that Leo and I would be together forever," she admitted. "But things just weren't the same between us. And I was heading to Virginia for college in August, and he was headed for Harkness in Connecticut. So it was going to be weird anyway. And I just *dreaded* the idea of a whole summer of Leo watching me to make sure that I was okay." When graduation day came, she'd reached her limit. Splitting up with him felt like simply accepting the inevitable. "So I told him that after such a sad, scary year, I needed a clean break, that I wanted to start fresh in college. And that there was no reason to drag it out. That it was just going to hurt more later."

Becca cringed. "What did he do?"

Georgia swallowed hard, and the wine she'd drunk seemed to turn to acid in her stomach. "He got all teared up. But he said, 'It's not what I want. But I understand.' And then he went home."

With a shaking hand, Georgia set down her glass and took another bite. At the time, Leo's quiet acceptance of this decision had shocked her. She didn't know three years of love and togetherness could be undone so quickly. But Leo stayed away like she'd asked him to. And she cried herself to sleep sporadically for the next several weeks, wondering if she'd been crazy to send him away.

The summer had dragged on in the same sad way, only lonelier. Then, on the Fourth of July, she'd gone to the fireworks show on her dad's boat. And on the docks she'd spied him with a girl from their graduating class. The two of them had been eating ice cream and laughing about something.

Seeing that had practically killed her. On the one hand, watching Leo smile at another girl had made her feel enraged. But the worst was knowing he hadn't smiled at her like that for months.

That's why she'd had to cut him loose. But knowing it was the right thing to do hadn't made it easier.

"Do you ever talk?" Becca asked.

Georgia shook her head. "Nope. I never wanted to. He's probably got a girlfriend, maybe even a fiancée. This was almost six years ago. I don't want to know. His brother and I are still friends, but I never ask about Leo. I guess that's pretty weird, right?" If you'd asked Georgia twenty-four hours ago whether or not she still felt any pain when she thought of Leo, she would have said no. But there was obviously still a sore spot there.

Becca set her wine glass down with a thunk. "Georgia Ann Worthington, I think he's the reason you don't date. I think you're still in love with this boy."

"*Man*," she corrected quickly. "And it was a long time ago, Bec. We were just kids."

Her roommate's scrutiny was a little more attentive than Georgia would have wished. "If you say so. Unfortunately, Leo Trevi went on record today to tell the whole world that you're the love of his life."

It was Georgia's turn to cringe. "Leo was shocked to see me, I think. And O'Doul had just referred to me as a bitch. He just . . . snapped a little."

"He can snap on my behalf any day of the week," Becca said. "I took seventy calls from the media this afternoon, and plenty of them were questions about Leo."

Georgia set down her fork and tossed her napkin on the table. Then she lay back on their area rug. "I'm in such deep shit, Bec. Nate and the general manager are going to have to hire someone over me now. My press conference was a shit show, and some of those reporters are going to ask about *me*." She picked her head up off the cushion and squinted at Becca. "They are, right? I'm not just vain to think that?"

Becca cringed. "You are the least vain person I know. And unfortunately, I was asked by three people whether you were the subject of the argument between O'Doul and the rookie."

Georgia dropped her head back down and groaned. "The publicist isn't supposed to be part of the story."

Becca was silent for a moment. "Well, Nate left for Midtown about an hour and a half after the press conference. So he doesn't know that I had to cover your phones all day. Not unless Hugh mentions it to him."

The general manager wasn't the type to micromanage Becca, so Georgia's freak-out had probably gone unnoticed. "Thank you, by the way," Georgia said to their antique plaster ceiling. "I don't know what I would have done if you hadn't screened for me." Once it became obvious that she'd receive press inquiries about the hot mic incident, she'd forwarded her line to Becca's desk, hoping to stay out of the story. "This is so bad, though. Will you help me strategize?"

"Sure," Becca said, her voice cheery. "First. Remove all your clothes, and then borrow my trench coat. If a hottie like Leo Trevi called me the love of his life, I wouldn't be eating takeout on the living room floor with my roommate. At least one of us should be having sex with someone who doesn't require batteries."

Georgia didn't rise to the bait. Leo was crazy to have said such a thing today. It didn't mean anything. They didn't even know each other anymore. More years had passed since she'd said good-bye than they'd even been together. "I just need to keep my job, Bec. How do I keep the media focused on the Bruisers without focusing them on Leo and me?"

"This story just has to wear itself out." Becca gestured grandly with her wine glass. "In the meantime, you can send your man Leo out on the town. He can do some interviews about how much fun it is to be a rookie. Did you see that some blog wants a photo shoot with Leo?"

Georgia had spotted it on Becca's lengthy call sheets. A widely read fan blog called Pucker Up wanted Leo for a spread entitled Hockey Hotties. "Sure, I can make Leo out to be Mr. Eligible Bachelor, even if he isn't one. I can send out his head shots like seeds in the wind. But that won't change the fact that news of the new coach just isn't as interesting as a scuffle between the captain and a hot young rookie. This is going to be a Page Six shit storm. *Rookie Bruiser Threatens Captain.* Film at eleven." Or worse—*Arrogant Rookie Bruiser Declares His Love For Mystery Girl.* That one would show up on the fan sites, with links to Leo's Instagram feed, if he had one.

And here she'd thought she could get a lot of coverage for the team's new direction in coaching.

"My office received Leo's scanned HR forms this afternoon," Becca said. "He listed his parents as his emergency contacts. No girlfriend."

Georgia's heart did an inappropriate twerk. Not that she'd admit it. "Tell me this story will blow over soon."

"If by 'soon' you mean next month," Becca mused, "Because nobody believed me today when I fed 'em your line about O'Doul and Trevi arguing over a pop song. They all saw you run out of there like your panty hose were on fire. You won't be able to convince anyone that there's no story there. But what you *can* do is serve up Leo on a platter. Send him to a movie premiere with an A-list date. Make him do the Pucker Up thing, and then maybe one of those beefcake calendars. And bring home a couple copies, okay?" She nudged Georgia with her toe.

"Not funny," Georgia grumbled. "God, we need a few wins. Is it too much to ask?"

"Ask Daddy for it as a birthday present," Becca teased.

"Sure. Coach Karl can change the narrative for me. He can rescue his foolish daughter from the gossip columns' clutches." At least she hoped he could. "But even if he does, I'm drowning in work. The team missed out on two publicity opportunities last week because I couldn't be in three places at once. I need help, but I'm not willing to ask for it. If they'd just confirm me as the permanent PR director, I wouldn't have to tiptoe around the issue."

Becca clicked her tongue sympathetically. "I know you don't want them hiring anyone new. Can you shift any of it onto the interns? Can you get a temp?"

She shook her head. "Writing press releases and setting up interviews isn't something I can delegate. Even when I ask them to blast out a bunch of stuff on social media, I have to spend an hour on it first, so the message is right. And then there's the charity stuff. It's actually my favorite part of the job, but I don't have enough time to plan for it now."

"You mean like the benefit next week?"

Georgia rolled her head, trying to get the knots out of her neck. "Yeah. Thank god for party planners. I'd like to do more with charities but I don't know how to stop spinning my wheels. It's hard to think big when you're always putting out fires."

"Poor baby." Above her, Becca leaned over the coffee table, gathering the empty cartons. She put the last dumplings on Georgia's plate, because her appetite was legendary. "You need anything?"

"I'm good," Georgia insisted, sitting up. "And you don't have to clean up. You've already done enough of my work for one day."

"So I answered a few extra phone calls. Big effing deal." Becca disappeared into the kitchen, returning with a new bottle of wine. "I'm topping up our glasses," she announced.

"Why? Tomorrow is open practice." And goddamn, what lousy timing. She didn't want to face fans on a Saturday morning.

"I need to get you drunk so you'll tell me whether the new rookie is any good in the sack."

"We are *not* discussing that." Reminiscing was exactly what she did not need right now. A girl could get really distracted remembering those hot nights in the back of Leo's car. And it was startling to remember just how reckless she'd once been. When she and Leo were teenagers, things had escalated in a big hot hurry. He'd been eager to please her and she'd been eager to let him try.

Nnnngh. They'd had so, so much sex. And it had been glorious.

Becca giggled. "He was, wasn't he? Hell. Teenage boys aren't known for their sexual prowess. But you should see your face right now."

Georgia bit her lip and fought for a more neutral expression. "I really don't need to be thinking about that tonight."

"Pity." Becca twisted off the top of the bottle and angled it toward Georgia's glass. "Whether you want to think about you and Leo together or not, both your faces are going to be on all the puck bunny blogs tomorrow."

"God, I hope not. And I hope the top brass won't notice how much thunder it's stolen from their big announcement. Crap. Nate probably has some kind of ninja web alarm that sends every mention of the team straight to his Katt Phone."

"You're not going to lose your job," Becca murmured.

"But maybe we should hold off another month on buying the new sofa."

"The universe does not want to show us any job security, Bec. Why is that?"

"I wish I knew." Becca had a good job running the Bruisers C-suite. But she *used* to be Nate's personal assistant at his skyscraper in midtown. When he bought the team, he shipped her out of the thirtieth floor office tower to work in Brooklyn. That's how she and Georgia had met, almost two years ago. Even now, Becca still wasn't sure why Nate made the switch. He said he needed a trusted employee in Brooklyn, because he didn't make it to the Bruisers' office every day. But Georgia knew she often fretted that he'd been dissatisfied with her work.

"That movie you wanted to see tonight starts at nine," Georgia said from her position on the floor. "But we're not really in the mood to go out, are we?"

"Nope," Becca agreed. "Why spend the money when we can drink wine and watch Netflix?"

"Truth."

"So get over here. The world's ugliest couch is calling your name."

Two hours and one chick flick later, Georgia climbed into her bed and shut off the light. She tucked the comforter around herself to keep out the chill. Theirs was a small, drafty apartment in an old building which had changed purposes so many times that it was difficult to say whether her little bedroom had once been someone's office or their servants' quarters. Her double bed barely fit into the space. But she wouldn't trade it for a high-rise in a less interesting neighborhood. Dumbo was pricey but scenic. And the short walking commute to work was something every New Yorker dreamed of.

She lay there in the dark, waiting for sleep to come. But the difficult day still held her in its stressful clutches. Leo's handsome face drifted through her consciousness for the first time in years. There was an ocean of time between them now—four years of college plus two more afterward.

Georgia never let herself think about him—it was too painful. She'd lost so much during her senior year of high school. Her peace of mind. Her fearlessness. And the love of the boy she'd always cherished. In order to bury those bad memories, she'd had to pack away the fun times with Leo, too. But today it had all come rushing at her like an avalanching closet. All the good, the bad, and the handsome, chiseled chin. The warm brown eyes . . .

Yikes.

Leo was going to be difficult to ignore—all two hundred glorious muscular pounds of him. Just the idea that he could pass by her office door at any moment was distracting. If she saw him almost every day, that tide of memories would not be held back.

At least there'd be a lot of good mixed in with the sad and the scary. They'd had so much fun together. Looking back on it with a few years' distance, Georgia realized they'd probably been one of those couples that lonely people hated. Whenever they were in the same room together, they were always touching. His hand on her knee under the table at the diner. Her fingers ruffling the hair at the back of his head.

And the stolen kisses . . .

Georgia squirmed in her bed. The memory of Leo's hands on her body was potent, even after all this time. Whenever they'd found a moment's privacy, they'd always attacked each other. The combination of natural chemistry and teenage enthusiasm had been practically combustible.

In hindsight, it was a miracle they'd never had a pregnancy scare. By the time Georgia turned eighteen and promptly snuck off to get an IUD without her father's knowledge, they'd been fooling around for many months already. The generous bench seat of Leo's old truck was their favorite place in the world. It was there that they'd kissed for hours on end, their hands wandering and exploring as far as they dared in a parked vehicle.

But the first time they had any real privacy was in Georgia's bed, on a night when her dad was out of town at one of his away games. Georgia had sworn to him that Leo would not come over while she was home alone. And yet the minute his car had backed down the driveway, she'd called Leo to tell him the coast was clear.

After hanging up, she'd removed all her clothes and climbed into bed. She'd laid there, the sheets silky against her heated skin, listening. Ten minutes later she heard the sound of Leo's truck engine. Then the slam of his door as he got out.

Georgia had clutched the sheet to her chest, where her heart did the mambo—not out of fear, but expectation. She heard the muted sounds of Leo moving through the house, looking for her.

When he finally appeared in the doorway to her bedroom, the look in his eye was hot enough to melt her everywhere. He kicked off his shoes and stalked over to the bed. Without a word, he tossed his hockey jacket aside and climbed onto the bed, pressing her down into the mattress with his hips, his mouth landing on her neck.

She gasped, pulling him closer with both her bare arms. His warm mouth did marvelous things to her throat while she fumbled with the hem of his T-shirt. "Off. Now," she'd demanded.

"Me or the shirt?" he'd rumbled in her ear.

"The shirt! And the jeans. All of it." She said what she wanted, and she was not embarrassed. That's how it was between them. Easy. "You're the only one here who's wearing any clothes."

Leo's eyes had widened, then he'd shot up to his knees and yanked off his T-shirt, revealing the lean, muscular chest she'd always admired. Then his fingers had gone to his fly, and he caught on to the fact that she was watching. Maybe another boy would have gotten shy. But his eyes had locked on hers, his expression blistering. When he'd shoved down his jeans and boxers, his erection had bounced free, slapping him in the stomach.

Georgia's stomach shimmied. Then she'd reached out slowly and wrapped her hand around him. He'd been impossibly hot and hard in her hand.

Leo dropped his head back and gasped with happiness. So she'd moved her hand slowly up his shaft, her thumb making an exploratory sweep across the tip of him. Leo had made a helpless, guttural sound, so she did it again.

After a moment, his hand had closed around hers. "I'm about thirty seconds away from making a big mess," he'd panted.

"I don't care," she'd whispered. Making Leo lose his mind was the best thing ever.

"Not yet," he'd returned, gently removing her hand from his body. He'd shucked off his jeans and socks. Then Georgia made the bold move of tossing her sheet completely aside.

Leo's eyes had practically bugged out of his head, then. For a moment he forgot how to speak, and Georgia didn't breathe. Then Leo exhaled all of a sudden. "Goddamn, I love your body," he said. He'd dropped a hand onto her flat stomach, and paused, as if he couldn't decide what to touch first.

"Then come here," she'd whispered, moving over to make room in her twin bed.

"Right." He'd slipped into the bed beside her, his eyes laughing. "This is already the best night of my life," he whispered.

Georgia couldn't wait any longer. She'd reached for his face with both hands and kissed him.

He'd gasped, deepening the kiss. Then he'd rolled, spreading himself out on top of her. And finally, they were skin to skin. Everywhere. He'd pushed his tongue into her mouth and she'd felt herself absolutely flood with desire . . .

Unnng. Georgia rolled over, alone in her cold Brooklyn bed. She was never going to get to sleep if she kept thinking about that. Now she was sleepless for two reasons—the Rough Day Blues, and her libido had shaken itself awake for the first time in years.

Thanks, Leo Trevi. Thanks a ton.

FOUR

TOP TEAM HEADLINES:

Can a New Coach Save the Bruisers?
Or Is it Too Little Too Late?
—ESPN

WATCH as Hot-Headed Bruisers
Rookie Tangles with Surly Captain
—Puckrakers Blog

"Again!" Coach Karl barked from the sidelines.

Leo looked up into O'Doul's snarling face for the tenth time in as many minutes. They were doing a three-on-two drill, designed to practice those crucial minutes when the team was engaged in penalty killing. He was partnered with Jason Castro, another young forward. All the two needed to do was get the puck past O'Doul and two of his ornery, iceberg-sized henchmen.

They'd managed it a few times already, but not as many as Leo would have liked. And unfortunately, his partner had just flaked as one of their practice competitors bore down on him at top speed. He got the pass off, but it was a weak shot. Leo lunged, caught it with the tip of his stick and flicked it away again.

The puck *almost* sailed between O'Doul's legs. But in the last hair's breadth of a second, he'd closed the gap and nabbed it.

Fuck.

"Nice try, college boy." O'Doul chuckled.

After some sprints an associate coach asked the forwards for a final sprinting drill. So Leo bore down and turned on all the burners. His thighs were screaming and his lungs burned as he wove past the cones set out on the ice. But he welcomed the challenge. Hockey was an orderly world. Sure, any game or practice had a million possible results. But there were rules, and those who didn't follow them got ejected. For sixty minutes of timed play, Leo always knew what to expect. Hard hits. Exhaustion. He always got out of it whatever he put in.

Not like real life.

When Georgia had left him, the betrayal had astonished him. He'd loved her as hard and as thoroughly as a boy could. He'd put everything he'd had into it. Then he'd been shoved aside.

But hockey didn't work that way. If you were the best man on that sheet of ice, you'd eventually prevail. And a good teammate was always valued.

Off the ice, a guy could have his heart broken. On the ice, you lost a game, it sucked. You won a game, it was great. And there was always another game somewhere, even if it wasn't in the league you'd hoped.

This right here was pure living.

The final whistle blew, and Leo's first practice with the Bruisers came to a close.

There was sweat dripping into Leo's eyes as he took a couple of cooldown laps. Leo had skated like a wild man that morning. Not only did he need to prove himself to Coach and the team, but it helped to sweat away some of his frustration. His body was heavy with hard-won exhaustion. And nobody could say that he hadn't put in a hundred percent.

It wasn't easy being the new guy. Every time he made a jump in his hockey career, the bottom rung of the ladder was still a shock. In high school he'd thought he was hot shit. Then he got to Harkness College and learned a valuable lesson while getting his ass handed to him at every practice for an entire season, before pulling it together sophomore year. Things went well after that, and he'd worked harder than he ever had in his life. The reward was an excellent run in the NCAA championships his junior and senior years. They won the Frozen Four five weeks before graduation.

Achievement unlocked.

But then he'd signed on to the minor league team, and the process began again. Bottom rung. Big adjustments. He had to prove himself on an entirely new level. Last year had gone well, though. Instead of taking a year to make a real contribution to the Muskrats, it had taken him two months.

This time? He figured he had two or three weeks to prove himself. And if Coach and O'Doul both decided they hated him, even that wouldn't be fast enough.

The team filed off the ice while Coach stood by the open door with a word or two for each player as they stepped onto the mats. "Glad to see that wrist is strong again," he said to O'Doul. "Looking forward to working with you," he said to Castro.

Then Leo stepped up, and Coach's mouth slammed shut. A tight nod was all he got.

Shit.

Tired legs carried him toward the locker room. There was a big crowd at the practice rink today, and Leo had skated too hard to even notice them before. It was trippy to think that people wanted to spend a Saturday afternoon watching the team run drills.

No player ever got into hockey for the roar of the crowd. You had to love the game itself, because the first fifteen

years or so was just you and your competitors. And maybe
your parents, who had to drive your skinny ass to the rink
in the first place. Not until college had he played in front
of screaming fans, and usually he hadn't even noticed
them.

But now there were fans of all ages leaning over the
chute where players passed on their way toward the locker
rooms. They waved and thrust jerseys and programs
toward the veterans, a few of whom stopped to sign autographs and shake hands.

Leo scanned their faces as he dragged his tired body
toward the doors. There was only one person who could
snag his attention right now—a certain kick-ass tennis
player with long legs and wide hazel eyes.

He didn't know what to think about her sudden reap-
pearance in his life. She'd been so standoffish yesterday.
That wasn't like her. The girl he remembered had a bright
smile and an easy way about her.

Letting Georgia go was the hardest thing he'd ever had
to do. And he'd only been able to manage it because he
was sure it would help her be happy again. He hated wondering if she'd become a bitter person since they were
together.

If she wasn't happy, he was going to need to know why.

Leo didn't spot her in the crowd, though. Maybe she
wasn't needed on open practice days. As the new guy, he
had no clue how the organization worked. It was hard to
say how long he'd be in Brooklyn. But one thing he knew
for sure—he was going to talk to her, and soon. He didn't
want to leave here without knowing if she was okay. The
next time he spotted her, he planned to ask for a little of
her time.

When he reached the locker room, it was already loud,
the guys busy with their smack talk and teasing. As the
new guy, he stripped off his pads in silence, replaying the
practice in his mind. His effort today had been truly solid.
And he'd been having a great season with the Muskrats,
so he was in top shape.

All he could do was persevere, and hope the right people noticed.

Silas, the backup goalie, sat down beside Leo. "Hey, you did all right out there. But you weren't joking. Coach is not your biggest fan, eh?"

"Is it that obvious?" Leo pulled off his skates.

"You got a plan?"

"Skate my ass off. And avoid signing a long-term lease."

Silas laughed. "Where are you living, anyway?"

"Dunno. Got any suggestions? My folks are less than an hour from here, but that's probably too far. Can you imagine if I'm late for practice because I'm sitting on the LIE? That's not what I need. Though Coach is coming from the same neighborhood. Maybe if I offer to be his chauffeur, he'll like me more."

"Offer to *wash* the car." Silas snickered. "And maybe paint his house. Anything to keep on his good side."

O'Doul came to a halt in front of their bench. "Watch yourself," he said to Silas. "The college boy doesn't like advice."

Well, damn. "Look, I'm sorry about yesterday. I'm calm on the ice, but not so good in a room full of reporters," Leo offered. He'd said the same thing yesterday after that disaster of a press conference, but O'Doul had flipped him off and walked away.

"No big," Doulie said now, his mouth grim. "I don't get offended. But seems like our new fearless leader doesn't like you much. That's your real problem."

Apparently nobody in the universe had missed it. "I'll take that under advisement."

O'Doul gave him one more ornery look and stalked off to the showers. The guy was awfully hard to read. He seemed to work hard projecting a laid-back image, but Leo was pretty sure the captain was wound tighter than a drum.

"Shit," Silas said. "It won't help if he can't stand you either."

Leo privately doubled the workout he was going to do

tomorrow morning. He'd better impress everyone. Immediately. "What time does the practice facility open?"

"Seven. But before you lift there's yoga."

"There's . . . did you say *yoga*?"

Silas grinned. "Welcome to Brooklyn, man. Don't worry. You'll only look like an awkward chicken the first twenty times. And it's not like they're gonna make you do a beet juice cleanse afterward."

"Whatever. I'll be there." If the Bruisers did Jell-O wrestling or Falun Gong, then he'd do it, too.

"Look—I got an idea for you," Silas said. "The guy you replaced on our roster was renting a room in my place on Water Street. That's two blocks from here. Now that he's gone, I'm out the cash. I'd give you his spot without a lease, because I can't really afford the place alone—I'm on a two-way contract. Getting paid minor league money until they pop the question."

"Huh. Two blocks away?" That sounded like a slam dunk.

"Yeah, the commute is awesome. But you should still think it over. You might not want to say yes."

"Why? You snore? You have a thing for disco music?"

Silas shook his head. "Negative. It's just that the room has kind of a revolving door on it. You'd be the fourth guy in there in as many months."

Leo chuckled. "It's cursed? Take Silas's second bedroom, and get booted from the Bruisers?" That was silly. But . . . *four* guys?

"People believe in stupider shit than that," the goalie pointed out.

"Yeah, they do. Thanks, man. I'll sleep on it. Sounds like an easy decision, though."

"Take your time deciding," Silas said, stripping out of his garters and socks. "I wasn't gonna put it up on Craigslist until after our next road trip. If I'm not around to show it, there's no point in advertising."

"Cool. I'll let you know." Leo dropped the last of his

clothes and headed for the showers. The Bruisers had a gorgeous practice facility. He'd played in some pretty nice places, but this one was downright luxurious—generous rooms, good lighting, and a sleek design. The shower stall that Leo entered was done up in white marble tiles, and the dispenser on the wall held several different bath products with expensive-looking labels. The shampoo he chose purportedly contained "sea palm extract" as an ingredient. "For rich, shiny hair."

Good to know.

While he showered, he decided to take Silas up on his offer. He didn't really have time to shop for an apartment. If his contract held, money wouldn't be tight. He didn't need a roommate. But the coach could still send him down to the minors at his whim, where Leo would be one of the best paid guys who still wasn't playing for an NHL team. That would suck, but at least if he'd been renting from Silas, he wouldn't be leaving another signed lease behind.

And, hey, if things suddenly started looked up, Leo could get his own place in a few months if he felt like it.

As for the room's curse—or jinx, or fate—Leo wasn't going to worry about that. If he got sent down somewhere again, it wouldn't be a bedroom's fault. It would be either Karl's or his own. To believe otherwise was ridiculous.

He got dressed slowly, wondering where he could find a late lunch in this neighborhood. He'd need to fuel up if he was going to run his engine at a hundred percent, day in and day out.

Tonight he'd stay in the hotel, and tomorrow he'd be lifting weights by eight. Whatever it took, he'd do it.

FIVE

What a difference a day made.

Georgia sat hunched over her desk in jeans and a hoodie, wondering if she should update her resume. Spread out on the desk was the call log from yesterday's fiasco. Fully half of all the callers had asked about Leo Trevi's hot mic incident.

And today? There had been two dozen *more* inquiries. She jotted down every single one on her pad. The requests to interview Leo had come pouring in, and not always from the most reputable news sites. When she'd followed up with the Hockey Hotties request, she'd learned that they wanted him to pose nude for a charity calendar.

They did not, however, ask for an interview with the team's new coach.

Alone in her office, Georgia grumbled to herself as the phone began to ring again. It was Saturday, and technically the press office was closed, so she didn't have to answer. She let the call go to voice mail. A minute later the message light lit, so she picked up the receiver to hear what the caller wanted.

"Hello, this is Randy Fenning, a fact-checker for Page Six. I need to confirm that the Georgia Worthington who appears in the Huntington Northern High School yearbook alongside Leo Trevi is the same person as the publicity director for the Brooklyn Bruisers. Please return this call at 212 . . ."

She groaned so loudly that the sound echoed off the lonely walls of her office. It would be bad enough to see her name pop up on blogs with nothing better to do than to speculate about a high school relationship. But her *picture*? This would be a total disaster. And it wasn't just the embarrassment factor—a publicist could not be effective when she'd *become* part of the very story that she was supposed to manage.

If they hired a new publicity director by nine AM on Monday, she wouldn't even be surprised.

And that *picture*. Ugh. Georgia really didn't want to see her eighteen-year-old smiling face on a newspaper's website. She didn't have the yearbook on hand, but she guessed the picture the reporter referred to was the one with Leo's arm encircling her shoulders as they sat on the bleachers before a pep rally. Georgia remembered that picture well. It captured two heads tilted together like a couple of lovesick fools, their smiles wide. Youthful enthusiasm practically rose up off the page. It was a portrait of a happy, easygoing moment before she'd known what real life was like.

That picture was taken just a few months before her attack in Florida.

Georgia did not want to see it plastered everywhere. She didn't want to see it at all. And as ornery as she was about Leo's hot mic error, she'd bet cash money that Leo didn't want to see that picture, either. He didn't need the distraction, and if he had a girlfriend, that bit of public speculation was going to make things awkward at home.

At least he'd learn a valuable lesson about mics and press conferences.

After draining her coffee, she finished responding to every last e-mail. To be fair, many of the questions and interview requests were for her father and the team's general manager. At least the announcement of the new head coach was getting *some* of the attention. She made a few notes to ask her father to return the most pressing calls to *Sports Illustrated* and *ESPN*.

Now what to do about all the requests for Leo? It was easy to grant access for something like a photo shoot. But interviews were trickier if she wanted to downplay the incident at the press conference. Interest in a player *ought* to be a good thing. Georgia's job was to channel public interest in the team and its players. A publicist was there to amplify the team's brand and message. But the fact that Leo had seemed to *threaten* the team captain made this a delicate situation. She would need to ask O'Doul to sit down with a few journos, too. Maybe he could give an upbeat interview about how great the rookies were fitting in . . .

Someone tapped on the office door, startling her. "Come in!"

The door swung open to reveal none other than the big man himself, Nate Kattenberger. "Afternoon," he said while Georgia's stomach dropped. "You're holed up at your desk on a Saturday?"

She cleared her throat. "Lots of media inquiries. The *Times* wants to talk to you and Hugh about your choice for coach." *Also? A dozen professional gossips want to upstage your multimillion dollar decision with a story about my high school boyfriend.*

He shrugged. "Okay. You can set something up. Shouldn't you be down at open practice?"

Why yes, I should. But Georgia had been avoiding the rink today, even though open practice was a good time to reach out to loyal ticketholders. She usually liked to stop in and make sure the staff was handing out the game schedules she'd had printed.

"Of course, I'm heading there now," she lied, getting to her feet and grabbing her clipboard. She wasn't about to look like a slouch in front of Nate. And while she was down at the rink, she'd remind the players about the benefit dinner they'd be attending in a week's time.

Nate held open her office door. She followed him out into the corridor. Their path took them through the lobby and down a tunnel built from brick and glass block, toward the brand-new practice arena that Nate had built here on the edge of the Brooklyn Navy Yard.

Her high-ranking companion didn't say anything as they walked together. At first, working for a man like Nate had been intimidating. But his casual ways had eventually won her over. Today he wore his trademark hoodie and sneakers. Of course, the hoodie was a cashmere model from Bergdorf, and the sneakers were Tom Ford.

His silence made her feel a little edgy, though the stress may have been all in her head. With Nate you never knew what he was thinking. He might be inventing the next bit of software that changed the way your cell phone connected to the Internet. Or he might be deciding which global aid nonprofit would most benefit from a hundred million dollar grant.

Or? He might be trying to decide how to break the news of her demotion.

"That was quite a gaffe Leo Trevi made at the press conference yesterday," he said eventually.

"I'm sure sorry it went down like that," she said quickly, as her stomach dove toward her knees.

"I know." He actually chuckled. "At least it wasn't a *boring* press conference."

Georgia would have preferred that. But since they were having this carefree chat, she probably needed to confess something. "Um, as it happens, Leo Trevi and I dated in high school. So there's, uh, going to be a picture circulating on the gossip rags."

Nate gave her the side-eye as he held the rink door open for her. "A *compromising* picture? Your father won't like that."

"*God no.*" She took a very deep breath and let it out. "No—one of the reporters dug up our high school yearbook."

"Ah." Nate chuckled. "So it's just bad hair and a cheesy caption. The team has survived worse publicity."

His relative indifference to this circus was not what she'd expected. "Uh, true," she stammered, passing him as the icy rink air enveloped them. "And I'll, um, set up that interview with the *Times*."

"Excellent. Chin up, Georgia." He gave her an unreadable grin and walked past her.

So she might survive the week after all. Who knew?

Camera bulbs flashed as Nate made his way through the crowd and into the guts of the training facility. Fans were almost as curious about him as they were about the players. Though practice had already ended, and the rink staff were busy making sure that bystanders stayed behind the velvet ropes separating the public area of the rink from the lockers, treatment rooms, and gym. Last year they'd found some puck bunnies waiting naked in the team hot tub after an open practice, so constant vigilance was necessary.

Georgia pulled up the hood on her sweatshirt just in case any of the bystanders were with the media and happened to recognize her from yesterday's press conference. Then she approached the staff members guarding the entrance, where a lengthy line of patient fans waited to see who'd emerge to sign autographs.

It was a rink employee they called Old Bob who unhooked the rope for Georgia as she approached. "Hello, sweetheart."

"How was practice, Bob?" *Did either my father or the captain come to blows with my ex-boyfriend on the ice?*

"Lookin' good, Miss Georgia. I like our chances against Tampa tomorrow night."

Whew. "So do I. See you there, all right?" Leaving the crowd behind, she walked quickly down the brightly lit hallway. She passed through another set of doors and proceeded toward the locker room. But she stopped just outside it.

Entering the locker room was something she had to do from time to time. But it wasn't her favorite place to speak to players. In the first place, it was difficult to know where to put her eyes while waiting for some dude to put on his underwear and speak to her. All that male hotness in one place made a girl a little dizzy.

And today the whole issue was suddenly ten times trickier. Because *Leo* was in there. She did *not* need to see Leo naked. It was bad enough knowing that they basically worked in the same building now. The team had a series of home games this week, and it was weird knowing that she could turn a corner at any moment and come face to face with the only man who had ever loved her.

Naked Leo would be more than her poor heart could take. She'd probably burst an artery if she spotted all six-foot-two, two hundred muscled pounds of him (thank you, stat sheet) across the locker room. Her imagination kept wanting to veer off and picture Leo 2.0 without his clothes on. As a teenager, he'd already been strong and fit. She used to admire his biceps while sitting in the passenger seat of his truck.

Now? If she stood in that locker room while he stripped, they'd have to surgically remove her gaze from his muscular ass.

She could never go in that room again. Obviously.

Fortunately, players began to emerge from the locker room in ones and twos, their hair wet from the showers. "Massey!" She stopped one of them in the hallway, her clipboard poised. "You didn't RSVP for the Brooklyn Arts Benefit next week. Don't forget about it."

The big defenseman paused to give her a grin. "Yes, ma'am. I'll be there. And I'm bringin' someone, but I haven't decided who."

Georgia made a note on her pad. "Okay. E-mail me her name at least forty-eight hours before, okay? You don't want to stand around while they hunt for your date's name on the last-minute list."

"Will do." He lumbered off and she snagged one of the next two guys to emerge, asking him the same question.

When she next looked up, Leo was standing just two

feet away, looking down at her with those sweet brown eyes she'd always loved. "Hi, Georgia," he said.

"Hi," she attempted. But the word only made it halfway out, and the result was something more like a halting gasp.

"Look," he said, shifting a duffel bag on his broad shoulder. "I'm really sorry about the press conference. I didn't think—"

"I know," she said way too quickly, cutting him off. Reliving that moment was not something they should do. "Let's just move on." And that came out snappishly. *Damn it.* "Um, there are some promo things you're going to need to do in the next few weeks. I need to e-mail you a list. Where should I send it?"

He studied her for a second before answering, a serious expression on his rugged face. "My e-mail hasn't changed, Gigi. Send me anything, anytime."

"Right." She swallowed. "Okay. The, uh, first thing you need to know is that the entire team is required to attend the Brooklyn Arts Benefit a week from tonight. It's black tie—a cocktail party. And you need to send me the full legal name of your date, so that she'll be admitted to the party without a delay."

He frowned. "I don't have time to find a date. What if you went with me? Are you spoken for?"

"Uh . . ." *What?* "I can't," she snapped, her shock getting the best of her. "That's, um, nice of you, but I could never date a player." *Jesus.* He didn't ask to date her. "I mean, I can't *appear* to be dating a player," she rambled. This was getting worse by the second. ". . . And I work that night anyway. Hard. Long hours."

Holy hell. She couldn't even string a coherent sentence together. If anyone overheard this halting conversation she'd never work in PR again.

And now Leo was staring at her as if she'd sprouted two extra heads. "Well, all right. If that's the way it's going to be." He sighed, and she crumbled a little inside. The heap of awkwardness between them was piled higher than the ice shavings outside the Zamboni door. It was so tall she couldn't even see over the top.

She clearly needed to get out of there before sticking her foot in her mouth again. Taking a step toward the door, Georgia mumbled something about calling if he had any questions, then she made her escape.

Or she tried to. But Leo wasn't having it. He used those long legs to keep up with her. "Wait, Gigi." He put a hand on her elbow just before they reached the double doors. "Can we have coffee sometime? Just to catch up?"

Her heart did the tango around the inside of her chest. He wanted to have coffee together. That's something a well-adjusted woman could do with her ex-boyfriend, right? "Uh, okay? I usually have a publicity meeting with new players. We should do that anyway." It was yet another tepid response. *Way to go, Georgia.* But she couldn't bear for him to know just how hard the whole situation was for her.

His expression flattened. "Fine. Okay. We'll do that." He opened the door and held it for her. Gratefully, Georgia slipped past.

But neither of them made it very far before an ear-piercing shriek split the air, and a flying body shot past the rink workers and launched itself at Leo.

"Treviiiiiiii!" The girl's voice was pitched almost as high as a dog whistle. "Oh my God, baby! You looked so good out there!" As Georgia stared, a beautiful woman attached her body to the front of Leo's. Then she attacked his mouth with hers.

Leo took a staggered step backward before finding his balance. And even though he looked quite astonished to be suddenly kissing this girl, the sight of her lips on his mouth was actually sickening. Something went wrong in Georgia's stomach as the stranger grabbed Leo's rugged jaw in both her hands and leaned in even farther. Her fingernails were perfectly painted, shiny and rich-looking. And her hair fell in silky sheets down her back as she held him.

Georgia had the sudden urge to use her clipboard to whack the back of the girl's perfect head. And even though she knew she should just walk on past them, she couldn't have looked away for any amount of money.

After a minute, Leo eased the woman to her feet on the floor. "Amy," he huffed when he pulled his mouth free. "This is a surprise. It's been, how many mon—"

"But you're here!" she squealed. "In New York! I couldn't believe it! I wasn't going to miss your first practice! Omigod, why didn't you *call* me? When did you get in?"

"Uh, yesterday," he said, catching her hands as they wandered his body. "It was, um, sudden."

At least Georgia wasn't the only one capable of stammering.

"Well, let's go!" the interloper said, grabbing his hand. "We can have a late lunch, and you can tell me everything."

"I think I've got a meeting," he said.

Later, Georgia would wonder why she intervened. "The training meeting isn't until four," she heard herself say.

Amy leapt on this bit of wisdom without even a spare glance to see who'd offered it. "So you've got an hour and a half!" she said, tugging on him.

"Leo," Georgia added before the girl could succeed in either pulling him out the doors or dislocating his arm, "don't forget you need a date for the Brooklyn Arts Benefit."

The girl's head whipped around then. "A benefit? Where?"

"Brooklyn Academy of Music. This coming Saturday."

"Wow, I'm free on Saturday. I'll have to get a new dress! This will be awesome."

Finally, Georgia got a grip. She tore her eyes off the couple and headed back toward her office.

On the way it occurred to her to wonder what *she* was going to wear to the benefit. And she hated herself a little for worrying about it.

SIX

TOP TEAM HEADLINES:

Brooklyn Hosts Tampa at 7pm
—ESPN

It's All in the Family on Team Bruisers.
Players Fight Over Coach's Daughter
—Pucker Up Blog

Leo sat down for what felt like the first time in a year. Yet he only had a few minutes to relax before it would be time to head over to the stadium.

Installing himself in Silas's apartment had been the easiest part of his week, though. All he'd brought to Brooklyn was his gear and some clothes. He didn't even have sheets for the king-sized bed in the room he'd just rented. He'd had to borrow a set from Silas.

From his seat in the center of Silas's giant L-shaped sofa, he admired the high ceilings and the hip, industrial look of the room. The goalie's apartment was nicer than Leo had expected, and now he knew why the guy was so eager for a roommate. Leo's half of the rent was double the rate he'd paid for his own place in Michigan.

"This neighborhood is pricey," Silas had admitted when he told Leo the price. "But we're a five minute walk from the practice rink, which is pretty sweet."

And all that money bought a lofty interior and a sleek, modern kitchen. The place had floor-to-ceiling windows, great light, and a giant TV hung from one of the exposed-brick walls. He could get used to this place.

Leo's room was a decent size, too, though rather empty. It needed a rug and a dresser. Maybe a desk. But Leo knew it would be foolish to run out and furnish the place. He'd told Silas he wasn't superstitious, but it was hard to think of this pad as home when it was obvious that Brooklyn was still trying to eject him.

On the belt parkway there was a highway sign reading: *Leaving Brooklyn. Fuhgeddaboudit.* Every time he looked up into Coach Karl's angry face, Leo felt like he should have that sign tattooed on his own ass.

What did that man want from him, anyway? Blood? Sweat? Tears? Whatever it was, Leo would give it for a chance to stay in the big house. He'd shown up at the rink both mornings for the workout of a lifetime. First there'd been an hour of yoga, which was just weird, but at least it had loosened him up. And then a long, sweaty practice.

"Good energy," the trainer had said this afternoon. "You're killing it," the associate coach had added. "You have the fewest trouble spots of anyone on our roster," the team therapist had said when Leo went to his office for a primary consultation.

Karl Worthington had said nothing at all.

Leo leaned back against the cushions and closed his eyes. He was tired. And it was hard to know which of his many issues to try to resolve first. He had to impress the coach. That was a given. But then there was a long list of loose threads in his life that needed his attention. Should he worry first about sending movers to clear out the apartment he no longer needed in Michigan? Even if Coach Karl demoted his ass to the minors, it would be to one of the East Coast teams that the Bruisers controlled. Or should he worry about Georgia, and the awful tension between them? Or—and this only compounded the other problem—the sudden appearance of his ex-girlfriend Amy?

Leo and Amy had dated for all of his senior year of college. But she'd lost interest when Leo moved to Michigan to play in the minors. That league apparently didn't make the cut as far as she was concerned. And weirdly, Leo hadn't spent any time missing her. He'd chalked it up to being busy. But now that she'd reappeared and seemed ready to pick up where she'd left off, he wasn't feeling it. Not at all. Yesterday she'd dragged him to lunch, but all she wanted to talk about was herself and the clubs she hoped he could get her into. As if he had time to go clubbing.

He'd given her a polite kiss on the cheek good-bye, and then begun preparing his Dear Amy speech. *You're great, but I'm going to be really preoccupied settling in here for a while. And I just can't be who you want right now.* Or something like that.

But he'd forgotten about that fricking charity benefit Georgia had brought up and basically invited Amy to. And when Leo had turned on his phone today after his workout and two hours of watching tape of Tampa with the team, he'd found twenty texts from Amy, a quarter of them photos of dresses she'd tried on.

The last one was some kind of strapless shimmery thing, and she'd written, "I chose this one!"

So it looked like he'd be seeing her at least once more. But after the function he'd be sure to tell her that, sorry, it wasn't going to be a regular thing. And wouldn't that be a fun chat. Amy didn't like hearing the word no.

Leo opened his eyes and checked his phone for messages. There were three hours left until the puck dropped on tonight's home game against Tampa, and he had no idea whether he'd be suiting up for it. The past hour had found him checking his phone every three minutes like a teenager waiting for a girl to text him back.

It was pretty ridiculous.

There was one message that helped, though. He found an e-mail from his old college coach, the guy who'd seen him through his first trip to the Frozen Four junior year. Coach had retired after that season, and Leo had missed everything about him—his crusty exterior, which concealed an empathetic man, his rueful smile when they lost, and his speeches, which always quoted one or two dead presidents.

> Leo—
> Can't believe I saw your name on the *New York Times* website yesterday. One of my guys in the NHL? I live for moments like this.
>   Whether your career is one game or a thousand, I'll always be proud of you. Not only are you fast as blazes but you have a steady character and a good heart. Make sure you use all those gifts, and not just your slap shot. Congratulations, kid. You deserve this.
>
> All my best,
> John

Damn. That could help a guy get through the day.

"Want to head over to the rink soon?" Silas emerged from his own room and crossed to the kitchen with his coffee mug. He patted his stomach. "If we go now, there will be food."

Leo stood up, happy to have his new roommate break up his grim train of thought. "Sure thing. You can help me find the ice level door." As the new guy, he didn't even know where to flash his shiny new Bruisers ID to get in.

"Cool. I'll change."

Leo went into his own room to put on a suit. Now *that*

was an unfamiliar ritual. In the minors, you could still roll up to the rink in your sweats. The idea of glamming up the sport of hockey was pretty amusing, really. They could sell $200 bottles of champagne in the corporate boxes, and they could charter jets for the road trips. But down on the ice, the game itself was just the same. Leo would bet any amount of money that the refs still kept the pucks on ice in an Igloo cooler in the penalty box.

Back in the living room and waiting for Silas, Leo wandered over to the window to look down at the street below. The late afternoon light cast a purplish hue on all the brick buildings. Water Street was narrow, and one of the last streets in New York City to be paved with old bricks. It was a hell of a lot more atmospheric than the town he'd called home three days ago.

A bright yellow taxi slid to a stop at the curb, its door opening. As Leo watched, Georgia Worthington got out. Even from this peculiar angle, revealing the top of her head, he knew immediately it was her. Something inside his chest lifted at the sight of her. She clutched a shopping bag in one hand and paid her fare with the other.

Leo looked down, subconsciously giving himself a once-over. Maybe his new apartment's buzzer would ring in a moment. She might be stopping by to finish the conversation that had been aborted yesterday at the practice rink. She must realize how badly they needed to talk.

His forehead against the glass, Leo watched the taxi slide away. Georgia looked once to the left and then to the right, taking a moment to check her surroundings. It was good that she did that—a woman alone on the city streets as dusk fell. He hoped she wasn't fearful living here. But it was still a good idea to be aware.

Then Georgia turned her back to him, shaking out a set of keys. She climbed two steps onto the stoop of the smallest facade on the block—a walk-up sandwiched between two larger buildings. Fitting her key into the lock, she let herself in, disappearing inside a moment later.

"Okay!" Silas called from behind him. "Are you ready to head over?"

"Guess so," Leo mumbled, disappointed. He realized how ridiculous it had been to imagine Georgia was on her way to see him. She couldn't even have known where he was staying. And she sure as hell hadn't asked.

His gut told him they had unfinished business. But maybe that was just wishful thinking.

He pulled on his overcoat and followed Silas out the door. The two of them took a short ride down the building's shiny elevator from the fourth floor to the lobby. Like the Bruisers' headquarters, this apartment building was a converted factory, so all the ceilings were fourteen feet high except for the soaring lobby, which was doubly tall, with leather club chairs and oriental rugs. The place was gorgeous. A uniformed doorman greeted Silas and offered to fetch him a cab.

"That'd be great, Miguel." He and Leo followed him outside while he flagged one down at the corner.

Leo looked up at the little apartment building where Georgia had disappeared. The third floor had an illuminated window where he was pretty sure there'd only been darkness before. Is that where she lived? It made sense that someone who worked for the team would choose this neighborhood.

A taxi pulled up, and he folded himself into the back seat, following Silas. "You know any of your neighbors?" he asked the goalie.

"Nah," the goalie said as the cab accelerated. "It's New York. The only way to survive the crowds is to pretend the other eight million people don't exist."

Leo looked out at the darkening streets and wondered whether he could put Georgia out of his mind, at least for tonight. Worrying about her wouldn't do either of them any good if it got him kicked off the team.

"Oh, *man*." Silas chuckled. "This can't be good for you. Fucking gossip rags."

"What?" He turned to see Silas grinning at his phone. He took it from the goalie's hand and squinted at the screen, which showed a page from the *Post*. The headline was

NEW ROOKIE AND CAPTAIN FIGHT OVER A GIRL. BUT CAN THEY FIGHT OFF TAMPA?

There were two photos. The first was a shot of himself sitting beside O'Doul on the dais at the press conference, both of them wearing sour expressions. The second picture was one that Leo hadn't seen in years—he and Georgia seated together on their high school bleachers, their arms around each other, smiling gleefully. He couldn't remember what they'd been laughing about that day. It had been more than six years since they'd been that young and carefree.

Jesus. It hurt to look at it. He passed the phone back to Silas without comment.

"So that's why Coach doesn't like you?" Silas asked. "You were involved with his daughter? And that's why you jumped down O'Doul's throat."

Leo sighed. "Yeah. It was a long time ago, though. If I'd kept my trap shut the other day, this picture wouldn't have surfaced."

"Where'd they get it?"

"Our high school yearbook, if you can believe it."

"*Dude*," Silas said, the word full of sympathy. "That shit should stay buried. I do not want to see my eighteen-year-old mug in the news."

"Live and learn," Leo grunted.

"Hope Coach doesn't see it before he makes the lineup for tonight. 'Cause now you're the guy who got his little girl on all the gossip blogs."

Fuck. "I'm ready to play. Hope he doesn't scratch me."

"That's the tune I'm singing every night, dude. And yet I've played four games all season."

"I hear you." Backup goalie was a tough gig, though. It wasn't the same thing, and they both knew it.

"Did you cheat on this girl, or something?"

"Never," Leo said quickly. "We were together a long time, until she cut me loose on graduation day."

"Bummer." Silas laughed.

Leo said nothing. That year had been so hard on the both of them, but it wasn't something he should talk about. He hoped Georgia had healed as best she could, but it was her private business.

"Can you pull around the corner?" Silas asked the cabbie as the car slowed down. "We need the side entrance."

A minute later they both got out, and Leo waved off the goalie's ten dollar bill. "You can get the next one." He paid the fare and pulled out his shiny new team ID.

"Afternoon, boys," the security guard said as he waved them through. "Beat Tampa."

"We will," Silas said, although it was iffy whether either one of them would have a say in it. Leo followed the goalie down a set of stairs and through a bright hallway beneath the stadium. They came to a stop outside a locked door. "Try your ID," Silas suggested. "See if it works."

With a nervous chuckle, Leo held his card up to the scanner. The light flashed green and the door clicked open.

He was in. At least for today.

"Guess I'm your tour guide," Silas said. "Treatment rooms and the stretching gym are all the way at the end of the hall. But the locker room is in here." Leo followed Silas into an antechamber with traditional wooden lockers. "Coat goes here, and you can hang up your suit and change. Hey—they already gave you a spot." He opened a locker that already bore a brass-framed nametag reading TREVI. Silas pointed out a pair of black shorts and a gray T-shirt with the Bruisers' logo. "They've got you all set up with a training kit. I'm gonna change." He moved down the row to his own locker.

After they both changed into warm-up gear—pads and jerseys would come later—Leo followed Silas into the next room, which was where it all really happened. The Bruisers' owner had built a state-of-the-art oval dressing room, where every player had plenty of room for his gear and everyone could see and hear everyone else.

Once again, he found TREVI, #55 on a locker. All his pads were here—arranged by a team minion in his locker, which was beside Castro's. And what's more—a jersey hung from it. Purple, of course, with T R E V I stitched on in white. It was impossible not to stare at it. His whole life he'd been waiting for this.

"You can snap a picture," Silas said. "I won't tell."

"Nah." Leo's little sister would want him to, but Leo was too superstitious. If he got to stick around, there'd be plenty of time to get that picture later. "Where is everyone?" They were the only two in the room.

"In the treatment rooms getting stretched and taped. And in the lounge getting a bite or a protein drink. Let's go. It's right back here."

They went back the way they'd come and then a bit farther down the hall toward a door marked BRUISERS PLAYERS AND STAFF ONLY BEYOND THIS POINT.

Silas pushed it open, calling, "Hey, ladies. What's for eats?"

"Taco Tuesday!" O'Doul yelled. And sure enough, there was a spread of Mexican food on a kitchen counter at the far end of the lounge. In addition to the kitchen and dining tables, there was a carpeted area with leather sofas and a big-screen TV. A half dozen players were scattered around the room, snacking and talking to one another.

"It's Saturday, dumb-ass." Beringer, another veteran defenseman, pinched O'Doul's ass and then plucked something off his plate and stuck it in his mouth.

"Get your own," O'Doul complained, sidestepping him. He sat down in the center of a leather sofa that was just off to the side of the room. "Hey, rookie!"

It took Leo a beat to realize he was being addressed. "Hey."

"Bring me a water, would you?"

Seriously? "Sure thing," Leo said. But then he took his sweet time. In slow motion, he turned around, locating a spoon and a carton of yogurt. He wouldn't eat a real meal this close to game time.

When he was good and ready he crossed the kitchen to open the beverage refrigerator. "Does our captain prefer the still water or the bubbles with his cuisine?"

O'Doul snorted. "Just chuck me a bottle of the plain stuff."

Leo took out two, then walked over to offer one to O'Doul. "Here, man. Sorry about that bullshit at the press conference yesterday. I'm not usually a loose cannon." He locked eyes with the man and waited to see what the captain would say.

The guy studied him, giving nothing away. Leo was pretty good at reading people, but O'Doul was a tough nut to crack. He seemed to blow hot and cold on everyone. "Thanks," he said, taking the bottle and twisting it open. Whether the gratitude referred to the water or the apology, he didn't say. And then the captain looked past him, watching someone else come through the door. "Bayer! How's the shoulder feel?"

Dismissed. Ah, well. He'd tried.

Leo took a seat at one of the tables. But as he ate, he listened to the conversations around him. The most interesting part was the discussion of Bayer's injury.

"Got a massage after warm-ups, but it's still a little sore. The trainer wants me to sit out another game," Bayer complained. "But I don't need it. We both talked to Coach, but I don't know what the new guy'll decide."

A silence fell over the room as all the smack talk died. While Leo had probably the worst case of new-guy anxiety, the truth was that every guy here would be a little on edge today. A new coach could shake things up in ways that wouldn't be appreciated.

O'Doul looked at his watch. "I say we hit the soccer early." He stood up. "Let's go."

To a man, everyone stood up and followed him out. So Leo pounded the rest of his water and brought up the rear of the procession. The parade of hockey players threaded the length of the hallway until O'Doul pushed through a door marked LOADING DOCK. By the time Leo got through it, the guys were already forming a circle on the concrete floor. The room was cavernous and cold, due to a set of garage doors lining one side. But Leo felt his spirits lift as he stepped into the circle of men, each of them dressed identically to him in Bruisers warm-up gear. He felt the age-old tug of being on a team, with a common goal and a common enemy.

And elimination soccer was a blast, anyway.

"Heads up, boys," O'Doul said with a grin. Then he dropped the ball to his sneaker and popped it across the circle to Bayer. Who headed it to Silas. Who kicked it to Beacon, the starting goalie.

Who went for it with a knee. And missed.

"Aww!" the men yelled together.

"I'm savin' it for later!" the goalie protested, but he backed out of the circle with a smile.

Leo gave over his consciousness to this silly pursuit. He headed the ball to O'Doul the first time it came to him. He managed a good knee bump the next time. The rules of elimination soccer were simple: the ball doesn't touch the floor. And smack talk is a hundred percent legal, and encouraged.

Players in the circle dwindled down to four. There was only Leo, O'Doul, Bayer, and Silas. Leo felt loose and ready to play, whether it was hockey or this silly warm-up game. He'd take it.

O'Doul kicked to Silas who headed it toward the space between Leo and O'Doul.

"Got it," O'Doul yelled, so Leo let him take the shot. The captain only got there in time to bump the ball with his shoulder toward Leo.

The heavy trajectory of the ball meant that Leo couldn't get an ordinary kick in. But he got a knee under it, boosting that sucker into the air, sending it sailing across the circle, but too high for Bayer to get a head on it.

"Fuck." Bayer chuckled. Instead of letting it go, though,

he backed up three big paces and sort of slid his body onto the concrete floor for a bicycle kick.

It almost worked. Almost. But the ball sailed over the tip of his sneaker. And on his way down, Bayer's foot collided with a forklift that was parked against the loading dock wall. "Arrrgh!" Bayer yelled, and Leo couldn't tell if the sound came from frustration or pain. Either way, Bayer rolled away from the machinery and up onto his feet. "Thanks a fuck ton, rookie."

"Yeah, sorry," he said, knowing it wasn't really his fault that Bayer's toe collided with heavy machinery. But he was the new guy, and therefore honor bound to take crap from the veterans. He trotted off to collect the ball, which had rolled toward the door, unattended.

As Leo nabbed the ball off the floor, a pair of dress shoes stepped into his line of vision. He stood up to find Coach Worthington standing in the doorway, a clipboard in his hands. "Evening, Coach," Leo said, spinning the ball on his finger.

Worthington stepped past him to greet the team. "Evening, hooligans," he said with a smile. "Are you ready to have a big night?"

Leo's teammates turned toward the coach's voice like flowers toward the sun. Karl Worthington was well-liked in hockey. While he was known to be occasionally gruff, he could also be magnetic and inspiring.

Coach grinned at them for a moment, taking everyone in. "I know we don't know each other so well yet. But I can already see you're a team who's going to do great things heading into the postseason. Let me tell you a little story about new coaches.

"You guys have all had the pleasure of working with my daughter, Georgia, for a while now. Maybe you don't know this about Georgia but she's a hell of a tennis player, and she started winning tournaments when she was seven years old. She was a fierce competitor, and my nickname for her was Killer."

That got him a few quiet chuckles.

". . . So when Killer was nine, her coach went out on maternity leave, and a new one came in. The first practice with the new guy, she really struggled on the court. She forgot how to use her backhand, and she didn't return balls that she should have gotten. Poor kid was falling apart out there. I didn't know that playing for a new coach would be a terrifying experience for her."

Leo scanned his teammates' faces. Some of them were smirking, wondering where Coach was headed with this.

"After practice I was real careful to ask her nicely about what went wrong. I said, 'You were really stinking it up out there, sweetie. What happened?'" The players laughed. ". . . And she said, 'Daddy, I already knew all the stuff he was telling us. But he only gets one practice with me before the tournament. So when I win that sucker next weekend, he can still feel good about helping me.'"

The other players roared, and Leo found himself smiling, even though he'd heard this story a dozen times before.

"So don't do that," Worthington said with a chuckle. "We don't know each other all that well yet. But I'm just going to take things slow, and watch how you work together. No hasty decisions will be made, guys. I need you to relax out there tonight and do your thing. To that end, our starting lines tonight will be exactly how they were in your last game."

He held up the clipboard and began reading names. And with each name that was read aloud, Leo's heart sank a little further. He was not on the player card tonight.

The soccer game started up again, but Leo sneaked out to head back to the quiet locker room. He sat on the bench and pulled out his phone. The signal down here was a little sketchy, but he wanted to tell his family not to make the trip into the city for the game tonight. That there was no point. The last call he'd received was from his brother DJ, so Leo hit redial on that one.

"Hey!" His little brother's voice filled his ear. "It's Mr. Unreachable! Wait—is this really Leo on the line? Or is this, like, his personal assistant calling?"

"Very funny, asshole," Leo grumbled. Though DJ had phoned him several times, Leo had been too busy to get back to him. Or he'd thought he was too busy. But look at all the free time he suddenly had tonight.

"The fam is on its way to see your game."

"Tell 'em not to come," he said quickly. "I've been scratched."

"Shit," DJ whispered, all the teasing gone from his voice. "That sucks."

"It really fucking does." If there was one person to whom he was willing to confess his disappointment, it was DJ. The two of them hadn't always been close. As kids they'd sparred as often as they gotten along. But when shit got real, the two of them always dropped their enmity and pulled together. "Coach Worthington hates my sorry ass."

His brother was silent for a moment. "I don't really understand why. But forget about that for a second. If he ships your ass back to the AHL, what does that do to you?"

Leo groaned. "It makes me look like damaged goods. And it makes me too expensive to trade to another AHL team. Unless I let 'em out of my contract, which my agent will not want me to do."

"Shit," DJ repeated.

"Yeah." There was another beat of fraternal silence, then Leo cleared his throat. "Looking on the bright side, I might be able to take you out for a beer or two while I'm still in the tristate area. I hope you guys didn't buy tickets for tonight already."

"Well." DJ chuckled. "Dad bought tickets to every home game for the rest of the season."

"*Why?* If this does work out, I could score him free seats."

"I told him that. But he said he needed extra for his buddies at work. And anyway—I wasn't ever making it there tonight. I'm out west, skiing with Lianne."

"Really?"

"Winter break."

"Oh." Leo vaguely remembered what it was like to take vacations. "Lucky."

"Yeah. But dude—we've been on the phone for five minutes, and you haven't told me if you saw Georgia."

Another tricky topic. "Get this—she works for the team."

"I know."

"You do? You saw that stupid press conference?"

"Nope." DJ cleared his throat. "I talk to her sometimes. We keep in touch."

"You—really?"

"Yeah. It started about two years ago—when I was in trouble at school. I wanted her opinion, so I called her. At the time, she'd just applied for the job on the Bruisers. And afterward we stayed in touch."

Leo's head spun. "Dude. You never told me that."

"It wasn't meant to be a secret," DJ said. "But, honestly. It's *you* who never talks about her. Like, never."

Leo felt himself getting irritated at his brother. Did DJ and Georgia talk about him behind his back? "Does she mention me?"

"Never," DJ said immediately. "And that's my point. You two treat each other like the other one is dead. It's weird."

"No, I don't," Leo said immediately.

"Uh-huh," DJ said. "When's the last time you mentioned her to me or the parents?"

Leo leaned back against his pristine, unused locker and banged his head into the expensive wood. "I don't know." *Never.*

"Do you ever think about her?"

"Sure." *More often than I'd like to admit.* "What the hell difference does it make? What's your point?"

"My point is that neither of you is over it. If you were, you'd be able to say her name out loud. You'd talk to her once in a while. You'd ask what she was up to."

"But you do that, apparently." Leo was not enjoying this line of conversation. "So fill me in. What's the 411 on Georgia?"

On the other end of the phone, DJ cracked up. "God, the two of you . . ."

"You going to tell me or what?" Leo growled.

"Fine." DJ chuckled. "She works in PR for the Brooklyn Bruisers."

"You're a funny, funny man."

"She lives a few blocks from the office with Becca, the office manager. Um, no pets. Travels with the team. Loves Ed Sheeran's music, unfortunately. But she can still do all the lyrics to Eminem's 'Rap God.' Seriously, very few women can—"

"Off topic, little bro." He'd forgotten that DJ and Georgia had a relationship based entirely on their mutual love of music.

"Fine. She's *single* . . ."

Keep talking.

"That's what you really wanted to hear, right?"

Leo sighed. It probably was. "Is she . . ." He didn't know how to ask. "Is she okay, though?" That was the real question—the thing he needed to know before he could accept whatever fate the gods of the NHL doled out.

DJ was quiet for a second. "Yeah. I mean, she doesn't walk around afraid all the time. It's not like that. She took a whole lot of judo and tae kwon do, starting in college."

"Yeah?" That made him smile. Georgia was an incredible athlete, and he could only imagine how well that would translate to the martial arts. His girl in a gi on the attack? She'd be fierce.

"Yeah. She's doing well. Good job, and a temporary promotion that she's trying to hold on to. Nice friends. But sometimes I think she's a little lonely."

Leo didn't know what to say about that. "Happens to the best of us."

"Uh-huh." There was a hint of snark in his brother's voice. "You talk to her yet?"

"I tried. She kinda blew me off. And then it got weird because Amy showed up out of the blue."

"*What?*" DJ yelped. "You land in New York, and the first person you call is *Amy*?"

DJ had always hated his college girlfriends. Particularly Amy. In fairness to DJ, Amy had never given him the time of day, because DJ wasn't a hockey star. "I didn't call her," Leo pointed out, feeling defensive. "She showed up at open practice. There was this press conference . . ."

"Yeah. Lianne told me about that. She caught it on Gawker. See—I wasn't even going to bring that up. You called her the love of your life?" DJ chuckled.

Leo winced. "Uh, well, anyway. Amy found out I was in town, and she came to the open practice. And when I was trying to talk to Georgia, she sort of attacked."

DJ laughed again. Apparently Leo's life was fricking hilarious. "I've *seen* Amy's attack. And yet for a year, when we all said, 'What do you see in her?' you didn't acknowledge the problem."

It was definitely time to change the subject. "Georgia didn't look happy to see me, anyway. Apparently the Worthington clan would prefer if I just crawled off back to the minors."

"Try again," his brother said immediately. "I really think you and Georgia need to talk. She's in a bind right now, trying to hold on to the top job in PR. Can't imagine that your hot mic moment made her job any easier."

Well, fuck. "I didn't know that."

"No kidding. That's why you need to . . ."

"Talk to her. Got it. I'll try again."

"You do that, bro."

SEVEN

Georgia hadn't meant to be a few minutes late to the rink on game night. But she'd gone to the dojang for a class and then done a little shopping.

By the time the cab had dropped her off at her apartment building, she had very little time to shower and change. And then none of her game-night outfits seemed satisfying.

"Does this look sleek and mature, or just boring?" she asked Becca, spinning around in a pencil skirt and a drapey silk blouse.

Her friend's eyebrows shot up. "I wonder why you're suddenly so deep into fashion crisis mode. It wouldn't have anything to do with a certain rookie player, would it?"

Damn it. It did. "Becca, friends don't try to headshrink friends when they're late for work."

Becca set down the handbag she'd been sorting for her own adventures tonight and came to stand in front of Georgia. She reached up, unbuttoning two of the buttons on Georgia's blouse, exposing a bit of cleavage. "It's perfect now."

"Thanks, I think. Are you ready to go? We can split a cab."

* * *

An hour later, Georgia was in the owners' box, trying not to speed-eat the Brazilian cheese puffs a food-service worker had just dropped off. But she was both hungry and nervous—a dangerous combination.

Fifty yards away in the press box, reporters were waiting for the starting lineups to be announced. And it was taking longer than usual tonight. They were getting grumbly, and fast.

And they weren't the only ones. Nate paced like a lion, watching his phone for updates. He didn't say anything, but Georgia could feel his impatience with her father. The big boss was chugging imported water, his drink of choice. That was something she and Nathan had in common—neither of them liked to drink at games.

"Honey?" Becca said as Georgia grabbed her seventeenth cheese puff. "Sorry to interrupt one of your regular feedings. But the reporters in the box are getting antsy for the starting lineup. The guy from the *Post* just asked me if there was some kind of problem."

"Ugh." Georgia drained her water glass. "It doesn't help that I've been ducking them all night. Excuse me." She skittered out of the room, down the hall, and then stuck her head into the press room. A dozen heads swiveled around to see whether anyone important had appeared. Usually those heads would swivel right back again. It wasn't that Georgia wasn't often useful to them. It's just that she wasn't newsworthy.

Unfortunately, the reporters' glances lingered tonight. "Is there any word on whether the rookie will play tonight?" a guy from ESPN called out. "All the women on my staff are asking about him."

She held back her groan. "The new coach is settling in," she said. "He's taking his time speaking with the players tonight, making sure everyone knows he isn't going to run in and start knocking heads together. I'll get you the lineup as soon as I have it."

The answer satisfied no one, not even her. The men who came out to cover games were hard-core sports writers—not gossip columnists. But she hated the feeling of being sized up for newsworthiness. That's why she'd been avoiding the press box all evening.

When the PR chief had to duck the press, it was always a bad sign. But she didn't know how else to play it until her name and face dropped out of circulation.

Standing around in here was uncomfortable, though. It would be fine when the game started, and the press had something to watch. But for now, she was going to bail out again. She pulled the door open again and took a step outside. But she didn't get far, because a big wall wearing a purple tie was suddenly in the way. And she walked right into it.

"Oof," Georgia said.

"God, I'm sorry." The rough timbre of the voice in her ear made her neck tingle.

Georgia leapt backward, removing herself from Leo Trevi's chest. "Sorry," she echoed, her voice a squeak. "Didn't, uh, watch where I was going."

Leo grinned at her, his smile spreading slowly across that handsome face. "I was just looking for you."

At close range, it was hard not to notice how broad his shoulders were now, and how massive his arms looked inside the sleeves of his suit jacket. She was staring. "Um, what?"

His smile became a chuckle. "I was looking for you. We really should talk."

"Talk?" Apparently she was only capable of speaking in one-word sentences.

"Yeah, Gigi. Talk—for once in six years. I suggested coffee. But you wanted to have a publicity meeting, right? Well here I am."

Here indeed, sucking up all the available oxygen with his smile and all that muscle. *Pull it together, Georgia.* "Um, sure. Where shall we talk?"

He lifted those massive shoulders in a shrug. "I'm the new guy. You're supposed to know these things."

Right.

Georgia glanced around herself. Privacy was at a premium in the stadium, even on the VIP level where they were now. There was a very posh bar just down the corridor, but anyone might be in there. Instead, Georgia led him several yards down the giant, curving corridor and over to an upholstered bench along the wall. She sat down and crossed her legs self-consciously.

The bench shifted slightly under Leo's weight when he sat down. It was a roomy enough place to sit, but still it felt unbearably intimate. Even from this distance his scent was distinctive—clean shirts and a woodsy aftershave.

She put her damp palms on her knee, over the hem of her skirt. "So." Where to begin?

"So," he echoed, his voice warm. "This is your meeting. What does the queen of PR do to break in the rookie?"

Was it her imagination, or was the question meant to sound so . . . suggestive? *Gah.* "Well, um. There are some events you'll be asked to do. There's the, um, benefit I mentioned the other day. Those black-tie events don't come up that often, though. It's usually a hospital visit, or skate with the team to raise money for cancer research . . ."

"That doesn't sound too hard," he said, his hand landing on the cushion between them.

Georgia lifted her chin so she wouldn't have to think about all the marvelous ways that hand used to touch her. But that was a mistake, because it meant she was now looking right into his beautiful brown eyes. There was heat in them, too, or was she crazy?

Yep. Definitely losing her mind. And her train of thought.

Damn it. She cleared her throat and got back to business. "There's a spiel I give everyone about being in the public eye. I'm sure you've heard this all before, but the stakes are higher now, because people will pay more attention." She relaxed a little bit now because she'd delivered this speech many times before, and it was a comfortable topic. "Whether you like it or not, you're representing the team at all times. So when you're in a public place, always assume that someone may photograph you. Anything you say online will be scrutinized. I always follow players' social accounts just to make sure there aren't any red flags."

Leo stopped her with an elbow nudge and a grin. "But you unfriended me on Facebook, Gigi."

And, *crap*. She had. After she'd said good-bye to Leo, he hadn't changed their relationship status. So every time she logged in, it made her heart hurt. For some reason, she just couldn't click that box to make it say "single" again.

Then, during their freshman year of college, her feed began to fill with pictures of Leo surrounded by new faces. Teammates she'd never meet. Girls. Those photos made her crazy. That's when she'd done it. She'd unfriended him completely so she wouldn't have to see that he'd moved on.

She swallowed hard. "Well, uh, I meant Instagram, Twitter if you use it . . ."

Leo snorted. "Not a fan."

"Okay," she said quietly.

"Look, I won't be your problem child. I'm easy. So long as your father doesn't ship me back to the minors, I'll be a good boy."

"He won't," she said automatically. Even though she hadn't been ready to see him again, she wasn't ready for him to disappear, either. Leo's eyes widened, and she realized too late that she'd made it sound as if she had inside information. "I meant, I hope he won't. Or, uh, I think he won't. Just, uh, speculating."

Leo nodded, his eyes boring into hers. When he looked at her like that, the years just fell away. They'd been so close for so long. Even if this was all very complicated, Georgia felt herself lean toward him by a few degrees. The connection between them was still there. Like the fishing line her father used when he took the boat out on the Sound. Invisible, yet strong.

Someone cleared a throat, and Georgia sprang up off the bench, as if she'd been caught doing something wrong.

"Sorry to startle you," Becca said quickly. "But Coach is looking for Leo. He needs you to suit up."

Now Leo leapt to his feet, too. "Really? Why?"

"Bayer isn't going to play tonight. They want to give his shoulder one more night's rest."

"Wow. Okay." Leo held Georgia's eyes, and there was so much warmth and happiness in that gaze that Georgia could barely breathe. "Guess I'd better go then."

"Get on down there," she whispered. His whole life he'd been working toward this moment. Skating in the NHL. How amazing that it was finally happening, and she was actually going to witness it.

Leo gave her one more smile, and it was so full of joy that her heart skipped a beat. Then he turned around and strode off, his long legs eating up the distance toward the elevator bank around the bend.

"Come back to me, George," Becca said. "Don't go toward the light."

"What?"

"Exactly." Becca snapped her fingers. "Stay with me, babe. Don't let the hottie who stole your virginity send you into zombieland."

"Becca!" Georgia shout-whispered. "Lower your voice!"

Becca gave her a Cheshire cat smile. "He did, didn't he? Aw! You guys are so cute."

"Shhhh!" Georgia chided. All she needed was a reporter overhearing this fun little conversation. "Stop."

"Only if you give me juicy details at home later. Because memories are all the action that you or I are getting lately."

"Sad but true."

"So, you have to promise not to freak out, but there's a cover-up at work here."

"What?" Georgia asked, trying to shake the Leo-fog out of her head.

"The doctors cleared Bayer's shoulder. But they think he sprained a toe during the soccer warm-up."

"Oh, hell," Georgia swore. "That can't get out, or we'll look like idiots. Big Strong Hockey Player Kicks Soccer Ball Too Hard, Misses Game."

"Be that as it may," Becca said with a grin, "your ex is having his big-league debut, in spite of the fact that your father hates him." She put her hand on Georgia's arm and tugged her toward the owner's box. "Why is that, anyway? Is it because Leo popped your cherry?"

Yikes. "Not really. You'd never believe it now, but they used to be pretty close. Dad used to give Leo one-on-one sessions at the rink, just for fun. I think Dad kind of looked the other way, you know? Plausible deniability."

Becca laughed. "I guess if you were a dad, you'd have to."

"Right. But then after I was raped, I think Dad just couldn't deal with the idea that I wasn't a little girl he could protect anymore. The blinders came off. And since Leo was a man . . ."

"Leo was dangerous, or something."

"Or something," Georgia said. "And it wasn't just Leo that Dad treated differently. You know how he calls me Princess now?"

"Yes, and I'm thinking of calling you that, too."

Georgia poked her in the ribs. "Not if you want to live. Well, he never called me that when I was little. I was Killer to him."

Becca barked out a laugh. "Oh my god. I have to say— Killer suits you better than Princess. I like that nickname for you."

"I'd prefer to have no nickname at all. But apparently that's not an option."

Becca clapped her hands. "Can I tell Page Six that your nickname is Killer?"

"No!"

She giggled. "Ah well. I would have liked to see that in print."

"We can't have everything we want," Georgia grumbled. "But we can have cheese puffs."

"*You* can. Some of us gain weight when we eat things."

"So I've heard. *Hell*. Now I'm nervous about this game. Leo in the NHL! How am I going to watch?"

"Aw. You've got it *bad*, girl."

"Do not."

"Do so."

Georgia gave Becca a little shove.

"Easy, Killer," Becca said. Then they both burst out laughing.

When game time came, though, Georgia retreated from polite company.

She watched the Tampa game alone, from the back corner of the press box. The isolation was exactly what she needed, since no game had ever made her so horrifically nervous before in her life. She watched the game with her seventeen-year-old self, heart in her mouth, fists clenched. Every time Leo took to the ice with the third line she stopped breathing.

Supersized Leo was a sight to behold on a pair of skates. He skated with the same ease he'd always enjoyed, but now it was fueled by even more impressive power and speed. There were years of estrangement between them now, but it was clear that he'd spent most of those years at the rink. He was nimble, even with Tampa's most aggressive defenseman bearing down on him. Time after time Georgia bit her lip as one enemy or another tore after him only to see Leo escape with the puck, creating opportunities where none had seemed to exist.

It was breathtaking. Georgia said another little prayer of thanks for the privacy of the darkened corner where she stood, because her face was plainly crisscrossed with emotion as often as hockey sticks crossed on the ice. She couldn't have hid her interest for all the dumplings in Brooklyn. The first two periods passed in a blur. The game was hard fought, and deep into the third period the score was tied 1–1.

Watching him was both amazing and painful. She

wanted this for him so badly it hurt. Right in the center of her chest, like a tightness that couldn't be soothed. The trouble, though, was that *wanting* was contagious. Wanting him to succeed felt a lot like wanting *him*. And that wasn't on the table. *It's just nostalgia*, she told herself.

She'd had him all to herself once, and it was wonderful. But then, when he'd *stopped* looking at her with passion in his eyes, it had hurt with a fire so bright that she'd never wanted to experience that again.

Never.

Never ever.

Leo vaulted over the boards to take another shift, and Georgia filled her lungs with a shaky breath. *Come on, baby. This is for all the marbles.*

His teammate passed the puck to him, and Leo took a run toward the net. But Tampa swarmed and he just barely got the pass off to Castro, who then got into trouble, coughing up the puck to Tampa's defense.

The clock ticked down, and Georgia wasn't sure she could stand the pressure as Leo gave chase. The other team closed ranks, and retrieving the puck looked impossible. But when Tampa passed to avoid the other winger again, Leo pounced, making off with the puck and crossing into the attack zone, then passing it to Castro.

Who shot. And scored.

The hometown crowd surged to its feet as the lamp signaling a goal lit up. Georgia's smile was so wide she thought her face might crack. Leo had his first big league assist. It wasn't a goal, but it was pretty damned impressive. How many of his high school games had she watched, wondering what the future held? A hundred? Dozens, at least.

A little voice whispered in Georgia's head. *Sometimes people* do *get their heart's desire.*

Not often, though. She was living proof.

The game ended without another goal, and the Bruisers had beaten Tampa. It was a notch in their belt that the team absolutely needed.

Feeling jubilant, Georgia sped out of the press box ahead of the reporters, taking the private elevator downstairs to organize the happy chaos of a postgame press conference. Usually, she'd set up ahead of time, watching the final moments of the game from a monitor downstairs. Tonight she was late to her own party.

But her minion Roger had seen to their little basement pressroom. She skidded to a halt in front of the podium. The wall behind it was already lit with Bruisers footage. (The team had the snazziest press conference setup of any team in the NHL, thanks to Nate's obsession with technology.)

"Thank you, Rog," she said, panting. "I couldn't tear myself away from the action."

He chuckled. "I gotcha covered, boss. Who are we bringing in for interviews?"

"O'Doul." Then Georgia hesitated. A rookie's first assist was newsworthy. But it made more sense to bring in Castro for the goal, and let the media forget about Leo for a night. "And Castro."

"I'll get 'em." He turned to leave the room.

"Thank you!" she called after him.

There was the usual commotion in the hallway outside the room. Georgia stuck her head out to try to convince reporters to come into the pressroom instead of waylaying players in the dressing room or the corridor. She needed those soundbites to happen in front of the Bruisers logo rather than a scuffed-up hallway wall. "Let's go, guys and gals!" she called cheerfully. "We'll bring you the players."

A couple of heads turned, but nobody moved. It was the same routine every game night.

When O'Doul and Castro appeared, moving toward the pressroom, the reporters closed in with their microphones, hoping for an exclusive comment. The slow-moving parade of journos followed the players toward the pressroom.

Georgia stepped out of the way, allowing everyone to pass her. When the horde was through, she stuck her head out into the hall, looking for stragglers. But it was the usual crowd of wives and girlfriends with VIP access. The locker room door kept opening and shutting again as players came out to greet family or retreat inside. Then Georgia saw Leo emerge for a split second before he was promptly tackled. This time, the tackle did not come from his shrill girl-friend, but from Leo's mom.

At the sight of Mrs. Trevi, Georgia's heart tripped over itself almost as clumsily as it did whenever she saw Leo himself. The look of joy on Marion Trevi's face was so pure and lovely that Georgia felt a tickle at the back of her throat. And there was Leo's sister, Violet, grinning beside her. Georgia was startled to see how grown up she looked. When she'd broken up with Leo, Vi was headed for her freshman year of high school, and had a mouth full of braces. As she watched, Leo grabbed his sister and squeezed her, while their dad beamed from a few feet away.

Georgia made herself look away. This was Leo's moment with his family. She stepped back inside the press-room, where her own father was taking the podium with his two players. But her heart was still out in the hallway.

There'd been a time when Georgia had considered the Trevi clan to be her family, too. She loved how loud and happy the Trevi household was. Three kids. Three hockey practice schedules (because DJ and Violet played, too). A refrigerator full of leftovers, homemade cookies on the counter. While Georgia and her father had always been close, Leo's home was lively with affection. She'd spent many a happy Sunday in their den watching football, or on the back patio in the warmer seasons. When she'd cut herself off from Leo, she'd cut herself off from her second home, too.

They were never hers, anyway.

Georgia focused her attention on the podium, and did not look into the hallway again.

EIGHT

TOP TEAM HEADLINES:

Brooklyn Falls to New Jersey in
First of 3-Game Road Trip
—NBC Sports

It didn't matter how old he got—Leo was never going to forget that first game.

The memory fueled him through the rest of a very long week. Coach Worthington's piercing whistle continued to object to half the plays he made during practice. And then Coach benched him for the game against New Jersey.

The Brusiers lost that game, which left the whole team grumpy.

Not Leo, though. Because he had an assist on the winning goal against Tampa. And nobody was ever taking that away from him. His family had yelled themselves hoarse in the stands that night. Afterward, his mom and sister got a photo with his sweaty jersey, reading T R E V I on the back.

And—most important—he'd gotten to show a coach who didn't want him that he could be valuable, given the chance.

It was going to take a lot more than some more grumbling from Coach Worthington to bring him down. Every hour he spent as a member of the team cemented his chance to stick around. Leo figured that if there was an easy way for Coach to invalidate his new contract, he would have done it already.

"It looks like you might be stuck with each other," his agent had said, chuckling.

Thursday night they played their last home game before a three-game road trip across the country and Canada. Leo played that game, against Pittsburgh, because "we're resting Bayer's shoulder for the road."

Whatever, Leo thought to himself as he'd tied his skates. If Coach wanted to make it sound as if Leo was just a stand-in, just let the man try to talk him down. Whether Coach was happy with him or not, he'd play his second NHL game with everything he had.

They battled Pittsburgh to a tie. Leo wasn't entirely impressed with himself. He missed a few opportunities that he should have capitalized on. And he couldn't always anticipate his new teammates' moves the way he'd learned to do with the Muskrats.

If it takes time, it takes time, Leo coached himself. If only he had more of it.

On the morning of the black-tie benefit the team had a morning skate and then a good, heavy workout in the weight room. After grabbing lunch in a deli, he went back to Silas's apartment—he still didn't quite think of it as his own—and took a nap. While he was sleeping, his tux was dropped off with the concierge of the apartment building. He'd had to rent one from a formal wear company that had come to the practice rink to fit him. Leo's own tux was in a box somewhere, packed up by the movers he'd hired to liberate his stuff from his place in Michigan.

Padding around the apartment as the afternoon slid into shadow, he still felt exhausted. It had been exactly eight days since he'd landed in the middle of the team's regular season play. The Bruisers were finishing up a February slate of twelve games, while March promised an astonishing sixteen matchups. Dropped feetfirst into this brutal schedule, he was supposed to get to know his teammates, contribute to their scoring power, move from a thousand miles away, *and* develop as a player.

He hadn't managed to see much of Georgia since that chat they'd had before the Tampa game, either. But he hoped she'd be at the fundraiser tonight. He could hardly believe he had to button himself into a penguin suit and smile for the cameras the night before a weeklong road trip. He hoped this boondoggle was going to raise a cargo-load of money for some worthy cause. Otherwise? Not worth it.

And then there was Amy. She'd texted him about twenty times while he napped, with pictures of the pedicure she'd gotten and the tiny underwear she'd found to go under her dress. His heart dropped when he saw those pics, because it was pretty obvious that her expectations for tonight did not match up to his own.

This night was going to end with Leo in his own bed, alone. The end.

If he was honest, it had become increasingly obvious all week that he should have already called Amy to let her down easy. He should have manned up and disinvited her to the function he'd never really invited her to in the first place. But he was trying to be nice. Amy was a puck bunny of the highest order, and a glitzy night in the company of two dozen professional hockey players would be like her best fantasy come to life. He knew she'd see it as the selfie event of the year with the best bragging rights in town. She'd have a blast, and it didn't have to mean that they were a couple.

But now, squinting at the sexy selfies she'd sent to his phone, staying quiet seemed like a mistake. After tonight's function, he needed a good sleep and a clear head for the road trip. What he did not need was further entanglement with Amy.

He'd just have to tell her tonight. Gently.

In an hour, she'd pull up outside his apartment building, and he'd need to be ready. On the advice of one of Becca's office assistants, he'd sent a limo into Manhattan to pick Amy up. When they'd made that arrangement via text, he'd explained that he needed to pack for a week on the road, and she'd said she understood why he couldn't pick her up in person.

After this shindig tonight, he'd tuck her back into that car and send her on her way again. And there would be no further misunderstandings.

In the meantime, Leo went into his rented bedroom and pulled out his suitcase. It was time to pack.

Two hours later, Georgia stood in the middle of the sumptuously decorated ballroom at the Brooklyn Academy of Music, surveying the crowd. So far, the event had gone off without a hitch. The passed hors d'oeuvres were tasty. The bars at either end of the room were plentiful and well-attended, but not overcrowded. And the florists hired to turn the hall into a winter wonderland had gone out of their way to make the place look stunning. There were silver birch branches with tiny strings of lights, and glittering snowflakes hanging from the ceiling.

It was magnificent. Even so, Georgia was perfectly miserable.

"Man, there she goes again." Becca sidled up to Georgia, giving her a subtle nudge with her elbow.

"I don't want to look," Georgia grumbled. She knew Becca was referring to Leo's date. The two of them were out on the dance floor, sliding through a slow, sultry song together.

This was one of those rare nights when Georgia wished she was more of a drinker. She needed something to numb the burn of that woman's hands all over Leo's body. Since alcohol in public wasn't her style, she'd taken to drowning her sorrows in mini quiches and duck confit en croute.

"She slid her hand *right* up his thigh, and he removed it." Becca snickered. "She's like an octopus in Prada."

Georgia only growled and shoved a mini empanada in her mouth.

"Don't be that way," Becca chided her. "The man is grinding his teeth so hard it's going to leave permanent damage. He'll have to order applesauce for supper from Denver to Phoenix. All the smack talk she's been dishing out is getting to him, too."

"What smack talk?" Georgia hated herself for asking.

"She told Bayer's girlfriend that they'd been together 'since college.' Which is really funny, because earlier I heard him ask her how she'd been since graduation. And that was more than a year ago, right?"

"Almost two," Georgia corrected.

Becca grinned. "You just gotta see the humor, George. This too shall pass."

Georgia cut her eyes toward the girl—Amy was her name. She'd arrived in an entirely glamorous silver dress, her boobs practically popping out everywhere. She was stunning, if Georgia was honest. The girl was both tall and curvy, with smooth, bronze skin, shiny hair, and a rather sleek makeup job of the sort that Georgia had never mastered.

Except . . . Georgia squinted. The girl's mouth was a little too big. And not just figuratively. It was *wide*. Like a muppet's.

Ugh. And now Georgia was picking apart the appearance of a perfect stranger, and all because she was hung up on her high school boyfriend.

Pathetic much? Because while Becca might be right about this girl—that Leo wasn't really enjoying her company—it didn't really matter. If it wasn't Amy then someday soon it would be another girl. Georgia had no claim on Leo. The girls would stick to him like flies in honey. He'd had his picture taken about a hundred times already tonight, by both the charity's photographers and the ticket-holders. Rich fans who'd paid a thousand dollars a head tonight were interested in the cute rookie.

Especially the female fans.

Sitting in Georgia's inbox right now was a reminder

from Hockey Hotties to set up Leo's nude photography shoot. She still hadn't asked him to do it. How she was ever going to have that conversation without blushing like a tomato, she really had no idea.

"I want to see you two fight over him," Becca teased. "You'd go all third-degree black belt on her ass—she wouldn't know what hit her."

Georgia snorted at the image. While it was true that Georgia could, at this point in her training, probably break Amy in half like a board, that wasn't how a man's heart was won.

"Incoming," Becca whispered. "Single, attractive yet egotistical defenseman at nine o'clock."

"Ladies." O'Doul stopped in front of Georgia and Becca. "You both look beautiful tonight."

"Thank you," Becca crowed. "You do that tux some justice, too, mister."

For her part, Georgia bit back another grumpy remark. O'Doul might be handing out compliments tonight, but she hadn't forgotten how he'd spoken about her at the press conference, when he thought she was out of earshot.

"He has a big crush on you," Becca said after he'd slipped away again.

"No way!" Georgia yelped. "You're high."

"You are the most clueless human alive, you know that? Half these guys are in love with you. O'Doul especially. And he asked you out for dinner last month when we were in Vancouver."

"Oh." Georgia frowned. "I think he meant, like, a group thing. There's some restaurant he really likes there."

Becca rolled her eyes. "It was a romantic seafood place on the waterfront, and he was asking you out on a *date*. I overheard the whole thing. Buddy, you are seriously out of practice at this whole boy/girl thing. We need to find you a dojo where they teach male/female interaction."

Georgia snorted. "Can you imagine the drills? How to flip your hair."

"How to lean in for the kiss." Her roommate snickered. "The boob brush that's so subtle it looks like an accident."

They both giggled. "Maybe I do need lessons."

"Just don't take them from *her.*" Becca pointed with her drink.

Leo's date was shimmying on the dance floor, pancaked against his body.

"Damn you! You made me look." Georgia yanked her eyes away from the happy couple, spotting a uniformed waiter exiting the kitchen, his tray freshly filled with tiny shrimp pot stickers. *Come to mama,* Georgia coached. *I need a fix.*

"Girl," Becca said, nudging her elbow. "Step away from the passed hors d'oeuvres. Why don't you ask Silas to dance? He looks a little bored."

Georgia spotted the goalie across the room, leaning against the wall, a drink in his hand. He did, in fact, look a little bored. "His date bailed at the last minute. That happens to him a lot. It's weird." And the players were obligated to attend these functions a few times a year, whether they wanted to or not.

"See?" Becca prodded. "He needs you. And what would it hurt?"

"I don't ask the players to dance."

"But there's no law against it, right?"

"Why don't you do it?" Georgia challenged. "And, omi-god, are we fourteen? I'm pretty sure the last time I had this conversation I was in ninth grade. And Green Day was playing in the gym. 'Boulevard of Broken Dreams.'"

"Good song. But you know hockey players aren't my type," Becca insisted. "I like 'em thin and artsy. And don't go trying to tell me they're not your type. Because I'm calling bullshit on that."

Georgia didn't try to argue the point. "Silas would faint from shock if I asked him to dance."

"He'll know you don't mean anything by it. Just do this, okay? I'll clean the inside of our refrigerator if you do."

"Really? Even the fruit drawer?" Georgia had been

dreading that task. The overripe mango was still in there, seeping slowly into its own swampy ooze.

"Even the fruit drawer." Becca gave her a shove. "Go. Before I change my mind."

Georgia walked in the general direction of Silas, taking her time. Asking him to dance was probably something she wouldn't really have the finesse to do. She was technically working right now, and practically everyone she knew was in this room. Too many eyeballs, too much pressure. It was different when she was a teenager. Dancing with Leo had always been fun. But in the past six years, she'd only danced at the occasional wedding. And only with relatives.

Yikes, she thought as she made her way around various clots of partygoers. Six years was a long time to be a homebody. That's how a habit became a rut, wasn't it?

That wasn't a fun realization.

In college, Georgia had played it safe. She'd kept to herself the first year, staying away from strangers and crowds while rebuilding her confidence. Her tennis teammates became good friends, and since they knew the difficult history of her last year of high school, they'd been understanding. Nobody ever made Georgia feel like a loser for staying in on Fridays and Saturdays. And during tennis season, she'd had plenty of company. They all worked too hard to party much.

As the years passed, she stopped being afraid. Georgia felt strong—happy, even. But solitude was habit-forming. Parties now seemed too loud and overwrought. She preferred dinners out with small groups of friends.

Sometimes there were dates, and sometimes more than once with the same guy. But nobody she'd met after Leo really clicked, or she held herself aloof. One or the other. In either case, she hadn't had a boyfriend since Leo. Funny how she'd never stopped to do the math until he turned up, either. Almost six years she'd been single now. And it hadn't seemed pathetic until tonight.

"Hi, Silas," she said, stopping beside him.

"Hey, Georgia. Is there somewhere I'm supposed to be?"

"Nope," she said, smiling to put him at ease. Geez, was she really as frosty as that? She said hello, and he assumed he'd done something wrong? "There's no place I'm supposed to be, either. So I decided to hold up this section of the wall beside yours. Just in case you needed help."

"Ah," he said, touching his drink to her water glass. "I'm just tired. And the next week is going to be nutty."

"True." It was the longest road trip on their schedule. And the backup goalie had to practice just as hard as any player on the team, even though he expected to play only occasionally.

"When's the earliest that I can sneak out of here without getting in trouble?" Silas asked.

Georgia peeked at her watch. It was only nine o'clock. "After the president of the charity speaks. But that should happen in thirty minutes."

"Awesome," Silas said, grinning at her. "If anyone stops me, I'm going to say you told me I could go."

"Do you want me to write out a hall pass, like in high school?" The question seemed appropriate since apparently high school was the last time she'd had a life.

"Sure," he teased.

Georgia found herself smiling back at him. She still wasn't reckless enough to ask him to dance. Becca was probably chewing off her fingernails across the room, wondering what she was waiting for. It was sort of fun to torture her pushy roommate this way. But even if she didn't fulfill their bet, chatting with Silas got her mind off Leo for a few minutes. And that had been the point, anyway.

"How shall we pass thirty minutes, then?" he asked.

"We're very busy holding up this wall," she pointed out.

He extended his drink, indicating the band playing in the corner. "I like this song. We could hold down the dance floor instead."

"Okay," Georgia said quickly. Becca wouldn't even know she'd chickened out and she'd have to scrub rotten mango juice out of the fruit drawer anyway. Georgia bit back a smile at this little deception as Silas removed the water glass from her hand.

Guiding her toward the dance floor, Silas put a hand at the center of her back. She didn't mind the warm pressure of his palm. It was steadying. There was something cheerful and open about Silas that she'd always appreciated. He didn't have the intensity of Leo, but he was approachable. Dancing with a player under the scrutiny of the whole entire world just didn't seem as weird as it should have. Because this was Silas, with his scruffy beard and easy hazel eyes.

She put her hand lightly on the shoulder of his tuxedo jacket as he stepped closer. With a quick grin, he adjusted their dancing stance and turned her easily to the left.

"You're a good dancer," she heard herself blurt out.

He laughed. "You were expecting me to suck?"

"No," she said quickly. "Never mind me. I don't dance much."

"Maybe you should dance more," he suggested. His tone was light, and his smile easy.

Holy crap, I'm actually having fun, she thought as he guided her around to the beat. *And Becca has to clean the fridge.* Winning!

"What's so funny?" Silas asked.

"Not a thing. Did you take dance lessons?" she asked, just to turn the conversation away from herself.

But Silas didn't answer, so she studied his face. "Can I trust you?"

"Sure. I'm a vault," she promised.

"My mother made me take six years of dance lessons. Seventh through twelfth grades."

"What?" she yelped. "Why?"

"Because she's from the South," he said, as if that explained it. "Cotillion. Everyone had to."

"That is bizarre."

"Not where she's from."

"That's what I mean . . ." She had to pause because Silas lifted her hand above her head, and Georgia knew she was supposed to turn. "What's bizarre is that a southern gentleman like you became a hockey player."

"True," he said. "But my mama likes dancing and white gloves, and my daddy likes violence. So it's all there."

Georgia smiled at him again, and was happy for the distraction, however brief.

NINE

"So tell me," Amy said to Bayer's girlfriend. "How does the wives and girlfriends' club work?"

The low hum of a headache that had troubled Leo since they stepped into the room rose in pitch to a dull throb. It had been a mistake to invite Amy. She'd been busy trying to worm her way into his life—and his pants—since the moment he and Silas had joined her in the limo.

Silas was clearly the smarter of the two residents of apartment 407. He hadn't brought a date. ("I don't date," he'd said with a shrug when Leo had asked.) And now? The young goalie was dancing with Georgia. Leo knew he shouldn't watch, and he shouldn't care. But his eyes kept drifting over to the two of them. They both looked about a hundred times more relaxed than he felt right now.

And since his attention had drifted, Amy was getting her hooks in, absorbing all of the other women's attention and advice. "Meet us for cocktails on the road!" one of them was saying. "We're good at sneaking into the hotel after curfew. It's a blast."

That's it. He couldn't let this go on. "Amy?" He took her hand. "Let's dance. I want to talk to you."

She sort of slithered into his arms, smiling up at him. "I'm all yours."

Oh hell.

He led her a short distance away, where they could chat privately. Then he took her hand and met her eyes. "I'm really glad you could come out tonight. This event is pretty crazy, and I thought you'd find it fun."

"It's amazing," she agreed. "I got a picture with O'Doul and his cute little date." She slid her free hand into his jacket and over his abs. "And I got to reacquaint myself with *you*. Almost." She grinned. "When can we go home?"

He caught her wandering hand. "Amy, we're not going home together tonight. I told you that."

"I know you need your sleep." She took a step forward until her tits met his chest. "But it's early. We could get started now."

Leo held back his sigh. He'd said it nicely a dozen times already, but Amy had selective hearing. So now he was going to have to be a little less subtle. "We're not going home together. Not tonight, and not another time. We were finished after college, Amy. That was your choice, anyway."

She looked up at him with wide eyes. "But you moved to the Midwest. And even so, it was a bad decision. I've regretted it ever since."

Ever since last Friday, she probably meant.

"I've moved on," he said as gently as possible.

"Really?" She took a half step backward. "Where is your invisible girlfriend, then?"

"I just mean . . ." *Fuck.* "We're over. It was good while it lasted, but we're not getting back together. I'm sorry. There's too much going on in my life."

Her eyes narrowed. "I was going to surprise you on the road. In Montreal. When have you not wanted a quick hotel fuck, Trevi?"

Trevi. He'd always been a name on the back of a hockey jersey to her. That used to be fine with him, too. It wasn't anymore, though. Maybe this wasn't all Amy's fault. But he was allowed to change his mind, right?

"I'm sorry," he said slowly. "I don't want to argue. But I didn't mean to start something up with you."

"Fine," she snapped, her eyes dampening. "So you were okay using me for sex in college, but not anymore."

"Amy," he whispered. "I was good to you in college." If anyone had been used, he was pretty sure it was mutual. And once they'd gone exclusive senior year, he'd never looked at another girl. Even though she'd been awfully high maintenance, he'd put up with all her antics with a smile.

"But you never *loved* me," she spat. "I can't *believe* I wasted so much time on you."

Now heads were turning in their direction. That couldn't be good for anyone's dignity. "Let's walk out to the car," he said gently. Thank God he'd asked the driver to wait, even if it was costing him a fortune. "We can talk more if you want."

"'Talk' is not what I came here for." She'd raised her voice. And now she tossed her hair in that age-old show of female defiance. "You are clearly too dumb to recognize a scoring opportunity when one comes around. Hope your teammates know. It doesn't bode well for your stats on the road. Best of luck, rookie!" This last bit was delivered at a shout. And then Amy stomped away on her glittering high heels, her ass sashaying in that shiny dress. Dancers lost the beat on the dance floor, and the crowd parted for her.

Then dozens of eyes landed on Leo, standing there stupidly.

His neck was hot and his head throbbed. And he wanted nothing more than to tear his constricting bow tie off and hurl it across the room. Naturally his gaze fell right on Georgia, who was no longer dancing with Silas. She was staring at him in horror.

Shit. Another PR disaster. Who knew the NHL would turn him into the kind of guy who caused a scene at least once a week? And he couldn't even leave right now, because Amy might still be collecting her coat in the entryway and locating the car he asked to wait for her.

Another drink, then.

Leo took a deep breath and headed for the bar against

the wall. While he waited for the bartender's attention, he tried to imagine what his brother was going to say when he heard about this. The kid was going to laugh his ass off, probably.

"Scotch, please," he said when he reached the front of the line. He dug a couple of singles out of his pocket and tucked them into a brimming tip jar.

"Leo," a soft voice whispered.

After taking his drink, he turned. There stood Georgia, looking both ridiculously hot and absolutely pissed off. All night he'd been trying not to notice her in that dark blue dress, which skimmed her taut body with one long sweep of fabric. She'd worn dresses dozens of times when they were young. But this one made it painfully obvious that she wasn't a teenager anymore. It was sophisticated. Something a smart, sexy *woman* wore.

Jesus. He found it impossible to stop his head—and other body parts—from revisiting the past.

"That was quite a performance," Georgia said, putting one hand on her silk-clad hip. Leo was envious of her palm. "Since when are you a spotlight hog? If I have reporters asking about the rookie and his messy dance-floor breakup tomorrow, you'll officially be the most time-consuming player on my docket. God forbid my office should talk about hockey."

He heard every unfortunate word, even as he admired the pink tint to her cheeks and the fiery look in her eye. "Yeah, it was a lot of fun for me, too. I'm thinking I should just call it a night and slip out the back."

"Good plan," she fired back.

He took a big swig of his scotch, which was excellent. "Right. But if you do get calls tomorrow, try to remember that *you* invited her tonight."

Leo thought he'd gotten the last word, except he'd forgotten that Georgia always won a volley. "You dated her in the first place," Georgia returned. "Or do I have that wrong?" Her big blue eyes narrowed, and she crossed her arms in front of her perfect chest. Hell, a guy could forget what argument he'd been making.

That's when he threw in the towel. When they were together, he always let her win the fights. Georgia was a smart girl, she never steered him wrong. And the makeup sex had always been spectacular. "Fine. I think it's pretty clear tonight that I'm an idiot. Maybe the girl made a few good points there at the end."

Georgia's lips twitched. Then she gave in and smiled. And it was like the sun came out. There was more warmth and humor in Georgia's smile than he'd seen anywhere else in six years. His heart said, *This. This right here.*

His brain didn't weigh in at all, unfortunately. That's the only explanation for the way he stepped forward to cup her cheek. His fingertips slid into the silky hair behind her ear.

Those clear, pretty eyes widened slightly. But that didn't stop him. For the first time in way too long, Leo leaned down and claimed her mouth in a kiss, right on her very sweet lips. Georgia made a soft, bitten-off sound of surprise. Damn, how he'd missed her. This was too much and yet not enough, either. He deepened the kiss, stroking her cheek with his thumb, his groin tightening at the feel of her skin under his hand. She tasted like the happiest years of his life.

She tasted like *his.*

But Georgia had more sense than he did—as always. She put one perfect hand in the center of his chest and gave him a little push. "Leo," she warned softly as they broke apart. This wasn't the time or the place for the reunion he craved, though neither his body nor his heart really cared. He straightened up, though, because her eyes asked him to. But he couldn't have looked away—not even if he'd been promised a Stanley Cup win.

And that was unfortunate. Because if he'd looked around, he might have seen the approach of Coach Worthington and his angry red face. Or at least his fist, which came shooting out to catch Leo square in the jaw.

Leo's head snapped sideways from the impact, and he stumbled back a step, his ass hitting the table beside the bar, where a hundred or so wine glasses were lined up, waiting for the next thirsty guests. The ensuing crash and tinkle of glass was deafening.

As a reflex, Leo clapped a hand over his face at the point of connection. But he had to hold on to the bar with his free hand because the room seemed to tilt from impact. He closed his eyes, hoping he wouldn't black out.

"No!" he heard Georgia gasp, and the frightened edge to her voice helped him focus.

He lifted his chin and opened his eyes, and the room righted itself.

But people were scrambling around to stare. Heads turned from every direction to take in the latest scandal. Hugh Major, the general manager of the team, hustled over and tugged Coach Karl back a step. The man's meaty hand on Georgia's father's arm was either a calming influence or a threat. Or maybe both.

Glass continued to tinkle musically to the floor from the table behind Leo, and the pop and flash of several phone flashbulbs went off, the light bouncing erratically off the glass shards and guaranteeing that the newest Brooklyn Bruisers fiasco would make tomorrow's gossip rags.

Somehow, Silas slid between the growing cluster of gaping people, arriving at Leo's side. "Come on," was all he said before pulling him out of the scrum.

Leo obeyed, straightening up to his full height and dropping his hands to his sides. After a few deep breaths he was steady on his feet as they entered the lobby.

"You have a coat check?" Silas asked.

"Uh . . ." Leo dug into his pocket, coming out with the paper tag.

Silas took it. "Wait here. Two minutes."

His jaw throbbing, Leo leaned back against a pillar and looked up at the ornamental ceiling far above him. Someone had gone to the trouble to make the room look like a forest in winter. Tomorrow the place would be back to looking like a music hall.

He had to wonder whether he'd be back to looking like a minor league player in the morning. Getting punched by the coach? Not an auspicious sign.

By the time Silas got him home in a cab, his phone had lit up several times with numbers he didn't recognize. He didn't answer any of them. The lights in the hallway outside their apartment were all too bright. He just wanted to put some ice on his aching face and go to bed.

"How old is Georgia?" Silas asked as the door swung open, and Leo realized they hadn't spoken all the way home.

"Twenty-four," Leo mumbled, his jaw stiff.

"Can't punch a man for kissing your daughter unless he's robbin' the cradle."

"Apparently you can." It hurt to speak. Leo headed straight for his room.

Silas chuckled. "You need anything? Motrin? Water? A lawyer, maybe?"

"Just ice."

"I'll bring you a pack."

Leo waved a hand. "You don't have to, man."

"I know."

He stripped off the tux and got ready for bed, ignoring his phone. In the mirror, his jaw looked swollen already. So he stopped looking at it. He took a pain reliever and lifted his suitcase off the bed and onto the floor. First thing tomorrow morning he'd be getting on a plane with the team and Coach Worthington. Wouldn't that be cozy.

Silas walked in, an ice pack in one of his hands, a phone in the other. "You're not answering, apparently. The team's doctor is looking for you."

"Thanks," Leo grunted, taking the ice and—reluctantly— the phone. "Hello?"

"Mr. Trevi, I hear you took a punch to the jaw."

"Yessir," he said, trying to enunciate so the doctor would know he was okay, and leave him alone. He sat down on the bed. "It's not too bad, though."

"How are your teeth?" the doctor asked. "Any looseness?"

"No."

"Did the skin break or abrade either inside or outside your mouth?"

"Don't think so." He didn't feel like getting up to check, either.

"Are you experiencing nausea or dizziness?

"No. Just pain."

"On a scale of 1 to . . ."

". . . Just a three," Leo broke in, inventing a number. "Hurts at the point of impact. I took a couple of Advil. I'm icing it."

"Tell me exactly what medication you took, please."

Didn't he just do that? "Two ordinary Advil. Nothing fancy."

"Okay. I'm worried about a concussion, Mr. Trevi."

"Leo," he corrected. "And I really don't think it's that bad."

"All right," the doctor said mildly. "If you have nausea or dizziness, you can call me, and if it's serious, you should always go to the ER or call 911."

"Got it," Leo promised. He sure as hell hoped he didn't have a concussion. What player ever sat out an NHL game because the coach punched him? It was almost impressive how many brand-new ways Leo seemed to have found to fuck up a pro career.

"We'll speak tomorrow morning," the doctor said. It was a demand, not a question.

Leo hung up, handed over the phone, then climbed into bed to put a terrible evening to rest. What a disaster. *Except for that kiss . . .*

He fell asleep remembering the taste of Georgia on his lips.

* * *

"Hey. You okay? Can you wake up a sec?"

Leo swam through the stillness of his dreams. He did not want to wake up.

"Earth to Leo. Come in, Leo."

His eyes opened to find a figure sitting on the side of his giant bed. "Silas?" He sat up in a hurry.

"Sorry to startle you, dude. The doctor asked me to wake you up every three hours. Aren't you glad you moved in? You get a bedroom, a big rent bill, and a wake-up at two in the morning."

"Shoulda stayed at the hotel," Leo mumbled.

Silas laughed. "Let's make a deal—I'll tell the doctor I woke you up several times, but instead we'll both sleep."

"'Kay. I'm fine, anyway." *Except for the pain in my face.*

"I'm sure you are. They take concussions pretty seriously, though. Don't be shocked if they put you on the injured list a couple of nights just to be sure."

"Fuck." He needed to make a contribution to the team, like, yesterday. He couldn't do that without playing. "Fucking Karl."

"Dude, you could get Coach in some serious trouble. Shit—you could get that man *fired* if you go to the commissioner with this."

Leo cringed, which hurt the muscles in his face. "Sounds like a bad career move." He didn't want to be the rookie who got the coach fired. "O'Doul gets hit worse every other game."

"O'Doul knows those fights are coming. And he's wearing a helmet."

Those were good points. But there was still no way he was going to make a big deal out of this. If anything, he was more determined than ever to play for Worthington. That asshole was going to give him scoring chances and learn to be grateful for it.

That was the idea, anyway.

"You want another hit of Advil?" Silas asked.

"Good idea."

Silas disappeared into the bathroom and returned a minute later. "Heads up."

Leo raised his hand just in time to catch the bottle sailing toward him.

"Nice. I can text the doctor that your reflexes are top notch."

Leo popped the top off the bottle and poured out two pills. He capped it again and then dry-swallowed them.

Silas handed him a glass of water, which he drank gratefully. "Thanks, man. Really."

"No big. Can I ask you something?"

"Shoot."

"What's the coach's problem with you, anyway?"

Wasn't that the question. "I think it's the usual protective father crap. Georgia and I started up pretty young. I mean . . ." Leo chuckled to himself. "That man has no idea."

"Or maybe he does."

Leo lay back on the pillow and closed his eyes. "Maybe. We broke all the rules he set. Not just me, either. Georgia was a party girl. Sometimes I'd be tugging on her hand, saying, 'We have to get you home.' And she was the one saying, 'One more dance.'"

"Huh."

"What?"

"I've never seen Georgia party."

"What do you mean? You danced with her yourself tonight." Shit. He hadn't meant to say that.

Silas laughed in the dark. "You noticed that, huh?"

"Maybe."

His roommate laughed again. "I was as surprised as you, man. That girl doesn't drink, she doesn't party, and I've never seen her dance. I only asked her because we were both standing there, bored. Couldn't believe she said yes."

Leo didn't like the sound of that. "Maybe it's because she's always working when you see her out."

"Maybe." Silas didn't exactly sound convinced. "So

Coach hates you because you broke curfew? That'd be a hell of a grudge."

No kidding. "Nah, something changed. He used to like me a lot. We got along great. He was this big college coach and I kind of idolized him. He'd come to our rink sometimes and run workshops for my high school team, and it was because I asked him to do it. When recruiters started showing up to watch me play, that's when he really supported me. He made a lot of calls to those guys. I'm pretty sure I wouldn't have made it onto the Harkness team without his help."

Silas gave a low, appreciative whistle. "That's pretty awesome. So what the hell happened?"

Leo wasn't sure what he could say without violating Georgia's privacy. "Spring of senior year is when it all went to hell. The college deposits were in, and life was good. But then Georgia went away to tennis camp over spring break, and she was the victim of a crime." That was all he would say on the matter, but even that sounded like too much. Just mentioning it felt like uncorking an old bottle of bad juju. *Shit.* Perhaps that's why Coach Karl was coming unglued. Maybe he and Georgia hadn't had to think about this for a long time. And then Leo showed up and stirred up all the old anguish . . .

That was something to think about when he was less tired.

"A bad crime?" Silas asked.

Leo sighed. "Yeah. And nothing was ever the same. Georgia kind of lost it for a little while, and I did everything I could for her, but it was just a really bad time. That's when Karl started giving me the evil eye. He'd come home from work and see me sitting there with Georgia, even though we weren't supposed to be alone together at his house. I knew I wasn't welcome anymore. But at that point Georgia really needed the company and I just didn't care what he thought. But it was like he woke up when someone hurt his little girl. And he didn't trust anyone anymore. Not even me."

Silas was quiet for a long moment. "That's a hell of a history, dude. And then you two broke up?"

"She dumped me after all that. She said she wanted to start fresh in college." Leo relaxed in the bed, his head sinking into the pillow.

"Ouch."

"Yeah. Ouch. But Karl has no legitimate beef with me. I was good to Georgia."

"Except when you were breaking rules and keeping her out late in your lovemobile."

Leo snorted. "I drove a Ford F-150 with a pimped out stereo. Thought I was a total stud."

"I drove a battered hearse."

"What? An actual hearse?"

"Yeah."

Leo was feeling really sleepy again. "Could you get girls to climb into the back of a hearse with you?"

"You'd be surprised."

He fell asleep mid chuckle.

TEN

TOP TEAM HEADLINES:

*"Brooklyn Bruiser Bruised by Coach? Tuxedos and
Trouble at Benefit for Brooklyn Arts"
—Pucker Up Blog*

"Do you have your cell phone charger?" Becca prompted.

"Got it." Georgia zipped her carry-on bag shut. The car she'd hired was waiting downstairs.

"I'm not even going to ask if your gym stuff is in there. I know you wouldn't forget that. But how about your round brush? This road trip is no time for flat hair."

Honestly, a burka sounded like a better choice. Georgia would just as soon go into permanent hiding after last night's fiasco. She was surprised there wasn't a message on her phone telling her not to bother to show up at the airport this morning. Georgia peeked at her messages one more time. Nothing from the GM. Everything in her inbox was from news sources asking for a statement about last night's rumored scuffle between a player and the new coach.

It was going to be another long week.

Becca loomed over her in her bathrobe. While Georgia always traveled with the team, her roommate usually stayed behind to man the office. "Do you have condoms?"

Georgia looked up quickly. "God, why?"

"Duh!" Becca grinned. "Don't you want to see where that kiss could lead?"

"It led to a punch in the face! God, I don't even know if his *jaw is broken*."

That last bit came out in an anguished squeak, and Becca's face softened. "He'll be okay, honey. If it was that bad you would have heard already. You could call him, you know."

Now there was a terrifying idea. *Hi, Leo. That was the only truly good kiss I've had in six years. Was there any permanent damage on your end?*

Georgia shook her head. "I'm the last person he wants to talk to right now. And unless he's decided to sue my father and quit the team, somehow we have to travel on the same jet for six straight days."

"And five straight nights," Becca said, waggling her eyebrows.

"I love you, but you're crazy," Georgia said, checking her bag one more time and then standing up.

Becca threw her arms around her. "I love you, too, Georgia. And I don't think you say those words very often."

Surprised at this uncharacteristic emotional moment, Georgia put her arms around Becca and gave her a squeeze. Becca was right, too. She didn't ask people to dance and she never told anyone she loved them. And damn that Leo Trevi for showing up and making her notice all the ways she'd changed since high school. "You're going to DVR our shows, right?"

"Of course." Becca released her.

"And if I need you to return some calls to the press today . . ."

"I'll do it. Just forward the e-mails and tell me what to say. Now let's go. Your car is outside."

Georgia stepped into her shoes—flats, of course—and picked up her carry-on. Becca rolled the big suitcase toward the door. "I'm helping you carry this down the stairs. God, it's heavy."

"Six days is a long time."

"And I want *frequent* updates."

After they wrestled the suitcase down the stairs, Georgia handed off the bag to the driver of the black sedan who was waiting at the curb. She climbed onto the leather seat in back and shut the door, waving at Becca one last time.

Just as the driver climbed back into his seat, another black car pulled up behind them. Georgia eyed the ridiculously fancy condo building across the street. Usually the hired cars stopping on this block were here for people who lived in the posh building across the street. And given the timing, it might even be Silas who emerged from the front door.

Sure enough, a doorman with shiny buttons on his uniform stepped out, holding the door. Silas followed, wearing his suit, his purple tie, and rolling a big duffel bag behind him.

We should have shared a car, Georgia thought. *What a waste.* But then another figure appeared behind Silas—a tall, beautiful man with an enormous purple bruise all over the side of his face.

Leo. Her heart gave a whimper at the sight of his injured face.

Her driver picked that moment to accelerate, and the car slid away from the curb and down Water Street. Georgia actually felt a rush of nausea. She gripped the door's handle and debated with herself whether she might need to ask the driver to pull over. She fixed her eyes on the horizon and took three slow breaths.

What a tangled mess she was in. And she had no clue how to escape.

One of Brooklyn's blessings was the quick trip to LaGuardia airport, so Georgia was only allowed half an hour of brooding before the car pulled up to Marine Air Terminal.

"Morning, Georgia," her father greeted her as she rolled her suitcase into the gate area. "Can I get that for you?"

Georgia gave her head a shake and tried to keep on walking.

But he reached out and grabbed her hand. "What, you're not talking to me now? I brought you an apple turnover from Reinwald's."

"Dad," she said, forgetting her vow to call him Coach at work, "don't try to butter me up. My inbox is full of reporters who want to know if Coach Worthington socked one of his players in front of three hundred guests. A pastry isn't going to make that headache go away."

He gave her a sheepish face. "I'm sorry about that, Princess. Didn't mean to make your job more difficult."

"Then what *did* you mean to do? I don't get it. Not at all! What did Leo do that was worth jeopardizing your career, my sanity, and his face?" Georgia felt herself getting all worked up. If Leo stuck around Brooklyn, he and her father were going to have to sort some things out. Whatever issues they had probably involved her. So wouldn't that be fun.

Her father lifted his chin in that maddening, closed-off way that men had. "That's not your concern."

"Isn't it?" Georgia pressed. "I'm telling you that it is. And I need you to fix it. Tell him you're sorry." She pointed at the bakery bag. "In fact, you should give that pastry to Leo and commence groveling." Then she rolled right past him, taking up position against the wall and arming herself with her phone and a don't-talk-to-me face. She kept her head down, because it was too tempting to watch for Leo, and to worry about that awful bruise on his face.

This was going to be a long trip, and she could not spend it staring at Leo. There were other things to worry about. Her stomach gave a grumble, which only made Georgia more irritated with her father.

Because now she was also thinking about apple turnovers from Reinwald's. Only pride kept her from snatching it out of her father's hand.

* * *

While last night Leo had been That Guy Who Caused Two Scenes at One Benefit, this morning he was That Guy Whose Name Wasn't on the Flight Manifest. His record for causing difficulty within the organization was approaching epic proportions. For once, at least, it wasn't his fault. None of the office minions had remembered to add his name to the list. But that didn't stop the grumbling and the overt checking of watches before his twenty-two teammates and assorted staff were ushered onto the plane without him.

Leo stood there, passport in hand, watching the last of them disappear down the Jetway and tried not to feel that the universe meant it as a sign.

When eventually his status was sorted out, Leo boarded the jet to find that most of the seats were taken. He kept moving down the aisle, and toward the back he spotted a couple of empty seats, one of them beside Georgia Worthington. He'd snuck glances at her in the terminal while she studiously ignored him. She wouldn't be able to avoid him now, though. He quickened his pace toward the seat.

"Leo Trevi?" He looked up to see Hugh Major calling to him from a narrow doorway at the back of the plane. "Can you come in here a moment, son?"

Foiled again.

Leo continued down the aisle, his eyes on Georgia. And when he passed, she glanced up, her eyes creasing with something like sympathy.

He must look pretty frightening.

Ducking into the little room in back, he found a small but attractively appointed room featuring a table and leather-upholstered built-in seating—like a restaurant booth for rich people. In fact, the jet was a marked upgrade from long hours on a bus with his AHL team. And now he'd been called into the inner sanctum. Coach Karl sat at the table, looking surly.

"Have a seat," the GM said, taking his own seat beside Coach Karl. "Coffee?"

"Um, yes, please," Leo said, fitting his big frame into an open seat on the opposite side of the table. It was a bit like being called into the principal's office. Although if the news were very bad, they wouldn't have had him on the jet at all.

"How's the jaw? The doctor look at you yet?" The GM opened a Starbucks bag and pulled out three sealed cups of coffee, passing one to Leo.

"I'll live," he said, uncapping the coffee. "Haven't spoken to the doctor yet, but he won't find anything other than a real ugly bruise and a scrape. Nothing my cosmetic surgeon can't fix."

Nobody laughed. And Coach Karl sat stone still in his chair, wearing an expression like someone had just force-fed him something bitter. Leo sipped his coffee and was grateful to have it. Maybe it wasn't worth getting punched in the face, but he'd never underestimate the healing power of French roast.

Hugh cleared his throat. "Son, we need you to know that the club does not support the actions of a coach who lays his hands on his players. Or vice versa, of course. What happened last night shouldn't have. And it won't happen again."

"Okay," Leo said, his gaze leaving the GM and landing on the coach. It was all well and good for Hugh to give that speech. But Leo was pretty sure that a direct apology should be forthcoming right about now.

"Karl?" Hugh prompted.

"I apologize for my rash temper and the unfortunate result," Karl said woodenly.

Never was such a lackluster apology issued. And even though none of this was funny, Leo found that he had to fight back a bitter laugh. "Thank you." . . . *For that inadequate sentiment.*

Coach pushed a white paper bag across the table. "Here," he said gruffly.

He took the bag. "What's this?"

"An apple turnover from Reinwald's."

"Um . . . thanks?" This morning got weirder by the second. "Is it poisoned?"

Nobody laughed.

"Son," Hugh began. "We need to know if you plan to pursue any legal action against the coach or the team."

With that question the conversation moved rapidly into the ass-covering portion of the morning. *Careful.* Leo's agent wouldn't want him to promise anything. "If that's the last of my difficulties with Coach Worthington, I don't see why I would pursue anything," he said.

The manager tilted his head back, studying Leo over the end of his shrewd nose. "All right." He shuffled a file folder in front of him and drew out a page. "Then would you mind signing this?"

The plane had begun accelerating down the runway for takeoff. Leo took the paper from Hugh and read the first few lines. *Regarding the altercation between myself and Karl Worthington on the evening of* . . . He skimmed. *I will not pursue regulatory nor legal action, nor seek damages* . . .

He sighed, then set the paper down on the table, which was now rattling as they went airborne. "Tell you what. We both know my agent would spank me for signing anything without getting his eyes on it first. But we don't need this piece of paper."

"We don't?"

Leo shook his head. "If Coach gives me a fair shake, treats me like the rest of his players, and doesn't trade my ass, then this conversation is moot."

The GM gave a slow blink. "Are you blackmailing Coach Worthington? If he trades you, then you'll sue?"

"No," Leo argued. "Don't put words in my mouth. I don't want lawyers, I want to skate. And I want the same shot as every other guy on the plane. It's not that complicated."

Hugh surprised him by smiling suddenly. "Good answer, kid."

Coach Karl said nothing.

Leo shouldered his duffel bag. Then he took the pastry bag and the Starbucks cup. Because good coffee was good coffee, even if assholes gave it to you. "We're done here, right?" He looked at his coach, who only stared back at him for a long moment.

Then he nodded.

"Thank you." Leo got up and slid the door open with his index finger, ducking carefully out of the little room. The jet was still gaining altitude, so he held the ceiling with his pastry bag hand and carefully eased down the aisle. When he got to the row where Georgia sat, the seat beside her was still empty. Feeling the eyes of nearby teammates on him, he slid into it and fastened his seatbelt. Beside him, Georgia looked with a steadfast gaze out the window at the hazy white sky.

He opened the bakery bag and pulled out the pastry. He hadn't had one of these for years. His mouth watered just looking at the flaky thing on the sheet of waxed paper. "Georgia," he whispered.

"What?" she whispered back.

"Any idea why your father gave me a punch in the face and then an apple turnover?"

"Nope."

"Was this supposed to be for you?" he asked. "You always liked filled things."

"What?" She finally turned her heart-shaped face toward his. It was hard to be angry when those clear eyes were looking at him.

"Filled things," he repeated. "Turnovers. Samosas. Dumplings."

She swallowed. "You're killing me right now."

He grinned, nudging the pastry. "Halfsies?"

Slowly, Georgia nodded.

Leo folded the waxed paper carefully around the pastry then tugged it in half. He picked up one of the pieces himself, then placed the other on the white bakery bag and slid it onto Georgia's tray table.

They ate in absolute silence. Chewing was uncomfortable for Leo, as it made his jaw ache. But the pastry made it worthwhile. Reinwald's was a bakery about a mile from their high school. It opened at six thirty in the morning, so a guy could get a donut even before an early practice. After Georgia had been attacked, he'd gone there every day after school on his way to Georgia's. He'd choose whatever cupcake or cookie had the best chance of making her smile.

Those were grim days, before she was ready to go back to school. Before the cuts on her face had healed. She wouldn't talk about it, either. A couple of times he'd tried to get her to open up about her attack, but she'd only change the subject.

So he brought her a cupcake every day for two weeks until she complained that she was going to get fat. That was such an unGeorgialike thing to worry about that it felt like a slap in the face.

But Leo didn't give up on her. Not ever. Instead of treats, he'd switched to bringing her funny videos on his phone. That hadn't worked so well, either. But he'd tried.

He would have waited forever to see her smile at him again, but she didn't give him the chance.

Leo looked down to find that he'd balled up the empty white bag and was squeezing it so hard that his knuckles were white. Funny thing—he hadn't realized that after all this time he was still angry. What was the point of that? It was a long time ago. And he knew Georgia had had her reasons. He'd known it even then, but he'd still been mad.

"Does it hurt?" Georgia asked suddenly.

Hell yes, he nearly answered. But then he realized she was referring to his face, not his heart. "It's fine. Looks worse than it is."

"I'm sorry," she murmured.

He turned to look at her, forcing her to do the same. Georgia's sweet eyes were so tentative. He hated that. They never used to be uncomfortable with each other. Not Georgia and Leo. That's not how it was supposed to be. "I'm sorry, too," he said finally. "I'll bet you wish your father would hurry up and trade my ass."

For a moment, she didn't say anything. "I want you to get your shot, Leo. You deserve it."

"Guess I shouldn't kiss the boss's daughter, then."

She gave him a small, secret smile. "I guess you'd better not."

There it was. The rejection. *Ouch*. Kissing her like that had been a loopy thing to do, though. Maybe he was looking at this the wrong way—he was lucky Georgia hadn't hit him herself. Just like his gaffe at the press conference, it was a dumb-ass, hotheaded thing to do. "Lesson learned," he said, keeping his tone ten times lighter than he really felt.

Georgia turned to look out the window again. As she did, he could swear she looked a little disappointed. But that was probably only wishful thinking.

ELEVEN

A six-day road trip with Leo aboard? Pure torture.

Even worse—they'd been assigned adjacent rooms at the first hotel in Denver. After a noon skate, the team went back to the hotel to rest. Georgia spotted Leo from the end of the hallway, letting himself into what turned out to be room 614. But the time she passed his door, it was already closed.

But she was hyper aware of him during her short stay in room 615. Georgia used the hour of downtime to return some e-mail. Sitting against the headboard, her computer in her lap, she couldn't stop listening to the stillness of the room beside hers, wondering if he was stretched out on the bed . . .

Gah. An overactive imagination was not what she needed right now.

But it was all too easy to imagine Leo on a hotel bed. The fall of their senior year in high school, Leo had been so bold as to reserve a room for the two of them on homecoming night. They couldn't sleep there, of course. Neither her dad nor Leo's parents would have allowed it. But they left the dance early, sneaking out the side door of the gym so that their friends wouldn't complain that they'd ditched.

That had given them three unforgettable hours before curfew.

They'd barely made it inside the room at the Motor Inn before they were all over each other. Leo had pushed her up against the door, his hard body demanding her attention, his mouth all over her. Maybe it was the unaccustomed privacy. Maybe it was their eighteen-year-old hormones. But the two of them had been wild that night. She'd removed his tie with feverish fingers, and he'd unzipped her dress as if it was on fire.

Stumbling out of their clothes, they'd barely made it onto the bed before Leo was inside her. When he'd pinned her hands to the bedspread, she'd moaned loudly enough to be heard across the Long Island Sound. There was no shyness between them—only loud, encouraging gasps.

Looking back, it was astonishing how utterly unselfconscious Georgia had been in her foolish youth. After a couple of minutes of eager thrusting, he'd rolled the two of them over, leaving her on top. "I'll last longer," he'd panted. "Ride me."

She had, while he watched with a sexy gleam in his eyes, his hands cupping her breasts, his full lips muttering dirty, encouraging words. Then he'd skimmed a hand down her belly, lowering his fingertips right to . . .

Arrrrrgh. Georgia stared, unseeing, at the same paragraph she'd been trying to write for ten minutes. She wasn't getting any work done. So she gave up and went to take a shower, instead.

That night, the team doctor benched Leo just as a precaution. Georgia watched his face fall when the doctor delivered the verdict. "We can't have you take a hit tonight and develop symptoms of concussion," he'd stressed. "One night of caution is crucial."

Leo watched the game from a seat behind the penalty box, his jaw set tightly. Georgia could see his displeasure all the way from the press box. The team won 2–1 with a lucky breakaway in the third period, which Denver couldn't answer in the remaining two minutes of the game.

Afterward, while Georgia was handling the reporters who had waited to get a few minutes with O'Doul, Leo slipped away with some teammates, probably to a bar.

That night Georgia lay awake in her hotel room bed. Sleep wouldn't come to her because Leo hadn't returned to the hotel yet. It was past midnight. Where was he? She pictured him in a club somewhere, dancing with a female fan. Maybe the girl invited him over . . .

She rolled over, annoyed. Torturing herself was not healthy, damn it. And maybe he'd snuck in and gone to sleep next door. Maybe she was killing herself for nothing.

Finally she heard the click of his hotel room lock and the closing of the door again. Feeling like the worst kind of snoop, Georgia held her breath, listening. To her immense relief, there were no voices. Leo had come back alone. And after some plumbing sounds, she heard the television. She fell asleep to the voice of a late night comedian.

The next morning, the team decamped for Phoenix.

After a full practice at the arena, they checked into another hotel. This one lay on sprawling grounds and boasted several swimming pools. It was forty degrees warmer here than in Brooklyn.

But *again* she and Leo had adjoining rooms. There were two differences. This time, they were on the eleventh floor. And this time Leo noticed. "Hi, neighbor," he said mildly as they opened their side-by-side doors.

"Hey there." She swiped her key card and pushed into her hotel room, her heart dancing the cha-cha. The universe was clearly out to make her crazy.

Or maybe it wasn't the universe's fault.

Georgia dropped her rolling duffel. Grabbing her phone, she tossed her handbag on the bed. Then she went into the bathroom and closed the door.

Her roommate answered on the first ring. "George! Are you enjoying your hotel stays so far?"

"Becca!" she hissed. "Do you monkey with the hotel room reservations after the travel team makes them?"

"I put my hand in from time to time." She giggled.

"Make it stop! You're killing me."

Becca got quiet. "Why, sweetie? I just wanted to give you an opportunity to talk to him. I think you need to."

After checking to make sure that the lid was down, Georgia sat down on the toilet. "Bec, I could talk to him without even opening the door. It's weird to listen to him on the other side of the wall. Last night I was worried he'd bring a puck bunny home and I'd have to listen."

"Ugh," Becca said. "I didn't think of that. Is he the type?"

"Like I'd know? People change, Bec. It's been six years."

"Yeah? So how have you changed in six years?"

Georgia snorted. "My jokes are better now."

"Really? They must have been pretty scary before."

"I set that one right up for you, didn't I?"

"Yup. And I appreciate it."

There was a comfortable silence for a moment before Becca spoke again. "Before, when it was easy to talk to Leo, what was your currency?"

"Our what?"

"Your currency. The little things you shared. You and I have a currency—it's trash TV and dumplings on the coffee table. What did you have with Leo?"

"A whole lot of sex," Georgia said immediately.

Becca let out a dreamy sigh. "While that does sound amazing, it couldn't have been the only thing. The day is long."

"I'll have to think about it. I've spent a long time trying not to remember all the little things."

"Why?"

She was going to make Georgia say it out loud. "Because I have always regretted it, okay? Breaking up with him was something I did because I had to. Not because I didn't love him."

"Oh, man," Becca said, and Georgia could picture her shaking her head. "You *still* love him, don't you?"

"I don't know about that." *Liar.*

"When you got on the jet and saw his face, how did you feel?"

"Lousy," she said immediately. "Is it awful that I just don't even want to be friends? That sounds childish, but it's so hard to look at him and not remember so many things. He was there when I was the happiest I've ever been. And then he was there for the aftermath of the worst days of my life."

"That's a pretty potent combination. No wonder you've been acting a little cray cray."

"Have not."

"Have so. I watched you put six pairs of shoes and four dresses into your suitcase. I didn't think you owned six pairs of shoes."

Georgia only grunted. Her roommate was entirely too observant.

"Go hit some balls, babe. The hotel you're staying in right now is next door to a tennis club. Lessons are only thirty bucks. I picked that hotel for you."

"Omigod." Georgia laughed. "So you *can* be helpful."

"You have no idea. Now go burn off some of the Thai food the team is having for dinner later. I picked that for you, too. There are four different dumplings on the menu."

"I take back all the nasty things I said about you."

"Go already."

Georgia did as she was told. She made an appointment with a tennis pro for half an hour later. Then she took out her computer and tried to catch up on those e-mails.

TWELVE

TOP TEAM HEADLINES:

Scrappy Brooklyn Team Breaks Our Spree. Meanies.
    —Denver Sports Network

Leo lay on the bed in his hotel room and tried to rest. But there were several things on his mind that were making it impossible.

The doctor had finally cleared him to play tomorrow night. Yet Coach Karl had not weighed in yet. He knew that bastard wouldn't, either. Not until Leo had suffered through the next twenty-four hours, wondering what would happen. He just knew he'd be made to wait.

So that was fun.

The other bramble in his side was the fact that Georgia was right next door. And that was just weird. There was a wall between them. A fucking metaphor if there ever was one.

He picked up his phone, which had a new text from his brother DJ. *Did Karl seriously punch you? Please tell me Twitter is wrong.*

Leo tapped his brother's name and then hit Call. When his brother picked up, he said, "It's actually true. I have a bruise the size of Montana on my jaw."

"Chicks dig that," DJ joked.

"Hope you're right."

"But, Jesus. What did you do to make him so mad?"

Leo was thoroughly sick of this question. "Big picture? No idea. But that night was a shit show. First I told Amy that we weren't getting back together. She made a big scene. Go ahead. You can say I told you so. I won't even get mad."

DJ just laughed. "I'm going to take the high road here, but only because you finally manned up and sent her packing."

Leo grunted unhappily. "So that was fun. And then Georgia started in on me for making a scene. She got all fiesty . . ." Leo could still picture that fiery look in her eye. *Hell.* He'd kiss her again right now for it. Some lessons just couldn't be learned, even with a punch to the face. "And then I . . ."

"What?" DJ asked.

"I . . . I kissed her. Planted one right on her to shut her up."

His brother erupted with laughter. "Smooth, slick."

"Right? And that's when Coach tried to take my head off in front of three hundred people."

"Man, I miss all the good shit," DJ complained. "I'm coming to a home game in a couple weeks. Make sure it's eventful."

"No can do," Leo grumbled. "I'm done making waves. Gonna keep my head down and score some goals from now on. Lesson learned."

"Nah," DJ argued. "You haven't learned shit. If you go back to dating Teflon girls, I'm going to punch you in the jaw, too."

"Dating . . . what?"

"The Amys of the world, moron. I call them your Teflon girls—they're tough as nails and completely heartless. You'll never love one of 'em, but they can't really hurt you, either."

"That's ridiculous," Leo sputtered. "What, like you know everything about relationships now? You find the rare, perfect girlfriend, and suddenly you're an expert? Maybe Amy wasn't right for me. But it wasn't a fucking *trend*."

"Uh-huh. Remember Lori? She had an ego bigger than that bruise on your face. Thought she was God's gift because she was in charge of that a cappella group. And before her there was Emily, and also Stacia your sophomore year. Every one of those girls was an ice queen. And I'm not talking about the hockey kind of ice."

Leo cringed. "So what? They were kind of frosty. Doesn't mean anything."

"Just a big coincidence, then," DJ scoffed. "Your taste changed after high school, right? You just happened to start liking women who never smile, except into the mirror."

"You're a pain in the ass, D." Leo was tired of being psychoanalyzed.

"That's probably true. But I'm your pain in the ass. Stop dating bitchy women already. I'm begging here."

"I'm not dating anybody." Ever again, probably. "Too much on my plate, anyway."

"Fair enough. Is Coach going to play you tomorrow?"

"I wish I knew."

"Good luck!"

"Thanks."

They hung up, and Leo was even grumpier than he'd been before. So he gave up on resting and put on a pair of shorts and a T-shirt. The hotel undoubtedly had a gym. He would find it, maybe run a couple of miles on the treadmill. Obviously, he needed to burn off some of the shit swirling around in his head.

But when he left his room, he saw Georgia step into an elevator, wearing tennis clothes and carrying her racket case over her shoulder. Before he could get there, its doors closed.

It was almost like seeing a ghost.

He waited for another elevator, and when one arrived, Silas was on it, wearing workout clothes, too. "Hey, man! Coming to the gym?"

Leo hesitated. "I have a sudden urge to play tennis. You think there's a court?"

Silas shrugged. "Dunno. Ask the concierge. You know we're doing Thai food later, right?"

"Sure. I saw it on the schedule." Leo chuckled.

"Well, bring your gold card. It's the first restaurant meal on the road. O'Doul's gonna order every expensive thing on the menu and leave you with the bill. Rookie dinner. It's a tradition."

Ah, of course it was. "Good to know." The elevators parted in the lobby. "Catch you later? Come hungry, I guess."

"Sure thing."

Leo sought out the concierge desk. "Hey there. I heard there was somewhere to play tennis nearby?"

"Right next door—it's a good club. They take walk-ins." The woman in the gold blazer smiled at him.

"Great." He smiled back at her. "My next question is whether you have any rackets back there for idiots who forgot theirs."

"Of course we do."

Five minutes later he was armed with a cheap racket and directions to the tennis club in the next building over. He found Georgia warming up opposite a preppy young man in tennis whites, who was blatantly staring at her chest. "So what do you want to practice?" the guy asked her, his eyes like lasers on her cleavage. "Have you worked on your slice yet?"

A flash of barely concealed amusement flashed through Georgia's eyes. Leo could almost see her wheels turning. Her gaze said, *I'll school you on your slice . . .*

That would have been worth watching, too. Except that Leo's inner caveman couldn't stand by and let another man practice with Georgia if he was available. "Hey there," he heard himself say. "Can I play, too?"

Both Georgia and her ogler turned at the same time. "Private lesson," Preppy Dude said dismissively.

Georgia raised an eyebrow at him, as if to ask, *What are you doing here?*

"That's a shame," Leo said. "Because now I won't know if I can still beat her in straight sets."

"What?" Georgia yelped. "That is not how I remember it." She crossed her arms under her sports bra, and Leo had to look away to avoid becoming an ogler of her cleavage, too.

"I won sometimes," he insisted. "I'm pretty sure."

She rolled her eyes. "Get over here. Somebody needs a spanking."

Holy hell. She didn't mean it like it sounded, but he liked hearing it anyway.

Leo moseyed over to the opposite side of the court, and the tennis pro reluctantly stepped back. "All right, guys. Let's see how well you're matched," he said.

"You need to warm up?" she asked, giving the ball a bounce. "Wouldn't want you to strain anything."

"Serve it up. Or I'm going to think you're stalling."

Her eyebrows furrowed. "Love all," she said.

Leo only had a split second to wonder how the word "love" had ever come to mean "zero" in tennis talk before the ball came flying over the net. He swung, returning it. She sliced the ball back nice and easy, and just like that they had a pretty good rally going. They used to hit together pretty frequently when they had just started dating. Not only were they both athletes, but the tennis club was somewhere they could spend time together and nobody questioned anyone's motives.

Although, back in the old days, Georgia never took things easy on him the way she was now.

Leo returned the ball harder and right on the singles line, catching her by surprise. She didn't quite make it there in time, and the ball was in. So it was his point.

Without comment, she retrieved it. "Love, fifteen," she said calmly. Then she served it a bit faster than last time. And it was on. The battle slowly escalated, each of them ramping up their foot speed and effort. The first game got to deuce before Georgia edged him out. He won the second game, but the third went to her after she aced him on the last serve.

"I guess your slice is pretty solid," the tennis pro mumbled at one point.

They were both sweating now. Georgia walked over to the side and grabbed a water bottle, taking a gulp and then holding it out to him.

"Thanks," he said, taking the bottle, admiring the light sheen of sweat on her chest. But then she stalked back to her corner and frowned, ready for the next game.

Leo bounced the ball and caught it again, preparing to serve. He'd forgotten how this felt—the single-mindedness of tennis. Playing Georgia quieted the worrying in his head, because whenever he forgot to focus on that fuzzy little ball, it always went poorly. And this was *fun*. Sports without life-altering consequences on the line. What a revelation. There was a time in his life when hockey had been just a game, but that time was long gone.

They played on, and Georgia took the first set. "Had enough yet?" she asked.

"Fuck no."

The tennis pro frowned at him for cursing. But that dude was just jealous. He'd been reduced to just standing there while Leo had the pleasure of getting sweaty with the hot chick who knew how to hit. Even if it wasn't his favorite kind of sweaty.

"Okay, tough guy," Georgia said taking one more swig from the bottle. "Let's see if you can make a comeback."

He bit back the innuendo on the tip of his tongue and readied himself for the next attack. He would never get enough of getting bested by the beautiful creature running around on the other side of the net. It wasn't just her long legs in a short skirt, or the flush in her face. He might even be more turned on by her look of determination than the view of her cleavage when she leaned down to tie her shoe.

He'd dated quite a few women in college, but he'd never gotten to know any of them as well as he'd known her, had he? He'd never felt the same connection, or shared so much in common with anyone else.

What would his annoying little brother say about that? Leo wasn't sure he wanted to know.

Focusing on the game again, he stayed even during the second set. It was four games to four, and he'd remembered how to use his longer reach to retrieve the ball when she wasn't expecting him to. But Georgia wasn't having that. For two more games she dug deep, finding some kind of extra mojo, and she handed his ass right over the net. And when she lunged hard for the ball on the very last point, the guttural sound she let fly was a force to be reckoned with. It was a sound so soulfully deep that he felt himself start to go hard.

Fate listened, and that ball went sailing past the end of his racket with no more than an inch to spare. *Jesus.* He might be the first guy in history to get all boned up while losing a tennis match. *Down, boy.*

They met at the net, both of them winded. "I guess you've still got it," he panted. He'd meant her tennis game, but somehow it came out sounding X-rated. And damn if her nostrils didn't flare.

To get even with her, Leo wiped his face with his T-shirt. When he caught her eyes on his six-pack, he had to bite back a smile.

Oldest trick in the book. He used to pull that shit back in the day, too.

Georgia thanked the tennis pro for his not-quite-useful time. And then the two of them walked back to the hotel together. They didn't speak, and Leo tacked it up to sexual tension.

Either that, or Georgia was just tired from giving him a beat down. It could really go either way.

"Leo," she finally said in a low voice, just as they crossed the hotel lobby, "there's a favor I need."

Please let it involve nudity. "What's that?"

"There's some people shooting a 'Hunks of Hockey'

calendar tomorrow. They asked for your participation specifically."

It took a second for the disappointment to sink in. But then Leo barked out a laugh. "So this request *does* involve nudity?" *Just not the kind I was hoping for.*

She raised an eyebrow. "That's generally how those things are done. Nothing, um, vital will be shown."

"Right." He crossed his arms. "I'll hide it behind a hockey puck."

Georgia cleared her throat and studied the grip on her racket a little more closely than necessary. "No, probably something a little . . ." Her eyes lifted all of a sudden. "That was a joke, wasn't it?"

He grinned. "Just a little one."

"Oh Jesus." She rolled her eyes, but her cheeks had become even pinker. "Will you do the damn calendar or not? I'm supposed to let them know."

"Dunno, Gigi. I thought you were sick of me being such a . . . 'spotlight hog' were the words you used, I think."

She bit her lip. "I'm sorry I said that. I know you're not really a diva, Leo."

"Thank you."

"You can let me know either way by tonight."

"Sure."

They walked the rest of the way through the lobby together, another silence gathering between them. His desire for Georgia was a living, breathing creature. And maybe it was just wishful thinking, but he could swear he saw it reflected back in her. The way she held her breath when he got near her. And the way her eyes seemed to be asking for something before she looked away again.

He dropped off the racket with a nod and a smile at the concierge. Georgia was holding the elevator when he returned to her side.

The silence had stretched on pretty long by the time the elevator doors closed. Leo punched the button. "Hey," he said, turning to her. He meant to say, *Thanks for the game.* But he forgot the rest of his sentence when he saw the flush of her cheeks, and an expression heavy with longing.

"Leo," she whispered, her chin rising toward his.

"Yeah," he whispered back. It seemed as natural as anything to take a step toward her, slipping a hand onto her waist. The curve of her body under his hand was exactly the way he remembered it. She was actually trembling a little. He reached up with his other hand and grasped the elastic in her hair, sliding it down, freeing all those silky strands, and she gasped right in his ear.

Without thinking too hard about it, he pressed his lips to her temple. That just felt *right*. He inhaled, and the familiar fruity smell of her shampoo misted his already hazy mind. Slowly, she lifted her chin, her nose tracing a line up his cheek. Then their lips found each other's effortlessly, like magnets realigning.

The first kiss was soft and slow. Their lips slid tenderly together, as if they both needed a moment to just remember how this felt. But the sensation was so perfect that Leo heard a rumble from his own chest. He pulled her head closer and slanted his mouth over hers. Georgia opened for him, and he groaned at the first sweet taste of her.

"Mmm," she replied. Warm hands found his chest.

Leo deepened the kiss again, needing more. Needing everything.

Then the elevator dinged its announcement that they'd reached their floor. They parted as the doors slid open.

"Goddamn it," he heard her swear as she took off down the hall.

Was that a good "damn it" or a bad one? he wondered, following her. She hurried ahead, reaching her door, swiping into the room before he got there.

And she let the door fall shut behind her.

THIRTEEN

Jesus Christ almighty, why did we have to go and do that?

Georgia stalked into her hotel room with shaky knees. Leo's kisses made her feel crazy and out of control. She hadn't felt that way in a long time.

And now she'd gone and sprinted away from him like some kind of drama queen. But she hadn't known what to say after a kiss like that. If he'd asked her a question, she'd probably have ended up babbling, or speaking in tongues.

She heard the sound of a bolt turning in a lock, and then a tap on a door. Leo was knocking on the door that joined their two rooms.

Georgia just stared at the door for a moment. If she opened it, anything might happen. Was that good, or terrifying?

Their currency, as Becca had put it, came back to her in a rush. It was *speed*. Their skates on the ice. The tennis ball flying back and forth over the net. And kisses so hot they could leave contrails in the sky.

"Gigi," he said from behind the door. "Let me see your face."

But that's what had started this mass confusion in the

first place. For six years she hadn't see Leo Trevi. She didn't have to *feel* so much.

"Gigi," he said again. "Please."

Hell.

She crossed to the door and unlocked it. Then she opened the door, and he was there, looking hot and enormous, leaning one elbow on the frame, his hand in his hair. He took a step toward her. "Can we talk . . ."

Her heart in her mouth, Georgia launched herself at him. Her mouth collided with his, and she heard him emit a grunt of surprise. But Leo Trevi had always had natural reflexes and an athlete's ability to read the game. So his hands closed around her waist only a nanosecond later. He took over the kiss as Georgia stood on tiptoes, wrapping her arms around his neck. His mouth was firm and welcoming, and she closed her eyes and let go.

He smelled like clean sweat and *Leo*. When she parted her lips, his whiskers tickled her chin. But that was the only truly unfamiliar part of this moment. When his hungry tongue swept inside, meeting hers, it felt like coming home. How many times had she kissed Leo Trevi? A million? Never had she appreciated it more than right now. She pressed closer, her hips and chest fitting against his hard body, extinguishing all the distance between them.

Leo moaned, long and low, and the sound vibrated throughout her body. Strong hands slid down her rump and then squeezed.

God. Her little tennis skirt and his thin workout shorts didn't put up much of a barrier. He was *right* there. And hard for her. She let out a desperate whimper.

"Fuck," he rumbled into her mouth. Then he lifted her, forcing Georgia to break their kiss and just hold on tight.

She was airborne, and they were moving. And all the while, Georgia kept her eyes slammed shut, as if the moment were a dream that might disappear if she opened them.

A moment later she landed on his lap. He'd sat down on whatever upholstered chair the hotel room contained. Her knees splayed to either side of Leo's lap, landing on the cushioned seat. She was straddling him. He pulled her close and kissed her again.

Georgia let her hands wander over his broad chest, reacquainting herself with all the muscle she found there. Her fingertips swept downward, skimming his six-pack, then up again until her thumbs brushed hardened nipples behind his T-shirt.

He groaned. Loudly. They'd always been vocal about their desires, and so free with each other's bodies. That was before Georgia had known to appreciate what an incredible gift it was to have wild, uninhibited sex with someone who loved you.

"Innocent" wasn't a word many people would have used to describe their sexual relationship. But in so many ways it was exactly that. They'd pleasured each other in every possible way, with gusto and without fear.

Until the day they hadn't anymore.

Georgia pushed that idea right aside. She swept her hand under the hem of Leo's shirt, finding hot skin. And everything was better again. Her mind was free of distractions. There were only his wet, open-mouthed kisses on her neck and her wandering hands.

Forgetting herself, Georgia pressed her aching body against Leo, trapping his erection right where she wanted it. She caught his face in her two hands and fitted her mouth against his, where it belonged. His tongue invaded immediately, and she let out a moan that could probably be heard throughout Phoenix. She felt her body gathering itself in, tightening the strings of expectation. His hands cupped her ass, encouraging her to move. She slid up the length of him and then back down again, and he groaned.

Clinging to him, she moved against him with increasing urgency, and Leo rolled his hips to meet her. And all the while their kisses were deep and desperate. They were teammates who'd played the game together so many times they knew exactly what the other needed. Her desire coiled more tightly with every successive kiss.

"Georgia," he rasped between kisses. "Look at me."

Her eyes popped open on command, but she wasn't quite ready for the fiery look in his heavy-lidded eyes. He was burning up for her. It was something she'd never thought she'd see again.

"Missed you," he rumbled before taking her mouth in another scorcher.

That was all it took. Her hips shook even as Georgia felt her heartbreak crest and overflow. She buried her face in Leo's neck and came with a sobbing gasp.

He made a soul-deep noise and then clamped his arms around her back. She shuddered, and his grip tightened, just holding her. His big strong arms were like a warm cage, and she didn't want to be released.

Her heart rolled around in her chest like a milkmaid in a haystack. But as she began to calm down, the awkwardness of the moment crept in. She'd just thrown herself at her ex and ridden his dick until . . . *Gah.* It was the first orgasm she'd had with another person in the room since the last one he gave her when she was barely old enough to vote. And all without taking her clothes off or managing to have a proper conversation that lasted as long as the crazy make-out session she'd just inspired.

It was all horrifically embarrassing. And yet it somehow seemed perfectly rational to keep her face jammed into the hollow between his shoulder and his ridiculously attractive jaw.

Leo held on tight, stroking her hair with one of his oversized hands. Just as he pressed a single kiss to the side of her head, there was a knock on the door.

"Princess? I thought we were having coffee. Did you forget about me?"

Georgia sat up fast, almost clocking Leo in the chin. Scrambling off his lap, she stood on shaky knees, panic in her stomach. "Dad? I, uh." Her eyes cut involuntarily to the open doors bridging her room with Leo's.

He took the hint, standing up beside her. Leo looked

flushed and rumpled from all the pawing she'd done. He raised his palm to touch her cheek in a silent leave-taking.

"Princess?"

"Just got back from playing tennis!" she called, tiptoeing after Leo to shut the door behind him. "Need a quick shower!" *And someone to slap some sense into me. And probably a new job.*

"Meet me in the coffee shop. Don't primp all day." Her father chuckled and then his shadow retreated from under the door.

Georgia stood there on the carpeting a moment longer, just listening. She really should say something to Leo. Apologize for throwing herself at him. But the shower started up on his side of their wall. So of course her mind was flooded with images of Leo getting naked and stepping under the spray as water droplets ran down his pecs . . .

Lord. She would stay on her own side of the door. Joining him in the shower was *not* the right way to untangle this mess.

Instead, she went into her own bathroom. Avoiding her own sex-flushed face in the mirror, she took the quickest shower in history before joining her father in the coffee shop.

"Good workout?" he asked when she sat down in front of him ten minutes later.

"Yup." *Don't you dare blush*, she coached herself.

"Decaf or regular?" he asked her. "It's sort of late in the day, so I didn't want to guess."

"Decaf," she said quickly. "Thanks."

When her father got up to get her a cup of coffee, she wrote a two word text to Leo's old number. *I'm sorry.*

The reply was quick: *I'm not.*

Georgia stuffed her phone into her bag and tried not to wonder what that meant. Her father returned with coffee for her and a cookie to share. He broke off a corner and pushed the little plate toward her. "What's up in the world of PR?"

She looked up into his gray eyes and tried to decide if she should be honest, or if that was just picking fights. "Damage control, of course. Lots of questions about the rumored skirmish between the new coach and his player."

He waved his hand as if he couldn't believe that anyone would bother with such trivial matters. "When we win, they won't have to bug you with that bullshit."

"If you play Leo tomorrow, the questions will stop." The comment just popped out before she could think better of it. Good grief. It was really not her place to weigh in on coaching decisions.

Her father's eyes widened at her audacity. Then he snorted. "No, they won't. Gossip follows its own rules. I'll play Trevi when I'm good and ready."

Yikes. Georgia couldn't decide if that sounded encouraging or not. "Why *wouldn't* you play him, though?" she pressed. This was a dangerous conversation. But they'd gone years without mentioning Leo, and now she was starting to realize how odd that really was. He'd been such a big part of her life for so long. "I'm not trying to influence you, but I just don't get it. What do you have against him, anyway?" It felt risky to bring up the past. Neither one of them wanted to relive the worst days of her life. But Leo was here amongst them, and thinking about it was inevitable.

"I don't trust him," her father grunted.

"Why?" The word hung in the air over their heads. This was the most they'd said about Leo in six years.

His gray eyes squinted down at his cup. "I just don't."

It was hard to imagine a less satisfying answer. But Georgia had pushed him as far as he was going to go.

So she changed the subject, which was the same thing she'd done with anyone in the last six years who asked her about Leo.

FOURTEEN

A cold shower wasn't going to cut it. So Leo took a lengthy, soapy shower wherein he relieved some tension in a crucial way.

Then he turned off the water and took a deep breath of the steamy air, which seemed to be tinged with optimism. He and Georgia were going to get back together and stay that way. Maybe she didn't quite realize it yet, but it was clear as ice to him. Their spark was still there, and stronger than ever.

She seemed skittish as hell, but he'd figure out why and then fix it.

Her job was one obvious question mark, though. *I can't date a player*, she'd said when he'd asked if they could go to the benefit together. And, sure, a woman had to be professional at work. But he wasn't just some player she might have hooked up with in the locker room. He and Georgia had known each other all their lives. If they were together, it would hardly be a cheap scandal.

He toweled off, humming to himself. Georgia had broken his heart once before, but he'd survived it. The summer after graduation hadn't been the worst of it, because he'd held out hope that she'd come to her senses before it was too late.

But then September had come with no reprieve, and he'd gone off alone to his first days at Harkness College. He was so homesick and lonely he could hardly breathe. The skaters on his team were wicked good and none too nice to the rookies. The first year had sucked, and at the core of his misery was the empty place in his chest where her love for him had been.

He'd been nineteen years old and absolutely floored by the pain she'd caused him.

That was a long time ago, though. Now he was stronger in every conceivable way. Georgia wasn't immune to him, either—that much was obvious. She wanted him, even if she didn't yet see that they were meant to be back together.

He could work on that.

Leo put on khakis and a nice shirt. He knocked on Georgia's door, but there was no answer. So he texted Silas instead, and the two of them walked a block to the team dinner at a Thai restaurant. The hostess led them to a private room in back, where players were already gathering.

"Rookie!" O'Doul called out. "Hope you brought your credit card." His laugh was rough. "I'm ordering a twenty-five-year-old bottle of single malt. I think they just sent the delivery boy across town to buy it."

"Aw, yes!" Bayer chuckled. "I love a good rookie dinner."

This particular ritual—ordering the sun and stars at a team dinner and leaving the rookie the check—was familiar to Leo, though it had been over a year since the Muskegon Muskrats pulled the same crap on him.

Whatever. At least they were at a Thai place and not some top-shelf steak joint. He was getting off easy, considering.

Leo ended up in a corner on a bench, hemmed in by Bayer, O'Doul, and Silas. The guys gleefully ordered every fucking thing on the menu. "Sure, we'd love to try the sea scallops. Better make it a double order. Scallops are small."

He would be a good sport about it, of course. The smiling faces around the table were just beginning to feel familiar. Berreki with his three missing teeth. He never wore his bridge. And Johnson, who was the grandpa of the team at thirty-eight. He had a daughter in college but he was a wild man nonetheless.

Leo hoped he'd get the chance to really be a part of this team. It was all up to him, of course. And Coach Karl.

Neither Coach Karl nor the GM turned up for the meal. But the associate coaches showed, and a couple of other guys from management.

But not Georgia.

The table was crammed full of food. There literally wasn't enough room for all the dishes the guys had ordered. There were roasted filets of fish, Panang beef curries, and several different flavors of pineapple and coconut rice. And—this made him think of Georgia—dumplings in several different colors.

Leo pulled out his phone and texted her. *Where are you? It's dinnertime. There's a ton of food. They're running up the bill on me.*

It was only a minute or two before she replied. *I wasn't going to come. Catching up on some work.*

You must be buried, Leo teased, *if you're missing out on Thai food.*

I am! Sorry to ask but I need to know if you'll do that calendar. They need a decision.

Smiling to himself, Leo replied: *Which calendar?*

The only one we discussed. The naked calendar.

Oh, right.

You just wanted me to write *naked* didn't you?

Now he was grinning like a lunatic. *Yep.*

She sent him an emoticon with pink cheeks. It was like being in high school again—in the best possible way.

He went in for the kill. *I count four kinds of dumplings on this table.*

That's just mean.

No it isn't! Get down here. I bought all these dumplings, apparently. Here's the deal: I'll do the calendar if you come down here.

There was a pause before she replied. *So we've stooped to bribery?*

Yep.

Ten minutes later Leo was happy to see Georgia ease into the room. And God bless the warm climate of the Southwest, because Georgia wore a sleeveless top showing off smooth, golden shoulders that he wished he could nibble on instead of the Thai food. She hesitated in the doorway, though, probably because the table looked pretty crowded already.

But the goalie, Beacon, saw her standing there. "Hey, it's Killer!" Georgia's eyebrows shot up in surprise at hearing her dad's old nickname, but then she smiled. "Get in here," Beacon said, beckoning. "Yo—Castro, move down for Killer." They made room on the bench for her.

Leo was basically trapped at the opposite end of the table. But he took three dishes, each with a few dumplings on it, and began to arrange them on one plate for her. When it was assembled, he handed it to O'Doul. "Pass that down to Georgia, please. And no sampling."

O'Doul took the plate with a raised eyebrow. "That's a lot of dumplings."

"My girl likes her dumplings. And she has a monster metabolism."

O'Doul passed it to Bayer who passed it to Silas, who actually got up and delivered it to Georgia at the end of the table.

Kiss-ass, Leo thought grumpily. But at least she got her dish.

From her seat on the far end, Georgia looked up at Leo. *Thank you*, she mouthed.

For what? he replied, with an eyebrow wiggle.

She dropped her eyes and blushed. Immediately, Leo felt blood rushing south, even though she was ignoring him now. She picked up a napkin and tucked it into her lap while he admired her long, toned arms. He knew exactly how those felt clinging to him. She was strong, and it was such a turn-on. Earlier today he'd been mesmerized by the sight of her hands wrapped around the handle of her racket and it was all too easy to imagine them wrapped around something else.

Fuck. He had it bad.

"So . . ." O'Doul said, swirling the scotch in his glass. "You two used to be a thing?"

Leo had to stop himself from protesting O'Doul's use of the past tense. This afternoon had sure felt like a present-tense situation. But Georgia was skittish. So he forced himself to downplay it, and also to ignore the faux-casual tone of O'Doul's question. "Yeah. Long time ago."

"So you must like 'em uptight?" Bayer laughed.

"Guess so," Leo said lightly. They didn't need to know that earlier today he'd seen her be anything but uptight. Although . . . His eyes scanned the table. It hit him all at once that Georgia was the *only* female face in a sea of teammates and club employees. There were other women working for the organization. He'd met more than a handful already. But it couldn't be easy to be the only chick traveling with all these men. Even if you were gorgeous, smart, and an athlete, too.

No wonder she was touchy about the way they saw her.

That was something to think about later.

He waved down a waitress who'd stopped to exchange some flirting with Castro. "Excuse me, but that young lady needs a drink," he said, indicating the only young lady at the table.

A few minutes later the waitress brought Georgia what looked like a Diet Coke.

He'd rather buy her a glass of champagne and drink it naked in bed. But a guy had to start somewhere.

The final bill at the restaurant was a doozie. Leo didn't remember the limit on his credit card. Handing it over, he only hoped that the amount wouldn't be declined. That would mean splitting it onto two or three cards while the team laughed.

It went through, luckily.

In the unlucky department, Leo didn't get to talk to Georgia at dinner. And on the short walk back to the hotel, she chatted with Silas.

Georgia was avoiding him. There was really no other way to look at it.

Back inside the hotel lobby, they all headed in the obvious direction—the bar. Leo took a spot at a high table, leaving space for her. She was near the doorway, finishing up her conversation with the backup goalie.

And then? She disappeared.

His teammates had obviously decided that Leo's wallet had taken enough of a beating tonight already, so they began buying him beers. Castro bought Leo a shot of good tequila, and wanted to talk about college hockey. They'd played against each other in the Frozen Four once. An hour slipped by in casual conversation.

But Georgia did not reappear.

Pleasantly drunk, Leo took a second to text her. *You okay?*

The reply came quickly. *Yes, and thanks for the dumplings.*

Where'd you go?

In for the night.

Didn't *that* just give him ideas. He could picture her in the king-sized bed in her quiet hotel room. He wanted to spread her out on the bed and . . . Yeah. He'd need a few hours just to check off the top few items on his to-do list with her. *Can I come up and visit you?*

The reply was immediate. *It's not a good idea.*

He thought it was. *Seemed like a good idea earlier today*, he pressed.

That was a mistake, was her quick reply.

Leo groaned out loud.

"Your girl disappear on you?" Silas said from beside him.

He looked up quickly, shoving the phone in his pocket. "Maybe. But I can be patient."

Silas laughed. "Can you? 'Cause you don't look patient to me. You planted one on her in front of a couple hundred people, like sixty seconds after breaking up with what's-her-name. And let's not forget your hot mic moment. It was stylish. But it *wasn't* patient."

"Shit." Leo took a pull of his beer and grimaced. Silas's thoughts on the matter were unfortunately valid. Since stepping off the plane from Michigan, Leo had behaved like an ornery toddler more times than he cared to count. "You make a few good points."

His roommate laughed again. "Calm down, dude. She's single and she has been as long as I've known her. Most of the team is lusting after her, and she doesn't ever notice."

Now that was more interesting than Leo wanted to admit. "First time I ever asked her out, she didn't believe me. Mighta been my cheesy pick-up line, though."

"This I gotta hear."

Leo chuckled. "We were sixteen, and had the same physics class together."

Silas snorted. "Please tell me you didn't offer to get physic-al."

"It was *almost* that bad," he said while Silas laughed. "The teacher was trying to get us all to understand circuits. So he said, 'Who wants to be part of a human circuit? I need two volunteers.'" Leo could picture the scene like it was yesterday. Georgia sat a couple of rows ahead of him, and he usually spent physics class watching her instead of the teacher. He'd had his eye on her for a while before he got up the nerve to make his move. "So Georgia raises her hand. She was always fearless." He chuckled at the memory. "Like, *hell yeah I want to conduct an electrical current with my body.* So I raised my hand, too."

"Of course you did."

"Right? I'd take an electrical shock to stand close to the prettiest girl in tenth grade. So the teacher puts us side by side, and he asks us to hold hands, so I knew I made the right decision."

Grinning, Silas killed his beer.

"Then we each put our free hand on this metal conductor on a special battery the guy had. He switched it on, and nothing much happened. 'But Leo—don't let go if you don't want to be shocked,' the guy said, because if we broke the circuit, I'd feel it on my end."

"So of course you let go," Silas guessed. "Because sixteen-year-old boys are all geniuses."

"Wait, were you there?" Leo joked. "Of course I let go. And it wasn't a big shock, just a little zap. And Georgia just shook her head. After class I followed her to her locker and asked her to go to the homecoming dance with me. 'There's a real spark between us' is what I said."

"Smooth."

"Right? And first she looked at me like maybe I was making fun of her. So I asked her two more times and she finally said yes."

Silas pointed his empty beer bottle at Leo. "And that's why you made it to the big leagues. Never give up, dude. Tomorrow could be a big day for you."

"You never know." Leo finished his own beer. "But just in case, I think I'd better pack it in for tonight. Gonna need to hit the morning skate hard if Coach is going to decide I'm indispensable."

Silas gave him a salute. "Go on, soldier. At least you

have a fifty percent shot of playing tomorrow. It could always be worse. You could be the backup goalie."

"Right. Sorry."

Silas shrugged. "See you in the morning. We have yoga first."

"Of course we do." Leo walked out of the bar, shaking his head.

FIFTEEN

TOP TEAM HEADLINES:

*"Arizona Favored to Win Against Brooklyn Tonight
at Home, Adding to a Three-Game Streak"*
—Phoenix Eagle Sports Page

Georgia carried her yoga mat into the room that Nate had reserved and took a spot in back, like she always did.

The team's yoga classes were taught by Ari, the team's massage therapist, which meant that yoga classes were held at least three times a week even when the team was on the road. Georgia hadn't been to a class in a while, though. Last week she'd bailed on yoga twice, because the idea of watching Leo do sun salutations was distracting as hell. And then the whole team had missed a couple of sessions, because Ari had taken some sick days, which was unusual.

The exotic, tattooed instructor, in her trademark pink leotard and tights, gave her a cheery wave from the front of the room, which Georgia returned. But then she noticed Ari's blue boot cast on one foot.

Well, that explained the massage therapist's absence. Bummer.

Georgia unrolled her hot pink mat and sat down to stretch. Up in front she spotted Nate. The owner had flown out to see tonight's game, probably on his private jet. He was already limbering up in the front row on his purple Bruisers mat. Nate was a little nutty about his yoga. There were other NHL teams who had yoga and meditation as part of their training program. But this class had been Nate's own initiative, and he liked to get the whole organization involved. Coaches—and publicists—were encouraged to participate.

Which was why, to Georgia's amusement, her father wandered in a minute later, wearing an ancient track suit and a scowl. It hadn't occurred to her that Dad would have to do downward dog and the warrior pose with the rest of them. Maybe next time she'd smuggle in her phone and snap a few pictures. Her aunt Joanie would be so amused.

Inevitably, Leo arrived, entering the room with a yoga mat in hand. And inevitably, Georgia's heart tripped over itself at the sight of him. She watched his eyes sweep the room and land on her. Then he walked right over and positioned himself in front of her. "Morning," he said under his breath.

"Morning," she repeated, feeling a prickle of sweat under her arms. Really? She had to spend the next hour trying not to stare at his butt? He'd worn a pair of Harkness College sweatpants to class, but instead of hiding everything they seemed to cling to his muscular thighs.

As he unrolled his mat—lime green—she wondered where he'd gotten it. She could hardly picture him wandering into one of the boutiques in Brooklyn and purchasing it. But who knew? Maybe Leo was a yoga pro. Maybe he had mats in every color of the rainbow. She needed to keep in mind that they didn't really know each other anymore. Aside from a hot and heavy make-out session and a few texts, they'd been apart for longer than they had ever been together.

In fact, if Ari asked them to meditate later, Georgia

would choose *restraint* as today's guiding principle. Control. Distance. Reserve. They were all good words, and she would rhyme them into a mantra if it made it easier to rein in crazy thoughts about Leo Trevi.

He'd sat down on his mat and was currently rolling his wide shoulders, the same ones she'd gripped with both hands while they'd tried to fuse themselves together at the mouth.

Gah! *Restraint.*

Restraint.

Restraint.

Even if her unruly little heartstrings still vibrated whenever he walked into a room, their former connection was just that. Former.

Luckily for Georgia, Ari brought the class to attention. "Good morning, yogis! Let's have a seat, please, cross your left leg and then your right. If you have tightness in your hips or lower back, please feel free to sit up on a block or straighten your legs at any point . . ."

Georgia assumed the position, then lifted her clasped hands in imitation of the teacher. Ari began the familiar series of wrist and forearm circles that always began her classes. There was a comfort in this, and Georgia understood why Nate made yoga a part of their routine no matter where they were. Living out of your suitcase was disorienting, and at least once a season Georgia gave herself a bruise or a stubbed toe while trying to find the bathroom in the middle of the night in a strange hotel room. But the geography of her yoga mat was always the same. And Ari's soothing voice and warm-up routine were a pleasant way to wake the body.

The players still joked about Ari's high-minded language. They felt weird "centering" themselves or "finding inner peace" in yoga-speak. ("I'll show you my inner piece, babe. Heh heh.") But that was just trash talk. After they got used to the routine, they always stopped fighting it. An hour from now, everyone leaving this room would have warm, limber muscles and a calm attitude.

At the front of the room, Nate sat comfortably in the Sukhasana position, his lean body displaying perfect posture. Later, when the poses became more difficult, he'd be inverting himself with statuesque form while the highly paid athletes around him shook and shimmied like a pack of wet dogs. The boss man was ridiculously good at yoga.

At the side of the room, Georgia's father grimaced through a simple forward bend. Georgia looked forward to watching her father try to tackle the tougher poses, but she was suddenly robbed of this fun about fifteen minutes into the class, when the cheater actually bailed. "Please excuse me," he said to Ari. "I have a conference call."

She gave him a look that said, *Conference call my ass.* Ari may be the queen of yoga but she was a Brooklynite through and through. You don't bail on her class. It simply wasn't done.

But her father marched through the room with as much guilt as Napoleon exiting Mount Tabor. He gave her a grin, but it snagged when he noticed Leo right in front of her. As he passed, his sneer seemed to say, *Stay away from my daughter.*

Leo didn't even glance up at him. *Point Leo.*

The class progressed to sun salutations, and Georgia managed not to laugh when Leo fell out of the transition into downward dog. It was entirely distracting to have him in front of her, though. His reverse warrior made his T-shirt ride up, giving Georgia an oblique view of his happy trail as his muscled torso twisted to the side . . .

Turn away from the light, she ordered herself.

But there was something about the warm room and her increasingly limber body which began to make her a little crazy. As her body moved and stretched in close proximity to Leo's, it took only a short leap of imagination to reposition them in fun and interesting ways. His long arms put every perfect muscle on display when he moved, and when Ari invited the class to "find your center," Georgia felt like begging Leo to find hers.

It was a long hour, and when the minutes of private

meditation and visualization arrived at the end, Georgia's visualizations were much more stimulating than usual.

When the class finally ended and Leo turned around, he gave her a look hot enough to heat the place for a bikram class.

Yowza. None of that. Georgia rolled up her yoga mat and beat a fast retreat back to her room for some alone time. It was bad enough that she'd have to take him to a naked photo shoot in a few hours.

A tepid shower helped. Then she sat down to her over-stuffed inbox, which proved to be the perfect libido-killing distraction. It was only nine in the morning, and already there were fires to put out at work. She took a minute to call Becca to check in. "Hey, lady!"

"Hey, babe! How was yoga?"

"Well, I think I'm ready to start dating again."

Becca was momentarily shocked into silence. "*Really.* That's awesome, sweetie! I need to say up front that I deserve details—juicy, juicy details."

"Good luck with that. Okay. Who should I date?"

There was another silence on the line. "I thought we were talking about Leo Trevi. Georgia? Who is this?"

"Bec! I can't date a *player.* I mean—professionally it's a horrible idea. And there is zero privacy in the clubhouse. Can you imagine?"

"So it's not the ideal setup. But *he's* perfect, right? And that's what matters?"

Georgia sighed. "I'm really rusty, though. Out of practice. Atrophied. I need a warm-up date. Someone to limber me up."

Becca laughed. "There's nothing like dating a guy you don't actually *like* to limber a girl up. And a year ago you swore off dating apps for good. So where are we going to find this warmer-upper man?"

Those were good points. "I'm screwed."

"No," Becca insisted. "But you should *get* screwed. Tonight if possible. By a hot rookie forward."

"Don't think I'm not tempted."

"So, God. Just do it."

"Really, Bec? Of all the people on the planet, that one is the—" She *almost* said *the scariest choice*. But Georgia didn't get scared. "—the riskiest one."

"Risky how? I thought you dumped him."

"Oh, I did. But not because I wanted to. I was just accepting the inevitable. He fell out of love with me, but you can't dump the weepy rape victim. So I did it for him."

"How nice of you," Becca said, her tone just barely on the right side of patronizing. "So what the hell was that kiss, then? I saw that boy make his move. Hell, everyone saw it."

That was true. And confusing as hell. Then there was yesterday's shenanigans . . . "Maybe he wants the last word," Georgia suggested. "Leo is competitive. I dumped him, and now he wants a turn."

"Oh my God. You are the most cynical girl alive."

Was she? It hadn't always been true, but being a rape survivor at eighteen could do that to a girl. "I hate this. I hate that he's making me think about everything that happened in the past. Two weeks ago I didn't have to look at his ridiculously handsome face and wonder if he was attracted to me. And then wonder why he stopped being attracted to me."

"You're right, there's no cure for that kind of torture. Oh wait. What if *you asked him*?"

No can do. "I'll take it under advisement." But seriously—she and Leo were never having that conversation. It was ten times worse than asking a man, *Do I look fat in these jeans?* Before her attack they'd had sex constantly. Afterward he'd taken to giving her dry pecks on the cheek. As if he couldn't retreat fast enough. Sure, he'd hold her on the couch when she was sad, which was all the time. But if she ran her hand down his chest and left it tauntingly on his inner thigh, he'd pick it up and move it elsewhere.

His body language said, *Yuck*. And she'd died a little inside every time he'd pulled away from her.

"I don't know what to tell you, sweetie." Becca sighed. "At least one of us shouldn't be lonely."

"But we're not!" Georgia insisted. "So what if we don't have a guy? We have a great roommate. We have great jobs . . ."

". . . Decent jobs, which we're both in danger of losing."

"Okay, *decent* jobs. Fine. And an apartment in one of the nicest neighborhoods in the world."

"There's a mouse in the kitchen again."

"Damn it! You're not making this whole pep talk thing easy."

Becca laughed. "It isn't, though. Because I *want* a guy in my life. I want a partner, and kids. I'd go gay for you, hon, but adoption is expensive. And then there's the matter of your not having a dick."

"It's always something with you." Georgia wished she could just fly home now and sit on the ugly couch with Bec. Where things were easy.

"Did Nate make it to yoga? He was worried about flight delays out of Teterboro."

"He made it. Looking Zen as ever."

"In his I-am-not-afraid-to-wear-tight-shorts shorts?"

"Yep." Georgia hesitated. "Do you think he has the technology to hear everything we say on these things? Maybe he monitors us."

"Maybe. Did I tell you that I plan on working an extra twelve hours today? And I'm skipping lunch just to get some extra work done."

"Uh-huh."

"Love you, George. I have to go get some actual work done."

"You're very convincing. Bye!"

Georgia waited in the hotel lobby for her calendar boys. The blog had asked for Castro as well as Leo for their au naturel pictures.

Castro was the first to arrive. "Hey, Killer," he said with

a smile. Castro had quite a nice smile, actually. He was a winger who'd been Nate's first trade after he'd acquired the team. He had the most unusual coloring Georgia had ever seen on a man—flawless brown skin and unexpectedly pale hazel eyes. No wonder Hockey Hotties wanted to photograph him. If he left hockey, he had a future in modeling.

"Hey, Castro. I guess that nickname is going to stick around."

"Seems so." He grinned.

Thanks, Dad. She surveyed the busy lobby, and her vision snagged on a tall, dark, sharply dressed man coming toward her.

Leo.

You'd think after a couple of weeks she'd be used to the sight of him. But no such luck. He wore his game-night suit and cocky smile, and her heart did a slutty shimmy just at the sight of him. She was thoroughly confused about what it meant to have him back in her life, but her subconscious wasn't confused at all. Whenever he appeared, all her senses leapt to attention. And now she knew what that muscle felt like under her hands when they kissed . . .

"Hi, gorgeous," he said, looking as dashing as ever.

Yowza. It was going to be a long afternoon. "Hey there. Are you ready to play tonight?"

His smile faded. "We'll see."

"How was practice?"

"Epically bad."

Noooo. "Did something happen?" She didn't know how much more drama she could take.

He gave his head a slow shake. "Nope. Just not my day. And I can't afford to have days like that. Not even one."

"I'm sorry," she said. No matter how confusing it was to have Leo around, she wanted him to have his chance.

"Where are we headed, anyway?" He held the hotel's front door open for both her and Castro. "Some photography studio?"

"Nope. The rink. These are going to be action shots."

Leo scratched his chin, which was sporting a delectable amount of scruff. "Like, in the locker room?"

"Probably," Georgia hedged. She didn't really know what the photographer had in mind, but they were about to find out.

The three of them got into the waiting limo. "There's only twelve months in the year," Castro pointed out. "And thirty NHL teams. Are they seriously going to use two of us? Or am I going to get cut in favor of pretty boy here."

"Better to be cut from a beefcake calendar than from the team," Leo pointed out.

"True." Castro chuckled.

"That's probably why there's two of us," he grumbled. "In case one of us gets sent down before this thing goes to print."

"That's the spirit," Georgia said, poking him in the knee. His muscular knee . . . *Focus, Georgia.* But it was hard to mentally keep her distance when they were in the same vehicle together.

It was a short limo ride, thankfully. They showed their Bruisers IDs to the security guard at the stadium door, and a staff member led them through the bowels of the arena to the visitors' dressing room, where the photographer and her two assistants waited.

"I'm Gloria," the photographer said. She was a stocky woman with a beautiful face, a dozen earrings, and a militant flattop. "You must be Georgia. Thank you for bringing me these two healthy hunks of man meat."

"Um . . ." Georgia sputtered.

"I'm Castro," the player said, holding out his hand. "How do you want this to work?"

The photographer sized him up from head to toe and up again. "Nice," she said. Then she turned to Leo and did the same. "Okay, let's start on the ice itself. You've got your skates, right? Follow me." She pushed through to the chute door and led them down to the visitors' bench. "I'm going to set up, and then Gracie here will help you prep. I've got someone standing by to change the lighting." She waved a hand vaguely toward the mezzanine level. "So who's first?"

"He is," Castro said quickly, pointing at Leo.

"Aw, hell," Leo grumbled.

"Okay." The photographer rubbed her hands together. "I want to put you on the rink in nothing but your skates."

"Brrr," Castro said, cackling. "Things are gonna be shrinking, then."

Georgia bit her lip, and Leo scowled.

"You'll be holding your helmet in a very strategic place," the photographer continued. "The shot will be sensual, but not pornographic."

"Good to know," Leo said under his breath.

"Stop your whining," the photographer said with a grin. "I'm going to make you look like a super stud. Now drop trou and my helpers will get you oiled up."

Leo spoke up. "Um, why the oil?"

"You have to *glow*. Look at this." The photographer took a binder out of the side of her giant camera bag and handed it to Leo, who flipped it open to a spread in the middle.

Everyone went silent, because they'd all misjudged the photographer. She was a freaking *artist*. These shots showed a series of football players posing in various sporty locations—a locker room, lounging on bleachers, or standing on turf at night, the stadium lights illuminating their sculpted bodies. They had a surprisingly ethereal quality, each image a moody masterpiece. The light played over each man's musculature, making the athletes look like a race of superhumans.

"Whoa," Georgia breathed.

Castro snickered. "Somebody's a fan."

Georgia stepped back quickly, hoping she wasn't drooling on herself. "Stop. You can get any girl in America with one of these shots. Don't pretend that doesn't interest you."

"Fine. They can oil my brown ass up. At least it makes a good story for the bar later. C'mon Trevi. Strip. We don't have all day." He grinned at Leo.

Still frowning, Leo began to loosen his tie. "Can you take this?" he asked, handing his jacket to Georgia. "I don't need to get oil on my suit."

"Of course." She took the suit jacket and waited for his tie. And all the while she worked on her game face. It was not going to be easy to look casual while Leo stripped.

"Crazy job you've got here, George," Leo said in a low voice as he unbuttoned his shirt.

"Just another day at the office," she said, pulling her phone out of her bag and attempting to look bored. As if watching a hot athlete pose for a sensual photograph in the middle of a hockey rink was really not all that interesting.

"Do I really have to do this?" he asked under his breath.

"Nope. You don't," she said immediately. She wouldn't force him to. "Baring your ass for charity is a pretty personal decision."

"What's the charity again? It better be something important." He handed over his shirt, and she absolutely *did not stare at his abs.*

Okay, she only took one *tiny* peek. Just a glance, really. "It's, uh . . ." What was the question? "The charity is called Everyone Play. They help spread awareness to keep sports free of homophobia."

He sighed, kicking off his dress shoes. "Sounds pretty worthy. So will you be the one oiling me up?"

A shiver ran right through her, and she hoped Leo didn't notice. But of course he raised a cocky eyebrow. *Busted.* "Nope." She shook her head. "Sorry."

He made a pouty face. The same one he used to give her when she had to leave him to make it home in time for curfew. "I think I deserve some kind of reward, though. A kiss good night, later." He picked that moment to drop his trousers and his boxers on the floor.

Georgia gulped and focused her gaze on his ear. *Must. Keep. Eyes. On. Ear.* She could feel her heartbeat accelerating. As soon as he handed her those trousers, she would get out of there.

"Um, George?" He asked, frowning. "Is there something wrong with my ear?"

"Not a thing," she said shrilly. "I'll just go hang this stuff up for you." She grabbed at the trousers, turned her back, and fled into the empty dressing room, locating the locker reading TREVI and taking a few moments to hang everything up.

When she returned, Castro was signing a photo release form, but Leo was buck naked except for his socks, facing the wall of the tunnel while a female assistant rubbed oil down his thighs with two hands.

"Stay away from my ankles," he coached. "We need to keep the oil off my skates."

"Sure thing," the assistant chirped. She stopped to douse her hand in more oil from a bottle sitting nearby. Whistling to herself, she ran her hands all over Leo's calves, knees, hamstrings, and up his gorgeous muscular . . .

Gah. Georgia took a deep breath and looked out onto the ice, where the photographer had positioned a tripod.

"Uh, that's getting kind of fresh," Leo complained. "Kind of . . . ticklish there," he said through gritted teeth.

"Just doing my job, sir," the assistant said.

Do. Not. Look, she ordered herself. "Are you ready for your skates?" she asked him without turning her head.

"Yeah, but they're right here." In her peripheral vision, he turned, sitting down on a folding chair to lace them up. "Shit that's cold!" He laughed. "And I almost slid off this thing." He bent over and laced up one skate and then the other.

Georgia allowed herself one glance at his gorgeous upper body, his muscles shining like an oil painting come to life. "I'm going to check the security," she said suddenly. "We don't need some staff member snapping naked pics of you two and passing them around on Twitter."

Hearing this, the photographer stood up from peering into her camera. "Let me see if I can spot anyone." She turned in a slow circle, studying the stands. "I think we're good. I've got a guy in the lighting booth, but he's supposed to be the only one up there."

Georgia stood up on the visiting team's bench and scanned the mezzanine level. "I don't see anyone, either."

"We should get hazard pay for this shit," Castro said. "And now you've oiled up that chair. So thanks for that."

"Whew," Leo said, straightening up, and giving an exaggerated shiver. "It's a bit nippy in here. Hope that camera doesn't capture goose bumps." Then he stood, stark naked, and Georgia scrambled to find somewhere to put her eyes.

"Where'd my helmet go?" he asked, looking around.

Right. Stay focused. Find Leo's helmet. Georgia dropped her eyes to the floor and searched.

"Hey, George?"

"Yeah?" her voice was hoarse, her eyes scanning the walls of the chute.

"You have my helmet in your hand."

"What?" She looked quickly at her hands. Sure enough, one of them was clutching the strap to Leo's helmet. Great. Now she was practically losing all executive function. "Uh, sorry," she said, thrusting it in his general direction.

"Now all I need is my stick," Leo said. "My *other* stick." Everyone except Georgia laughed. He grabbed his stick and stepped onto the ice with a smile that said, *I'm making the best of this.*

The photographer beckoned from behind her giant camera. "Okay, HOUSE LIGHTS OFF! And Leo, take a warm-up lap. Then I want you to skate past me with one leg in front of the other, so we can't see your peen."

"You won't see it anyway," he called, heading down the ice, the muscles in his gorgeous butt pumping. "It's gone into hiding." Georgia tried not to swallow her own tongue as a spotlight came up on Leo as he curved at the end of the rink and gracefully skated back toward the photographer, in full naked glory. "This gives new meaning to 'dangling the puck,'" he said.

"You are having way too much fun with this," Castro pointed out.

"Fun is the point," the assistant said. "Be a crime not to

have fun with that body." Leaning forward for a better view, she sighed as Leo made another nude loop on the ice.

Thank heavens the rink was mostly dark, so that nobody could see Georgia's face. Leo had always skated beautifully and he'd always had the body of a god. But watching him skate around in the altogether was more than a girl could really be expected to take. *Don't look at his package*, she coached herself as he came around the oval again. *Don't look . . .*

She looked, but was too late for the full monty. All she saw was a dark trail of trimmed hair down his belly, where it dove toward a V of pure muscle. Then his statuesque thigh swept forward, hiding the good stuff. She slammed her eyes shut. Self-torture was really not her style. But it was hard to believe that he used to be hers. That she'd once been the first woman to touch him.

No, the first *girl*. They'd been so young. It was important to remember how far in the past it all was.

"Yeah, like that," the photographer was saying. "Now do it again, passing me closer. And slow it down just a notch. Drop your left shoulder and raise your chin . . ."

Georgia gave herself a little shake. In mere minutes they'd be done. The lights would come up, and she'd be standing here with her tongue hanging out like a Saint Bernard. She tore her eyes off of Leo's perfection and went back to the locker room to find the poor man a towel to wear on his way to the showers.

SIXTEEN

G eorgia spent ten long hours at the rink, but the day only
got more exciting after the photo shoot.

After another nail-biter of an afternoon, her father had
put Leo on the game card. Then Leo did it—he scored his
first NHL goal.

It was the third period of the game, which was tied
2–2. Coach had switched up the lines midgame—probably
trying to keep their opponent from getting too comfortable
with their offensive style. Leo was skating with Bayer and
O'Doul, who got a breakaway. The captain couldn't find
his shot, though, with both the opponent's defensemen
suddenly in his face. So he'd crossed the puck backwards
to Leo.

Who snapped it right past the goalie's elbow into the net.

Georgia had practically gone hoarse from screaming.
Not that Leo could hear her all the way up in the press box.
When she came to her senses, she pulled up a document of
Leo's bio and minor league stats. With shaking fingers,
she'd e-mailed it to every journalist on the premises.

In the hallway after the game, they'd all stuck their
microphones into Leo's face. Their camera spotlights illuminated his sweaty, victorious expression. "How does it
feel to sink your first NHL goal?" the journos had asked.

"It feels like pulling a win over Arizona," he'd said.

Not only had he scored the winning goal, his soundbite was humble and supportive of the rest of the team. He really was the perfect man.

Georgia hadn't even spoken to her father after the game, for fear of saying something that sounded exactly like a giddy teenager. So she went back to her hotel room alone. She put on a Bruisers T-shirt and pink flannel pants and got into bed. But she was too buzzed to sleep. Her head and her heart were too full to do anything but relive the day.

She couldn't even call Becca because it was already midnight, and the poor girl would be asleep. She sat back against the upholstered headboard, hugged her knees to her chest, and groaned. How *did* people fall asleep on nights like this? Was counting sheep passé? Had Nate come up with an app to solve this problem yet?

There was a light knocking sound on the wall beside her head. *Tap. Tap.* Georgia held her breath, listening. Then it came again, this time in a familiar rhythm. *Shave-and-a-haircut.*

Georgia reached up to finish the pattern: *two bits.*

Her phone rang a second later. It was Leo calling.

She answered at a whisper. "Hi."

"Hi. Everything okay? I heard you groan."

"I'm fine," she said quickly.

"Yeah? Then was it a good kind of groan?"

She laughed. "No! Mind out of the gutter, Mr. Trevi."

"Mmm," he said, his voice roughened. "That's too bad, because I'm laying here naked, groaning your name."

The hair stood up on Georgia's arms, and she suddenly felt warm all the way to the center. "Leo!" she scolded.

"Kidding!" He chuckled. "I'm watching sports high-lights on TV, actually."

"Geez!" she squealed, embarrassed.

He laughed. "I'm sorry! I could make it happen for real. Come over here."

"No way." She gave a little shiver at the idea.

"Gigi, I'm awake because I'm too hyper to sleep. I just

saw a clip of *myself* on the fucking television. It was entirely surreal. I need someone to talk to me, because I'm bouncing off the ceiling here. Please? Just come and watch TV with me. We'll watch whatever you want. Here . . ." There was a pause and she thought she heard movement on the other side of the wall. Then she heard the sound of a lock sliding open. "I opened my door. Come visit."

She hesitated. "You make it sound so simple," she whispered.

"It is. I miss you. It doesn't have to be a big deal. Just get over here and I'll raid the mini bar. I think I saw Combos. Hang on . . ." There was the sound of rustling chip bags. "Got 'em!"

Georgia was on her feet before her brain could really weigh in. "Cheese or peanut butter?"

"Uh, Sweet and Salty Caramel?"

Rawr. She ended the call and tossed the phone on the bed. *I'm just doing this for the Combos,* she told herself as she opened the door to his room and went inside.

He was sitting on the bed, mirroring her former position exactly, phone still to his ear. Lowering it slowly, he gave her a shy smile. "Midnight snack?" He tossed the phone aside and picked up the bag, tugging it open.

Again Georgia hesitated. Should she just climb up on the bed with him?

He patted the spot next to him. Then he picked up the remote and nudged the TV volume up. The announcer was talking about college basketball now.

Georgia sat down and swung her feet up. Leo handed her the open bag. They sat there crunching together for a couple of minutes, listening to the talking heads argue about who had the best chance to do well during March Madness. They finished the Combos quickly.

"Carolina looks good this year," Leo said, balling up the bag.

"They look good every year. And yet it's been a while." She took the bottle of water he passed her and cracked it open. They watched several clips of unbelievably tall men flying toward the basket like gazelles.

That's when déjà vu set in. This used to be them on any given weekend. Snacks and commentary. Sports and snark and easy conversation.

On the television, the presenter launched into the week's sports bloopers. Leo drained his own bottle of water and tossed the empty onto the distant nightstand. He leaned back, his big body comfortable against the cushions. One of his hands fell onto her knee and gave a casual squeeze, then relaxed. He let out a chuckle at something funny on the screen. His big body was *right there* beside her. Close enough that she took in the scent of laundry soap and warm skin.

Georgia closed her eyes and just absorbed the moment. It *was* simple. Georgia and Leo, parked beside each other after a long day. A moment of late night peace. How many times had they sat like this together? A thousand?

The scene was so familiar, with one big exception. She wasn't the same girl she'd been when they'd first watched the sports recaps together. That had been a different Georgia. Teenage Georgia thought that life would always be that easy. That her boyfriend would always love her. Weirdly, even though her mother had passed away when she was little, Georgia hadn't really understood the power of loss until she was eighteen. She and Leo had probably watched this same television program the week before she'd been raped. Maybe they'd snacked on chips or passed a bottle of water back and forth. Maybe it was even the same brand.

Struck by a pang of dread for her younger self, Georgia felt a ripple of despair. That teenager sitting on the couch had had an easy laugh and a generous spirit. She thought everything would always be easy.

But it wasn't. Not at all. She hadn't known how everything could blow up so completely. That two people who'd always been so close could suddenly have a wall of fear and discomfort between them.

Her eyes began to sting, and the TV went into soft focus. Damn it.

Georgia slid off the bed and headed for the bathroom—Leo's bathroom. So it wouldn't look like she was sprinting away. She closed the door and flicked on the light, catching herself in the mirror. Her eyes were red and her face was flushed. Ugh. She sat down on the edge of the tub, annoyed at the older Georgia. This one fled into bathrooms and got teary.

That was the problem with Leo turning up. Two weeks ago, if you'd asked Georgia whether or not she was doing well, she would have answered *hell yes*. She had a good life in Brooklyn and she didn't walk around scared all the time. She'd *healed*, goddamn it. So what if she hadn't dated anyone more than twice in six years? Good men were thin on the ground. It wasn't because she was damaged goods.

And yet . . . Leo waltzed into town and threw everything into high relief. Suddenly it was impossible not to compare her old life with her new one. And the new one didn't stack up so well.

Georgia pushed her fingertips into the corners of her eyes and took a deep breath.

There was a tap on the door. "Gigi? You okay?"

"Yeah," she bit out. A tear escaped its prison and trickled down her finger.

The door opened a crack, and one brown eye looked down at her. Then the door opened further to reveal Leo's concerned face. He held out a hand. "Come here, Gi. Come sit with me."

She shook her head. Sitting beside Leo would just make it *ache*.

"Please," he whispered.

Georgia stood up. Her plan was to beat it to her own room before the trickle turned to a river. She'd never been a cryer, either. Not until after she'd been . . . A sob forced itself out of her chest.

Two arms pulled her against the warm wall of Leo's chest. She took a deep, shaky breath and bit her lip, trying to stop the fricking tears. But she'd been holding it all back for days. And he felt so good. Her eyes dripped like leaky faucets, and she pressed her forehead into his T-shirt so she couldn't see her own miserable face in the mirror. "I'm sorry," she said, the words garbled by the fresh-smelling cotton.

"Nah," he said softly. "Come on now." He bent his knees and lifted her a foot off the ground, his forearm catching her under her backside.

She closed her eyes and pressed her hot cheek against his shoulder. There was the sound of effort as he flung the comforter aside and deposited her onto the bed. Then he clicked off the lamp.

Since the TV was already black, the room became dark, except for the low light shining through the open door from her own room.

Leo traveled around to the opposite side of the king-sized bed and got in. His voice came through the dark, the sound a cross between a growl and a whisper. "Let me hold you."

She rolled, depositing her chin on his shoulder. Strong arms pulled her closer, until she was half on his body. It felt divine. Except for one problem. "I don't even want to count all the times you've held me while I cried." The words sounded bitter. But she *was* bitter. To be with Leo meant going back to that place where they both felt bad about what had happened, and what they'd lost.

His hand sifted through her hair while she waited for him to say something. "I don't like it when you're sad," he admitted. "But we had a lot more good than bad."

That was a ridiculously optimistic way of looking at it, considering how all the sadness at the end had killed off their special bond. But Georgia didn't want to argue the point. She stretched an arm across his broad chest and sighed.

"Why are you upset, Gigi?" he asked. "Tell me so I can make it better."

You make me ache. She didn't say it out loud, though.

Because Leo would ask why, and it wasn't really his fault. She didn't feel like admitting that she hadn't recovered quite as thoroughly as she'd thought. "I'm overwhelmed," she said instead.

"Mmh. Okay." His big hand slid down to her back, its heel pressing reassuringly between her shoulder blades. "Just try to relax."

A kiss landed on the top of her head. Georgia took a slow breath and let it out again. His heartbeat beneath hers was slow and steady. Leo Trevi was the source of all her stress at the moment. How odd that he could also be a source of comfort, too. She closed her eyes and let herself drift.

While she flirted with drowsiness, his fingertips continued to stroke her back. Her mind began to revisit the rink, with its crowds and lights. The white oval of ice danced in her sleepy mind. Just as she fell asleep, it almost sounded as if someone whispered, "Come back to me, Georgia."

SEVENTEEN

TOP TEAM HEADLINES:

*"Brooklyn Beats Arizona on the Road. Can They
Make It To the Play-offs for the First Time since the
Franchise Was Reborn?"*
—The Post

Leo woke up to the pleasant sound of someone else padding around his hotel room. In his sleepy cloud, he didn't think too much about it. He knew that it was someone he loved. And that the room was still mostly dark and quiet. The soft footsteps retreated to the other room, where they mingled with the sound of water running. The muffled flush of a toilet. The sound of a toothbrush in use.

Georgia.

Her name in his conscious mind woke him up. He opened his eyes, finding only gray predawn light filtering under the hotel curtains. He'd slept well all night, occasionally reaching out to place one lucky hand on the warm, sleepy body on the other side of the bed.

Having her next to him had been perfect, though he wished he'd woken up in time to appreciate it.

Leo got up, too, and spent a few moments in his own hotel bathroom. He felt stumbly and half-awake, and unwilling to entirely let go of last night.

Still in his boxers, Leo went to stand in the open doorway between their two rooms. The bathroom door opened, revealing Georgia in a towel, her hair clipped to the top of her head the way she sometimes had it when taking a shower. Random memories of waiting for her to get ready to go out with him hit like a punch to the gut. *How're these jeans?* she might ask him, turning in a circle to show him the full effect. *Perfect*, he'd answer.

They always were, as long as she was wearing them.

Now she stood across the room, blinking at him, looking unsure.

"Come here," he said, his voice thick with sleep. She obeyed, and he opened his arms to pull her in. Her chin landed on his shoulder. "You sleep okay?" he asked. Not the most creative inquiry, but he just wanted to hear her say something. To tell him that she wasn't going to run away again.

"Yeah," she breathed, wrapping her arms around him.

Leo's heart skipped a beat at the feel of her warm body aligned with his. This right here was exactly what he needed. He tilted his chin and dropped a gentle kiss on her bare neck. And Georgia shivered in his arms.

Jesus. His awareness of her was dialed up to eleven. Slowly, he traced her jaw with his lips. Her skin was velvety and damp from the shower.

In the stark silence, he heard her breath catch. That little sound was all it took to get him going. His desire for her would forever be waiting on the bench, geared up, ready to leap into action. Even now, his cock began to feel nice and heavy.

Down, boy. He needed Georgia to know that she was his, but it didn't have to be about sex. "It's early," he said, his voice pure gravel. "Let me hold you a little longer."

He expected to be shot down. In the cool light of day, Georgia might go back to keeping her distance.

But she did not, in fact, pull away. Another moment ticked by while he hugged her in the doorway. Then he took her hand and led her back to his bed. He slid onto his back in the still-warm sheets. When Georgia curled up beside him, her head on his shoulder, he thought he might burst from happiness.

She was wearing only a towel, and his body wasn't about to forget it. So he tucked her against his side, where it wouldn't be so obvious that barely touching her had left him raring to go. He smoothed his hand down the silk of her hair and sighed. "It's been too long, Gigi," he whispered. "I like having you beside me."

Georgia didn't say anything, but she spread her fingers across his stomach. The weight of her hand was delicious. They'd always been one of those couples who'd had to touch each other. All that clinginess had driven their high school friends nutty, but that's just how they were. He'd had several girlfriends in college, and never felt this way about any of them. It had never made him feel such bone-deep satisfaction to lie quietly beside anyone except for Georgia.

And why was that? His irritating brother probably had a theory or two. Leo pushed that out of his mind and concentrated once again on the way Georgia's soft hair tickled his jaw. He kissed the top of her head again, just because he could.

Georgia's smooth fingers played with the hem of his T-shirt, which had ridden up. Then her hand slipped beneath the fabric, meeting his skin.

Leo held his breath. He'd take her touch any way he could get it. But the thumb which had slowly begun to stroke his abs was pure, sweet torture. "Mmm," he hummed.

"Mmm," echoed a soft voice. And then a pair of soft lips arched to meet his neck, kissing sweetly in the sensitive place just beneath his chin. And the magic of her touch began to seep through his consciousness, heating his skin, lighting every nerve ending in its wake.

Leo bit the inside of his cheek to keep from moaning. Georgia curled in even closer to him, nuzzling his jaw. Meanwhile, he was hard and getting harder.

There had been so many times he'd wished for this—waking up beside Georgia in bed. It's something they'd never managed as teenagers. It was strictly against everyone's rules. So he was living out a fantasy right now. Part of one, anyway.

Georgia slid her hand farther up his chest to tease his nipple. Then she began to suck on his neck.

Leo gave in and groaned. "I love that, baby. But you're giving me big ideas." Then, unbelievably, her naughty hand skimmed down his chest again, then over the waistband of his boxers where her fingertips grazed his aching dick. "Ungh," he grunted, shocked.

Georgia had always been able to reduce him to a throbbing heap of need with a single hot glance. That obviously hadn't changed. Although one thing had. He turned his head and cupped her chin so he could see her better. Temporarily blocking out the awesome feeling of her hand on his dick, he asked her a question. "Are you sure?" he asked. If this encounter ended up with another text telling him it was all a mistake, he'd be crushed.

Her gorgeous blue eyes blinked back at him. The whisper was so low he was almost lip-reading. But the words were unmistakable. "I need you, Leo."

Jesus, Mary, and Joseph, she was going to kill him. "I'm yours anytime you need me," he whispered. He turned onto his side, his finger tracing a slow line across the upper swells of her breasts, just over the edge of her towel. "But is it okay? I mean . . ." He cleared his throat, his head muzzy with desire. "Can you . . . ?"

She reached up and tugged at the corner of the towel, and her breasts broke free of their confines, spilling out to meet his palm.

He groaned, rising up on one elbow. Then he dipped his head to kiss first one breast and then the other, lapping at the nipple, then sucking gently on it. The first time he'd done that they'd been sixteen and at a drive-in movie. Now as then, she arched beneath his hungry mouth and gasped.

His groin tightened with longing as he lifted his chin to take in her flushed face. He didn't want to rush—the moment was too important. But tell that to his overeager body.

Georgia reached for him, tugging him close, finding his mouth with hers. The kiss went molten immediately, their faces slanting for a more perfect connection, their tongues tangling. He repositioned himself over her body, propped onto both elbows. He sank his hips toward hers, his aching dick cradled between her thighs. Heaven.

But then she made a desperate noise so he pushed off her body, breaking their kiss. "You okay?" he asked immediately.

Two hands grabbed the waistband of his boxers and shoved them down. "I'm fine," she insisted. "Don't you dare stop."

Well then. He kicked off the shorts, then sank down again. They were skin on skin, and everything was heat and friction. They might as well have been eighteen again, with their eager hands and ravenous kisses. Before this morning, Leo had believed a few years of maturity had made him more patient in bed. But now he knew that was wrong. Georgia still made him crazy. Her soft skin and firm body stripped him of his ability to slow down and think.

Maybe that was the reason he'd put his foot in his mouth so many times these last two weeks. Georgia was his Kryptonite. Nobody else made him feel so alive. He never wanted it to end.

But it was going to, and all too soon if he wasn't careful. Kissing her and touching her was almost too much.

Leo wrapped his arms around Georgia and rolled onto his back. The change in position told his body to slow the fuck down. And the view was pretty spectacular, too. He looked up at a flushed and beautiful woman, her breasts heaving, her eyes burning up for him.

She was amazing. And she was going to be his again. He just knew it.

EIGHTEEN

Georgia stared down at Leo, her heart dancing the jitterbug. He was smiling up at her, his big brown eyes sparkling. Confident as ever.

Meanwhile, she was practically quaking. Who knew that it was possible to be absurdly turned on, and also incredibly nervous? *Note to self: Six years was too long to wait to do this again.*

Leo pulled her into another doozie of a kiss, the kind that made her forget her own name. Her nerves weren't quite so distracting with his tongue in her mouth and a pair of big hands running lovingly up her back. The throaty, approving moans Leo made vibrated in her chest.

She knew she could slow this down, and he'd understand. He would hold her all day if that's what she'd needed. But Georgia was sick of counting up all the things she missed about her old life with him. *This* had once been their currency, too. When it had disappeared, she'd been crushed.

But Leo was here right now in all his naked glory. And he wanted her. The evidence was obvious and also torturing her. She slid her body slowly along his shaft, just testing the idea for soundness.

The result? Both of them moaned.

Leo's hips jumped with excitement as she did it again. "Fuck," he murmured into her mouth. "You feel so fucking good."

But she knew it could be even better. And—just as in skydiving—hesitating wouldn't make the plunge any easier.

Georgia lifted her hips, lined him up and sank down on Leo's cock, filling herself in one glorious motion.

He gasped, bucking his hips a single time, flinging his big arms out to either side. "Holy . . ." he panted, canting his head back, too. "Fuck, don't move for a second."

But she couldn't have, anyway. Gripping Leo with her knees, Georgia buried her face in his neck and held on tight, the sensations overwhelming. Happy tears rimmed her eyes. If she could, she'd hold on to this moment forever. She was so very *alive* right now. And she was making love to the one person she'd always wanted.

Leo groaned, slowly lifting his arms and wrapping them around her back again. "Whew. Okay. Carry on." Strong fingers traced her spine. "Sorry." He chuckled, kissing her ear. "It's been a long time for me."

You have no idea. Georgia turned her head and pressed her lips to his cheek. She dropped kisses across his face, threading her fingers into his thick hair. When she thought she was ready, she rose up and kissed him again. He moaned immediately, shifting his hips beneath her.

Georgia took the hint. She pressed her elbows into the bed and began to move slowly.

"Oh, Gigi." He grabbed her hips, encouraging her. "Ride-me-oh-hell-yes." His voice was smoky and desperate, and the sound of it was so achingly familiar. He rolled his pelvis to meet her again and again, his big brown gaze taking her in. And his expression was full of love and something else. *Joy.* It shone so brightly that Georgia felt its heat each time he moved. She heard it in every whispered encouragement, and in the little groan he made when she picked up the pace.

Such a simple little word, "joy." And so hard to come by.

But not at the moment. Georgia took a deep breath and

ground down on Leo. He raised his hands to her breasts, stroking his thumbs across her sensitized nipples. "So fucking good," he said, and she shivered. He'd always been a talker in bed. Sexiest thing ever. "Now give me that mouth."

Georgia would have done anything that voice commanded her to. She leaned down and kissed him again. Her jitters were long gone, burned away by sweet friction and heat. Her brain clicked off, and she let herself fall into the easy groove they'd always shared. The steady beat of Leo's heart and the way his strong arms braced her body were all she needed to know.

Time slipped. There was no more worry. There was only pleasure and the pleasant sound of heavy breathing, punctuated with the occasional quiet click of their teeth as they kissed.

"Mmm," he ground out, and she loved the sound of strain in his voice. "Missed you, baby. So much."

That did her in—the words and his reverent hands and six years of pent-up sexual frustration. Georgia felt all her senses gather together. She took one more deep breath and then gasped, tipping over the edge, bearing down on him, letting the pleasure sweep her under. She heard herself utter something nonsensical. It didn't matter what.

Leo pulled her down onto his chest, kissing her and thrusting with abandon, all that muscle pumping under her while she held on tight. Then, with a deep gasp he grabbed her hips one more time and slammed their bodies together. He shuddered and moaned and it was the most beautiful sound she'd ever heard.

It was quiet after that, except for the sound of their ragged breathing. Big, clumsy hands swept the hair off her sweaty neck while he slowly kissed her.

After a moment, Georgia tucked her cheek against his chest and smiled. She may have just greatly complicated her life. But now was not the moment to worry about it. She was too busy feeling lucky.

She lay on his chest a long time, with Leo playing with

her hair. No words were spoken, but eventually Leo gave a chuckle.

"What?" she asked, her voice hoarse from disuse.

"Just occurred to me to wonder if you still have that IUD you got in high school."

She lifted her head and looked into eyes so ridiculously attractive that she almost forgot the question. "Absolutely." She put her head on his shoulder again. "I wouldn't do that to you."

His arms tightened around her back and he sighed. "I know. And, anyway . . ." The sentence died.

"What?"

"Eh. You won't want to hear it."

She picked her head up again. "What?"

He gave her a slow grin. "The idea of making babies with you always made me hot."

"Really? Geez." Now there was a crazy idea. "Bite your tongue. We were babies ourselves."

"Maybe so." His smile widened, but he looked up at the ceiling. "I used to think about it, though. Still like the idea."

Her heart wobbled. "This is not the right time for that discussion."

Leo gave her a squeeze. "Knew you'd say that."

"Seriously. We can't just pick up where we left off. Pretend like six years didn't happen."

He gave her ass a friendly slap. "My dick is inside you right now. Seems like we picked up just fine."

Well, damn. Georgia felt a happy throb between her legs which made it hard to argue the point. She lifted her body a few inches, separating them, and Leo gave a sexy groan that made her toes curl again.

She needed to get out of this bed and put some distance between herself and Leo. But he pulled her onto his chest again, and she instinctively relaxed against him. They'd been champion cuddlers back in the day. And—as with all sports—muscle memory wasn't so quickly lost. Their bodies still knew exactly how they were supposed to fit together, with her head tucked under his chin, and their legs intertwined.

Seriously. If cuddling after sex was a medal sport, they'd own that podium. And why did this not feel strange? *It ought to*, she reasoned. *I'm lying naked on Leo Trevi*, she thought, trying to shock herself.

Nothing.

Weird.

But even if sex with her high school boyfriend wasn't scary in and of itself, missing the jet to Dallas was. And dawn was already lighting the edges of the hotel curtains. "We have to get up," she said, still boneless and splayed all over Leo.

"Uh-huh," he said, not moving a muscle.

"We can't be the last people stumbling onto the bus, together and with sex hair."

His chest wobbled beneath her ear as he chuckled. "If you say so."

She gathered the tattered remains of her Type A personality together and pushed herself up. "I mean it. Gossip is not what we need right now. We can't have everyone whispering about our one-night stand."

Leo reached up with one of his long, edible-looking arms and tugged her back down onto his spectacular chest. "Fuck that," he said. "You and I don't have one-night stands. We have forever-night stands."

Georgia's heart took an hour-long tango lesson when he said that. When she'd been young and deep in puppy love, she and Leo had used the word "forever" with each other. And then when they hit the skids, it had hurt worse than anything. She turned her face to the side, turning away from all the brilliance that was Leo. It was hard to think rationally while lying on his body.

But Leo only began nuzzling the back of her neck. "You can run, but you can't hide, Georgia girl. Even if you give me the cold shoulder on the plane today. Even if you go all shy on me. It's *on*."

She slowly sat up again and gently disentangled herself from Leo. But the cold air was a shock, and she missed the hard press of his body immediately.

Gah. *Make up your mind, crazy lady.*

"I need another shower," she said. And it was certainly true.

"Mmm," Leo growled from the mattress. "Wonder why that is?" He sat up, too, and pulled her into his embrace. He kissed her neck, and she shivered *everywhere*. Leo was hard again. She felt him pressing against her hip. Her latent teenage bad girl considered ignoring the lateness of the hour altogether.

But that wouldn't go well for either of them. "Let me up, hunk. I have twenty-five minutes to try to look like a professional."

"Uh-huh," he said between kisses to her neck. "You know, the whole sexy publicist look really works for me."

"Leo," she grumbled, but it was just posturing. It had been a long time since she was someone's object of attraction. It made her feel young again.

"That tight skirt you wore to the game last night made it hard to concentrate."

"I'll wear something baggy to the next one. We need the wins." She slid off his lap and moved toward the edge of the bed.

"Wait." His long arms reached for her hips. "I need to say good-bye to the tatas."

Georgia's heart squeezed as Leo leaned down to nuzzle her left nipple. "Later," he said, the word muffled by the swell of her breast. Then he dipped his head to have a word with the other one.

It was absolutely ridiculous. And yet Georgia's eyes got hot. Because he used to do the same thing after they'd fooled around in high school. When it was time to get dressed and take Georgia home to meet her curfew, he'd say good night to her boobs. Although both of them enjoyed it, it was a *joke*.

Except it wasn't anymore. Now it was just one more

thing to remind Georgia how much time had passed. Was it their ritual alone? What other sets of knockers had Leo conversed with over the past six years?

Don't go there, she coached herself.

Leo lifted his chin and gave her a very sweet kiss on the lips.

Then, with a lump in her throat, she pulled away, retreating to her own room to shower and dress.

"Morning, Princess!" Georgia's father greeted her in the hotel lobby with a peck on the cheek.

"Hi, Daddy," she said with forced cheer. She was a girl with a secret. And even if it was a damn good one, she felt a tiny twinge of guilt.

"How did you sleep?" her father asked.

Gulp. "Just fine. You?"

"Eh. Can't wait to get home on Friday. I see the bus outside. Shall we?"

She sat beside her father at the front of the bus for the ride to the airport. And even though she conveniently looked out the window when Leo boarded, she felt him pass by. In the harsh morning glare of the hotel parking lot she could hardly believe her own daring. She'd been the instigator of the morning's festivities. She'd touched him through his clothes, her hand stroking his erection as he'd hissed. She'd been the one to rise up above him, lowering herself down on his . . .

"Princess?"

"Mmm?" she said, shaking off the memory. "What?"

"I was just asking if you were okay. You look a little flushed."

"It's just, uh, warm in here."

The Deep V of Trouble deepened in his forehead. "It's actually freezing in this can of a bus. Hugh just complained to the driver."

"You know, this sweater is *really* warm," she babbled. "It's cashmere."

He gave her an odd look. "Good to know, Princess," he said, pulling out his Katt Phone.

Georgia did the same, and was greeted by a text from Becca. *Guess where I am! I'll give you three tries.*

Georgia was too distracted to play the game. *I give up.*

You are a drag. Now I'm not going to tell you.

Fine. Be that way, Georgia replied.

"Georgia?"

"Yeah?"

"Why are you frowning?"

"Um, just texting with Rebecca," she said, raising her eyes to her father's. "Why?"

He was studying her with narrowed eyes. "You're acting strange today."

"How do you figure?" Was she? Georgia had been a skillful liar during her teen years. But she was probably rusty these days.

"Are you all right?" her father asked.

"Perfectly."

"Is it hard on you?"

"What?"

Her father glanced around, the special scowl he saved for Leo creeping onto his face. "Traveling with *him*?"

No blushing, she reminded herself. "He's fine." *Damn.* "I mean, *it's* fine. I'm fine." *We are all fine!* She needed to stop talking now.

He chewed his lip. "Let me know if he bothers you in any way."

"Um, okay." It felt traitorous not to stick up for Leo. Her father was the one acting strange. But her father would not like to know what had happened between them, and Georgia was too uncertain about what it all meant to make any bold declarations. So she sat there, mute, until her father finally gave up and went back to pecking at his Katt phone.

When Georgia got onto the jet a half hour later, the first

face she saw was Becca's. Her roommate beckoned frantically. "Sit with me! I've missed you."

"But of course." Georgia put her bag into the overhead compartment, her eyes flicking to the rear of the plane, where the meeting room door was already closed. But if Becca was here, that meant Nate needed to huddle up with the coaching staff and the GM en route to the next game. Was that weird? They'd won last night. That should put the boss at ease, right? She sat down beside Becca. "Everything okay?" she asked quietly. If Nate was worried about her father's coaching, would he hover like this?

Becca shrugged. "I don't know what the boss man is up to. He called me last night and asked me to pack a bag. So here I am. Maybe he just wants to watch the new coach in action. It doesn't have to mean anything," she said, reading Georgia's mind.

Georgia wanted to believe her. "Okay. What's up with you?"

"The mango is gone. And there are no new science experiments in our kitchen."

"Yay!" Georgia clapped.

Becca narrowed her eyes. "That is a lot of excitement over a clean refrigerator. You look awfully cheery today."

"I don't know what you're talking about," Georgia insisted. But heat began to climb up her neck.

Her roommate's eyes bulged. "Holy shizzle. Georgia Worthington got *laid*."

Georgia reached over to clamp her hand over Becca's mouth. "Shut it. I swear to God. You are going to get me in so much trouble." Becca stuck out her tongue in retaliation, wetting Georgia's hand. "Ew!" She released Becca's mouth and wiped her hand on Becca's wool Bruisers scarf.

"Ladies," a deep baritone said. "Is there a problem here?"

Georgia turned to look into Leo's handsome face. And the look he gave her could only be described as "smoldering."

"*Damn*," Becca breathed.

"Everything is fine," Georgia said hastily. She made a little motion to wave him on. *Move along.*

He winked, then disappeared down the aisle.

Becca grabbed the in-flight magazine out of the seat back pocket and began to fan herself. "The heat pouring off you two is hazardous. I'd better make sure I know where they keep the onboard fire extinguisher. Because, safety first."

Georgia grabbed the magazine out of her hands and shoved it back into the pocket, while Becca laughed.

NINETEEN

Leo: Is it something I said?

Georgia: ?

Leo: Your friend Becca put me in a room with Silas. And O'Doul is in the adjoining room. He won't cuddle me. :(

Georgia: Have you asked nicely?

Leo: Yeah. So now I have a black eye.

Georgia: You crack yourself right up.

Leo: Thank you, folks, I'll be here all week . . .

Georgia: You are bunking with Silas because Nate decided to travel with us to Texas and this hotel is full.

Leo: So your room, then? :)

Georgia: Nope.

Leo: But I need a word with the tatas. There's something I forgot to say.

Georgia: I'll put them on Skype.

Leo: Really?

Georgia: No!

Leo: Your room number is . . .

Georgia: . . . is the same one as Becca's. See above explanation about the full hotel.

Leo: Fuck.

Georgia: Not so much.

Leo: I need to kiss you. Today.

Georgia: Is this some new superstition thing? Like your lucky jock strap in high school?

Leo: Fuck no. I need to kiss you. Everywhere. Soon. Before you invent a bunch of reasons why we shouldn't.

Georgia: Too late.

Leo: Not funny. We'll talk later. I miss you.

Georgia: What ever happened to your lucky jock strap? Please tell me you finally washed that thing.

Leo: Nope! I don't wear it anymore tho.

Georgia: Thank god

Leo: It's in a zipper bag at the bottom of my gear duffel. It was ten feet from the bed where we . . .

Georgia: Ew!

Leo: :)

TWENTY

TOP TEAM HEADLINES:

"Dallas Has a 7-1 Record vs. Brooklyn in Recent
Match-ups. Let's Make it Eight?"
—The Dallas Tribune

Leo caught himself humming in the showers after the
morning warm-up. Everything had gone right for a
change. He didn't know whether his attitude had been
buoyed by last game's goal or yesterday morning's perfect
reunion with Georgia. Maybe both. But whatever the
cause, he'd killed it at practice yesterday and this morning.
Even during the three-on-twos at the bitter end, he'd sliced
past O'Doul and made the puck his own.

After the morning skate he'd stayed behind a few minutes because the associate coach wanted to talk to him
about Dallas's defensive habits. Leo was the last man off
the ice, and he thought he caught even Coach Worthington
wearing a look of grudging approval.

Finally. A little momentum.

He shut off the tap and reached outside the stall for the

towel he'd hung there. But his hand met only a hook and cool air. So Leo stuck his head past the discolored shower curtain and checked the hooks on either side of his stall. They were both empty.

Fuck.

He stepped out anyway, dripping wet, wearing nothing but his shower shoes. Someone had decided he needed a little middle-school-grade hazing. The stack of clean towels he'd seen on the counter ten minutes earlier was missing, too.

Whatever.

Leo walked into the dressing room, where several guys snickered. As he passed O'Doul he made sure to shake himself like a dog, sending droplets of water flying everywhere.

The snickers turned to full-out laughter, except from O'Doul, who swore. "It wasn't me, asshole. Castro loves to pull that shit."

"Good to know." He crossed to his locker and looked for something—anything—to dry himself off. Yesterday's T-shirt? Good enough. He swatted at the drops of water on his chest and neck.

"Hey, naked boy." O'Doul stood beside him, frowning.

"Yeah?" He dug his underwear out of his duffel.

"We gonna win this thing tonight?"

Leo chuckled. "That's the plan, right?" Though Dallas was a tough team, and the Bruisers' record against them wasn't the best.

"Sure. But there's a defenseman on this crew who has it in for me. One of their guys was injured in our game last season. Career-ending. You remember Burkowski?"

"Yeah. Broken femur?"

"That's the one. It was a clean hit, but they still blame us. And then I embarrassed this other asshole in a fight during the preseason. He wants a rematch. You're the new kid so he'll probably fuck with you to draw me out."

Great. Leo wasn't exactly known for his fighting. Unlike so many other NHL players, he'd skipped Juniors in favor of college hockey, where fighting was illegal. "You want me to take a swing at him?"

"Fuck no. Just put the biscuit in the basket, college boy. I'll follow up. Just watch your back."

"All right. Thanks."

Leo got dressed, wondering if O'Doul had decided to count him as a real teammate after all.

When the player card went to the refs before the game that night, Leo half expected his name to be missing from it. In spite of his big night in Arizona, he wouldn't put it past Coach to try to teach him a lesson in humility.

But apparently not. Because his name was on the card. And he was ready.

The mood was a little slap-happy in the locker room. Castro hid several players' protective cups during elimination soccer, and was chased around the dressing room and pelted with them when they were eventually found. But O'Doul wasn't part of the pregame shenanigans tonight. Instead, the captain sat in the corner, his head bowed. And every few minutes he muttered to himself.

Leo nudged Silas. "He okay?"

Silas shrugged. "Guess so. That's how he stirs up the crazy before a rough game. He'll be okay after we start."

Leo felt buoyant, in spite of his team's edgy attitude toward its opponent. His phone was full of well-wishes from his family and friends. This was it, ladies and gentlemen. The highest level of play a guy could see in professional hockey.

They gathered around for a last-minute chat with Coach Karl, who looked even more ornery than usual. "This could be a real shit storm. Just let the refs do their thing and don't lose your cool, boys. Revenge doesn't get us to the play-offs, you hear?"

There were murmurs of agreement, then the chute door opened and it was on.

As predicted, the game got ugly early. Lots of tripping

and slashing in the corners. Leo found himself playing dirtier than he liked to. And he took two minutes for tripping before the first period was over.

Coach had a few choice words about that during intermission. "If you're gonna fight back, rookie, don't be so fucking blatant. Even my aunt Sally would have called that penalty."

Leo barked out a laugh. "I've met Aunt Sally and she's hella sharp."

Worthington only growled.

Leo's sense of humor took a hit early in the second period, though. The faceoff positioned him against an opposing wing with a snaggle-toothed snarl. "That face won't stay pretty tonight, boy. Rookie's gonna get ass-fucked up by my enforcer," he threatened.

"You kiss your mother with that mouth?" Leo barked without taking his eyes off the ref's hands. Seconds later, the puck came flying out of the circle in his direction. Leo snapped it out of the air with his stick, winging it back to his own defensemen in a blur of motion.

"Cocksucker," the other wing growled, jamming the end of his stick into Leo's ankle.

Fuck. A bright shimmer of pain radiated up his leg. And since the action had already traveled down the rink, the ref didn't notice the illegal jab. Leo skated off in pursuit. It was only pain.

But they weren't done with him. The jackass wing side-swiped Leo at every opportunity. It was irritating, but nothing he couldn't handle—or so he thought. Avoiding that dude proved dangerously distracting.

Leo never even saw the big hit coming.

One second he was scraping the puck off the boards, looking for the pass, keeping clear of the wing with an attitude. The next moment he went flying into the plexi, helmet first. For an odd, frozen moment, he locked eyes with a girl seated in the front row while the force of impact kept him hovering over her. Then he crashed to the ice in a heap.

The air got weirdly cold and *loud*. It took a moment for Leo to realize that his helmet had popped off. He was lying on the ice feeling stunned. He opened his mouth to take a breath, and it didn't quite work.

Shit.

The noise in the rink pressed in on him, and the lack of oxygen to his lungs began to freak him out, too. But just as panic threatened to set in, he heard an old familiar voice in his head. *Give it a second, son.* That's what his retired college coach used to say whenever he or someone else got the wind smacked out of them. So Leo waited out that awful moment when his lungs forgot their job. O'Doul was somewhere nearby, cussing up a storm. "Illegal fucking hit to the *fucking head*!"

Leo's self-preservation instincts kicked in. Even before he could properly inhale, he began scrambling upward, digging a blade into the ice and rising to his feet. Only a pussy stayed sprawled on the rink. And he was okay. He hadn't even blacked out.

Standing up, Leo finally got a breath of air. The bench swam into view, and Leo could see the trainer opening the door, about to walk across the ice to check on Leo.

That would not be necessary, Leo decided. He pushed off toward the bench and found that his legs worked fine. The trainer stayed where he was and held the door open for him. During the ten-second journey, the rink came into sharper focus. Coach was leaning over the wall, in a full rant at the referee. "Bullshit! Major penalty. Game misconduct at least!"

O'Doul was there, too, gloved hands clenched into fists, yelling at the linesman.

The ref told them both to calm the fuck down as Leo stepped over the threshold. The trainer pushed him onto the bench and began to ask him questions.

Leo tuned him out, concentrated on breathing and waiting for the haze to subside enough for him to figure out exactly where it hurt.

"Any dizziness?" the trainer asked.

"Uh . . ." *Pull it together, Trevi.* "Just got the air knocked out of me. I'll be okay in a minute."

"Is it your head or your chest? Where's the impact?"

"Shoulder took it pretty hard. But I think it's okay." Leo lifted his elbow and slowly rotated the joint.

The trainer grasped Leo's upper arm and dug his fingers in among the pads. "This hurt?" he asked. "Lift your chin."

When he did as he was told, the trainer's fingers pressured collarbone, checking for a reaction. "I'm solid," he said. "Hurts like a nasty bruise, that's all." *I hope.*

"Stretch it out for a minute," the trainer advised. "Test your range of motion."

"All right." Leo took a few more breaths.

"Castro. Bayer. Crikey," Coach Karl barked. "You're up next."

His teammates vaulted over the wall a second later. Karl had changed up the lines. Leo was initially grateful for the reprieve. The trainer came over again and questioned him about his head and chest. "Any lingering dizziness? How's your vision?"

"Fine," Leo insisted. "My head is fine."

Someone picked that moment to deliver his helmet to him. Since he'd forgotten it on the ice, his I'm-sharp-as-a-tack argument took a hit. "Thanks," he mumbled, grabbing the thing.

The player who'd flattened him had gotten only a two minute penalty, which meant that Coach Karl kept up his cursing. Leo turned his attention to the game, where Bayer and Castro were passing the puck back and forth in the attack zone, trying to capitalize on their power play. And Leo's vision *was* fine—fine enough to see the puck go suddenly winging past the goalie's knee and into the net.

"YES!" he yelled, standing up to see the lamp light. The fact that his team scored on the power play meant that the brutal hit he'd taken had served a purpose. The game was tied up now. They just needed one more goal before the buzzer. "We can do this," he said, unsnapping his helmet to put it back on.

But Coach called another shift that did not include him. "I'm good to go," he called down. "Send me out." Even though there were only six minutes left in the game, Coach couldn't keep rearranging the lines to leave Leo on the bench. That was ridiculous.

The coach wove his way down the bench toward Leo. He grabbed Leo's jersey and yanked it up, then stuck his hand on Leo's ribs and squeezed.

"Fuck!" Leo swore before he could think better of it. He practically flew backward, too, escaping the coach's clutches. The man had grabbed him right where he'd been hit.

"Yeah, I thought so," Coach Karl spat.

"I'm fine," Leo argued.

"Sit on the fucking bench when I tell you to, rookie."

Jesus. First he'd been ignored, and now he was being babied. Fucking Karl. Leo was beginning to doubt that he would ever win this man's approval.

TWENTY-ONE

The ten seconds that Leo was sprawled on that ice were the longest of Georgia's life.

Get up, get up, she chanted internally as the ref blew the whistle and teammates swarmed. The hit he took was ridiculously hard, and too high up on the body to be legal. The ref stopped the game. High hits were so, so dangerous. Players had been paralyzed by less.

When Leo staggered to his feet, she exhaled.

"He's okay," Becca whispered, reading her mind. Not that it was difficult tonight—she'd had her eyes glued to one player since the puck had dropped.

But Leo looked wobbly on the way back to the bench. On the rink, the linesmen were patrolling the ice, keeping a close watch on the faceoff circle, probably because O'Doul looked ready to blow like a volcano. Her father was practically foaming at the mouth down there, too. Maybe he didn't like Leo, but he'd never take it lying down if someone pulled a move like that against one of his players.

Georgia divided her attention between the action on the ice and the trainer who began to prod Leo. Only when the trainer left him alone did she really start to relax.

Luckily, all that tension lit a fire under Team Brooklyn, who capitalized on their power play at the one minute mark. Bayer fired a missile right past the goalie, tying up the game. That should have changed the tone down on the ice. But at the next stoppage of play, after the penalized player emerged from the sin bin, O'Doul threw off his gloves. Down went the other dudes' gloves, and O'Doul grabbed him by the jersey and swung.

The impact made Georgia wince. Fighting was not her favorite part of hockey. When she was younger, the fighting didn't used to bother her. But now that she saw the injured players right after every game, she was no longer so sanguine. Fighting *hurt*. So when O'Doul did his thing, she didn't like to watch.

"Thank God Leo isn't a brawler," she muttered. "I wouldn't be able to stand it."

"Yeah," Becca agreed. "That would be a tricky thing to explain to your future children. Daddy hits the other boys at work, but you still can't drop the gloves in kindergarten."

"Very funny," Georgia scoffed.

"Is it? Just let me know if I need to shop the spring sales for something to wear to your wedding."

"Shh! Stop trying to marry me off," she said. "So we spent one night together. It doesn't have to mean anything."

"Jeez, I wonder how loudly I can call bullshit?"

"Pretty loudly, apparently." Georgia looked over her shoulder to make sure nobody they knew was listening.

"In the past two weeks, have you strung together fifteen minutes without thinking of him?"

"Sure I have." *While I was sleeping.*

Becca snorted. "That's gonna leave a mark," she said, pointing at the action on the rink below. "Doulie just crushed that guy. Ooh, gross. There's blood on the ice."

Georgia didn't want to look. She studied Leo instead. Was he sitting funny? Several times he put a gloved hand up to his pectoral and seemed to probe it. Each time he did that, Georgia escalated her worries about him. Was he bruised? Broken ribs?

Heart attack?

Gah.

She watched the last part of the game with dread in her stomach. Her father kept sneaking looks at Leo, too. It was rare for him to take his eyes off the ice like that. So Leo *must* be injured. Except Leo was obviously pissed off at sitting out his shifts. At one point they stood toe to toe, faces red, arguing.

Leo didn't skate until there were only two minutes left on the clock. Georgia scrutinized his movements, looking for trouble. But when a world-class hockey player skates at 90 percent instead of full out, it's not easy to spot the difference, even for someone as invested as Georgia was. His skating was as powerful and fluid as always. She could watch him all night.

I still love him.

Ack. Now there was a messy thought.

When the buzzer rang the game was still tied 1–1. Five minutes of overtime went up on the clock, and the ice team came out to shovel. Reluctantly, Georgia made her way downstairs to prepare for the after-game press conference.

There was a monitor in the visitors' lounge, though, so she and Roger stood there, watching. After the overtime period began, nothing much happened for the first couple of minutes. But then Leo's assailant got hung up in front of the visitors' bench, trying to dig the puck out of a scrum of skaters and sticks. And all of a sudden Silas, sitting in his usual spot on the bench, jerked the door open.

His opponent went down fast and hard, sprawled halfway into the visitors' bench area, his legs splayed out on the ice.

"Whoa," Roger breathed.

Georgia moved so close to the monitor that her nose was only inches away. *Nobody touch him*, she begged. Emotions were running high down there, and she couldn't even imagine the bench-clearing fight that might break out if the Bruisers bench let loose on that guy.

The next two or three seconds seemed to last forever. Georgia didn't breathe while the player curled his body back onto the ice and then hopped to his feet.

Meanwhile, O'Doul had captured the puck and run it down to the attack zone, where he scored on a breakaway.

Georgia just stared at the monitor for a few minutes, trying to make sense of what had just occurred. Then she grabbed her Katt Phone and asked it a question. "Nate, is the bench door prank against NHL rules?"

Her phone couldn't find much mention of the bench door in the NHL rulebook. She learned that the benches for each team were required to be of equal length, with the same number of doors—two—for each side. There was nothing about yanking the door open to make the other team's man fall over.

How crazy.

Regardless of its legality, Georgia had a PR quandary on her hands. She didn't know whether to put Silas in front of every reporter in the stadium, or try to hide him and downplay the incident.

She had about ninety seconds to figure it out.

Georgia ran into the empty dressing room and out the other door. The first players were just clomping off the ice and down the rubber mats. Luckily, Silas was one of the first off the rink. She grabbed his arm and spun around to walk with him into the dressing room. "Nice work out there. But I don't want you to brag about it on camera."

Silas grinned. "Thought you might say that. I'm gonna say it was just an accident of timing that I happened to open the door then. Didn't know their guy would fall on his face at our feet."

"Perfect," Georgia said. "Now come say that out in the hallway. But I'm not bringing you into the press conference, because that makes it look too official for something that was an accident."

"Okay, boss." Silas removed his gloves and hurled them toward his locker. "Let's do it."

In the hallway, a local sports reporter pounced, and Silas gave his quote about the "accident of timing."

"That's really your story?" the reporter drawled.

"Sure is," Silas said, slowing down the words to match

the other man's southern accent. "I guess it's just the same kind of coincidence your guy had when he accidentally clocked my teammate in the head."

Georgia bit her lip to keep from laughing, then she sent Silas back into the locker room.

Of course, his teammates knew better. Their shouts could be heard even through the dressing room door. "Silas for president!" some player yelled. "Play of the year!" hooted another.

The hallway was chock-full of journalists looking for quotes from the winning team. When Georgia put her head into the locker room, asking for O'Doul, the GM told her that he'd refused to take questions tonight.

"He's feeling beat. Take someone else," Hugh said.

That made her job a little trickier, but if the captain had decided he was in no mood for polite conversation, she wasn't about to argue. She pried Bayer out of the locker room to say something about his goal. He made a little dig at the other team, something about "past grudges that some players couldn't set aside," but it wasn't too bad. Tonight would not be a complete PR disaster.

Lately that counted as a win.

A lot of time went by, though, without Leo showing his face. Georgia was worried about him. She checked her phone, but there were no messages. She could always go into the locker room and ask, but if something was seriously wrong, her father would be there, too.

Rock, meet hard place.

Georgia gathered her things together and went to find the bus back to the hotel.

TWENTY-TWO

Leo was prodded six ways 'til Sunday by the doctor and the trainer after the game. They did a battery of tests for concussion, shining a light in his eyes, asking stupid questions.

"What day is it?"

"Game day!" he answered cheerfully.

"Mr. Trevi . . ."

"*Thursday*, I'm pretty sure. But on the road, I forget sometimes. You should ask me who the president is, or something. And I'm fine. Really."

That went on for some time, and then they probed his ribs and shoulder, which were admittedly pretty tender. But he was used to feeling beat up after a game. "I'll take an ice bath," he suggested. He'd offer anything to get 'em off his back. The doctor and the trainer were also worried about cracked ribs, but Leo knew from experience that it would be a day before he was sure whether the soreness could be written off as muscle aches or not.

"All right," the trainer finally agreed. "We'll look at you again tomorrow."

Leo took a quick shower, trying not to hiss when the hot water hit an abrasion on his neck. Then he went to suffer in the ice bath, as he'd promised he would. At this facility, the thing was just a plastic tub and a cold tap, which some helpful soul had running at full blast. He put his hand in the water and then wished he hadn't. With a sigh he stepped in, one leg at a time, and then sank quickly below the surface, up to his chin.

Some people swore by the cold bath as a way of staving off muscle aches, but Leo had never been convinced that it accomplished anything more than shrinking his nuts down to pebble size. He counted to three hundred and then got the heck out of there, drying himself with blue-tinged fingers and cursing the inventor of the ice bath.

By the time he'd fumbled his shaking limbs into his suit and shoes, the press conference was over and the bus had already left with the first group of players. The dressing room was almost empty. And by the time he'd hefted his duffle bag to leave, the only other player in there was O'Doul. The captain sat fully dressed on the bench in front of his locker, his head tipped back, as if he were reading a treatise off the ceiling.

When he caught Leo watching him, his chin snapped down, allowing Leo a view of the bandages on the side of his face. "You okay, rookie?" he asked Leo suddenly.

"Yeah, sure. I'm not sure why everyone is freaking out over this hit. It's just another day at the office."

"Maybe 'cause you didn't see it." O'Doul tapped his fingers on the bench. "Looked reckless as hell. If your body had been positioned differently, coulda been ugly."

"Good thing it wasn't, then." Leo took a step to the side to see how big the bandage on O'Doul was. "You okay? That looks kind of brutal."

"'Course." O'Doul stood up quickly. "Just a flesh wound." His Monty Python accent wasn't terribly accurate, but Leo wouldn't call him on it. "Want to walk back? I don't feel like waiting for the fucking bus."

"Sure, why not." Leo held the dressing room door open for O'Doul to pass through.

"Are you the last ones?" a young man with a Bruisers' ID hanging around his neck asked in the hallway.

"Yeah, Jimbo," O'Doul confirmed. "Thanks."

The young man went into the dressing room they'd just vacated, probably to start packing up their gear. It felt strange to Leo to just walk away from his gear after a practice or a game. But these days it was someone else's job to pack up his pads and his equipment and transport them to the next facility.

Weird.

He and O'Doul exited the rink via the back door near the parking lot. Leo didn't know exactly where they were, but he could see some fans waiting over to the left, probably hoping the home team would come out and sign jerseys for them.

O'Doul pointed right, and the two of them wordlessly avoided the crowd in favor of a slightly longer walk around the exterior of the rink.

In his pocket, Leo's phone buzzed. He drew it out, noticing that O'Doul did the same. "You get this text?" Leo asked. It was an automated message from the travel team, asking his location and whether he needed transportation.

"Yeah," O'Doul grunted. "Just reply to it and they'll leave you alone."

Walking back, Leo texted. *Thanks.*

O'Doul shoved his Katt Phone into his pocket. "They've got the geolocation working all the time. If you ever rob a bank, leave the Katt Phone at home."

"Good tip."

"Though you must not be a criminal, or Kattenberg wouldn't bring you on board. He's the most sophisticated miner of data in the business, I'm told. He probably knows your shoe size, how many fillings you have, and your kindergarten teacher's first name."

"Millie," Leo offered. "But I think she's dead now." They reached the main drag, and the hotel lights were almost on them. "Thanks for, uh, throwing down for me tonight."

"Anytime. You're wearing the sweater, I'm gonna have your back."

Leo chuckled. "I know it's not personal. You'd defend even the most irritating rookie."

To his surprise, O'Doul gave him a playful check with his elbow and said, "You're not even the most annoying guy on the team. Gotta work harder if you want that title."

"Damn. Okay. I'm on it." A man in uniform opened the hotel door for them, and they went inside.

"Night, college boy," O'Doul said without a glance over his shoulder. Then he broke away, heading for the bar.

Leo almost followed him, because O'Doul made him curious. The dude was not easy to read. But he didn't feel like a trip to the bar. His ribs ached, and he was too tired to drink. So he headed to the elevator instead, where he texted Georgia. *Hi, honey, I'm home.* It sure would be good to see her face.

As soon as he reached his room, he got out of the suit and into his favorite sweats. With the remote in hand, he climbed onto the bed and wrapped an extra blanket around his body. Only then did he tuck the ice pack they'd made him under his shirt.

Silas walked in a minute later. "Hey! How's the ribs?"

"I'll live. Not partying tonight? I'll bet you won't have to pay for any drinks."

"I'm beat," Silas admitted. "Long road trips really take it out of me. Imagine what would happen if I actually played." He did a face-plant on the other bed.

Leo laughed, and then his phone buzzed with a text. He picked it up quickly, hoping to hear from Georgia. But it was his mom. *Are you okay? I waited 90 minutes to ask. My new record.*

He had to laugh. *Nice work, and I'm fine. I'd feel better if I'd scored, though.*

We love you no matter what. Even if you lose to the Rangers next week. But try not to.

I'll see what I can do.

The game is on my birthday. Can you have a late lunch with us beforehand?

Sounds great, Leo replied, feeling guilty that he'd forgotten that his mom's birthday was coming up.

There was a knock on the door, and Silas picked his head up. "You order room service?"

"No, but I like that idea."

Silas slid off the bed and went to open the door. Leo heard him greet somebody, and when he reappeared, there was amusement on his face. "Leo, a visitor."

Georgia appeared behind him, looking tentative. "Hi."

"Hi."

"I just . . ." She cleared her throat. "Are you okay?"

Aw. "'Course I am, baby. Come see me."

Silas pulled off his suit coat and loosened his tie. "You know, I think I'll have a drink downstairs after all. See you in a little while." He tossed his jacket on a chair and made a quick exit.

"I hope he doesn't tell the whole bar he's giving us a few minutes alone. You and Coach don't seem to be getting along as it is," Georgia said, still hovering near the door.

"Who cares? Come here and kiss me."

She approached him slowly, eyeing the ice packs under his shirt. "Are you really okay? Would you tell me if you weren't?"

"Probably." Leo chuckled. "Your dad got really weird about the whole thing. He wouldn't let me skate. He kept sending the trainer over to prod me."

"Maybe he was worried about you?"

"No way. I think he'd run me over with the Zamboni himself if given the chance. Tonight I felt like he wanted to make me look weak, or something."

Georgia shook her head. "He doesn't embarrass anyone. It's not his style."

Leo used to believe that was true. But he didn't want to trash Coach to Georgia any longer, either. It wasn't fair to make her choose sides. Instead he lifted his shirt. "See, it's not that bad. Give me a day, I'll be fine."

She made a low, concerned noise in her throat. And when she placed gentle fingertips on his bruised skin, something in Leo's chest tightened. It had been a long time since anyone he'd dated had worried about him. The Amys of his past had found the game-day bruises sexy. Like warrior's marks. But Georgia's touch was all worry, no glee.

"That wasn't a fair hit," she whispered.

"Coulda been worse," Leo pointed out, tugging her closer. She grabbed the headboard to avoid falling on his injured chest. But Leo would risk a little pain for a kiss. *I love you*, he thought, pulling her in. Their lips met softly, and the tenderness made for a wholly different sort of ache in his chest. He kissed her again, knowing that his meddling brother had been right. Nobody had ever mattered to him the way Georgia did. Kissing her felt like coming home.

He grabbed the backs of her knees and swung her onto his lap. "Missed you today," he whispered between kisses.

"Mmm," she said, her sweet lips brushing his. Then she tipped her forehead against his and peered at him seriously. "I hate that asshole who hit you."

"You're very loyal," he whispered. "Even though you avoided me at the rink earlier."

Her expression turned guilty. "You were busy."

"Uh-huh." Leo kissed her on the nose. "You had on a different sexy publicist outfit today. And I couldn't get close enough to you to admire it."

Georgia rolled her eyes. "You can't admire me with your hands, mister. That's not allowed."

"Sure it is." He gave her ass a little squeeze, and then wondered how long it would take for Silas to have that drink . . .

She caught him by the chin. "Be good."

"Baby, I *am* good. You said so yourself the other morning."

Another eye roll. "Leo, we can't be a couple right now. There are complications. It's not that easy . . ."

He grabbed her in a hug and buried his nose in her hair. "It's *exactly* this easy. You and me, alone together. There's not one thing about it that's complicated. You're mine, Georgia Worthington. I don't care what your fucking dad thinks. I spent six years trying to get over you, and it didn't take. Our time is now."

Georgia took a deep breath and seemed to relax against him. One soft hand stroked the whiskers on his chin. "The whole guns-a-blazing thing is sexy, hunk. But you need to remember that the trade deadline is in two weeks."

He grunted. "You think your father would trade me for spending time with you?" Though "spending time" was a euphemism, and they both knew it.

"Maybe. I don't know what he's got against you, but this couldn't possibly help."

He nuzzled her neck with his lips. "So you're saying we need to stay in the closet for two weeks? I can do that."

"At least." She sifted her fingers through the short hair at the nape of his neck. "Then there's *my* job to worry about."

"Why?" Leo moved his head back so that he could see her face. "Is there, like, a policy against it?"

"I'm not sure. I never had any cause to go digging through the employee guidelines for a fraternization rule."

He grinned. Maybe it made him a Neanderthal, but he didn't like the idea of Georgia dating anyone else in the organization. Surely she'd had boyfriends, but he didn't want to meet any of them.

"A few weeks before you showed up, the head of PR quit. Nate and Hugh Major aren't sure yet what they're going to do with the position. I only have the chief job on an interim basis. And that press conference you bombed? It was my first one."

He blinked. "Shit, really? I'm sorry."

"What I'm saying is that I need to at least string together a *short* stint where I manage to look professional."

Leo lifted her palm to his mouth and kissed it. "All right. I get it. If you need to be stealthy for a while, I'm not going to wreck things for you. But I need to see you. Often." He kissed her wrist, and then her forearm. "And I need to show you how much I missed you." He kissed the inside of her elbow. Then he leaned closer and kissed her shoulder. Her neck. The place beneath her ear that made her shiver.

Georgia whimpered against his shoulder. "You're making me crazy."

"Good." He put his fingers to the buttons of the silky blouse she'd worn tonight.

"No." She sat up a little straighter. "We can't. Silas will come back."

Leo held back a groan. He was pretty sure that Silas had made himself scarce for a while. But Leo wouldn't push it. He didn't want to make her uncomfortable. "Watch some TV with me, then."

"Okay."

"Can you get the clicker? It's a pain in the ass to arrange the ice packs."

"Sure, old man." She crawled away from him, toward the edge of the bed, and in her skirt it was quite the image.

"Wait. Just stop right there," he said before she managed to hop down. "This is a better view than TV."

She rolled her eyes at him and then fetched the remote. She chose a late night comedian.

"Not the highlights?"

She shook her head. "I don't want to watch your hit on replay."

"But I'm right here!" He put an arm around her shoulders.

"I know you are." A soft hand landed on his stomach. "Does it hurt here?"

"No, baby."

She swept her hand a bit lower. "Here?" Her fingers teased the sensitive skin just north of his sweatpants.

He chuckled. "I'm not sure. Touch me some more so I can figure it out."

Georgia slid her hand right underneath the waistband and wrapped her hand around his thickening cock.

"Ahh," he said, surprised. "No pain there."

"Good." She released him, sadly. But then she got off

the bed again and went over to the hotel room door. He heard a clunk, which he decided was the sound of Georgia repositioning that U-shaped barrier lock which frequently appeared on hotel room doors.

Yesssss. A nice little wave of lust rolled down Leo's groin just hearing it. And when Georgia came back to the bed, he reached for her again.

"No," she whispered, steering his hands away. "Just let me take care of you tonight." Then she reached into his sweats and pulled out his dick. "Mmm," she said, licking her lips. She leaned down and tongued the head of his cock.

Leo exhaled in a great gust. And when she opened her mouth and took him in, he pressed his back into the pillows behind him. "So fucking nice," he rasped, gathering her silky hair in one hand. She released him, but then licked him from root to tip. "Whew," he said, beginning to tingle everywhere. "Are you sure you don't want me to . . ."

Georgia chose that moment to swallow him, and he couldn't finish the sentence. She was working him over, and it was so, so good. When he finally caught his breath, he made another suggestion. "Flip around. There's only a skirt and some stockings in my way."

She shook her head, then tongued his tip. She raised her chin, and the view was straight out of his fantasies. His girl between his legs, looking up at him with lust in her eyes. "You've had a long night. Just let me soothe you. Tell me how you like it."

As if she didn't know. "I like it from you. That's how I like it."

"Mmm," she said, dropping a hand to cup his balls. Then she bent over him again, taking him into her heavenly mouth. She gave a good, hard suck, and Leo sank into the pleasure of it. He was a lucky, lucky man, and not about to forget it.

TWENTY-THREE

TOP TEAM HEADLINE:

"Bruisers to Face Boston,
Washington, and Rangers in Home Game Spree"
—New York Post

Going home to Brooklyn the following day had been a relief. But Georgia was still swamped at work. So on Saturday morning she went in to the office for a few hours to finish what she hadn't gotten done the previous day. But even that wasn't enough. There were still two hundred unopened e-mails in her inbox by the time it grew dark outside. There were media requests to answer and player bios to update. And the head of Nate's charitable foundation wanted to put the finishing touches on their next benefit dinner, slated for the following week.

She was still there at seven when the GM stuck his head in her office door. "Everything okay? When I see a publicist working on a Saturday night, I think, *scandal*." He chuckled.

"Everything is fine, Hugh," she said quickly. "Really."

He frowned. "You must need some help, though. We've been busy with the trade deadline approaching, but we need to find someone else for publicity."

"I'm good for now," Georgia said quickly.

Hugh gave her a thoughtful nod. "You're a really good sport is what you are. G'night."

Georgia listened to his footsteps retreating, then called Becca's Katt Phone. "Fire up the dumpling cannons," she said when her roommate answered. "It's been a long day, and I'm going to need some trash TV to relax."

"Buddy, I already ordered for you. Jade dumplings and spring rolls from Thai Me Up."

"Yes!"

"I won't be home, though. I have a date."

"Um, what?" Georgia wasn't sure she'd heard correctly.

Becca laughed. "You don't have to sound *so* shocked. I just figured you'd be spending all kinds of time with Leo now. And it made me realize I needed to get out more. So I let my sister fix me up with one of her coworkers. We're all going to a comedy club in Chelsea."

"Wow. Have a great time."

"I plan to. Get your butt home, though, because— dumplings. And I'm leaving another little surprise for you on the sofa."

"What is it?"

"Just come home." Becca hung up on her.

Motivated by dumplings, Georgia shut her computer down and finally left the empty office building. She hurried across the cobblestones and into her apartment building, then jogged up the stairs. She unlocked the door and pushed it open. "Hi, honey, I'm home!"

"Awesome," a voice answered. But it did not belong to Becca.

Georgia's heart did a backflip with a double twist. She peered around the corner to find Leo relaxing on the sofa in tight jeans and a form-fitting thermal shirt, drinking a beer. "Well hello there," she said, suddenly shy.

His smile was so warm that some of the strangeness of

the moment evaporated. "I rang your buzzer about a half hour ago, and Becca told me to just come up."

You can ring my buzzer anytime. Georgia's eyes got a little stuck on the long, muscular legs propped onto her coffee table. "No plans tonight?" she asked.

"Oh, I have a few," he said, his brown eyes flashing. "But you should eat your dinner before it gets cold. Becca left it in the kitchen."

Georgia's tummy fluttered as she scurried off to find the Thai food that Becca had left her. There was a note on the bag. *I won't be home until midnight.*

Everyone had big ideas for her evening.

She made a plate for herself and carried it into the living room, taking the spot beside Leo.

"Nice apartment," he said.

"It's cozy. That's Brooklyn for 'small.'"

"The brick fireplace is neat, though. Santa can visit you."

Georgia offered her plate to Leo, but he shook his head. "I went to Grimaldi's with Silas. He said I needed initiation into the Brooklyn pizza cult."

"Nice. You can lord it over DJ, too."

Leo grinned. "My brother, the pizza snob. Can't believe you two have kept in touch. That's cool."

"I love that kid," Georgia admitted.

Georgia took a bite of her first dumpling, and it got quiet between them. There had been many times during the past six years when she'd imagined how nice it would be to have Leo sitting beside her on the sofa. Now that he was actually here, she didn't know what to say. The silence felt heavy, and it gave her a twinge of nerves. Maybe there was only so much separation a relationship could bear before it collapsed under its own weight.

"This is a spectacularly ugly couch," Leo offered.

Smiling at him, Georgia relaxed by a couple degrees. "We call it the Beast. No uglier upholstery has ever been sighted this side of the Rockies. But it's comfortable as hell."

He lifted his eyebrows suggestively. "I'll bet."

Georgia felt her neck get hot. "Can I put on a movie?"

"Sure. Anything you want." He put a hand on her knee.

"Even a chick flick?" she teased.

Her knee received a squeeze. "I really miss you, Gigi. If you're going to let me crash your Friday night, you can put on *My Little Pony* for all I care."

"Let's not get carried away." She chose *Working Girl*, which she knew by heart, and sat back to watch the opening montage. The camera swept past the Statue of Liberty and New York Harbor. There were glimpses of the very Brooklyn shoreline where she and Leo now sat. And she'd always had a thing for Carly Simon's anthem about chasing dreams. This was her go-to pick for the evening after a tough week.

The weight of Leo's hand on her leg was almost as delicious as the dumplings she munched. She was living out her fantasy right now—holed up with Leo at home after a long day.

When she finished eating, Leo paused the film so she could clear her plate. She stopped on her way to the kitchen. "Can I bring you a drink? I say that not knowing what the choices are. I've been out of town . . ." That and they rarely had visitors. But she kept that to herself.

"I brought a six-pack," he said, holding up his empty bottle. "I noticed you don't drink."

"I drink at *home*," she argued, taking the empty from him. Though she never felt like drinking in public. A rape survivor was never supposed to blame herself for what had happened, and Georgia didn't. Many hours of therapy had made it clear that the only one responsible for a rape was the rapist. But that didn't mean she was comfortable with the idea of losing control in a place where she was vulnerable . . .

Leo studied her, his head tilted to the side, as if considering whether he wanted to ask a follow-up question. "Bring two, then," he said instead. And then his mouth curved into a smile that made her knees feel a little squishy.

She retreated to the kitchen to rinse her plate. The weirdness of having Leo back in her life hadn't worn off yet, even if he seemed immune to discomfort. *You're mine,*

Georgia Worthington. In between phone calls at work today, those words had bounced around in her head. They were exciting and more than a little terrifying. She wanted him. And there was little doubt in her mind where the night was headed. If Leo wanted to take her to bed, she wasn't about to say no.

But she wasn't quite as sure as he was that they were embarking on a forever-night-stand. She'd used the word "forever" with Leo before, and life had gotten in the way. She wasn't that naive anymore. There weren't any promises that couldn't be broken, even by people as wonderful as Leo.

She uncapped two beers and brought them to the living room. "The Brooklyn Brewery, huh?" she asked, handing one over.

"When in Rome," he said, patting the sofa cushion next to him.

Georgia started the movie again, hip to hip with Leo. After they finished their beers, he wrapped his arms around her, pulling her back to his chest. As the film progressed, he spread one big hand across her stomach. His fingers began to gently caress her ribcage. The light touch made her shiver.

Those naughty fingertips continued their ministrations, and then his thumb traced the swell of each breast. Georgia began to tingle *everywhere.* It wasn't long before she lost track of the film, her attention focused entirely on his touch, until her breasts felt heavy and overly sensitive in the confines of her bra.

But Leo's attention was on the screen, and he continued to laugh in all the right places, even as his fingers dipped lower. He skimmed the ticklish part of her belly, making her stomach muscles clench. Then his hand slid down between her legs and he just let it rest there, its heat seeping through the black skirt she'd worn to work today. Waiting.

She forgot to exhale. And when his hand finally retreated, she let out a shaky breath.

"I like this part," Leo said.

"Wha?" Her eyes swam over to the screen, where

Melanie Griffith was at the bar wearing Sigourney Weaver's dress. Harrison Ford paid her a compliment. And when everyone's favorite working girl said, "I have a head for business and a bod for sin," Leo echoed the line into Georgia's ear.

Check, please. With a whimper, she arched her body back against his, turned her head and kissed his neck. If his plan had been to ease her into the idea of fooling around, it had worked. She turned toward him and slung one knee over his.

"Hey, I'm trying to watch this movie," Leo complained with a chuckle. But his very hard cock argued otherwise. She ran a hand down his chest and palmed him, rubbing.

He groaned with appreciation, then kissed her. She forgot all about the movie then. Harrison who? There was only Leo and his big arms encircling her. She slanted her head to the side to improve the angle of their kiss and dove right in.

But Leo was in the mood to take his time. His lips slid over hers with sweet deliberation. He tasted her lower lip, then nibbled on it. Then he moved on to her upper lip, teasing and tasting it.

Georgia felt herself growing more impatient by the minute. So she tugged on the hem of his T-shirt, lifting it over his head.

Leo laughed. "Do you always get naked in your living room?"

Only when you're here. "Becca won't be home for hours."

"I see," he whispered, his voice like smoke. Beneath her, his superhero torso rippled as he lifted his arms to catch her in another kiss. She leaned in, eager for more. But again, he tasted her slowly, like she was a fine wine he was trying to evaluate, when she wished he'd just gulp her down like a Gatorade before an overtime period.

As they kissed, his big hands began to wander her body, his touch reverent. Georgia could work with that. She stroked his pecs and tweaked his nipples, earning a groan for her trouble. Their kisses grew deeper, and she began to float into a lovely place of pure arousal, where nothing mattered but this.

"Gigi?"

"Hmm?"

"Was it easy for you to have sex again after you . . ." He bit the end of the sentence off.

Noooo! her libido complained. *That* topic would only put her happy, sexy bubble in danger of bursting. Georgia leaned down and kissed him again, ignoring the question. He opened for her immediately, and she accepted the invitation, deepening the kiss. He tasted like the local lager. He tasted like happiness.

But when they came up for air, he pulled his head back and looked at her. "I need to know, Gi. So I don't do the wrong thing."

"You won't." She went in for another kiss, but he caught her cheek in his palm.

"I *love* you. And we are going to have *so much sex*. On, like, every surface of this apartment. But I'm asking for a little guidance, here."

For a few moments, Georgia just basked in that sentence. *I love you.* He'd said the thing that she was reluctant to admit. It just popped out of his mouth, the words easy and kind. She'd also enjoyed the *so much sex* part, too.

She did not, however, want to talk about her attack or her subsequent sexual history. The first thing was a libido killer, and the second was just embarrassing.

With a groan, she put her forehead against his. "I'm asking you not to bring that up. Because talking about it with you is . . ." *The only thing I'll admit to being afraid of.* ". . . not fun."

"I'm sure that's true." His thumb swept across her cheek, which felt divine. If only he'd stop talking. "But you never actually told me what happened to you in Florida. There's a lot I don't know."

"In Florida we lost to Tampa."

"Georgia," he chided softly. "Please."

Her temper flared. Her heart stamped its impatient foot and asked, *Didn't I just ask you not to go there?* "Please?" she squeaked. "I'll show you *please*. Please don't make me talk about this right now. Why would you want to?" The only reason she and Leo were fooling around again after all these years was because the ugly past had finally faded. Bringing it up again was just going to put them both right back to that unhappy place—holding hands on the sofa in her father's den, watching sports on TV and feeling sorry for each other.

That's where true love went to die.

"Baby, it's necessary," he whispered, his brown eyes sincere. And sincerely infuriating.

"The hell it is!"

Leo leaned back against the sofa, his brow furrowed. "Look, I really don't want to fight." He squeezed his beautiful eyes shut and then opened them again. "I wasn't asking you to rehash the blow by blow. All I asked was whether it was difficult for you now."

Well, damn. *Point Leo.* Though his question was another can of worms. "Did I make it look difficult the other morning in Phoenix?"

His chest bounced with a quick laugh. "No, baby. But you were in control then. See . . ." He tucked her head against his collarbone, lowering his lips to her ear. Then he began to whisper. "I have big plans for you." His breath tickled her ear. "I need to know if I can strip off your clothes and push you down on the bed and have my way with you. I want to feel you underneath me when I make you come."

Every nerve in Georgia's body quivered. "So let's practice that. I'm free now."

His hands slid around to her ass and squeezed. "Okay. But you didn't answer my question." He grabbed her waist and rolled onto his side, so they were face to face on the sofa. "So help me out here."

Grrrr. "Leo, you may be a ninja, and that's hot and everything." He grinned. "But I'm not a fearful person, and I don't see why we have to rehash our recent sex lives. I don't particularly want to hear about yours. And there's nothing to hear about mine. Absolutely nothing, okay? And thanks for making me say that."

His brown eyes widened. "You can't mean . . ."

She banged her head back into the couch cushion and groaned. "So what if I didn't have sex for six years? It's probably not even a world record. I wasn't terrified, okay? It just . . . there wasn't anyone I wanted to go there with."

Leo didn't say anything for a minute. But he lifted her hand and kissed her palm. "I'm sorry to pry."

"Your inner caveman likes my answer, though." She gave his ankle a little kick. "Admit it."

He rolled over on top of her, his big eyes looking down at her, his gorgeous shoulders in full view. "My inner caveman?"

"Yeah," she breathed, her tummy quivering at the gorgeous view of his bare, muscular shoulders hovering over her. "Don't deny that a little part of your fragile male ego is beating on its chest right now." He gave a snort, and his beautiful eyes crinkled with humor. Maybe she'd only had sex with one man in her life, and some people would consider that pathetic. It wasn't, though. She knew she'd been spoiled in the best possible way. The man lying on top of her right now was the MVP. No question.

"My inner caveman wants you naked, no matter the circumstances," he said.

She reached up to touch that gorgeous face. "You *say* that. But there was a time when all we did was think about the shitty things that happened to me. And—coincidence— we stopped having sex completely. It's really no wonder I don't want to go back to that awful time when you didn't want me."

Leo's eyes went wide. "Hang on a minute, missy. There has *never* been a day when I didn't want you."

Georgia dropped her head onto the cushion and sighed. She ought to be glad that Leo remembered it that way. But the sting of rejection still gnawed at her. "We didn't fool around for *months*," she whispered. "I'd try to kiss you, and after a minute you'd turn away." It had been the worst feeling in the world. And damn if her eyes didn't grow damp from the awful memory.

Above her, Leo's brow furrowed. "Well, no kidding. It wasn't the right time. But not because I didn't want to."

"Well I did." She hated the gruff, unhappy sound of her own voice.

"*Georgia*," he gasped. "What did you expect me to do? I wasn't going to be like, hey, baby, I know you're freaked out from being *violated*, but I'm used to gettin' it regular."

She turned to hide her face in the world's ugliest sofa cushion. It had been a mistake to bring this up.

Leo wasn't going to let it go, though. "Baby, look at me."

Slowly, she turned around to find him waiting for her with soft eyes. "It was a long time ago," she said.

"Yes and no." He leaned down and kissed her on the nose. "Sometimes when I look at you, it feels like five minutes. But I was just a punk-ass kid back then. I didn't know what to say to you then. I didn't know how to ask you about this. I wanted so badly to be a man for you. But I had no clue how to do that."

Crap, now her eyes were leaking. "You *were*, though. You were so patient with me, and I didn't appreciate it. I was afraid that you thought I was gross."

"No," he crooned, pulling her close. "God, I was so afraid to say the wrong thing. I was just so fucking scared. So I just stuck to you like glue and prayed for it to just get easier."

"It didn't, though. And I got so sick of being scared together, and waiting around for things to get better. It was like we spent two months at a funeral."

With gentle fingers he tucked a stray piece of hair behind her ear. "Is that why you dumped me?"

Was it? "I guess so. I felt ugly and all wrong. You and I weren't the same anymore. That stung."

Leo shook his head. "I'm so sorry."

"Me, too." She tried to flick her tears away. But they were stubborn.

"I think we could have saved ourselves a lot of pain if we'd talked it through."

"Because that's so much fun," Georgia said with a sniffle.

He chuckled, and she loved hearing it. Laughing is something they hadn't done that awful spring six years ago. "Let's never be eighteen again."

"Deal." Georgia snuggled closer to him. It was quiet enough to listen to his heartbeat.

"I want you to know that you can tell me the bad stuff, though," he said eventually. "I don't scare so easy anymore."

"Okay." She was all talked out, though. So she lifted her lips to Leo's jaw and dropped the gentlest of kisses there. Then she moved up slowly, his stubble teasing her lips. She kissed a path to his ear, nibbling on his earlobe.

Leo purred like a happy cat. He caught her cheek and tugged her into a kiss.

Yes, finally, Georgia inwardly chanted. *This*. She pulled him down onto her body and tried to put the old disappointments behind her once and for all.

TWENTY-FOUR

Go slow, Leo ordered himself. Georgia had said she was comfortable with this, and he believed her. But now that he'd been given the green light, he was raring to go. They finally had a night together at home—no interruptions. He wanted to make it last.

His girl was done being patient with him, though. Breaking their kiss, she sat up and shed her own top. Then she went for his belt, yanking the end of the strap out of the buckle.

Leo pitched in to help. "You'll tell me if I do anything you don't like?"

She put one palm in the center of his chest, and when she looked him in the eye, there was fire there. "I've never been afraid of you, and I'm not starting tonight."

Schwing! He'd always enjoyed getting schooled by Georgia. "Maybe it's time I got the tour of your bedroom." He pulled her onto his lap and then stood up.

Startled, Georgia yelped with surprise and then clung to him like a cat. "It's that one," she said, pointing.

Whatever. As long as there was a bed. He carried her around the hideous couch and into the dark room beyond.

"Watch out for . . ."

Something collided painfully with his toe. "Oof!"

". . . My suitcase," she finished.

Leo nudged the suitcase away and pressed onward. Light reflected from neighboring buildings spilled into her window, illuminating his destination—the bed. He set her down on the edge, and she went immediately to work on his fly. The metallic sound of the zipper made him even harder than he already was. Nobody could ever rile him up like Georgia could. She had always been fearless in bed, and to think that she was so eager to do this after all that had happened made him so fucking happy that he could die.

Soft but determined hands shoved down his jeans and boxers, exposing him to the cool air in the room. Immediately, Georgia grabbed his hips in two hands. Leaning forward, she licked the underside of his cock. "Oh my fucking god," he panted, wrapping a palm around the back of her head just to ground himself in the dark. She made a soft, happy sound and then engulfed him with her mouth. "Jesus," he said with a chuckle. "It's so good the way you take me. First time you ever did that? I knew I was the luckiest guy alive."

Georgia popped off him with a laugh. "I sure as hell didn't know what I was doing, then."

She *had* known, though. Maybe they didn't have any technique when they were teenagers, but it hadn't mattered. She'd *cared*, and it made all the difference.

Now she slipped a thumb over his sensitive tip, proving she knew *exactly* what was what. "I remember you were lying on the seat of your truck making noises like the world was ending. Best thing ever."

Ungggh. It really was.

Before he was ready, she parted her lips and enveloped him again, her hot mouth taking him all the way to the back of her throat. Leo exhaled with pleasure and surprise. Georgia gave a good, hard suck and his hand tightened instinctively on her hair. "You're killing me. I want all your clothes off, babe. Right now." Georgia moaned in agreement, and the vibration around his cock made him clench all his muscles in earnest. And when she backed off him, he couldn't resist giving his hips one delicious pump, and they both groaned.

"Okay," Georgia whispered finally. She grabbed the waistband of her skirt and fumbled with the button. He tugged it down and tossed it on the floor. There was enough street light coming through her window that he could see the heated gleam in her eye. His girl needed him, and Leo was just the man for the job.

He kicked out of the pants around his ankles and toed off his socks. Then he tapped Georgia's knee. "I want these gone."

Her hungry eyes held his while she shimmied out of her tights and panties. Her skin shone pale in the ambient light coming through the window. When she lay back on the bed, the smooth, curving line of her body was broken only by the little black bra she wore. He dropped a hand to her ankle then ran his palm up her shin, giving her knee a squeeze. "You have never looked more beautiful to me than you do right now."

"Then get over here," she said, nudging his leg with her toe.

Yes, ma'am. He climbed onto the bed, stretching out beside her, and she rolled to meet him. There was nothing tentative about their kiss. It skipped all the warm-up drills and went straight to a friendly scrimmage. Leo cupped her bare ass with his hand and squeezed. Georgia retaliated by running a hand down his body to cup his balls. When she rolled them gently in her hand, he groaned into her mouth.

Two could play at that game. He rolled onto his back, taking her with him. She dove in for the next kiss, and he spread her legs with his knees. With two hands, he dragged his fingertips tautly down her back. When she made a little whimpering sound he slid a palm over her butt and dropped his hand between her legs.

She was so wet that they both moaned.

"Christ," he whispered, giving his fingers free rein to touch and tease her. Though trying to torture her had surely backfired, because he was now as hard as a fencepost and so eager that it hurt. His thumb circled slowly, and she began to ride his hand. Her kisses lost focus. She was close. He could feel it.

Leo withdrew his hand, causing Georgia to growl. He kissed the corner of her mouth with a chuckle. "If you're okay with it, I want to feel you underneath me."

"Do it," she panted, sliding off his body, onto her back.

He sat up and knelt between her legs. Lifting one of her knees, he straightened her leg until her calf lay on his shoulder. Then he tugged her hips toward his body. He lined himself up at the door to paradise and pushed himself home.

The sensation of coming together was so intense that they both gasped. Below him, Georgia's lips parted as she tipped her head back, her arms outspread.

Looking down at her this way for the first time in years, it was hard to catch his breath. He'd been worried that time and circumstance had severed their connection. But there was so much trust on her blissed-out face right now. *We're going to be okay*, he allowed himself.

She caught him staring, and she tucked her hands behind her head. "Never saw you hesitate in the middle of a game before." She gave her hips a push, and he damn near shuddered with joy. "Where's your hustle?"

Leo smiled. Hugging her knee against his chest, he rocked his hips. The motion was subtle, but it emphasized all the places they were touching. The sensation amazed him—he could feel every soft particle of her body holding him. She was the only one he'd ever fucked without a condom, and he was grateful as hell that he'd saved that for her. He wanted nothing between them ever again. Forget hockey. He was going to do only this, forever.

Georgia moaned. "Yes. *More*." She ground down against him, and Leo's balls tightened. Okay, so doing this forever wasn't going to work out. Ten minutes would be a challenge if she made that sound again.

"Why are you so far away?" Georgia sighed. She lifted her arms, reaching for him. "Kiss me already."

"Soon," he teased. "I like the view from here." But he was just stalling. He knew if he could feel her sweet body underneath him, and her plundering kisses, it would be all over but the crying. Georgia turned him into a teenager again. Maybe they'd lost six years together, but his body didn't know that.

Georgia gave a sexy thrust, and he felt his pulse kick up a notch. Then she lifted her hands to play with her breasts, and he had to take a deep, slow breath in order to stay where he was. His girl knew she had his attention, too. He knew that even before she gave him a secretive smile and then slid a hand down her own body to the place where they were joined. She rubbed herself, and her fingertips brushed against his root, and he had to grit his teeth to keep from blowing his load right then and there.

But it was too soon, because he needed her closer.

Leo grabbed her naughty hand. In one smooth motion he eased her leg down to the bed and then stretched out over her body. When they were nose to nose, skin to skin, he kissed her, sliding his tongue into her tempting mouth. Georgia moaned and lifted her knees to squeeze his hips.

There was something primal about this position—his girl underneath him, right where she belonged. And since she was still making happy, encouraging noises, holding back was no longer an option. He had to move, had to fuck her in earnest. He jacked his hips while she panted into his mouth.

"*Leo*," she gasped. Her body squeezed him everywhere at once, and the sound of his name on her lips made him feel like a god.

That was all she wrote.

The next thing he knew, he was thrusting and shooting and roaring with sweet victory. A moment later he did a face-plant in her pillow while her arms clamped around his neck. Then they just lay there, breathing hard, wrapped up in each other.

And everything was right with the world.

TWENTY-FIVE

Grinning like an idiot into the darkness, Georgia did not want to let go of the big, sweaty man who had collapsed onto her body. There was nothing better than this. Especially because he didn't seem to want to let go, either. After they'd both calmed down, he made no move to untangle himself from her. Instead, he just rolled them both to the side and tucked her against his chest. His fingers threaded into her hair and he let out a sigh of contentment.

After a while Georgia began to drift into the drowsy, half dreams of the sexually satisfied.

"I want to stay," he whispered, waking her.

"Mmm." She sighed. "I'll find you a toothbrush."

"I brought mine."

She pinched his hip. "Awfully sure of yourself."

"I don't hear you complaining."

Point Leo. "You go first. Use anything you need in the bathroom."

While he was in there, she put on an oversized Bruisers T-shirt, then spent thirty seconds wishing she had sexy nightgowns like Becca's. But she wasn't a sexy nightgown kind of girl, and there was really no use pretending she was.

Leo shuffled back into the room a minute later, naked, and climbed into her bed. When she joined him after brushing her teeth, his eyes were closed. But he reached for her anyway, folding his arm around her body, pulling her close. His hand snaked up under the shirt, and he made a sound of approval. "I like this," he said with sleepy lips. "Good access to the tatas. Night," he said, giving her left a gentle squeeze. "Night," he repeated, cupping the other.

She fell asleep with a smile on her face. And she would have stayed that way, except some time later her phone began to vibrate beside the bed. She opened one eye. It was pitch dark in her bedroom except for the phone's glow. She closed it again, deciding that the phone was unimportant. Not only was she sleepy, she was warmer and more comfortable than usual. Leo's big body was stretched out beside her.

Heaven.

The damned phone buzzed again. Nobody called her in the night. In fact, she was pretty sure she'd set it to be silent after eleven PM, except for a couple of crucial phone numbers.

Crap.

Georgia woke up all the way now. If her phone was making noise, that meant it was important. She reached for it when the apartment's buzzer rang. Maybe Becca was locked out?

She swung her legs out of bed, grabbed the phone, and padded into the living room. The phone's screen said *Missed Call: Dad.* She tapped redial. While she waited for the call to connect, she noted that Becca's door was closed. So her roommate was home . . .

"Honey?" her father said into her ear. "Can I come up?"

"What? Why? It's . . ." She couldn't see any clocks. "Late," she guessed.

He chuckled. "I know, and I'm sorry. But I went out drinking and missed the last train to Huntington."

"Where's your car?" Georgia asked.

"Can't drive it," her father muttered. "For a skinny guy, Nate sure can drink. I don't know where he puts it."

"You're at the front door?" she asked, finally catching on.

Her father intended to crash in her apartment. Where Leo was currently sleeping naked in the bedroom. Holy hell.

"Yeah, honey. I promise not to make a habit of this." He gave a drunken chuckle.

Georgia leaned on the button which opened the door downstairs. "Tell me when you're in."

"I'm in."

She disconnected the call and then scurried into her bedroom for the extra set of sheets and the blanket she kept for visitors.

"Wha's the matter?" Leo asked sleepily.

"Nothing," she hissed. "Can you do me a favor? Be absolutely silent? My dad is on his way up."

"'Kay," Leo said sleepily.

She left her bedroom, pulling the door partially shut, then scrutinizing it, hoping it looked like it was *casually* half closed. When a tap came on the apartment door, she opened it to admit her father.

"Hi, Princess," he said, with a little slur. "Never drink with people half your age."

"I'll try to remember that." She moved over to the world's ugliest couch and dropped the folded sheet onto it. Holy hell. There were clothes all over the floor. Thank God it was pretty dark in here. Panicking, she kicked Leo's big shoes under the couch. "Why don't you use the bathroom? There's, uh, an extra toothbrush in the medicine cabinet. In the package. You can't miss it."

"Thanks," her father mumbled. "Dental hygiene isn't my biggest issue right now. You got any Advil?"

"Help yourself."

As soon as he lumbered into the little bathroom, Georgia dove for Leo's belt and their shirts. She scooped them into her arms and carried them into her bedroom, depositing them on the chair in the corner. How had she turned into someone's misbehaving teenage daughter again? This was ridiculous.

Back in the living room, she shook out the sheets and the blanket and put a pillowcase onto one of her throw pillows. It wasn't the Plaza Hotel, but her father could just deal with it.

"Thanks, honey," he said when he emerged from the bathroom. "Sorry to wake you. I really appreciate the favor. We were right in the neighborhood . . ."

"I get it." She sighed. "Sleep tight."

"I'll take you out for brunch tomorrow as a thank-you."

"Uh, thanks. Good night."

Damn it. There went her lazy morning in bed with Leo. Her heart thumping guiltily, Georgia tiptoed back into her own room and shut the door all the way. She slipped into bed again.

Leo rolled onto his side and pulled her in. "Hey. You okay?"

"Shh!" she whispered into his ear. "He's right on the other side of that door!"

He was quiet, but she could feel his belly shake with laughter. Then he put his lips right up to her ear, his voice a low growl. "Ours is the love that dares not speak its name. Does this mean there won't be any morning nookie?"

"Leo," she warned in the lowest voice she was capable of using. "Please. He can't know."

He licked her earlobe. "Are you ashamed of me?"

"No!"

Still chuckling, he pressed his face against her cheek. "Is it awful that I just want to be outed? You're mine, Gigi. I don't care who knows."

"Just a little while longer," she mouthed. "The trade deadline is *soon*. I don't want to lose you."

Leo rolled on top of her. "Okay," he whispered. "But I'd sure like to make a whole lot of noise right now." He kissed her neck.

She wrapped her arms around him and sighed. It really *was* such a pity.

When Georgia woke up next, there was plenty of sunlight in her room. And she was alone in the bed.

Shit!

She sat up fast, listening. She heard her father snoring on the sofa. And then the flush of the toilet. There was the creak of the bathroom door, followed by someone moving carefully through the apartment.

A moment later Leo slipped into the bedroom again, wearing his boxers and nothing else except a grin. It was a fine sight, but it still made Georgia anxious. He closed the door behind him, then crawled onto the bed, pushing Georgia down into the mattress.

"He could have seen you!" she whispered.

"The man is sawing logs out there," Leo said, nuzzling her ear. "I need to get going home, though, while the getting's good."

Except he didn't go. Instead, he began to drop gentle kisses onto her cheekbone. One of his hands wandered under the covers, skimming up her knee, sliding onto her thigh . . . It was the stuff of fantasies. Waking up with Leo on a weekend morning.

With her father in the next room.

Sigh.

She gave him a little shove on the chest. "Behave," she whispered.

He gave her a naughty smile. But then he got up and grabbed his jeans off the chair.

"Your shoes are under the couch," Georgia whispered. "That end," she said, pointing.

When he was finished dressing, Leo patted his pockets for his phone and keys. Then he kissed Georgia on the head. "I'll call you later."

She caught his scruffy face in two hands and held on just a moment longer. "Okay. Sorry about breakfast."

"Next time."

She stood up to watch him make his escape.

Leo slowly opened the bedroom door one more time. Her father's snores were loud, with a nice big honk at the end of each one, just like in a cartoon. Leo tiptoed over to the end of the couch and bent down. He slowly drew out first one shoe and then the other. He hooked two fingers into the heels and slowly rose.

That's when everything seemed to happen at once.

Her father's snore gave an extra loud honk and then stopped—going absolutely silent. Leo froze midstep toward freedom. And Becca's bedroom door snapped open. "Hi . . ." she said before breaking off, probably picking up on Leo's awkward body language.

From the sofa, Georgia's dad coughed and rustled the sheets. She couldn't see him from where she stood, but it was the sound of a man waking up. She gestured frantically toward Leo and the door.

Leo had been a natural at sports all his life. He knew how to spot an opening, and how to take a shot before the opening slammed shut. So now he hustled toward the door.

"Morning, Becca!" Georgia said loudly and with false brightness. "Sleep okay? My dad is here."

Leo was out the door by the time she got to the end of that sentence. But Georgia flinched at the sound of the apartment door opening and closing.

"Um, yeah," Becca said, wide-eyed.

"Princess?" her father called. "You just come in?"

"Yup!" she said with too much enthusiasm. "Checked for the newspaper, but it wasn't down there yet."

He sat up. "What time is it?"

"Excellent question," she said, her heart still pounding. "I'll just find out."

She escaped to her room with a pounding heart. And three minutes later she got a one line text from Leo. *I'm home now, but I forgot something.*

What??? she replied, hoping her father wasn't just about to discover Leo's watch in the sofa cushions.

I didn't get to say good-bye to the tatas, damn it. I miss them.

She practically slumped with relief. *They miss you, too.* There were, in fact, quite a few of her body parts she would have liked for him to have visited this morning. But you can't have everything. Georgia got dressed slowly, then went to see how her father was doing.

"It's quarter to ten, Dad. You can take me to brunch anytime you're ready."

"Okay," he said, getting up off the couch. "I'll take all my roommates out. Where do you like to eat, Becca?"

Her roommate snickered. "Oh, I didn't realize you meant me."

Georgia glared.

"Right. Of course you meant me," Becca said. "Let me just get my handbag."

The next week was both wonderful and exhausting.

Georgia was still buried by work, and Leo had every player's relentless schedule of practice and home games. The team tied Boston and beat Washington, D.C., with Leo earning a goal and two assists.

In the PR office, things hummed along. The interview with Nate and her father went live on the front of the *Times* sports section. "A Young Billionaire and His Young Hockey Team." Nate seemed pleased enough with it, so Georgia was counting it as a win.

Even though it wasn't easy for Georgia and Leo to find time together, they solved this problem by staying up late into the night. The only fly in the ointment was Georgia's exhaustion. She wasn't used to staying up until the wee hours with Leo to catch up on six years of lost sex and then getting up early to catch up at the office on six days of lost work.

And even when Leo slept beside her, Georgia fought to stay awake. The sound of him breathing quietly in bed beside her was precious, too. The comfort of sharing a bed with the man she loved was an entirely new sensation. She looked forward to the warmth of his sleeping form, whether they were at her place or his.

On Thursday night Silas had gone out drinking, so she

and Leo had the run of the loft. They watched about seven minutes of television on the big screen before attacking each other on the leather sofa.

Later, Georgia had set her phone alarm for an early Friday wake-up. When it went off, she was very disciplined. She only spent one or two minutes admiring the godlike body asleep in the big bed beside her before tiptoeing off to the glamorous glassed-in shower stall in Leo's en suite bathroom. She washed and shampooed, but then the bathroom door opened and Leo appeared, naked. He stepped into the shower, then, without a word, dropped to his knees.

"Good morning," he rumbled, before reaching up to palm her backside in two big hands.

"Good . . ." she got out before he leaned forward and placed an open-mouthed kiss right at the juncture of her thighs. "Unnnngh," she said, splaying her hands out onto the tile wall for stability.

"Mmm," Leo said, the sound vibrating right in the center of her suddenly needy body. He pressed forward, his tongue making a pass right where it counted, and she dropped a hand into his wet hair and moaned.

She hadn't gotten to work today quite as early as she'd planned, after all. And she was still tired from their late night frolicking the night before. That's why coffee was invented.

But even better than caffeine was the spark of possibility each day now held. Even if she rarely glimpsed Leo at work, just having him nearby filled her with excitement. Who needed skydiving when your secret boyfriend just might turn the corner in your office corridor and give a secretive wink that made you blush? And since it was Friday, and all the bullpen kids were chattering about their weekend plans, nobody expected her to be sharp as a tack anyway.

She worked late, of course, because the media invite list for their upcoming charity banquet for a Brooklyn women's shelter was not going to organize itself. But by six it was quitting time, thank God. She'd finished the most dire items on her to-do list. Finally. Before she left for the night she had to return a file of information on Nate's foundation to Becca's desk, so at least her own desk would be a clean and orderly place when she sat down there Monday.

Once again, Georgia had stayed later than any of the minion mob. As she passed the outer office, all their computer monitors were dark, except for one still displaying a screensaver of O'Doul scoring the winning goal in a game against Detroit last year.

Her Chuck Taylors made no sound in the corridor as she crossed to the C-suite. Becca was long gone—her computer dark, too. But just as Georgia set the folder on Becca's desk, she heard Hugh Major's voice coming from behind his closed door. And she heard him say, "The call was Vancouver. They want to talk about the rookie. Trevi."

Georgia froze like a thief in the night. She ought to just turn and go, but there was no way she could stop herself from eavesdropping now.

There was a pause, and she assumed that Hugh was on the phone, listening to someone else talk. But then she heard her father's voice. "Yeah? They want to show us a trade?"

Goose bumps broke out on Georgia's neck.

"Yeah," Hugh confirmed, and her heart seized. "Might be a shit trade, though. If they read the blogs, maybe they think you have issues with that player. They're probably going to show us a crap deal just to see if we'll bite."

The next silence was lengthy. *Please don't*, Georgia begged inwardly. She didn't know if she was begging her father, the universe, or Leo himself. But Vancouver was really, really far away. She held her breath.

"Let's see what they've got," her father said. "Might be something we need."

Georgia's heart staggered, then fell down on the floor.

"You heading out?" Hugh asked. A shadow moved behind the frosted glass of the office door.

That unstuck Georgia from where she was frozen in place in the middle of the room. She slipped out and went back to her office alone.

She sat down at her desk. The building was so quiet she heard her chair creak. The silence was all too familiar. For a long time, Georgia had kept her own counsel, and silence was so common she'd stopped hearing it. *Guess I'd better get used to it again*, she coached herself.

For a little while there, life wasn't so quiet. She'd been so swept up in Leo she'd forgotten that good things didn't last.

Sitting there in her office chair, Georgia no longer saw the point of going home. So she lingered a little longer, chin propped into her hand, wondering what the hell was going to happen. And the more she thought about it, the more complicated the situation became.

She couldn't tell Leo what she'd overheard. In the first place, it was highly confidential. Secondly, it would only worry him. It might come to nothing, anyway. Most trades managers and coaches discussed never happened.

So why was she gut-wrenchingly sure that this one would?

Several more miserable minutes passed while she pictured Leo on a plane to British Columbia, where the coach wanted him, and would give him more playing time immediately. She swore under her breath. If she leaked the news to Leo, he might actually do something rash, like throw himself at the mercy of her dad to stay in Brooklyn, thereby squandering the chance to play for a team that would let him reach his full potential.

Or, even more terrifying, he might *not* do that. He might leap happily on the first Air Canada flight and wave from the window.

Jesus lord, she couldn't decide which sounded worse.

Even though it was already six, her computer dinged with one last e-mail for the day. *Figures*. It was from Hugh Major, so she opened it.

Hey, Georgia—on Monday afternoon I'm
interviewing this candidate to add to our publicity
staff. On Monday morning would you let me know
what questions you'll have for him? Have a great
weekend!

Reluctantly, Georgia double-clicked on the resume that
Hugh had attached. *Please let her be a nineteen-year-old
intern*, she prayed.

Unfortunately, the candidate was a thirty-one-year-old
guy, currently the associate director of publicity for an
AHL team in the Midwest. As she scrolled down the page,
her heart staggered into the basement and slumped against
the cold, hard floor. The candidate had a degree in marketing from the Wharton School, and he'd played college
hockey for North Dakota while starting his own T-shirt
business in his spare time.

It was a good thing Georgia hadn't met any mob contacts in Brooklyn, or she might have asked if anyone knew
a good hit man.

She grabbed her Katt Phone and texted Becca. *Summon
the dumpling delivery drones. I'll bring the wine.*

Then she put on her coat and headed outside. When she
reached her block of Water Street, she risked a look up at
the building where Leo had been living. She was just getting used to the idea of having him nearby. Now she'd have
to adjust again. That building would be just a building.
And at work, she'd never turn a corner and spot Leo's
handsome face smiling at a teammate. She'd never hear
his laughter echo from inside the locker room.

An ache bloomed in her chest. She crossed the street
and let herself into her own building, where she would
spend the evening panicking, just like in the bad old days.

TWENTY-SIX

TOP TEAM HEADLINE:

"Bruisers to Face Rangers in Subway Matchup"
—The Times

In the thick of the season, sometimes morning skate was listed as optional on the team schedule. Players who were exhausted from seeing the most playing time could opt out.

Leo knew better than to take a morning off, though. It was no use looking like a slacker when you were fighting to keep your job. So in spite of the fact that he'd gotten drunk late into the night at a birthday dinner for Bayer at Peter Luger's, he got himself up and out the door for a brutal practice first thing in the morning. Then he'd seen Ari, the massage therapist, and spent some time discussing stretches with the trainer.

Now it was noon, and in five hours he'd need to be at the rink for a game. But first he had to drive Silas's car to Long Island for his mom's birthday dinner. They'd scheduled it around him.

Grabbing his suit in a garment bag and his keys, he stopped to call Georgia.

"Hello?" her voice was soft in his ear.

"Hey, babe. Are you ready? I'll meet you out front in five."

There was a silence on the line. "Leo, I don't think it's a good idea for me to go home with you today."

Something in her tone made a chill rise up his spine. "Why? What's wrong?"

Georgia didn't answer right away. "I think we need to slow things down just a little. Just . . . take a step back for a couple of weeks."

"Um . . ." Leo had no idea what to say. The last time he'd seen Georgia they were fucking like porn stars in his shower, and she was yelling his name. "Baby, we have to go sing *Happy Birthday* to my mom. It's her fiftieth. And then we can talk about whatever's bothering you."

"I can't go," she whispered. "I'm so sorry."

She actually disconnected the call, and Leo stood there like an asshole with his Katt Phone pressed against his head, trying to make sense of what just happened.

Don't panic, he told himself. He grabbed his bag and ran out of the apartment, taking the elevator down to the lobby where the concierge was waiting with Silas's car. "I'll be just five minutes," he said. "Be right back."

He darted across the cobblestone street and leaned on Georgia's bell.

"Hello?" a female voice called down. The sound quality was so bad that he wasn't sure it was Georgia.

"It's Leo. I need to come up."

The door rattled with its unlocking buzz, and he yanked it open then sprinted up the stairs. It was Becca who opened the door. Wordlessly, she beckoned him inside. Then she tipped her head toward Georgia's bedroom door.

Leo walked over and stood in the doorway. Georgia sat on the edge of the bed in slacks and a soft sweater. Her bag was beside her, and her coat lay across her lap. "Babe? Looks like you're all ready to come with me."

She lifted worried eyes to his. "I don't think I should. Your family . . ." She let the sentence die.

". . . Loves you," he finished.

"I don't have a gift for your mom," she argued, her voice dull.

"No problem. I'm bringing her a jersey and her favorite bottle of wine. We're covered." Georgia didn't look convinced. "Did I mention that DJ made lasagna?"

"Lasagna?" Her stomach growled so loudly he could hear it across the room.

He took two steps into the room and held out a hand for her. "Like I said, I don't know what's bothering you. But let's not be late for dinner. There's probably a birthday cake from Reinwald's. Chocolate with raspberry filling. And if there's something you need to tell me, I'll listen." He held his breath, waiting.

Georgia sighed. But she put her hand in his and stood up. "I don't find it easy to resist you," she whispered.

Something warm bloomed in his chest as his hand closed around her smaller one. "The lasagna and birthday cake don't have a thing to do with it, I'm sure," he joked. "Let's go. The car is waiting."

They went downstairs and across the street. He held the passenger door open to the black Volkswagen Jetta, then ran around and got in on the driver's side. Georgia's reluctance had cost him fifteen minutes, and he didn't have time to spare.

"Nice ride," she said as he pulled away from the curb.

"It belongs to Silas. But I drove this same car all through college. DJ has it now."

"Oh." She frowned. "Weird. I can only picture you in that old truck."

"I sold it after you broke up with me."

"Why?" she asked.

"Too many memories. Every time I got in that truck, I thought of you. I swear it even smelled like you."

Georgia turned to look out the window, as if she didn't want to hear it. He didn't know what had frightened her today. But if she thought she could just slink away from their troubles without it mattering to him, she had another think coming.

They were in this together, damn it. That's what he should have said when they were eighteen. On the other hand, when a girl who's been raped tells you to stay away, you do it. Even if you don't want to.

This time would be different, though. They weren't kids anymore. He'd ask her to own up to whatever was bugging her out. Later, though. He'd give her a couple hours' reprieve. "This is the way to the Brooklyn-Queens Expressway, right?"

"You got it." They rode in silence for a moment until he accelerated onto the highway. "I need to stop at the florist before we get to your house. I can't show up empty-handed."

"Mom is going to do backflips when she sees you. She doesn't need a gift. You're it." He hadn't told his parents that he and Georgia were an item, either. It was so new, and kind of a secret. And he hadn't felt like answering anyone's questions.

Georgia was awfully quiet, and so Leo turned on the radio and tuned it to WBAB. This rock station was the sound of his high school life. He chuckled. "It's still there. Some things never change."

She didn't answer but he could almost hear the echo of her thoughts. *Some things do change, even when you don't want them to.*

They pulled up to the house almost on time, and Leo parked opposite a stretch limo with a driver reading the newspaper behind the wheel. That's how his brother's girl-friend, an honest-to-god movie star, traveled.

He took Georgia's hand as they strode up the driveway to the kitchen door of the two-story Tudor where he'd grown up. She'd been there a million times before. He wondered if it seemed strange to be there again after all that time.

Leo pushed open the door and stepped in. "Hey, Mom! Happy Birthday! How does it feel to be thirty?"

His mom turned around to smile at him, but when she saw Georgia, her happy expression faltered. "Georgia, honey!" She gasped. "My God." She put a hand up to her mouth.

A few feet away at the kitchen table, Leo's little sister Violet let out a shriek and dropped the knife she'd been using to cut up a tomato.

Beside him, he felt Georgia stiffen.

Okay—this was a lot more drama than he'd meant to cause. Obviously he should have tipped off his mom that Georgia was coming today. Now they were gaping at her.

"Guys," he said gently. "You're freaking Georgia out. She hasn't risen from the *dead*."

Mrs. Trevi dropped her hand. "I'm sorry. I'm just . . ." She wiped her hands on her apron. "I'm really happy to see you, honey." She came over and hugged the startled Georgia.

"Me, too!" called Violet, who piled on, laughing. Georgia was squeezed so hard that Leo feared for her ribcage. "You don't understand," Violet said. "Leo dated the most *horrible* girls in college. They were, like, awful people . . ."

"God, Vi. *Shut up*. Jesus Christ," he complained.

"Don't swear, Leo," his mother said.

Georgia disentangled herself from the Trevi women, looking more than a little embarrassed by the avalanche of affection. "Wow," she said, glancing around the kitchen, likely measuring how much was exactly the same. There was even a plaque on the wall that she'd given his mom for Christmas one year. *Raisins in Chocolate Chip Cookies Are Why I Have Trust Issues.* Her gaze landed on Violet, and then finally Georgia smiled. "God, when did you get so *beautiful*. It just isn't fair."

His sister beamed. "Stop! The last time you were here I had *braces*, for fuck's sake."

"Violet," his mom said. "No F-bombs in my kitchen."

"Hey! Guys!" His brother's voice called from the family room. "Can somebody bring me a beer? The game is on."

"Get it yourself!" Violet yelled.

"I'll do it," Georgia said. She walked over to the refrigerator and opened it.

"Get yourself something," his mother said. "Or I could open a bottle of wine."

"Soda is great," she said, grabbing a beer and a Diet Coke from the rack in the door.

And now Leo had his own little déjà vu moment. Because Georgia used to be comfortable here, in the kitchen with his family. They spent a lot of time here, especially when they were younger, before sneaking off to have sex became their favorite hobby.

Georgia passed him without a glance on her way into the den. She was obviously pissed at him for forcing this weirdly emotional moment on her today. There were still sore spots between them—old wounds that hadn't quite healed yet. He should have realized that before now. *It's exactly this easy*, he'd told her the other night.

Maybe that was wrong.

Leo followed Georgia into the den, where his brother sat on the L-shaped sofa with his girlfriend, facing the TV. DJ turned his head and spotted Georgia. "Holy shit! Gigi! This is awesome." He jumped up to kiss Georgia on the cheek. Then he gave her a big hug.

The sight of his brother's arms around her made Leo inexplicably ornery. He cleared his throat. "Georgia, meet Lianne. She's great in spite of her blind spot for my brother."

DJ flipped him off, and Lianne raised a fist for Georgia to bump.

"Hey, lady," Georgia said, meeting it with her own fist. "How are you? Got any new playlists for me? Your slacker boyfriend hasn't sent me anything for a while."

"You two have met?"

Georgia finally spared him a glance. "Yeah. We had dinner in Manhattan last summer." Her eyes asked, *Where were you?*

Good question. Everything would have been easier if he hadn't let six fucking years get between them. *Note to self. You aren't half as smooth as you think you are.*

Georgia handed DJ his beer. He patted the empty seat beside him. "C'mere. I always wanted *two* girlfriends."

"DJ," Georgia chided him. "That's not nice to Lianne."

"You hold him, I'll hit him," Lianne suggested.

"Deal."

"Don't make me spill my beer," DJ said, kicking his feet up onto the coffee table. Then he put one arm around each of the beautiful women on either side of him.

"Who's playing?" Georgia asked.

"Kentucky. They're undefeated heading into the playoffs."

"Yawn," Lianne said, and Georgia laughed.

Since Georgia looked relaxed for the first time in an hour, Leo turned around and went back into the kitchen. His mother and Violet were finishing up the salad at the kitchen table. "Get over here," Vi snapped when she saw him. "We need answers."

He fetched a beer for himself from the refrigerator and joined them at the table. He sat down and looked into their gleaming eyes. "What if we didn't make a big deal about it?"

Vi rolled her eyes. "Where's the fun in that? And we love Georgia. It was never the same around here after you two broke up."

Leo shrugged, feeling self-conscious. Until today, it hadn't occurred to him that his heartache had rippled through his family, too. "Georgia and I have been spending some time together. It's not a big deal."

"I think it is," his mother said softly. "I hope it works out. But if it doesn't, at least you tried."

Ouch. His mom was pretty astute. Maybe too astute. "Where's Dad?" he asked just to change the subject.

"DAD!" Vi yelled. "LEO'S HERE!"

There were footsteps overhead which eventually clomped down the stairs. "Hey," his dad said, cuffing him on the shoulder. "Does this mean we can eat DJ's lasagna now?"

"Guess what?" Vi crowed. "Georgia came to dinner."

His father frowned. "There's plenty. Can we eat it now?"

At least one person wasn't going to put Georgia in the spotlight. Thank God for his clueless dad.

"Do you people *deliberately* miss the point?" Violet asked, sliding out of her chair. "Get the silverware, Leo. I'll get the plates."

TWENTY-SEVEN

Georgia struggled through the meal, laboring hard to convey good cheer. But her smile felt pasted on. There were ghosts all around her. Sitting in the Trevi family dining room was like watching a 3-D movie of her younger life. Just stepping into their familiar kitchen gave her an ache, and Marion Trevi's tight hug had seared her.

Even so, DJ's excellent lasagna and Vi's salad went down easily. Because it was mealtime and her metabolism didn't take a day off just because she was stressed out.

But sitting in this cheery dining room with its striped cotton napkins and happy faces made the ache worse. She'd once felt like an adopted member of this family. It was something she'd needed back then, and she hadn't even known it.

Her dad was a good man and a good father, but their home had always been quiet. Even before her mother had died, Georgia had wished for a baby brother or sister to liven things up. But their luck had once run only in the other direction. When she thought back to the misty days of her childhood, it was amazing how high-functioning her father had really been in the face of tragedy. Even right after Mom passed, he'd kept up the Christmas traditions. He'd made it to all her school events and taken her on vacation. The loss must have been staggering, but he did it for her.

Even then she'd known not to complain. But her heart had always yearned for more family. And when she and Leo became an item in their high school days, she became a fixture at the Trevi table. She was sitting, in fact, in the very same seat that she'd had in the past—the one nearest the napkin holder shaped like a sailboat. Whenever there'd been a spill, she'd been the one to leap into action. There were frequent spills, because when the Trevi siblings argued they used their hands.

Stepping back into this room was like a window on everything she'd once given up. Meanwhile, she felt Leo sneaking worried looks at her from one seat away. And when she finally looked into his waiting eyes, all the warmth there made her heart do a pirouette of joy, followed by a sudden face-plant.

He was beautiful. She loved him. And he was probably going to live four thousand eight hundred miles away (thank you, Katt Phone) by the end of next week.

She wanted to curl up into a ball and cry. But instead she sang *Happy Birthday*, including the mandatory verse about smelling like a monkey in a zoo. Vi had actually put fifty extra-thin candles on the cake, and Mrs. Trevi complained that it was going to set the house on fire. But her eyes shone when her kids sang to her, and Georgia could hardly bear to watch while she blew them out with a big smile on her face.

Leo ran out to the car for the gifts he'd brought. The jersey was a huge hit, except with DJ.

"Great. The family's professional athlete brings Mom a jersey with our fricking name on it. You're making the rest of us look like assholes."

"Where's mine?" Violet demanded.

"It's not your birthday," Leo reminded her.

"Just don't get sent down to the minors before I turn twenty-one," she grumbled.

"Your faith overwhelms me," he returned.

And then all of a sudden it was time to get going. "I'll check the traffic," Mr. Trevi said, leaving the table to grab his iPad. "I think you'll be okay on the LIE."

People in other parts of the world talked about the weather. On Long Island, traffic was the subject of choice.

Georgia went to the front hall to find her coat, and DJ followed her. "You okay?"

"Yeah," she said quietly. Though apparently she hadn't hidden her discomfort very well, damn it. "It's been an overwhelming month."

"I bet it has." DJ wrapped her into a hug. "I'm always happy to see you. If my bonehead brother isn't treating you right, there's room in my harem."

She pinched him.

"Ow."

"Are you and Lianne coming to the game tonight?"

"Of course. You can expect a full critique of the music in the morning."

"Awesome." She gave him one more squeeze.

"Call me," he said in a low voice that betrayed his concern.

"I will."

She and Leo got into the car after another round of hugs and well-wishing. "We'll be right behind you! And look for us in section three!"

"I don't even know where that is," Leo confessed, kissing his mother good-bye. "So yell loudly."

They pulled out of Huntington and Georgia watched the familiar sights pass by. When they'd made it onto the expressway, Leo said, "Okay. Now tell me what's got you so upset."

Georgia fiddled with the zipper on her jacket. There were several good reasons preventing her from telling him what she'd overheard. Eavesdropping in the C-suite endangered her own job, and if he did something with that information, it would endanger his. But Georgia had come to realize that the phone call from Vancouver was only a wake-up call. If Leo did well for the Bruisers, there would only be more calls like that. He'd spent much of his twenty-four years trying to arrive at this moment, when his fledgling pro career was just about to launch.

A week ago, being with Leo had seemed as easy as falling into bed in their conjoined hotel rooms. Now it seemed impossibly complicated.

"Gigi," he prompted. "I need to know what you're thinking so hard about over there. What's this bullshit about taking it slow?"

He sounded a little angry, and she didn't blame him. Once upon a time things were always easy between them. They played tennis and Scrabble and gave each other orgasms. In the past few weeks she'd given him lots of tears and indecision instead.

"Things are going badly for me at work," she said, and it was true. "Hugh is interviewing someone on Monday that looks a lot like a replacement for me."

A mile or two went by before Leo spoke. "That sucks, baby. I'm sorry. But I don't see what that has to do with you and me."

Good question. "This job is really important to me. For two years it's been my whole life." That sounded a bit pathetic when said out loud, but again it was true. "I need to concentrate on keeping it."

"I get that you're afraid . . ."

"I'm never *afraid*," she argued before she could think better of it. Maybe it sounded petulant, but she really did hate that word.

"*Right.*" Leo's voice was frosty. "So you're saying I'm a distraction, then."

"True."

He switched lanes and passed two tractor trailers. A few miles later he spared a glance in her direction. "Distractions are good things. They're supposed to be, anyway."

Of course they were. He wasn't going to buy the bullshit she was selling. But there was no way out of this hole that she'd dug for herself. She couldn't tell him about the trade. And she couldn't pretend that it wasn't going to happen.

After the game tonight, Leo would want to see her. He'd want to peel off her clothes and make love and make plans for the future. She'd have to nod and smile and pretend that it wasn't all for nothing.

Georgia wasn't that good of an actress. And faking things with him was the very last thing she wanted to do.

More miles slid by. The lights of Brooklyn were in view when Leo spoke again. "The thing is, Georgia, I love you. A lot. I don't know what the hell is bothering you, or why you won't level with me. But if you ask me to leave you alone for a while, I'll have to abide by that. Under one condition."

"What?" It came out as a scrape.

"You're honest about why. The way I see it, there's only two reasons you're pushing me away. Either you're scared . . ."

"I'm *not* scared," she argued reflexively.

Leo surprised her by pulling over into a parking lot. They were a few minutes from home. He put the car in park and turned to face her. Reluctantly she met his big brown eyes. "I loved you when I was sixteen, and I told you when I was seventeen. When I was eighteen, you cut me loose. But I never stopped. If you're not scared, then maybe you don't feel the same way. Tell me right now. I can take it."

Ohhhhh shit. Do not cry. Georgia took a deep breath in through her nose. He was waiting, patient as ever. The one thing Georgia knew for sure in that moment was that Leo was going to go far in hockey. Never was a player so fierce or fearless as he was right in that moment, calling her bluff like the competitive genius that he really was.

They weren't eighteen anymore, though. The uncomplicated love they'd enjoyed at eighteen couldn't last anyway. He should know that by now.

"Yes or no, Gigi," he said softly. "It's a yes or no question. Do you love me like I love you?"

Georgia's heart held a gun on itself. Then it pulled the trigger. She shook her head.

For a few seconds nothing happened. His laser gaze stayed trained on her face, as if expecting her to crack and admit she was a lying liar who had just lied.

She didn't crack, though.

Finally, he turned toward the steering wheel, put the car in drive and maneuvered out of the parking lot. Five minutes later they arrived in front of her apartment building. She unclipped the seatbelt with shaking hands. What did a girl say after she'd just stabbed a good man in the heart? *Thanks for dinner. The lasagna was killer.*

"I just have one more thing to say," Leo rasped from the driver's seat.

"What?" she whispered, afraid to look at him again. So she was startled when his big hand cupped the back of her head and tugged her toward him. The world's softest kiss landed on her lips, and she returned it on instinct. For one beautiful moment, everything went silent inside her. As his lips caressed her own, she stopped hearing the echoes of a hundred worries. All she heard instead was her own sigh, and the soft sound Leo made from deep inside his chest.

Then it was over. He pulled away, leaving Georgia bereft in the passenger seat.

"That will have to hold me," he said under his breath as he turned away.

Georgia got out of the car on shaky knees and grabbed the door. It took all her willpower to close the door and turn away.

TWENTY-EIGHT

Leo's head was not in a good place as he hung his suit in the locker and pulled on his Bruisers workout kit. Something was wrong, and it pissed Leo off not to be told what. It didn't seem fair.

But Georgia had always been fair. That was one of the things he loved about her. Whether it was tennis, gin rummy, or love, she'd always been honest and true. She always gave it to him straight.

So why not now? What could be so scary that it could not be discussed?

She wasn't afraid of sex. Commitment? That didn't sound like her. Was she afraid that he wasn't committed? Hell. He'd get down on a knee and pop the question if he thought it wouldn't scare her off. Her dad would have a coronary.

Leo chuckled to himself just imagining it.

He left the dressing room, but hesitated in the hallway. The lounge wasn't appealing to him, because food and company weren't what he needed right now. Instead, he headed into the stretching room, which was empty. He sat down on the mats and began to loosen up his hamstrings, reaching slowly for the arches of his feet and breathing deeply. The yoga instructor would be so proud. Then he got up on one knee to stretch his hip flexors.

The stretching routine almost worked. But Georgia's tentative face kept looming in his memory. The bittersweet smile she'd given his mother before they'd left after dinner . . .

Argh. Here he was worrying about her again. When there was a hockey game that needed winning.

"Hey," Silas said from the doorway. "Got a minute?"

"Sure." Leo flopped back onto the mat and lifted his legs to stretch his lower back. "What's up?"

Silas came into the room and sat on the neighboring mat. "Remember I told you that your room had a fucking eject button under it?"

"Shit." He remembered that all too well. "Why do you ask?"

"I have a buddy in Vancouver. We played together in college."

"Yeah?"

"He called me to say that he and I might be teammates again. There's a rumor that he's going to be traded to Brooklyn."

Leo sat up fast. "Wait. Traded for who?"

Silas winced. "For you, man. I wasn't sure I should even mention it. Don't want to throw you off your game tonight. But . . ." He cleared his throat. "I know you have some complications here. Thought you could use the heads-up."

Leo wasn't one to panic. It was one of the reasons that he did so well at hockey—he was calm whenever things swerved in an unexpected direction. So this news didn't throw him into a tailspin. If another NHL team wanted him, that meant his stock in the league was rising. But . . .

Georgia.

"Christ," he said. And then a chuckle rose up in his chest. A few things became clear to him all of a sudden. Georgia *wasn't* afraid of commitment. She was afraid that he was about to be shipped several thousand miles away. He laughed, feeling better than he'd felt all day.

"Are you going to let me in on the joke?" Silas asked. "I like gallows humor."

Leo shook his head. "It's just a cosmic joke, right? The universe is giving me the runaround today. But I'm good. It will all work out." Either he'd be traded or not. "You'll have a roommate either way, man. Me or your buddy from college."

Silas shook his head. "That's not the reaction I expected."

"Eh. There are worse things. Maybe this will get me out of the next black-tie benefit."

"Now that's looking on the bright side. I got that e-mail today, too. Don't forget to put your date's name in by the end of the week. Maybe that Amy chick is available to accompany you." Silas cackled.

"Aren't *you* funny. But you know what? Last time you didn't have a date at all. How'd you get away with that?"

"I could tell you my secret, but it'll cost you." The goalie hooked one ankle over the other one and grinned. "Your favorite publicist makes a date mandatory because she thinks it improves our behavior if there's women at every table."

Leo snorted. "Hell. She's probably right. How do you get around it? I'll pay up."

"This one's on me. But don't tell anyone. You just make up a name. Put any name on the list. Then, the night of the party, your fictional date stands you up. It's the simplest thing in the world. And the bonus is that if it's a sit-down dinner, you can eat twice. Some of these fancy caterers are stingy."

"God, that's so obvious. Why didn't I think of that?"

Silas pointed to his head. "Genius. Right here."

"I'm using that. Because it's been a shitty day, and I won't be able to convince a certain publicist to be my date."

"No?" Silas shook his head. "Sorry."

So was Leo. Although now he knew why Georgia was freaking out. She must have heard the trade rumor in the C-suite. Maybe Becca told her.

He'd just have to ride it out. Over the next few days the trade would either happen or not. And if it did, he'd make it clear to her that they still weren't over. Vancouver to Brooklyn was a hell of a distance. But the end of the season was just a few months away. They could have the summer together . . .

"Silas Kelly!" Coach Karl barked from the doorway. "Can you play tonight?"

The goalie shot to his feet. "Of course."

Coach tapped the doorframe. "Good. Because it seems that Beacon has a touch of food poisoning. He keeps claiming he'll be okay, but he hasn't left the bathroom stall for forty-five minutes."

"I'm ready," Silas promised. "I'll stretch out now."

"You do that. Then I want you huddled up with the goaltending coach. Puck drops in ninety minutes." He disappeared.

When he was gone, Silas cursed under his breath. "A little warning would have been nice."

"I feel ya." This would be Silas's first game for Coach Karl. Under ordinary circumstances, he would have been told yesterday or this morning that he'd be minding the net tonight. "You got this," he said.

Silas gave him a salute, then sat down in the straddle position to stretch.

Leo left him there and went to see if the elimination soccer game was in progress yet.

Ninety minutes later, Leo felt calm and ready to play. His head was in the right place, and he felt strong and in control during his first few shifts on the ice. If Coach was going to ship his ass to Canada next week, at least he'd go out looking like a champ.

The Rangers were a formidable team, but he knew if they kept their heads in the game they had a chance to prevail. The game was scoreless after ten minutes. Leo, Bayer, and the other forwards kept the pressure up, even if the opponent's excellent blueliners thwarted their best attempts at scoring.

Patience, Leo reminded himself. He'd keep taking shots, and create a scoring opportunity. Soon.

Or maybe not. Because when Bayer got pinched into the corner by the other team's defensemen, he lost control of the puck. Their opponents passed to a capable forward, who broke toward the Bruisers' net.

O'Doul positioned himself perfectly to intercept the guy. It should have been fine. But their sniper took a long wrist shot. It wasn't particularly fast or hard to read. But Silas adjusted his stance poorly, overreacting to the angle.

The puck edged past the butt of his stick blade and went in.

Twelve thousand fans yelled "NOOOOO" in unison, even as the lamp lit.

O'Doul skated down to Silas, and Leo heard him say, "Shit happens, kid. Shake it off."

Unfortunately for all of them, Silas did not shake it off.

He looked shaky during the rest of the first period, and although Coach Karl gave an inspiring sermon during the break, the second period was a complete disaster. The skaters fought hard, but the Rangers smelled blood between the pipes. The way they drew a penalty on O'Doul was practically an art form. Then they gave it everything they had on the power play, scoring during the first thirty seconds of their advantage.

Fuck, Leo whispered under his breath. The other team had played Silas perfectly, and now all the momentum belonged to them.

The second half of the game felt like the longest that Leo had ever played. He and the other forwards played their best, but all their shots were thwarted. By the middle of the third period, the score was four to zero. A green-looking Beacon skated out to replace Silas.

Beacon held off any further goals, but the damage was done. Leo, sweat dripping down his face, battled until the final buzzer without a goal. His hip ached from a rough check into the boards, and his quads were on fire. And with nothing to show for it.

Afterward, the locker room was quiet, and not in a good way. Leo took a long shower and tried not to wonder what the bad game meant for him personally. He got dressed slowly, and when the locker room door opened, he heard Georgia's sweet voice cajoling O'Doul into an interview with the *Post*.

He couldn't wait to go home and drop into bed. If only Georgia were there to curl up beside him. He had a strong urge to take her aside and plead his case. Kiss her. Bribe her. (Not that she was the type to be swayed by gifts. But he was desperate.) Whatever it took.

But he'd already shown her he cared—he'd done everything short of getting down on his knees and begging. If she needed her space until his future was sorted out, he'd be patient.

He'd have to be.

TWENTY-NINE

TOP TEAM HEADLINE:

*"Bruisers Look Forward to Road Trip and
Redemption in the Midwest"*
—New York Post

Georgia was probably going to lose her mind.

She'd stumbled through the past couple of days waiting for the other shoe to drop. NHL trades often happened quite quickly. There may be only a day or two between the initial interest and signing. The athlete was never given any notice. One minute he'd be lacing up his shoes for a session in the weight room and a few minutes later he'd have to throw a few essentials into a bag and leave the building. It was brutal, but it was all part of professional sports.

Whenever her phone rang, she dreaded answering it. And every time Becca came into her office, she expected her friend to bring bad news.

"Are you mad at me or something?" her roommate finally asked. "Every time I see you today, you look at me like I ran over your puppy."

"No! I'm good."

Becca gave her the side eye. "All right. I came to ask if you wanted to grab burritos with me for lunch."

"Great!" she said with false cheer. "I'll get my coat."

The following morning featured a yoga class, and Georgia ran in at the last second, scanning the backs of everyone's heads, steeling herself against the possibility that Leo would be missing.

From a corner she hadn't checked yet he turned around to meet her gaze. Busted. She braced herself for his look of disappointment or irritation. But he only winked.

Weird.

Ari started them off with a guided meditation. Georgia closed her eyes and tried to concentrate.

"You are sitting on the beach, on a warm, breezy day," Ari began. "The waves are lapping onto the sand in a soothing, rhythmic way that matches your breathing. Focus on your breath. Allow your breath to find its natural, unhurried pace. Let the ocean sync with your body. There is peace between you and the world . . ."

Georgia's eyes snapped open. Her father wasn't in the room. She flicked her eyes back and forth, double-checking. Where was he? On the phone to Vancouver?

"When you breathe in, it is clean, salty air. When you exhale, you rid yourself of worry and anguish."

No, Vancouver is three hours behind. It's five in the morning there.

At this rate, she'd make herself insane before West Coast business hours. And she hadn't breathed out a single breath of either worry or anguish, damn it. The hour passed slowly. Waiting on bad news was lonely work.

After class, Becca squeezed her elbow. "I'm going to Ohio with the team tonight. Nate is flying in from Silicon Valley to see the game."

"Oh," Georgia said, still too caught up in her own misery to really hear whatever Becca was saying.

"Look," Becca said suddenly, grabbing Georgia by both shoulders. "I'm sorry to do this, buddy, but it's time I staged an intervention. I'm calling an emergency meeting at noon today," she said.

"Wait, really?" Georgia squeaked. "For who?"

Becca's eyes grew round. "You and me! That's who."

"Why?"

"Because you're a freaking zombie and it's driving me insane. Be at the usual meeting spot. Noon sharp." Becca marched off to start her work day, leaving Georgia alone with her worries.

Three hours later, Georgia entered the nail salon and made her way to the back, where Becca waited in a pedicure chair. "Did you pick your color?" her roommate asked.

Georgia held up the random bottle of pink polish she'd chosen at the front desk. She didn't care as much about nail polish as Becca. But in this neighborhood, there were very few places they could go at lunch without fear of being overheard by others in the organization. The nail salon was a safe place to gossip. None of the Brooklyn Bruisers would be caught dead in here.

"Remember—this is an intervention." Becca took the bottle from her hand and set it down out of sight. Then she passed Georgia a different one.

Georgia squinted at it. "Purple?"

"It's a *subtle* purple," Becca argued. "You always choose the same shade of pink."

"So?"

"It's so *safe*. Be daring."

"Wait. Did you just dare me to use purple?"

"I double dog dare you."

"Uh-huh. Does this mean I can dare you to come along next time I go paragliding?"

Becca opened her mouth and then closed it again. "Would you like the pink polish back?"

Gotcha. "No. I'll go with the purple. But I'm just saying—fearlessness comes in a few different colors."

"Touché. I'm going with one of these two blues. What do you think?" Her roommate held up two awful shades.

Georgia kicked off her shoes and removed her socks. "I think you should choose whichever one makes you happy."

"But they make me happy in different ways," her friend said, staring at the bottles. "But enough about my issues. What the *hell* is on your mind? Because I know it isn't nail polish."

Georgia waited while the nail technician finished setting up her station. Then she climbed into the seat next to Becca and dropped her bare feet into the warm water. The nail technician gave her ankle a pat and then went to collect her tools. "Can I ask you a question?" Georgia said, dropping her voice. "If you heard that Leo was getting traded, would you tell me?"

Becca blinked. "*Shit.* Is that why Hugh has been on the phone with Vancouver?"

Georgia's heart tumbled down a flight of stairs. "*Damn* it."

"Oh, baby. I'm so sorry. Are you *sure* they're looking at him? It could be anyone."

Georgia nodded, miserable. "I overheard something I shouldn't have."

"No wonder you're as jumpy as a long-tailed cat in a room full of rocking chairs." Becca patted her hand. "What does Leo say?"

"I haven't told him! Publicists who leak trades? They get fired. And even worse—I haven't dealt with it well. I told him we need to cool it off."

"You are an idiot," Becca said immediately.

"Tell me what you really think," Georgia muttered, making the other nail technicians laugh.

"No, but you are. Because Leo has probably thought about this already. Maybe he has a contingency plan for this. Or maybe he'd like the opportunity to tell you how he feels."

Georgia groaned. "But I can't tell him. If I tell him, it endangers both our jobs. I wish I'd never overheard it in the first place. It's eating me up. I look at him now and just think of how hard it would be to get over him a second time."

"I'm sorry, baby."

"He just RSVPed to the next team benefit. His date is someone named Honey Cove."

"What?" Becca yelped. "That sounds like a prostitute."

"I know. She's going to be worse than the last one. I just know it."

Becca giggled, then clamped a hand over her mouth, and the nail techs all clucked their tongues in sympathy. Becca wiped her eyes. "Karma is a bitch, Georgia."

"Thanks for your unwavering support."

"Correct me if I'm wrong. But the last time you pushed Leo away, you regretted it later."

"Your point being . . . ?"

Her roommate leaned over and gave her shoulder a shove. "Don't be thick. If Leo gets traded tomorrow, you'll regret being cold. And if he doesn't, you're acting like a freak for no reason. Miss Honey Cove wouldn't be on the guest list without your help."

It was hard to argue with that logic. Except for one problem. "But every time I look at him, or let his mom hug me, I want to puke from nerves. And what if he survives these trade discussions, and then they start up again after the play-offs? It never ends."

"So you just *deal*. The next team that's interested could be the Rangers. They're across the river. Don't borrow problems when they're falling from the sky like a spring-time downpour."

"Speaking of downpours, Hugh just sent me *another* resume for a dude with twice as much PR experience as I have."

"This calls for dumplings," Becca sympathized.

"Ain't that the truth." She looked down to see the first stripes of purple painted onto her big toe. The color was surprisingly pretty.

When Georgia walked down the aisle of the jet that night, Leo watched her with kind eyes. And when they ended up on the same elevator at the hotel, he held the door while she stepped off. This time, Georgia was not at all surprised when their rooms turned out to be adjacent.

"Sleep tight," he said softly just before her door closed.

Georgia stomped into her room and dropped her bag. Then she went into the bathroom to perch on the bathtub and call Becca. "Really?" she grumbled when her friend picked up the phone. "Again?"

"I just wanted to make sure there were no barriers when you finally come to your senses."

"He's so freaking *nice* to me, even though I've basically dumped him," Georgia grumbled. "How does he do that?" If Leo was going to get traded, she wished it would happen already, putting them both out of their misery.

"Maybe he just isn't falling for your bullshit."

"But it's not bullshit! I don't want to do this again. It sucks."

"Then don't! Just admit to him that you're scared."

Georgia very nearly corrected her roommate. She *almost* argued the point. "I *am* scared," she whispered instead.

"Oh, hallelujah. An honest answer."

"But what does that fix? *He's* not scared. We used to be equals. But now I'm always going to be the one who's worried. It's still the same old problem. I used to be fearless, until one night I learned how to be afraid." Her throat closed around the words, so she had to choke out the last few. "And nothing was ever the same."

"Oh, sweetie," Becca soothed. "Are you in your room? I'm coming up."

After Becca disconnected, Georgia just sat there in the hotel bathroom feeling pathetic. There were tears running down her face. Again! She'd spent six years trying to prove she was still courageous. Then Leo Trevi came to town and it took less than a month to demonstrate just how small and cloistered her life really was.

There was a knock on her door, so Georgia left the bathroom to yank open the door. Becca stood there in a hotel bathrobe, her trademark black negligée showing at the neck. She clutched the sort of tiny wine bottles that came out of the hotel minibar.

"I jump out of airplanes," Georgia said in what must have seemed like a complete non sequitur.

"That scares the shit out of me," Becca said, pushing past her.

"But I am the worst kind of fraud." Georgia yanked the hotel wine glasses off the TV stand and was surprised when Becca laughed.

"You aren't," she said kindly. "All that scary shit you do is like a dialogue you have with yourself about bravery. It's not fraudulent. It's just not the kind of brave you need right now. That boy is crazy about you. Tell him you might be separated."

"But . . ." Georgia swallowed hard. When you've been stupid, it's hard to admit it out loud. "When I was eighteen and out of my mind, I sent him away and he didn't argue. Is it awful that I was so mad about that? I didn't think he'd actually just vanish like he did. That's what I wanted to avoid—him having to make some kind of high stakes decision. I didn't want to know what he'd choose."

"So you fired him first," Becca said. "Thereby guaranteeing your own misery." She twisted open both bottles. "Overpriced red? Or overpriced white?"

Georgia took the white because she knew that Becca preferred the red.

They poured. They sipped. Georgia's eyes watered still.

"Look," Becca said, sitting on the bed. "You are brave every day. There's no disputing that. You're the top female publicist in a malecentric organization. You're an athlete and a kick-ass single woman. But maybe this is one of those times when you have to go backward to go forward. Leo stirred up a lot of shit that you don't like to think about. I know you hate being scared. But if you can't be scared *with* him, you're just stuck."

"Ugh. I hate stuck."

"I know. Me, too. Let's watch some trash TV and criticize everyone." Her friend scrambled onto the king-sized bed and yanked the covers down. "It's late. You can get unstuck tomorrow."

"'Kay." Georgia changed into her PJs and got into bed beside her. They drank bad wine and then fell asleep beside one another. And Georgia had courageous dreams.

In theory, neither Georgia nor Becca was needed at the rink at seven thirty the next morning, the way the players were.

But that didn't stop someone from pounding on Georgia's hotel room door the next morning.

When Georgia staggered to the door and pulled it open, Nathan stood there in a suit, every hair perfectly in place. "Have you seen Becca?" he demanded. "She's missing."

From the other side of Georgia's king-sized bed, Becca sat up quickly, her face puffy from sleep. "Where's the fire? Who's missing?"

Nathan peered around Georgia, who saw his neck flush, possibly because Becca slept in those skimpy little bits of lingerie. "You two shared a bed? Are we that stingy with the travel budget?"

Becca shook herself awake. "No, Nathan. Slumber party! We did each other's hair and got wasted on wine coolers." She slipped out of the bed, and Nate averted his eyes, his neck flushing even more deeply. "What do you need, anyway?"

"Uh." He looked confused. "The, um, ticket sales figures for Thursday's game. Do you have them?"

"Give me fifteen minutes, sunshine," she said, heading into the bathroom.

After that unusual wake-up call, the day was the usual crazy ride. Georgia worked through the morning practice, then took O'Doul and Bayer to an appearance at a local radio station. She ate lunch while returning e-mails then put on some workout gear and made her way over to the stadium in time for a noon yoga class.

As it turned out, admitting to Becca she was scared to lose Leo unfortunately did not make her any *less* scared.

Even as she showed her ID to the security guard and began walking through the underbelly of the old stadium, her stomach quivered. Would today be the day Leo disappeared?

There were six days left until the trade deadline. How did athletes live with that axe hanging over their heads all the time? Every season was like a long game of Russian roulette.

Georgia wandered around the poorly marked venue hallways, wondering if maybe the whole team had been traded. The place was practically a labyrinth, and just as charming—the hallways were just concrete tunnels lit by caged lightbulbs overhead.

Sexy.

Just when she was starting to get frustrated, Georgia heard Leo's voice. She'd know the cognac tones of his laugh anywhere, and that was definitely him behind a partially open door marked VISITORS. She stopped walking, her shoulders sagging with relief.

"You okay?" someone asked.

Georgia spun around to spot O'Doul stretching in the shadows, against one of the barren concrete walls. "I'm fine," she said quickly. *Heart palpitations over the trade deadline are perfectly normal for someone my age, right?* "Is it time for yoga?"

"Almost," he said. "Walk with me." He tipped his head toward the far end of the hallway.

Since Georgia had no idea where the class would be held, she was happy to fall in step with him. "What's up, captain?"

He chuckled. "I hear that Hugh wants to make us all go out for karaoke next week. Singing is not really my idea of a good time, but listening to these guys stink it up on stage sounds like a blast."

"That's kind of the point of karaoke," she pointed out.

"You sing? I can't quite picture it."

There had been a time in her life when Georgia was

always the first one onstage. "I'm good at lyrics. I do Eminem pretty well."

"No shit?" O'Doul laughed. "I have to see that."

"Okay," she promised. Bravery came in many forms, apparently. Paragliding was one thing. But letting loose in front of the people you worked with day in and day out counted, too. Why had she never realized this before?

"You're thinking pretty hard over there. Trying to pick a track?"

It was her turn to laugh. "No, I like the song to be a game time decision. Although, if I'm choosing one to sing for you . . ." She couldn't resist making the dig. "I should pick 'Bitch' by Meredith Brooks." That's what he'd called her at the press conference last month.

O'Doul flinched. "God, I regret ever saying that. I'm truly sorry."

"It's okay," she said quickly. Even though it really wasn't.

"Naw. See, you shot me down a couple of times, and I'm not used to that. Turns me into a toddler, apparently. Lesson learned."

Georgia's face heated. "Um . . ."

"Don't apologize."

She let out a nervous laugh. "Okay. But I'm pretty clueless sometimes."

"No big. But, listen—I saw you at the dojang on Spring Street a couple weeks ago—right before the road trip. What is that—a third-degree black belt you're sporting? You outrank me."

"Do I?" she squeaked. "I didn't know you did tae kwon do. Isn't it a little too much like your day job?"

He snorted. "Maybe. But I'm a little touchy about the way people think of me as a heavy. I took up tae kwon do because it makes fighting orderly. It's an art form and a *skill*, you know what I mean?"

This was easily the most personal conversation she'd ever had with O'Doul. "It *is* a skill. And beautiful when it's done well."

He grinned. "People don't usually say the word 'beautiful' in the same sentence with me. But I know what you mean. Is that why you took it up?"

"Nope. I did it because I needed to defend myself. When I was eighteen, something terrible happened to me. After I was raped, this was how I learned to feel confident again."

His eyebrows flew upward. "Jesus. I'm sorry."

"Thanks. It was a while ago. I started with aikido first, but it felt too staged."

"Yeah, I get that," he said. "Hey—you can help me study for my next belt test. I need some one-step sparring practice."

Georgia grinned. Sparring with O'Doul could be a hoot. "Okay! Let's go. I see a mat in there." They'd reached the stretching room where yoga would be held. He waited politely for her to enter the room first, and she slid past him. "There's nobody else in here yet. Quick—drop me, Doulie."

"I knew you were fun." He chuckled. He gave her a quick bow then relaxed into a preparation stance, while she waited with a grin on her face.

THIRTY

Leo followed Silas and Castro out of the dressing room and into the dank basement hallway. "Classy place," he muttered.

"It reminds me of a horror movie set," Silas quipped. "Didn't *Psycho* have some basement scenes?"

"Dude, *The Silence of the Lambs*," Castro suggested. "It puts the lotion in the basket."

Silas snickered as they turned a corner, finding nothing but an old mop bucket and a dead end. "Shit, are we lost?" he asked.

"Wait, this isn't a horror movie," Castro said as they all spun around. "*This is Spinal Tap*." He stopped beside a door marked Steam Chute 17 and pounded on it. "HELLO, CLEVELAND! I always wanted to say that."

"Cross that off the bucket list," Silas agreed.

"Wait, I heard voices," Leo said as they approached another turn.

"I see dead people," Silas countered.

"Aren't you both just hysterical," Leo grumbled. "Hustle, though. I'm not getting left off the game card tonight just to hear more of your movie trivia."

"We all know I won't be playing," Silas muttered. "Might as well take the scenic route."

But there was no scenic route, and Leo picked up the pace. He turned left and spotted the long hallway they needed. And this one had an arrow stenciled in paint on the wall beside the words "training facility."

"Here we go," someone said as they all turned in the proper direction, finally.

They walked onward. And it was really just happenstance that Leo lifted his chin toward the distant end of the hall at exactly the right moment. He saw two figures through a doorway at the opposite end of the hall, and one of them was Georgia. He knew the shine of her hair and her supermodel posture even in bad lighting at a hundred paces. He might have called out a greeting, except the man beside Georgia raised an arm and grabbed her, yanking her out of sight, into the shadows.

Later, he wouldn't even be able to recall the fifty yard sprint down the hall.

The same instincts that allowed him to reach a puck traveling seventy miles per hour across the ice had him racing toward the shadowy place where she'd been taken. The sounds of his teammates' voices dimmed to only a warble on the edge of his consciousness. There was only his speed, and the acidic bite of bile in his throat as he launched his body toward the target. His vision tunneled down to include only the doorway where she'd disappeared.

Seconds later he flew through that doorway at the man who had Georgia around the waist, on the fucking *floor*. Not a half second after that, his own hands dug into the perpetrator's flesh. A shout of rage tore from his own throat as he threw the man aside.

But the next sound was Georgia's shriek. And as he fell to his knees beside her, she grabbed his arms and yelled "STOP."

She kept talking, but it wasn't possible to understand. He was too caught inside the moment—the memory of that arm yanking Georgia out of his sight, tossing her into the shadows. It was all he could see.

His teammates arrived a moment later, their voices

crowding his head. "Is Doulie okay?" "Shit—what happened?"

Someone helped O'Doul off the floor. The captain raised a hand to the back of his head, and came away with a smear of blood. And Leo's eyes finally focused on Georgia, in her yoga pants and a Bruisers T-shirt, babbling about "sparring" or something. His brain told him he'd made an error of judgment. But his stomach still wasn't sure. And even though he'd gotten to his feet again somehow, the weirdest sensation crept up his arms and legs. It was an unfamiliar chill in his fingertips, spreading rapidly up and toward his core.

"Leo? Are you okay? He's turning gray."

Standing up wasn't really working for him. So he put out a hand toward the nearest wall. But the nearest wall turned out to be Silas. So Leo bent over to clutch his knees instead.

Then his stomach heaved, and he vomited all over the floor.

Half an hour later, Leo sat on a table in the medical facility, leaning his head back against the cool wall.

The team doctor had come and gone. Leo had explained himself. Sort of. It was all a stupid misunderstanding. He was horribly embarrassed, and hoping for a chance to apologize.

If only his stomach would stop rolling.

He'd also insisted to the team doctor that he was okay to play tonight. They'd handed him some of the sports drink, and he'd choked part of it down. And he continued to clutch the half-empty bottle in case anyone else came into the treatment room. He didn't want anyone to notice his hands were shaking.

Jesus Christ. Of all the bullshit he'd pulled, freaking out on O'Doul was the worst yet. He'd bet any amount of money that they had the captain in another exam room right now so that they could evaluate him for a possible concussion. He'd thrown O'Doul on the fucking *floor.*

But the guy had had his hands on Georgia, as if . . .

Leo's gut clenched again and he swallowed hard as another wave of nausea rolled through him. *Don't go there*, he told himself. *Don't think about that.* It had been a simple misunderstanding. He'd reacted *very* badly. There would be repercussions, but there was also a game to win. If he could just stay focused on that, everything would be okay. He took another sip of the sports drink and closed his eyes, picturing the rink. Too bad he hadn't made it to yoga. Right now he could really use some positive visualization or what-the-fuck-ever.

The door opened after a minute and Leo opened his eyes, expecting the doctor. Only it wasn't the one he'd expected.

"Hi, Leo," said Dr. Mulvey, the team shrink. "How are you doing?"

"Fine," he said tightly.

"Your hands are shaky?"

Fuck. A chill ran through his body, and he did a poor job of fighting it off. "I think I might be fighting off the flu or something." Why else would he feel so shaky? Maybe they could give him a vitamin shot and some Advil before game time.

"The flu, huh?" The doctor perched on the table beside him. "You ever have panic attacks?"

"Fuck no," Leo grumbled.

"There's a first time for everything."

Leo pressed the back of his head against the wall and sighed. "Who's getting cleared for the game tonight? Is O'Doul okay?" *Please say yes.* In the first place, he really hoped that O'Doul *was* okay. And in the second place, if O'Doul really wanted to make a stink about it, he could get Leo in a lot of trouble. Shit, he could call the cops if he really felt like ruining Leo's day.

"He'll be all right," Mulvey said lightly. "He might need a night off. Doc will decide soon."

Leo groaned.

"Can you tell me what happened back there?"

No. Leo hesitated. "I misinterpreted something. It was a stupid mistake. It won't happen again."

"I get that part," the doctor said. "But then what happened to *you*?"

"Uh, I got . . ." Leo did not even have words to explain what he'd felt. He wasn't even sure he remembered it all that clearly. Maybe it *was* the flu. "My stomach is just a little upset."

The shrink clicked his tongue. "But *why* is it upset? I think *you* are upset, and you'll feel better if you can articulate why."

Right on cue, Leo's gut clenched. "I psyched myself out there for a minute. It won't happen again."

"Maybe that's true," the doctor said quietly. "But for you to have such an outsized reaction to a misunderstanding suggests a fear you haven't dealt with. Shake my hand."

"What?"

"Just shake." Doctor Mulvey held out his hand.

Leo shook.

"Your hands are cold and you're not steady," the doctor said. "That's *shock*, Mr. Trevi. It happens after physical or psychological trauma. Like a bone break, or witnessing an accident on the highway."

"But I didn't."

The doctor chewed on his lip. "I think you did, though. In your own way." The doctor got off the table. "Lie down on your back and bend your knees."

"I don't need . . ."

"You want to play tonight, or what?"

Fuck. Leo turned to stretch out on the table. If this is what they wanted him to do, he'd do it. The doctor put a foam stretching block under his feet, to elevate them. Then he put a blanket over Leo's chest, while Leo clenched his jaw to keep from arguing.

"I'm going to speak to the doctor for a moment," Mulvey said. "Hang tight."

"Don't let anybody else in here," Leo said, irritation leaking into his tone.

"Okay," the doctor said, looking down at him. "By 'any-body else' do you mean Georgia?"

Leo grunted his acknowledgment.

"Fine. But you and I are definitely talking about this later."

I can't wait. Leo folded his hands on his chest and willed them to stop shaking.

When the doctor came in a while later, he brought Hugh Major with him. Leo sat up quickly, ready to take his punishment. The room only spun a little bit. So that was progress.

"Brought you this," the doctor said, setting down a tray with a banana and some kind of protein bar. "If you can eat, you need something with some available sugars."

"Thanks," he said, waiting.

The GM was eyeing him with a frown. "O'Doul can play tonight," Hugh finally said. "No sign of a concussion. It's just a scrape on his head, and a big bruise on his ass."

Leo sagged with relief. "That's good to hear. Will he let me apologize to him?"

The GM cocked his head. "Sure he will. But are *you* okay to play?"

"Yeah," Leo said immediately. "Of course I am."

The doctor rolled his eyes. "We've heard that before, son. You eat something and we'll talk in an hour, okay?"

"Sure." Leo grabbed the banana and began to peel it. If everyone would just leave him alone for a few minutes, he'd be fine.

They left, but the goddamn door opened up again to admit O'Doul. "Hey," the captain said.

"Hey." *Christ.* "Look, I'm really sorry." How many times was Leo going to have to give this speech? He'd never fucked up so many times before coming to the Bruisers. Seriously. His life had gone pretty fucking smoothly until now. He hadn't realized that there would be some serious karmic payback for getting to the NHL.

The captain waved a hand in the air. "I, uh . . . I didn't know about Georgia before today."

"What about her?"

O'Doul lifted a hand to the back of his neck. "You know. That when you guys were together in high school, she was raped."

Leo couldn't stave off his flinch at the sound of that word. "She probably doesn't like talking about it." And he could seriously relate right about now.

"I'm sure." O'Doul hopped up on the counter top opposite him. "But that's some pretty awful shit. Kinda explains a lot. About both of you."

Did it? Leo wasn't sure he liked the sound of that. He didn't want to be explained. He wanted to stop freaking out all the fucking time. "I'm still sorry I overreacted. Be kind of nice if that stopped happening."

O'Doul actually tipped his head back and laughed. "You think?"

"Yeah." And a ripple of laughter wobbled through him, too. Although it felt a little like hysteria. "So am I getting out of this little jail? Are we going to mow down this team, or what? Where is Coach anyway?"

"With Georgia," he said. "But, yeah. I'm sure he'll be barking at all of us within minutes."

"Good to know." Leo finally took a bite out of the banana. He didn't feel like eating, but he'd take one for the team.

"You know Georgia is a black belt at tae kwon do?"

"She didn't tell me much about it," Leo had to admit. "She's good at everything she tries, though. So it's not a big shock."

O'Doul grinned. "She is, isn't she?" He shook his head. "I asked her out a couple of times and got the brush-off. Didn't know she was waiting for you." He hopped off the counter. "I'll see you in the dressing room later?"

"Yeah. And I'm sorry about your . . ."

"Stop, college boy." The captain laid a hand on Leo's shoulder on his way out of the room. "Let's just win tonight, okay?"

"Yeah." The door shut on O'Doul, and Leo eyed the protein bar with suspicion. He picked it up and sighed.

THIRTY-ONE

Georgia had never cried at work before. Not even when her dad had called to tell her that her grandmother had died. Not even while they were all watching the movie *Rudy* on the jet to Vancouver, and the team carried Rudy around on the field on their shoulders.

Because you can't cry at work. That just makes you into the *girl*, damn it.

So Georgia bit hard enough on her lip to make it bleed as two of Leo's teammates hooked him under the arms and dragged him away from the scene of the crime. O'Doul stood there feeling the back of his scalp and asking, "What the fuck just happened?" until Hugh Major swept in and hauled him off to have the doctor look at his head.

Other teammates began to circle her, trying to be helpful, asking questions which Georgia did not feel like answering. Somebody called down to maintenance for a mop. And someone else called Coach Worthington.

Georgia just stood against the wall feeling . . . terrified. But of what, she wasn't sure. She couldn't stop hearing the awful sound that Leo had made when he tore around the corner. He'd *thrown* O'Doul down in front of witnesses. And he'd been ready to break the guy in half. She'd never seen anything like it.

It was all her fault, most likely. No—her shrink would reject that idea in a half second flat. But still, she *felt* guilty. Leo had come unglued before her eyes. Seeing it happen made her heart ache. And it made her realize that he wasn't unscathed by what had happened to her. It had happened to both of them. She hadn't really understood that before now.

"Georgia?"

She looked up to see Roger beckoning to her. "Yeah?" It came out as a croak.

"Your father would like a word with you."

Her heart sank. Wordlessly, she followed him down another of the million hallways this place seemed to have. She was going to have to say something to him now about seeing Leo. If there was any way to shift some of the blame off him, she'd do it in a heartbeat.

And please let O'Doul be okay, she begged inwardly. She'd just begun to like the guy, too.

Georgia ducked into the little office her father and Hugh were sharing. She'd had enough of depressing, underground spaces today. What she needed was to see the sun.

"Close the door, honey," her father said.

She obeyed, and took a set across from him.

"What the hell just happened?" he asked. "Help me understand. Leo attacked O'Doul? Was anyone else there? I didn't see it. But . . ." He cleared his throat. "I *heard*."

Georgia felt a tremor just remembering the awful sound Leo had made. She never wanted to hear it again. "There was a misunderstanding," she said, her throat so dry it felt like it might crack in half. "Doulie studies tae kwon do, too. We were talking about one-step sparring for his belt test. So I let him drop me onto the mats. And Leo was quite a ways down the hall. I mean . . . what he saw was O'Doul grabbing me and throwing me to the ground."

Her father flinched. "Jesus Christ. And he thought O'Doul just grabbed you? Is that really logical?"

Georgia hesitated. She'd seen the look on his face, and it would haunt her. "I'm not sure *logic* was possible just then. His reaction was more, uh, visceral."

Her dad clasped his hands together on the desk and frowned. "He panicked."

"Daddy, he *freaked*. It was terrifying—for him as well as O'Doul."

"And how about for you?" her father asked quietly.

Georgia suppressed a shiver. "I'll be fine. But I think . . ." She sighed. "You and I never talk about my awful year, right?"

Her father winced, then nodded his acknowledgment.

"Well, at the time, Leo was my rock, you know? He stuck close, and he was one of the people who got me through it. But I think it affected him, too." It filled her with shame to realize she'd never understood it, either. "I think he's still hurting."

Her father grunted, then rolled his toothpick from one side of his mouth to the other. That was all the acknowledgement she was going to get on the subject, and it made her temper flare.

"Daddy, I have *no clue* what you've got against Leo, and I really haven't wanted to get into it with you. But I swear to God—if you're going to trade him to Vancouver, you should man up and clear the air with him first. He's not some stranger you can just toss away."

Her father's eyes narrowed. "Trades are none of your business, little lady."

"Right," Georgia snapped. "So send me to my room and ground me for what I'm about to say. You can pretend that you've given him the same chance as everyone else on the team, but we both know that's bullshit." She stood up suddenly, startling both of them.

"Honey," her father said, "hold on a fucking second. I'm sure Leo is a good man. But he'd be better on someone else's team. Somewhere he doesn't have history."

Her stomach dove off a cliff. Without a parachute. "That is *not* fair. His only history is being good to both of us."

"I think your memory is selective," her father said quietly.

"How so? Just spit it out, would you? What is your *issue* with him?"

Her dad shook his head. "I don't trust him, and that is a perfectly valid reason to send him packing. I need to trust *every* guy wearing the team sweater. And since he's landed here, he's tangled with me and he's tangled with O'Doul. That's not good for morale."

Georgia gasped. "That's *crap*, Coach. You greeted Leo with a snarl on his first day, and you want to blame the tension on him? That's really mature. Maybe I'd be better off working for a different team, too."

"Honey . . ."

"Don't," she warned. "I love this job. I've been very happy here. But if you trade Leo to Vancouver, don't be too startled if I go with him." She took a step and grabbed the door handle.

"What?" Her father's voice was full of shock. "Georgia! Get back here. Don't storm out of here like a teenager."

She gave him a glare over her shoulder. "You're in no position to tell me that my behavior is immature."

At that she left the room and slammed the door with a bang.

THIRTY-TWO

Leo lay on the table, irritated with everyone and everything. He closed his eyes and tried to relax.

Who knew that losing your shit was so exhausting? He closed his eyes for a moment. But when he next opened them, he realized he'd nodded off. Leo sat up fast, his heart hammering. What the hell time was it? His watch said 3:30. He let out a breath. There were still four hours until the puck dropped. That wasn't so bad.

Someone was tapping on his door, too. As his heart rate descended, he realized that the knocking had probably woken him up. "Come in," he croaked.

The door opened to reveal Georgia, her soft face looking in at him with concern in her eyes. *Shit.* The last time he'd seen Georgia, he'd watched someone drop her to the ground . . . Again, his stomach rolled.

"Hi," she said softly. "Can I come in?"

"Yeah. Of course you can." He sat up a little straighter, knocking the blanket aside. He hated how weak he'd looked today. A man wasn't supposed to have trouble keeping his shit together, no matter what.

But then Georgia was standing in front of him, her sweet eyes taking him in, her expression cautious. "Hey," he said, his voice cracking. Because even though she was perfectly fine, he was too raw inside to believe it. He could still see her body tilt off center, overpowered by an unseen attacker . . . His eyes were suddenly, uncomfortably hot. It didn't make a lick of sense that he'd associate it with a crime from years ago that he'd never seen and couldn't have prevented.

Breathe, Leo ordered himself.

"Honey," Georgia said softly. She stepped up between his knees, put both her hands on his face.

There was nowhere to run. He closed his eyes, a new tremor rippling through his chest. The fact that someone had once hurt her was like a knife through his heart. His precious girl. She had been vulnerable to a fucking psychopath, and there wasn't a fucking thing he could do about it.

Leo reached for her, pulling Georgia to his chest. He took a deep breath, but it hitched on the way in. And the sound escaping him was way too much like a sob.

She wrapped her arms around him and squeezed while Leo fought for control. And lost. He buried his face in her neck while his eyes sprouted faucets. "I'm sorry," he choked. "I'm just . . ." *Losing my fucking mind.*

"I love you so much," Georgia whispered. "Everything is going to be okay."

There were no guarantees, though. He'd learned the hard way already that he could bust his ass all day and all night until he was the strongest, most competent punk on the planet and it could all go to hell in a hot second. The more you had, the more there was to lose. He'd spent the last six years trying to forget that. But the truth hurt like a bitch.

He'd never stop trying, though. He'd do whatever it took to keep her safe and happy. If it could be done, he'd do it.

Georgia climbed uninvited onto the exam table, the paper crinkling under her. She sat beside Leo and turned to pull him into her arms. "I'm sorry you're upset. But what happened before was upsetting. I don't think I ever realized how it affected you."

Leo took a deep breath and let it out. "You're the one who really suffered," he said.

"That's not true." She shook her head. "My dad did, too. And you. But I didn't have any room in my head to understand it at the time. I was too busy being angry."

He clamped his arms around her and sighed. "I'm okay, Gigi. I swear."

"You," she said, kissing the place just under his ear, "are everything to me. I didn't say so when I should have, so I hope it's not too late to say so now."

The warmth of her body against his was starting to calm him down. "I love you, baby. Don't leave me."

"I won't."

He stroked her hair. "You did six years ago, and I still don't understand why."

"I was panicked," she said in a low voice. "I'd suddenly lost my faith in everything, all at once. And I thought you were just sticking with me because you felt guilty."

"No—"

"Shh," she chided. "I was so full of shame and so scared. I thought that would never go away. The funny thing is that graduation was only two months after it happened. When I was eighteen those two months seemed like a lifetime of waiting to feel better. But they weren't. Just a few lousy weeks. I didn't know, though. I didn't understand that time heals."

Leo had seen some evidence today that time doesn't always get the job done. But even so, he understood. "I would have waited a hell of a lot longer."

She sighed against him. "I didn't trust it, because I didn't remember how it felt to be happy. I didn't believe I'd get that back."

He pushed a strand of hair out of her face. "You make me happy, baby. Just you." He kissed her on the forehead. "The rest we'll figure out, okay?"

"Okay."

There was a knock on the door.

Fuck. "Later," Leo grunted, pawing at his eyes. There

were no more tears, but the red-eyed evidence was surely still there.

The door opened anyway, admitting the stone-faced Coach Karl. Leo didn't take his arms from around Georgia. He was done worrying about what her father thought of him.

"You weren't supposed to leave," Coach said slowly.

"What?" Leo asked. "Leave where?"

"Leave *her*!" Coach said with a snarl.

"Daddy!" Georgia complained. "What the hell are you talking about?"

Coach came all the way into the room and shut the door. He studied his daughter for a second. "You're the one who wanted the air cleared," her father grumbled. "So I'll clear it." He turned to face Leo. "I trusted you with my daughter, and I thought you were worth it. But on the worst night of her life, you told her it was over. My little girl freaks out, has a few too many, and gets caught by some sicko. Takes her *years* to recover, asshole. And now you're just gonna waltz in and pick up where you left off? That takes balls."

A stunned silence fell over the little room. Leo's mind whirled as he tried to figure out what the hell Coach was talking about. "I *never* left her," he said. "What the fuck are you talking about?"

"The phone call," her father growled. "That night—she talks to you on the phone. Then I call her and she goes off like a firework. 'Leo upset me. I don't want to talk. Call me tomorrow, I'm going out to a party.' Next call I get is in the middle of the night, from the *fucking hospital*."

"*Daddy.*" Georgia gasped. "Slow down. What are you talking about?"

"You were pissed!" he spat. "You said so yourself. At *him*." He pointed an accusing finger at Leo.

"Wait a fricking minute. I do not like where this is going," Georgia said in a voice Leo had never heard before. It was low and full of menace. "You paid thousands of dollars for therapy to convince me that the only person at fault was the rapist. So it's really nice to hear now that you think Leo and I are also to blame."

Jesus. Leo put a hand on Georgia's lower back and began to rub slow circles. As if he could calm her down by osmosis. But he was still confused. "I don't get it. We didn't have any fights." They didn't, did they? So much had happened right after that random phone call on an April night, he couldn't be a hundred percent sure. But if they'd fought, it had to be over something small. He'd remember.

Georgia turned to him with heavy eyes. "I *was* upset that night," she whispered. "But that is not your fault. I never thought it was. I didn't even remember until now."

"But why?" he whispered back.

"You said you wanted to talk about next year," she said. "We were going to different colleges and it was just inevitable that we'd have that conversation. But I was pissed off that you'd bring it up over the phone."

Leo closed his eyes and tried to think. "I'd been sitting at home looking at airfares." It was coming back to him now. "I'd figured out that it would be expensive for me to fly from Hartford to Charlottesville to visit you. But that it was pretty cheap to go from Newark. I wanted to talk about airfares."

He opened his eyes just in time to see Georgia clap a hand over her mouth. And then her eyes filled with tears. Wordlessly, Leo hugged her. How did two healthy people produce as many tears as they did? *By ducking all the important stuff,* his conscience reminded him. Ah, well. Maybe they might finally get it right this time. "I love you," he said to Georgia. "Always have."

"I never blamed you," she squeaked. "I swear. Even if I freaked out like an idiot, it was never on you."

"It's okay," he said, tucking his chin onto her shoulder. "We're here now. That's all that matters." He risked a look up at Coach, whose face was a stone. The man turned on his heel and left the room, closing the door behind him with a click.

They held each other for a while, until eventually Georgia spoke up. "You might get traded," she said in a shaky voice. "I don't know what's in his head."

"If it happens, we'll deal with it. As long as *you* don't trade me, Gigi, everything will be fine."

"There isn't a better player I'd want on my team." She sniffled. "You're the captain for life."

He kissed her neck. "Don't make me the enforcer, though. Turns out I'm not that good at figuring out who to hit."

"We'll train you up." She looked at her watch. "You don't need to be back here for more than three hours. Can we get out of here? If you're tired, we could take a nap."

Leo shook his head. "Can't nap with you. I'll get ideas. And I can't get ideas right before a game."

She rolled her red eyes at him. "Fine. The hotel has a climbing wall. I'm a little rusty but I can probably still take you."

"No you can't," he said, the competitive instinct speaking up right away. "I only have sneakers, though."

"Me, too," she countered. "So it's a fair fight." She slid off his lap and off the table.

He stood up for the first time in an hour. Maybe he was still a little shaky around the edges. But he felt mostly solid. "Fine. A quick climb to victory, and then we'll find a snack." Taking her hand, he followed her out of the room.

Leo lost the climbing wall race. But he won the coin flip to decide where to eat. He chose a Chinese restaurant, though, because his girl hadn't had a dumpling infusion in a couple of days, and he liked to watch her dip them in the sauce with her chopsticks.

When they were finished, though, he caught her eyeing him over the rim of her teacup.

"What?" he asked.

Her eyes dipped. "Are you, uh, bringing someone named Honey to the benefit when we get back? Any chance I could talk you into taking me?"

Aw. Leo set down his water glass and grinned at her. "Georgia, there's nobody with that god-awful name. You were supposed to figure that out."

"I was?"

"Hell yes. You know that joke? Honey Cove is your stripper name. Your first pet and the street you grew up on. I thought you'd know."

Georgia slapped a hand in front of her mouth and giggled. "That's funny. Except the dog's name was Sweetie Pie."

Leo barked out a laugh. "Really? Hell, I was close."

She tipped her head back and laughed. "Not close enough."

"Shit. You really thought I'd bring someone named Honey Cove to that party?" He balled up his napkin and tossed it playfully across the table. "You must think very highly of me."

"You are a catch. I swear."

Laughing, he signaled for the check.

By the time he made it back to the rink, the day's emotional turmoil had begun to fade. The ache in his chest was replaced by a healthy amount of pregame tension. He changed into workout gear and did some stretches in the dressing room. Then he followed a few teammates to the basement room where the yoga class had been held earlier—the one he'd freaked out in on his way to attend.

O'Doul stood holding a soccer ball under his arm as the circle formed. "You start, rookie," he said, chucking the ball to Leo. There was no malice in it, though.

Leo took a quick glance around the circle of faces and he liked what he saw. Just a bunch of guys trying to live the dream, the same as he was. With any luck, he'd get to stand in this circle for a good long time. "All right," he said. "Stay sharp." He tossed the ball up and then popped it with his knee across the circle to O'Doul. Who headed it to Beacon, who tried to kick it and missed.

"Goddamn," O'Doul said with a shake of his head. "Good thing he's good with his hands."

There was a round of chuckles, and then the game began again. Leo lost himself in the pure, silly pursuit of keeping that black and white ball in the air, and at least for now, all was well.

*   *   *

On the ice that night, though, everything was just a little off.

Passes didn't connect. Shots didn't go in. Coach Karl was a snarling, ornery wreck, and his attitude seemed to hang over the bench like a cloud.

Weirdly, Leo had a great night. He scored one of the Bruisers' two goals, and he did a good job of anticipating even the ill-timed passes his teammates made. Maybe everyone else was stressed out, but he felt more relaxed than he had in weeks.

It wasn't enough to save the game, but he helped keep their loss to a single goal. It was something. And he was in a mood to count his blessings tonight.

The dressing room was somber after the game. Before he got too far stripping off his pads, Georgia asked him to step into the hallway and talk to a reporter.

This he did without pinching her backside, although in her sexy publicist skirt, it was quite hard to resist. "We fought hard out there," he said into the microphone. "We'll get 'em next time."

It wasn't the most original statement, but he was too distracted by Georgia's smile to say anything meaningful.

Back in the locker room faces were long. And they only grew longer when Coach, Hugh, and Nate all entered the room, standing together, facing the team.

One by one conversations died as everyone gave his attention to the men in charge. "We have a change to announce," Hugh Major said.

Oh. Fuck. Leo braced himself.

"Silas Kelly will head to Hartford tomorrow morning. I would like to personally thank him for his service, and his excellent attitude at every turn. And if we make it to the postseason, we'll probably see him in Brooklyn again."

O'Doul began to clap, and Leo joined immediately. But his mind whirled. Silas gone? The last-minute roster changes had begun. Karl obviously wanted to give someone else the backup job going into the play-offs.

Across the room, Silas was already stuffing things into his duffel. They'd probably only told him five minutes ago. Now it was back to the minor leagues. His two-way contract made that an easy decision for the team. But then . . . Leo felt a cold chill crawl up his spine. If Karl went shopping for a goalie, he might trade Leo to get one.

And poor Silas. Leo felt terrible for his roommate of four weeks. This business was rough. Nobody was ever safe.

When Leo came out of the showers a few minutes later, Silas was beside his locker, tossing gear into a hockey bag. He'd have to carry it out himself tonight, and put it on a plane to Hartford tomorrow.

"Man, I'm sorry to lose you," Leo said. "This should have been the start of a beautiful relationship."

Silas gave a bark of laughter. "Don't get all teary on me now. And hey—my buddy thinks he's getting traded to Anaheim now. You might be off the hook."

"We'll see I guess." Leo wasn't counting on *anything* after Coach's outburst today. At this point, he was probably willing to trade him to a beer league just to get him the hell away from Georgia.

"If you make it through the deadline, would you think about taking over my lease? There's five months left."

"Sure I'd take it over," Leo said quickly. "But that's a big 'if.'"

Silas gave him a sad grin. "Let me know. It's a lot of rent but I'll miss that place."

"I sure will."

They shook hands.

Leo got dressed and wondered where Georgia was. The jet would take them all back to New York tonight on a late flight. Leo was looking forward to going home. He slipped on his shoes and went to find her.

But when he stepped into the hallway, someone stopped him. "Leo. Could you come here a minute, son?"

Leo's head snapped up with surprise. It was Karl Worthington who stood frowning at him. "Sure," he said, wondering why Coach's voice sounded so dire. *Here it comes*, he thought as he followed him down the hallway. "What's the problem?"

"No problem." The coach stopped and crossed his arms. "I just want to apologize to you."

Leo just blinked for a minute. "You do?"

"Yeah, for being an asshole." Karl stuck a toothpick in the corner of his mouth. "Georgia's senior year of high school was really hard on me."

"No kidding," Leo said quickly.

But Coach shook his head. "Not just the last part. The whole thing. You two were gonna fly the coop. I helped my little girl pick a college. Then I helped you get onto that D-1 team where I knew you could become great. And everything was fucking *over*. Georgia was my whole family. No—Georgia and *you* were my whole family. When I thought you two were going to break up, I was angry at you for leaving both of us. And then . . ." He looked down at the rubber matting on the floor, shaking his head. "I blamed you even though it didn't make any fucking sense. I just wanted to go back in time to where the two of you were happy, sneaking around boosting Georgia through her bedroom window after curfew."

Leo's chest was tight. "We broke a lot of rules. But I loved her."

Coach's voice was gravel. "I know you did. I trusted you completely."

Yikes. "Thing is . . ." Leo rubbed his chin and tried to form words that made sense. "Who knows what would have happened? Maybe Georgia would have gotten sick of the long-distance thing. It happens. Or maybe I would have. We were so fucking young."

Karl gave him a sad smile. "I know. But I met my wife in high school. She was the best thing that ever happened to me. And you had a good heart and you made her laugh. Meanwhile, I'd just spent a decade coaching some real punks in college. At seventeen, you were twice the man as most of them. I had faith in the two of you. Until I didn't anymore. I'm sorry."

Leo leaned back against the wall and tipped his eyes toward the ceiling. What was *with* his eyes today? They kept getting scratchy and hot. "Apology accepted," he said.

Karl exhaled. "Now go find my girl and make her happy. You both deserve it." He held out a hand.

But something—maybe it was his competitive streak, or maybe it was love—made Leo grab him for a hard, back-slapping hug instead. Then he left Coach blinking in the hallway and went to pack up his stuff, so that he could catch up with Georgia on the jet.

THIRTY-THREE

Georgia would have been the first to board the plane, but she was waylaid by Hugh Major. "Can we chat about the PR department for a second?" he asked. "I know it's late, but here we are . . ."

"Sure," she said quickly. If he was going to give her bad news, they might as well get it over with.

"You didn't get back to me about those two candidates," he said right away. "I liked both of them. But if you're going to be working with whoever I hire, I really want your opinion."

She held in her sigh. "I'm sure I could work with either one. They're both amazingly qualified." *More qualified than I am.*

"That's true. But you and I need to talk about the division of labor."

Here it comes. Georgia looked square into Hugh's eyes and waited for him to explain that she'd be working for the new guy. She'd take it like a champ, and maybe he'd see just how professional she really was. "How do you see the division of duties?" she asked calmly.

"I'm going to appoint two coheads of PR. You and a new guy. So—" He spread his hands.

Georgia visibly jerked at this news. Did he really just tell her she'd (mostly) stay in the top chair in PR?

"—You need to tell me whether you'd rather be in charge of player communications—finding and arranging their interviews, handling their scandals, you know. The usual. Or do you want the half of the job that deals with our nonprofit outreach? The hospitals, that women's shelter, the Brooklyn Arts efforts. My gut says you like that side of it more, but I want to hear it from you."

For a long moment, she just blinked at him. "Well . . ." *Pull yourself together, Worthington.* "I enjoy the nonprofit work the most. But I can handle either job."

"Of course you can. But if you want the nonprofit work, I'm going to hire the one guy, and if you want the player representation piece, I'll go with the other—the Wharton guy—for the nonprofit work."

"There will always be some overlap," Georgia pointed out.

"Absolutely. So what's it going to be, Miss Worthington?"

"I'll take the nonprofit piece. We could really do so much more on that front."

Hugh grinned. "Nathan will love that. He really wants to show the world the Bruisers are good for Brooklyn."

"They are," Georgia agreed. "Our next benefit is for a women's shelter. Fifty kids live there on a temporary basis. I want to have a skating party with some of the players. These kids should know that not all men are awful."

"I like it." Hugh held up a fist to bump, and Georgia bumped it. "That's good outreach without much expense."

"Ice time on the practice rink and a few refreshments. I've already done the math. And I think we could donate ice time to Boys and Girls Clubs of New York, too." She heard herself start to babble. Hugh didn't really need an entire business plan at eleven PM. "Anyway. I have ideas."

"Glad to hear it, Killer." He winked. "I think they're ready for us." He looked past her at the Jetway door, which had just been opened.

Georgia practically scampered onto the plane. She was incredibly relieved at what Hugh had planned for the HR office. Two coheads was a structure she hadn't considered, but it made a heck of a lot of sense. It meant that the PR exec working on the nonprofit projects wouldn't always be yanked into whatever gossip or scandal was brewing with the team.

And there would always be gossip. These were hockey players, after all.

Georgia was one of the first to board the plane. She chose a seat near the rear, scooting all the way in to the window seat for Becca, who came down the row just behind her. But Becca didn't take it. Instead, she slid into the seat on the opposite side of the aisle, and winked.

It wasn't long before the cabin filled with players. Leo appeared over her. "Is this seat taken?"

"Nope!" Becca said from behind his backside.

Leo grinned, and Georgia was pleased to see that he looked relaxed and happy. Tired, maybe. But that was just a given in the middle of the season. He stashed his carry-on in the overhead compartment and then sat down. Reaching for her hand, he lifted it to his mouth and kissed it.

Georgia aimed her smile at the window, but since it was dark outside, all she saw was her own reflection. She looked relaxed and happy, too.

"Will you come home with me tonight?" Leo asked quietly. "I'll probably help Silas pack, so it won't exactly be a party. But I want you in my bed."

Georgia squeezed his hand. "Absolutely. I've missed you."

He made a low growl. "That's what I like to hear."

"I'm sorry," she said, moving a little closer to him. "I heard you might be traded, and I panicked."

"I know." He chuckled. "You were in a tight spot."

"It could still happen."

"Let's wait until they shove a plane ticket in my face before we panic. Deal?"

"Deal."

Most of the seats around them were taken now. But the head honchos hadn't gotten onto the plane yet. When Silas did, all the other players clapped.

Georgia yawned, wondering whether she could fall asleep during the two hour flight. But Leo fidgeted in his seat. And that really wasn't like him. "You okay?" she asked.

"Yeah. But there's something I need to get off my chest."

That woke her up fast. "Really? What?" When she turned her body to face him, she saw Becca do the same thing across the aisle, curiosity on her face. Whatever Leo had to say, Georgia hoped it wasn't something too private.

He took a deep breath and let it out. "My timing probably sucks. But I just can't wait." He unclipped his seatbelt and rose from his seat.

"Where are you going?" Georgia asked. They'd be shutting the plane's doors in a minute.

Leo turned around to face her in the aisle, then knelt down. Georgia squinted at him, on the verge of asking him if he'd dropped something, when Leo grabbed her hand. "There's a real spark between us," he said.

Was he . . . "Oh my God!" She clamped a hand over her mouth.

"Will you marry me this summer?" Leo's big brown eyes sparkled up at her, waiting for an answer.

Georgia actually replayed his words in her head, trying to be sure she'd heard him correctly.

"I wish I had a ring," he continued. "I always wanted to do this right. I had it all planned out once. When I was eighteen, I thought I wanted to take you stargazing in my truck and pop the question. But I don't want to waste any more time . . ."

"YES," Georgia said, shaking off her shock.

Becca gave a loud, shrieky squeal and Leo grinned widely.

"Holy fuck, *what* is happening here?" Castro demanded from the row behind them.

Someone started to clap, and then someone else joined in. The sound of applause rose as Leo stood up, then leaned over the seat to kiss her.

Georgia lost herself in the taste of happiness for a moment. Leo cupped the back of her neck and angled his mouth to fit against hers. But he began smiling so hard that he lost focus, and Georgia laughed. "Love you, babe. Always have," he rumbled.

"Coach!" somebody yelled. "Looks like you're paying for a wedding."

"What?" her father's voice barked, and Georgia stiffened. The plane got quiet.

Leo stood up slowly, his hand still a warm presence on her neck. He cleared his throat. "I should have asked you first. But I've always been impulsive."

Georgia watched her father's face cycle through the entire range of human emotion in about four seconds. Then it reshaped into its usual crusty visage. "Boys, you'd better make it to the play-offs. I'm gonna need that bonus money to throw a party. If you clear the semis, I'll spring for the good whiskey."

The jet erupted with laughter.

Leo sat back down, and pulled her into a hug. "You gonna be a bridezilla?" Leo asked.

"What do you think?"

"My girl doesn't like a fuss. But I've heard that weddings make people crazy."

She turned and hugged him across the chest. "I've sworn off crazy. Let's hire a wedding planner and let her do everything."

"Sounds good."

It felt weird to cuddle Leo in public, but not weird enough that she wanted to stop. Though her phone, its top edge showing from the seat-back pocket, glowed a color she hadn't seen before. Pink? That was odd. She untangled herself from Leo to take a look.

CONGRATULATIONS, the text read. *—Nate.*

"How does he do that?" Leo asked.

"No idea. He's not on the plane, right?"

"Nope," Leo agreed. "Didn't see him at all at this game. Where does he live, anyway?"

"In a mansion on the promenade in Brooklyn Heights. He takes the ferry to his midtown office and walks to the

Bruisers HQ. It's a good setup he's got. Can we stay in Brooklyn?" Georgia asked. "I like it there."

"Sure, baby." He tucked an arm around her. "Maybe I'll take Silas's apartment for real when the lease is up. I guess I should have thought that through." He laughed. "I'm kind of impulsive. Should I have waited to propose until I had a ring?"

"No!" She buried her face in his collar. "I'm sick of waiting."

He gave her a squeeze. "Me, too, baby. Me, too."

THIRTY-FOUR

TOP STORY

"Area Teams Make Last-Minute Roster Adjustments
Heading Into Play-offs"
—The Daily News

The official trade deadline was three o'clock PM, Eastern Standard Time.

Georgia no longer worried that her father would trade Leo just out of spite. In fact, it looked as though her office wasn't going to be issuing any big press releases today. Though Hugh, her dad, and Nate were cloistered in Nate's office, taking any last-minute trade calls from other teams, it didn't seem that they were making any big adjustments. They'd traded one of their AHL players from Hartford to Anaheim in exchange for a second round draft pick.

She'd sent out that press release an hour ago—the new guy hadn't started yet, so she was the one on duty. But the trade wouldn't make the front page of the sports section, as the Rangers and the Devils had more interesting trades to report.

Still, Georgia sat at her desk, keeping up the vigil. Until three o'clock, anything was possible. Even Leo could still be traded if the other team offered something advantageous. That unlikely scenario would not make Georgia happy, but now she knew it wouldn't be the end of the world.

They'd decided to get married on July 4th, at a yacht club on the North Shore of Long Island. Apparently Fourth of July weddings weren't all that common, so that date was still open even though it was just four months away. She and Becca were interviewing caterers next weekend. "We have to hurry," Becca had said breathlessly. "Only four months to shop for the dress, the shoes, the lingerie!"

Privately, Georgia imagined she might pray for her own death if it took four months to buy an outfit for a single day of her life. But she'd let Becca have her fun, at least for a little while.

She took her ten-millionth glance at the clock today, noting that there were only a few minutes left until Leo's postseason slot on the Bruisers' roster was official. When her e-mail dinged a minute later, she leapt on the message. But it wasn't from Hugh or anyone in the organization. It was from Hockey Hotties.

Dear Miss Worthington, attached please find the proofs from our photo shoot on February 9th.
Please have each athlete approve the pictures before March 7th.

She clicked on the attachment and her screen filled with the most amazing photograph. Leo, skin and muscle shimmering in luminous icy light, his powerful thighs outstretched as he skated past the camera.

Georgia just stared at the unforgettable photograph of her fiancé. And she was supposed to let the world have this shot of him? She flipped to the photo of Castro, which was also glorious yet tastefully captured. She closed that picture's file, though, because it felt weird to gawk at the bare butt of someone she worked with.

Leo, though. He still filled her screen with his beauty. It made her want to run out of the office and find him right now.

"Hey," someone said from the doorway.

Georgia startled at the sound of her father's voice. She clicked so hard on the mouse to close the photo that her thumb cracked. Then she turned to face him as casually as possible. Had her dad seen? Did he notice that she'd been staring at Leo's naked body on her work computer?

"Hey," she squeaked, and then focused on the real problem at hand. "Why are you here? Is there another trade on the table?" One that he felt the need to tell her about himself? Her heart made the sign of the cross while she waited to hear what he'd say.

Her dad shook his head. "It's quittin' time, Princess. Let's go get a coffee. We're done here."

"Oh." Georgia's shoulders sagged with relief. "Okay. I'll get my coat."

They walked out into the late winter's watery sunshine, where Brooklyn's brick buildings rose up in every direction. They turned onto Hudson Avenue, but her father stopped in front of the only restaurant on the block. "Step in here with me for a minute," her dad said.

"Why?" She looked up at the restaurant in front of her. It was on the fancier side, and she never ate here.

"Humor me," her father said, opening the door and stepping inside.

She followed him, and the first person she saw inside was Leo. "What . . . ?"

"SURPRISE!" cheered several dozen people.

With her mouth open Georgia scanned all the faces before her. Becca and Leo's family, including DJ and Lianne. The team. Ari the yoga instructor. Even Silas was here. "Wow," she breathed. They were all here for her?

The next sound she heard was a cork popping, and that

was DJ's doing. "Gotcha," he said. "We just wanted to celebrate your engagement in style." He began pouring bubbly into a row of glasses on the bar.

Georgia was still stunned into silence, but Leo crossed over to her and her father, lifting a hand to squeeze his coach's shoulder. "Thanks. Well played." Then he kissed her on the nose. "Say something. I'm worried."

"This is . . ." she tried. "Wow." Two waiters had appeared carrying trays of something that looked delicious. "Are those . . . dumplings?"

"Of course."

She turned around to face her dad, who let a smile crack through his usual crusty facade. "Thank you."

"Of course." He chuckled. "Should have seen your face when I stuck my head in your office, though. Didn't mean to panic you."

DJ handed her a glass of champagne, then kissed her on the cheek. "Cheers, beautiful. I still don't know why you like my brother. But congratulations anyway. And my door is always open if you decide to throw him over."

She took the glass. "Thanks, I think."

"That won't happen," her father rumbled, taking another glass from DJ. "She even has a naked picture of him on her computer."

"Omigod, *Daddy*," she protested. "Shut up. That's, uh, a publicity photo."

On a bar stool nearby, O'Doul cleared his throat. "I'd like to make a toast. Just a quickie."

He tapped a spoon on his glass, and the room quieted down a little bit. The bartender hurried to pass out glasses to those teammates who didn't yet have one.

"Guys," O'Doul said, raising his glass, "We're lucky to have Georgia 'Killer' Worthington on our team, and now we've got College Boy, too. Maybe the kid made a few rookie moves this season . . ." There were a few guffaws at that, even from his coach. "But he made a great decision when he asked Georgia to marry him. So let's wish 'em all our best."

There was some more general hooting and catcalling, and everybody drank to their good fortune. Georgia spent the next half hour greeting everyone who had come out to wish her well. She accepted another tight hug from Marion Trevi, and kisses from Violet and Lianne. She took some hazing from the team, and ate some dumplings. Leo received his share of back pats and hugs and jokes.

After she'd thanked everyone in the room for coming out on a Monday afternoon just to say congratulations, she ended up in front of Nate Kattenberger, who'd come in late. He was catching up on his own glass of champagne and some of the exquisite passed appetizers that continued to circulate. "Number Three!" he crowed, holding up his glass. "Congratulations. I wish you all the best."

Georgia thanked him, wondering not for the first time if he'd ever find anyone. How did an overworked billionaire find a date? And if a woman was interested in him, would he ever trust it?

Note to self. Some people's romantic troubles were probably thornier than her own.

"Do you feel good about the roster?" she asked. "I have to say I'm a lot more relaxed about planning my wedding now that the trade deadline is passed."

He made a wry face. "I wouldn't sign off on a trade of Leo Trevi. He just got here."

"Oh," Georgia said slowly. "Well, never say never." Surely every player had a price. Nate was a businessman. He knew that.

But the magnate shrugged. "While never is a long time, he's a fabulous player, and I brought him to Brooklyn for a reason."

"And what was that?" Georgia hadn't quite cracked the code of why Nate did the things he did. She loved hearing any little insights into the famous Nate Brain.

Her young, genius, billionaire boss actually rolled his icy blue eyes. "The Bruisers aren't just a team, Number Three. They're a family. Remember that."

While Georgia stared, he squeezed her elbow then

crossed the room for another bit of salmon tartare on a wasabi rice cracker. After he shoved it into his mouth, he went over to Leo to shake his hand.

Her man smiled broadly, his sexy, scruffy jaw widening with humor at whatever the big boss said to him, the muscles in his forearm jumping as he pumped Nate's hand. She could watch him forever.

"Wow, you've got it bad." Becca nudged her, making Georgia realize she'd been staring at Leo with a swoony expression on her face. Her roommate offered Georgia one of the spicy homemade potato chips she held on a little appetizer plate. "These are amazing. It's a good thing we can't afford this place. Well—maybe you can now."

"Oh, sure. I'm marrying Leo so I can run up his credit card."

"You want to run up *something*." Becca wiggled her eyebrows. "But not his credit card, I guess. Do you really have a naked picture of him on your computer?"

"Did *everyone* hear that?" Georgia's face began to burn again.

"Only everyone here." Becca giggled. "And that's everyone you know. Oh well."

Georgia groaned. "It's a publicity photo. Swear to God. That eligible bachelor shoot for the charity calendar? They sent me the proofs."

"Ooh." Becca sighed. "Does that mean you have a shot of Castro's booty, too? I might have to swing by your office and help you approve it. You know . . ." She paused, looking thoughtful. "Leo isn't an eligible bachelor anymore. You should let the blog know. They might not use his picture."

"Omigod! You're a genius." Georgia hugged her roommate. "I'm doing that the second I get home. That picture is *mine*."

"Speaking of home. Can I ask you a question?"

"Sure. Do you think we should finally replace the Beast?"

Becca shook her head slowly. "Nope. My family—god love 'em—is onto its next crisis. It's my sister and my baby nephew this time. Now that you're getting married, could I give them your room? I mean—not until you're ready." She fidgeted. "She lost her apartment again. And she can't even afford half our rent, but I figure I'll just suck it up."

"Aw, crap. I'm sorry. And yeah—you guys can have my room whenever you need it. Let me just talk with Leo and see if he has any reservations about me moving in soon."

Becca snorted. "Are you kidding? He'd move you in tonight if he could. You practically live there already."

She practically did. "Okay. I'll ask him tonight."

"You're the best."

"No, you are."

"No, you."

"Wait, not me?" Leo asked, swooping in for a kiss.

Georgia forgot to argue as he claimed her mouth. There were catcalls in the background, and Georgia heard her father make an ornery noise. She gave his chest a gentle shove. "Later," she whispered, self-conscious. "Everyone is watching."

"They're taking notes," he said against her lips. "They want to see how it's done."

Georgia drew back. "Arrogant!" She smiled at him.

"You love it," he argued.

She did. She really, truly did.

Keep reading for a preview of Sarina Bowen's
next Brooklyn Bruisers novel

HARD HITTER

Coming soon from Berkley Sensation!

Standings:
3rd place in the Metropolitan Division
17 Regular Season Games to Go

I t was four more days until Ari got O'Doul onto her therapy schedule. At first he'd agreed to see her at the rink in Toronto during the pregame warm-ups. But then "something came up," and he rescheduled. *Again*.

Now the team was back home in Brooklyn. Ari waited for him in her treatment room at the practice facility. She was perched on the countertop, wondering if he'd show. He was five minutes late already.

A girl could start to take this personally. She'd held this job for almost two years without ever having the captain on her massage table. Before now she'd chalked up his absence to his exceptionally good health and flexibility. The wrist injury he'd had earlier in the season was not the kind of thing that sent a man off to the massage room, either. But now that he was in such obvious need of her help, it was odd that he wouldn't seek it. Many of the other players would book a massage *twice* a day if her schedule allowed it.

Not O'Doul.

She'd asked him once in casual conversation whether he saw a private massage therapist. There were a few players who were so into massage that they paid up to have a private masseuse visit them at home in the mornings. As a veteran, O'Doul would have plenty of money to hire a staff of thousands if he wished.

When she'd asked, though, he'd just shaken his head.

Ari had a theory about O'Doul, though. He didn't seem to like to be touched. During yoga class, she never corrected him with her hands, because she'd noticed early on that his postures got worse instead of better when she tried to adjust him. At first she'd assumed that it embarrassed him to be corrected by a woman.

But his reluctance to have a massage had shifted her thinking. Maybe O'Doul didn't like to be touched *at all*. She'd tested this theory the other night at the bar, laying a hand on his broad shoulder in passing. He actually flinched a little.

Weird.

The training team was worried about a strain to his right hip flexors, so they'd asked for her help. And now here she sat watching both the door and the clock. If O'Doul didn't show this time, she'd have to tell Henry—the head trainer—that she might not be the right therapist for O'Doul's needs. If the man was sensitive to being touched, it might work better if he chose his own therapist.

This possibility made her jumpy as hell, though. It shouldn't be the end of the world if one player snubbed the staff massage therapist. But job security was always at the back of her mind, and she really wanted to do well for this team. She wanted to do well, period.

Every hockey team had a staff therapist, but the role was usually held by a man. Ari was proud of her position on the Bruisers, and lately, the job was the best thing in her life. Since the breakup with her boyfriend of eight years, her job was the one steady thing in her life.

Luckily, this train of thought was interrupted when the door to her therapy room flew open to admit O'Doul. Right away she was struck by how absurdly handsome he was. It ought to be against the law to have a jaw that rugged and eyes the color of a tropical sea. As a massage therapist, Ari believed that all bodies were beautiful and miraculous. However, some were more miraculous than others.

But when she checked his expression, her confidence faltered. O'Doul was the only player who walked into her treatment room wearing the same expression that another man might wear to have a tooth extracted.

"Good afternoon," she said, hopping down as he took off his coat.

He turned to face her the way a guy might face the firing squad. "Afternoon."

"I'll step out while you change," Ari said, placing a sheet on the table. "If you'd feel more comfortable you can leave your undergarments on. When you're ready, lie down on the table, using the sheet as a cover."

"Got it," he said, pulling his team sweatshirt over his head.

Ari stepped out of the room for a moment. She tied up her hair and fetched a bottle of massage oil off the warmer where she'd left it. Then she took a minute to close her eyes and visualize how she wanted the hour to go.

The team often snickered when she led them through visualization exercises, but Ari knew their power. It was hard to achieve something if you couldn't *imagine* it working. With her back to the door, she first formed his name in her mind. *Patrick.* When meditating on her clients' needs, she always used first names because they seemed more personal. When you put your hands on someone's body, it was personal whether you wanted it to be or not.

Today I'm healing Patrick.

In her mind's eye, he relaxed on the table. With firm but gentle hands, she'd probe his trouble spots. She pictured his hip flexor muscles, overlapping one another, the nerves stretching toward his groin in one direction and around to his lumbar spine in the other. She visualized her hands bringing him comfort, easing the strain, recruiting the deeper hip flexors. She'd try to ease any pressure he'd been shifting to his lower back. At the end of the hour, he'd be looser and more flexible. He'd feel more confident whenever he moved.

Ari opened her eyes. She could help Patrick if he'd let her. She knocked twice before re-entering the room.

"C'mon in," came the gruff response.

She let herself in, then stopped for a moment at the stereo she kept on the countertop. She cued up a playlist and then washed her hands. "Daughter" had begun to emerge from the little set of speakers she kept on the counter.

"Pearl Jam?" he asked from the table.

"You don't like it?" she asked. She would have figured him for a grunge rock guy. He was thirty-two years old with a macho streak a mile wide.

"No, I love it." He chuckled. "Once I tried to get a massage at a hotel, and they were playing harp music. My ears were bleeding."

"Okay, no harps. Got it." Ari approached the table and looked her client over. Bodies were an everyday sight for a massage therapist. But this was a particularly stunning example. All athletes were muscular but O'Doul was *cut*. Even lying flat on a table he looked like a tightly coiled spring, ready for sudden physical exertion. The sheet had been casually draped across his waist, but everywhere else rippling muscle was visible, from his stacked shoulders to his thick calves.

He tucked his hands behind his head and stared up at the ceiling. "How long does this take?"

Ari laughed in spite of herself. "Sixty minutes, usually. And I haven't killed anyone yet. I swear."

"Okay. Sorry." His mouth formed a tight line.

Right. Ari rubbed her hands together to warm them. She was oddly self-conscious for someone who gave six or more massages a day. "I'm going to ease toward your hip flexor strain, okay? I'll want to relax the surrounding muscles, so they don't contribute to your pain. You'll let me know if anything hurts, and if you don't approve of the pressure." She folded the sheet back to reveal his thigh. She patted his knee to announce her presence, then used her left hand to palm his lower quad, and her right to slowly manipulate the muscle just above his kneecap.

The goal was to relax the athlete before working on the trouble spots. Though O'Doul seemed poised to make his escape at any moment. So she'd better not dawdle.

Slowly she worked her way up the outside of his hip. So far, so good. "Just checking in, here. How's the pressure?"

"Okay," he said tightly.

Hmm. Not exactly a rave review. She worked on, and eventually he closed his eyes and sighed, which was always a good sign. If there were no risk of being caught acting silly, she would have given herself a victorious fist pump.

Taking her time, she loosened up all the ancillary muscles, the ones connected to his trouble spot. Her beat-up old iPod played a Red Hot Chili Peppers song and then transitioned back to Pearl Jam again.

All was right with the world until Ari moved her hands closer to Patrick's inner hip. One by one, all his muscles tightened up until his entire body had the consistency of a concrete block.

"Patrick," she said quietly, and his eyes flew open. "Are you in pain? Massage doesn't have to hurt to do you good."

"No pain," he said quickly.

Liar. "You're fighting me, though. Why is that?"

"Uh." He sat up. "That's the . . . trouble spot, right? Why would I want someone touching it?" The expression on his face was cautious for once.

"Well . . ." Ari replayed the words he'd just spoken, trying to find a clue to his reluctance. "Because I can help you? I won't hurt you, I promise. Careful massage can reduce inflammation, and relax surrounding muscles, too. Is it possible that you had a bad experience with massage before?"

He gave his head a shake, as if her suggestion did not compute. "Nah. I just don't like having, uh, weak spots."

"Everyone does, though, right?"

"I suppose. But I don't grab yours."

She put a hand on his muscular wrist, the way she would anyone. But his eyes traveled down to that spot immediately, and she wondered if she'd just made another mistake. Had any other client ever been such a mystery?

"Hey," she tried. "You told me a few minutes ago that you'd tried to get a massage at a hotel once. What happened that time?"

"Didn't work out." He gave her a wry grin. "It's not you, I swear."

"*Why* didn't it work out? Besides the harps. Why did you book a massage?"

He gave what was supposed to be a casual shrug. "I'd slept funny on the jet, and my neck hurt. No big deal. So I booked a massage at the spa. Left after ten minutes. I guess I just don't like hands on me."

"You don't like to be touched."

He looked at his hands. "It isn't my favorite thing, no."

The hair stood up on the back of Ari's neck, and she had to restrain herself from asking why. Not liking to be touched wasn't a common attitude. "Everybody's different," she said softly. "But we still have to work on your hip flexors. I have one idea that might help you."

"Good." He made a sheepish face. "Because I'm fresh out."

She patted his wrist again—intentionally. If they were going to work together, he needed to become at least a *little* more accustomed to being touched. "Let's try a more active technique. It will feel more like a gym exercise and less like massage. Can you roll onto your good side and bend your knee for me?"

He complied, turning his broad back to her. She adjusted his bottom leg to be somewhat straight, and then wrapped her hand around his right ankle. "Bend this knee a little more for me." He did. "All right. I'm going to brace your outer hip. Like this." She gripped the muscle as far in as she'd gotten before he'd begun fighting her touch. "And you're going to put your *own* hand on the trouble spot. Show me."

He pushed his fingertips into his flesh between his hip and his groin.

"Now, don't use your back." She put one hand on his lower back and tapped. "Don't activate these. Instead, use your hip and leg. Press down and straighten that leg. Go."

With a lazy-sounding rumble from his chest, he did as she'd instructed.

"Good! How'd that feel?" She dug her hands into the accessible muscle at his hip, warming it, working it as best she could.

"Not too bad."

"You wouldn't lie to me, captain, right?"

He chuckled. "No, ma'am."

"Ugh. You ma'am'd me like an old woman. Just for that you're going to do it four more times." She grabbed his ankle again. "Bend."

"Yes, *ma'am.*"

"For that? Six times."

"Yes, master." She watched the taut muscles of his back shake with laughter.

Ari placed her hands on his body again, her palm warmed by the smooth skin of his lower back, the fingers of her other hand gripping his sturdy hip through the thin cotton of his navy blue briefs. "Ready, big guy?"

"Ready," he rumbled.

"Push and go." Together they worked around his trouble spot while he extended his leg. And the sigh he let out was a good sign. "Okay?"

"Yeah. It feels a little looser than it did a half hour ago."

Ari's small victory was like a warm tingle in her chest. Smiling, she made him repeat the exercise a few more times. "Now roll onto your stomach," she insisted. "For fifteen minutes I want you to pretend you enjoy massage. Just to stroke my ego, okay?"

Chuckling, he rolled over. She spread a bit of oil on her hands and went to work on his calves, slowly working her way up to his hamstrings. Bit by bit she felt his body relax beneath her touch. "How am I doing?" she asked. "Feel free to lie."

"Aw. This is the best massage I've had all year."

She let out an un-ladylike snort. "This is the *only* one, right?"

"Yeah, but still." He rolled his handsome face into the crook of his arm and sighed again.

Skipping his hips, she went to work on the muscles at the juncture of his lower back and his rather beautiful ass. "Do you have much pain here? The risk with a hip strain is that you'll overcompensate by using your lower back."

"By the end of a game, I'm feeling it there for sure."

The honest answer surprised her. She gave him a pat on the back. "Okay. At your next visit, we'll keep working on these trouble spots. Each time you put on a burst of speed on the ice, you demand a lot from these muscles. If we keep you loose, it's going to help. I'm going to work into your hip a little now—but only from the back. But I'm not going to hurt you. And you're lying on the trouble spot, right? No one can touch it." She hoped his defensive position on the table would prevent him from tensing up.

"Got it. Do your worst."

They were tough words from a tough guy, but now she knew better. Patrick O'Doul had some serious issues with having hands on his body. His reluctance probably stemmed from a refusal to make himself vulnerable.

She could work around that, though. She'd have to.

Eddie Vedder sang "Black" through her speakers and Ari hummed along, rolling the waistband of his briefs down just an inch, giving her better access to his skin. She oiled up her hands again and leaned into him, closing her eyes, applying all of her strength to the task at hand. Muscle and bone pressed against muscle and bone. Skin met skin. She let the oil do its work, reducing friction, bringing her hands into better contact with the body she was trying so hard to heal.

That's when she felt it—finally—that beautiful connection, the moment when the client opens himself up to the treatment. He seemed to go slack beneath her, his muscles relaxing beneath the rhythm of her hands. If it wouldn't have disturbed his newfound peace, she would have hooted in victory.

She finished up the massage at his big shoulders, now supple. His eyes were heavy. His breathing was steady. And if she checked his pulse, she knew she'd find it at a slow, relaxed rate.

It almost seemed mean when she had to pat the back of his neck gently and tell him that time was up.

His eyes widened. "Okay," he said a little sleepily. "Thanks."

"Here," she said, placing a towel on the edge of the table. "You don't want to get massage oil on your clothes."

She turned her back and washed her hands at the little sink in the corner, giving him a moment alone to peel himself up off the table and gather his things. "See you Saturday in Chicago," she said over her shoulder. "I'll text you a location. I think we'll be at the hotel."

"Right. I'll be on time," he mumbled. "Thanks."

"Be well!" As he opened the door to leave, she stole a look at his face. The expression she found there tugged at her heart. It was a little dazed, as if he couldn't quite make sense of how he'd spent the last hour. She gave him a smile, and the corners of his rugged mouth turned up, too.

Then he was gone, probably to the showers. The hot water would do him some more good, and keep him loose. But it would also give him a few minutes to pull himself together. Somehow it hadn't been easy for O'Doul to let someone touch his body. But he'd done it. He'd let down his guard. Now he'd have to pull it back up again for game night. In a few hours he was expected to mow down the visiting team from Quebec, and maybe take a few punches to amuse the fans.

While Ari found some aspects of hockey barbaric, she

had tremendous respect for the competitive demands these men placed on both their bodies and their psyches. While she was donning her coat and wondering what to eat for dinner before the game, two dozen men would think of nothing but victory for the next seven hours. Cameras would follow their every move on the ice, then reporters would argue afterwards about their odds of making the playoffs for the first time since Nate Kattenberger bought the team.

Ari walked home, heading north toward the tiny Brooklyn neighborhood of Vinegar Hill, where the streets were brick and the buildings were barely three stories high. The houses here were smaller and older than in almost any other part of Brooklyn. The townhouse where Ari lived dated back to the Civil War. Someone had put a rather pedestrian brick facade on it during the sixties, which dimmed some of its charm. But as Ari approached from a block away, its blue-painted wooden door beckoned her home.

She was lucky as hell to live here. The building was worth a couple of million dollars at least, in spite of the fact that a Con Edison substation blocked the entire neighborhood from having any decent views of the river. The townhouse belonged to Ari's great-uncle. He and the rest of her Italian family had decamped for Florida a decade ago. She looked after the building in exchange for paying only a very modest monthly rent.

As she approached, though, she saw something that made her slow down. The back end of her ex's dark red van was visible just around the corner. The sight of it made her stomach ache instinctively, but its presence wasn't necessarily bad news.

Three days ago she'd sent him an ultimatum—an e-mail notifying him that he had two days to finally clear the rest of his belongings out of her storage room. He hadn't replied at all. Just this morning she'd been wondering what to do about that.

But if Vince was finally clearing out his junk from her basement, that was progress.

Ari dug out her keys—still shiny from their newness—

and covered the rest of the block quickly. She jogged up the four steps to her front door and unlocked the brand-new deadbolt. Then she closed and locked the door. And listened.

The only voices she could make out were muffled, and coming from the rear of the building. She set her bag down on the bottom of her staircase and tiptoed through the dining room and on into the kitchen, stopping only to kick off her boots to silence the sound of footsteps on her hardwood floors. She hung back near the old refrigerator, taking a cautious, oblique glimpse out the back window.

Nothing.

Her heart was racing for no good reason. Vince was outside and she was inside, behind the safety of new locks. His presence unsettled her nonetheless. Vince Giardi was the embodiment of her worst, most embarrassing mistake. The grandmother who'd helped raise her—God rest her soul—had been right about Vince. *Thank you, Nonna. Sorry it took me eight years to notice.*

Ari leaned against the fridge, its hum at her back, and took a six-count breath, expanding her diaphragm. She wouldn't let Vince get her riled up today. There was no need, anyway.

She heard the distinctive slam of the exterior basement door, and stood on tiptoe to take another peek out the window. A beanie hat appeared. But when the man came into view, it most certainly wasn't Vince. That was obvious even with the guy's back to her. He was thin and wearing dirty jeans. Vince would never dress like that. And, damn it, the man wasn't carrying anything. If there were strangers coming in and out of her basement storage room, they'd better have moving boxes containing Vince's clothing and video games.

Damn. It. All.

More than a month had passed since the awful weekend their relationship finally ended. They'd had an epic fight. Her flight was late in from Ottawa, and she'd gotten home to find Vince waiting up for her, drunk and angry. He wanted to know where she'd been. Why she hadn't called.

This was nothing new, sadly. Ever since she'd taken the

job for the Brooklyn Bruisers, things had been heading downhill. But on that awful night he didn't bother to couch his jealous little jabs behind a tense chuckle. He flat out accused her of sleeping with a hockey player.

Even as she'd taken out her phone with shaky hands to show him the official arrival time of their charter flight on her Katt Phone, she'd understood that he'd finally gone too far. That she couldn't live under a cloud of pointless suspicion anymore. It ended right then, even if Vince didn't know it yet. But instead of playing it cool like a smart girl, she'd raised her voice. Blame it on her Italian heritage, but her top blew right off. "I shouldn't have to *prove* it, Vince," she'd said angrily. "If you think I'm a cheat, then leave me already! Go on! Just fucking *stop this*!"

He did stop it—by grabbing both her wrists and shoving her toward the stairs. In her wool socks, she'd slipped. Heart-stopping fear rose up in her chest as the staircase sliced into view. Her head bounced off the wall as she grabbed for the carved antique bannister.

Her foot stopped her fall, though—caught between two balusters. At first it was such a relief to stop falling that she didn't feel the pain shooting up her instep. And then, shaking with fury and freaked out, she'd tried to conceal it. But that's hard when you can't put weight on one leg.

At the sight of her injury, Vince had sobered up fast and used Uber to get them a ride to the ER. "I'm sorry, baby," he babbled. "Terrible accident." "Never happen again."

It wouldn't, either. Because the next night when he went to work at the club, she'd had an emergency locksmith come over to change the locks. She'd asked her tenant, a flight attendant named Maddy, to help put Vince's clothing into trash bags. It was possibly the most embarrassing favor she'd ever asked of anyone. It had been far easier to shake off the hospital staff's probing questions than Maddy's. "He did this, didn't he?" she demanded, pointing one long red fingernail at Ari's walking cast. "I never liked the look of him. Good for you for showing him the door."

Ari had neither confirmed or denied Vince's role in her

tumble. He probably hadn't meant to break a bone, but it really didn't matter. A bone was broken, and he'd been the cause of both her trip to the ER and her sudden wake-up call. With Maddy's help she'd hobbled around, doing her best to be respectful of his things even as she scrambled to get them all out of the house and into the basement storage unit. Maddy made all the trips down those back stairs herself, which meant Ari owed her. Big.

"You'd do the same for me," Maddy protested. And surely it was true. When the job was done, Ari gave her a hug and a pre-apology for whatever grief Vince might give her if he happened to show up when Maddy was coming or going. "I can take care of myself, hon. You do the same."

The four AM pounding on the exterior door had been awful. When Ari didn't come to the door to explain herself, he'd begun yelling terrible things up at her bedroom window. "Fucking cunt! Get down here and let me in."

Maddy's chainsaw voice had rung out from her third floor window. "Go away or I'm calling the police. You have ten seconds. Tomorrow Ari will tell you how to get your stuff."

"Meddling bitch!" he'd returned. But when Maddy told him she was dialing 911, he actually left.

In the morning she'd e-mailed Vince to let him know he could retrieve his own things from the storage room with his old key. The fact that he didn't answer or turn up for a week only made her more anxious. It was unlike him to give up and walk away. Especially if his collection of expensive suits was on the line.

But then one day she'd spotted his van nearby. And she'd heard the basement door open and close. It happened again a couple of days later. For the past few weeks he'd either been moving out one article of clothing at a time, or merely torturing her with his sporadic presence.

That's why her latest e-mail had threatened to change the locks on the basement door, too. She should have done that weeks ago. It's just that the basement was so inhospitable— its entrance barely a step up from the cellar door in *The*

Wizard of Oz—she thought he'd get sick of the lurker cha-
rade and leave her alone for good.

Maybe today was the day.

Hugging herself, Ari kept up her vigil by the fridge.
Eventually the door slammed again and Vince strode into
view, his back to the window, his swagger intact. He disappeared around the corner of the building. A moment later
she heard what had to be the van's engine start up and then
drive away.

Finally, she relaxed.

With her heart rate finally returning to normal, she
checked her messages and reheated a square of lasagna
she'd saved for dinner. She even poured herself a half glass
of wine to go with it. Everything was fine, or soon would
be. Tonight her team was going to beat the visitors from
Washington, D.C., and tomorrow she'd relieve their aching
muscles.

After her early dinner she lay down on the couch with
a book. The house was so very quiet. She still wasn't used
to living alone. She'd met Vince when she was just twenty-
one and bartending at one of his clubs. She'd never been
an adult on her own.

It was obviously time to start. She read her book and
tried to think soothing thoughts.

By six-thirty it was time to get ready for the game. She
went up the creaky narrow staircase to her bedroom and
chose a knit dress with three-quarter sleeves and tights. The
NHL liked its staff to look professional, even if she might
be called upon to give some last-minute attention to stiff
muscles. It had taken her a few months on the job to figure
out what to wear. Now her closet held four comfy game
night dresses in shades of eggplant (the team color). She
wore ballet flats to keep herself comfortable and mobile.

Ari grabbed her bag and headed out the door. Instead
of walking toward Water Street where cabs were more
plentiful, she walked around the block for a moment, cas-
ing her own block like a thief. She peeked into the alley.
The basement door of her little building was closed, as it

should be. There was nobody in sight. Checking over both shoulders like a paranoid fool, she walked around back, slipping her keys out of her pocket.

But she stopped at the rear door, confused. There, gleaming against the beat-up metal door was a new lock. Even though it didn't make sense, she tried her key anyway. This was her building, for God's sake.

The key wouldn't even fit in the lock.

Anger rushed through her veins like a drug. *Damn you, Vince!* He was like a cockroach that couldn't be killed off. If this was his idea of revenge, she was going to give him a piece of her mind. He'd locked her out. Of her own basement.

What the hell?

The only windows back here were narrow and just above her eye level. Shaking with fury, she stood on tiptoe to peek inside. She cupped a hand over the glass to try to reduce the sunset's glare. But it took her eyes a moment to identify the shapes in the basement's dim light.

The first thing she could make out was the lights of a computer modem, doing their little dance to announce their connection. And their light helped illuminate a sort of folding table which held the rest of a computer setup—a screen and a keyboard and mouse, with a chair pulled up to them. But the item which really drove home the problem was the wastepaper basket on the floor. There was something so freaking civilized about it that it could almost make steam come out of her ears.

Vince had set up an *office* in her basement. He was conducting some kind of business on her property! With a wastepaper basket!

She was mad enough to spit. She stomped toward the corner, calm mood ruined, and stuck her arm in the air for a taxi.

Two hours later she was feeling a little calmer, even though the problem remained unsolved.

But the game was about to start, and she was surrounded

by ten thousand fans. It was hard to feel crabby with so much expectation bouncing around the arena.

Ari had already given a couple of last-minute chair massages to players with upper body pain. By this point their fate was out of her hands. She stood in the owners' box, a soda in her hand, a notebook at her side. She would watch the first period of the game from this premium location and make some notes about who suffered the hardest hits, so she could follow up with those players during the intermission or tomorrow.

Hockey was pretty freaking exciting, too. Just because she'd never been a fan before eighteen months ago didn't mean she didn't enjoy it.

Beside her, the Brooklyn Bruisers office manager stood sipping from a glass of wine. "How's O'Doul today?" Becca asked, watching the ice team sweep the surface one more time. "I heard rumors that they sent him to you for his hip."

"He seemed fair," Ari said, considering the question. "A little rest would probably help him. But I don't think it's any worse than a lot of the strains the guys play on."

On a gut level, she'd never understand the risks these players took with their bodies every day. That was their job, and they were highly compensated for it. She'd never be rich, but she'd never take a punch to the face, either.

Though you let yourself be pushed down the stairs, her subconscious prodded.

"Is Doulie a diva in the treatment room? He's so freaking bossy. The travel team actually calls all the hotels where he stays and gets duplicate receipts to submit for him, because they've learned it's a bigger pain to ask for his cooperation than to just take over."

"Really?" Ari laughed. "Sounds like he has them trained." Everyone was supposed to submit his or her own receipts, or pay an assistant to do it for them. Ari did her own, but it was a pain in the gluteus maximus.

"He has an ego the size of the stadium. If you have any trouble with him, I'm happy to play the part of bad cop."

"You do that part well." Ari squeezed her friend's shoulder.

"Fuck," Becca moaned. "Do that again. Please? I spent too many hours at my desk today."

Ari set down her drink and stood behind Becca. She put her hands on the younger woman's shoulders and began to rub. "You only like me for my hands," she complained.

"Not true! You make a mean margarita, and you always turn in your personnel forms on time."

"I feel so much better now." She put her thumbs at the base of Becca's skull and rubbed. This was a brand-new friendship. Ari had always liked Becca and her sidekick, Georgia, the publicist. But Ari's ex had resented all the traveling that Ari did for the team, and when she was home in Brooklyn he got pissy if she went out without him.

His attitude had kept her away from developing normal friendships with the girls at work, and she hadn't even realized it until after she'd broken things off with him.

During Ari's yoga training, a wise yogi had told her that pain always brought new awarenesses. That pain brought gifts with it. Or, as her Italian grandmother would have put it—when God slams a door, he opens a window. Becoming friends with Becca and Georgia was that window.

"Marry me," Becca breathed as Ari rubbed her shoulders.

"I would, but I've sworn off relationships. Today was a good reminder of why."

Becca spun around, cutting off her massage. "Oh no, what happened? Did he pound on your door again?"

"No, but his stuff is still in my basement storage room, and . . ."

This conversation was interrupted by the arrival of Nate Kattenberger, the team's owner. He walked in wearing his trademark hoodie and dark wash jeans. Ari had heard that the old guard of the hockey league hated the young billionaire's personal dress code, and its governors occasionally made snide comments about his "athletic shoes" in the press.

Becca had let it slip that Kattenberger's Tom Ford sneakers ran six hundred bucks, though. The man liked expensive clothes, but he did not like to conform to a bunch of league rules. And Ari loved him for it.

"Evening, ladies," Nate said with a wave. He walked right over to the front of the box and looked down, surveying his dominion.

A young woman breezed in after him. Lauren was Nate's Manhattan assistant, not to be confused with Becca, his Brooklyn assistant. The contrast between them was more than a little amusing. Lauren wore a designer suit in an expensive shade of pink, stockings, and high heels. Her hair was swept into a glamorous up-do that must have taken forty-five minutes to accomplish. And at seven-thirty PM, it still looked perfect.

Becca wore Doc Martens, purple tights and a leather dress. Her hair was purple and her eyebrow and nose were proudly pierced.

The biggest difference, though, was in facial expression. Becca raised a hand to give the other woman a friendly wave. "Hi, Lauren! Want to have a glass of wine with us?"

The only acknowledgment that Becca had spoken was a sidelong glance flicked in their direction. As if she hadn't heard at all, Lauren went over to the drinks table herself and poured her boss a Diet Coke over three ice cubes. She perched a wedge of lime on the rim, snapped a cocktail napkin into her hand and scurried over to him to present it as if to royalty.

"I'm always nice," Becca whispered under her breath. "But I'm really not sure why."

"Because it feels better to be nice," Ari whispered. "And you're a beautiful person."

Becca shot her a grateful glance. "She makes ugly look pretty good."

It was true. Queen Lauren (as they sometimes referred to her) was beautiful. But Ari wasn't even a little jealous of that silky pale hair or those blue eyes. Lauren exuded stress and unhappiness. A decade of yoga might not even make a dent in Queen Lauren's steel facade.

"Rebecca," Nate called. "Do you happen to have tonight's ticket sales?"

"But of course!" she chirped. "Do you really think I'd stand here and slurp wine if I hadn't brought them with me?" She balanced her glass in one hand and dug through her briefcase with the other. "It's here somewhere. Ah." When she finally tugged a file out of her bag, Nate took the folder with a smile. "Anything shocking in here? Should I hit the whiskey early?"

"It's always cocktail hour somewhere, boss. But the numbers looked good to me."

Nate flipped the cover open and scanned the summary page while Lauren glared over his shoulder at Becca. "These are good numbers. And I like the time series graph."

"Thanks! I got sick of flipping backward to see the prior weeks' numbers."

When he was through, Nate handed the folder to Lauren for safekeeping. Lauren stashed it in a leather satchel while simultaneously attempting to incinerate Becca with her eyes.

"Thank you," Nate said in Lauren's general direction. "That's all for today, I suppose."

Lauren said good night to her boss and buttoned up her impeccable jacket.

"Aren't you staying for the game?" Becca asked.

"I hate hockey," Lauren said. Then she walked out, her heels clicking importantly across the walnut floorboards.

Ari exchanged a loaded glance with Becca. Her friend's eyebrows lifted as if to ask, *Can you believe Nate's assistant would say that right before a game?* Maybe the girl didn't understand how superstitious men could be about their sports.

The door opened again, admitting Georgia Worthington and the brand-new publicist, Tom. "How'd the press take it?" Nathan asked by way of a greeting.

"*Lots* of questions," Georgia said. "There's going to be speculation."

"'Take what?" Becca asked, voicing the same question that was on Ari's mind.

"O'Doul was scratched at the last minute," Tom said. "The trainers want him rested. That's our story and we're sticking to it."

Oh boy, Ari thought, staring down at the ice. The players were lining up for the national anthem now. She couldn't even remember a night when O'Doul had been scratched before. The only time she'd known him to sit out games was that brief span when he was on the injured list while his wrist was healing.

She didn't know him all that well. But she knew enough to say he was *not* going to like it.

Coming Soon From

SARINA BOWEN

HARD HITTER

A Brooklyn Bruisers Novel

As team captain and enforcer, Patrick O'Doul puts the bruise in the Brooklyn Bruisers. But after years of hard hits, O'Doul is feeling the burn, both physically and mentally. He conceals his pain from his coach and trainers, but when his chronic hip injury becomes too obvious to ignore, they send him for sessions with the team's massage therapist.

After breaking up with her long-term boyfriend, Ari Bettini is in need of peace of mind. For now, she's decided to focus on her work: rehabilitating the Bruisers' MVP. O'Doul is easy on the eyes, but his reaction to her touch is ice cold. Ari is determined to help O'Doul heal, but as the tension between them turns red hot, they both learn that a little TLC is good for the body...

sarinabowen.com
facebook.com/AuthorSarinaBowen
facebook.com/BerkleyRomance
penguin.com